LIAR QUEEN

Liar Queen

M.T. Solomon

GOLDEN SCALES
PUBLISHING

This book is a work of fiction. Names, characters, places and incidents are the product of the author's imagination or are used fictitiously. Any resemblance to actual events, locales, or persons, living or dead, is coincidental.

Copyright © 2024 by M.T. Solomon. All rights reserved, including the right to reproduce, distribute, or transmit any form or by any means. For information regarding subsidiary rights, please contact the Publisher.

Golden Scales Publishing supports copyright. Copyright fuels creativity, encourages diverse voices, promotes free speech, and creates a vibrant culture. Thank you for buying an authorized edition of this book and for complying with copyright laws by not reproducing, scanning, or distributing any part of it in any form without permission. You are supporting writers and allowing Golden Scales Publishing to continue to publish books for every reader.

Golden Scales Publishing, LLC
P.O. Box 150616
Brooklyn, NY 11215
www.goldenscalespublishing.com

Edited by Morgan Macedo, Glasswing Editing, LLC
Cover art and design by Stephanie Stott
Stock photos from Deposit Photos
Interior formatting by Jared Reid
Interior map art by Victoria Diaz

HC ISBN 979-8-9915303-1-6
Paperback ISBN 979-8-9915303-0-9
Ebook ISBN 979-8-9915303-2-3

Also by M.T. Solomon

Dual Moons Duology

All the Fragile Hearts

Whispers in the Dark

To those who once carried the weight of childhood baggage but chose to set it down instead.

Enduring Kingdoms of the Black Rains

Northern Kingdoms

Jeweled Realm
- Gabi's Cabin
- Narlès
- The Palace
- Roully Dam
- Valenbeuge
- Montnoît
- Vatou
- House Black Chateau

The Waste
- Great Crevasse

Ursa
- Husa

Golden Foot
- Valon
- Souzy
- Liroux

Bastia
- Colendos

Chapter One

Seven years had passed since she held a blade to her sister's throat. Seven years, and not a day went by that it didn't haunt her. The memory was pulling her away, making her forget what she was supposed to be doing. Her eyes caught the glimmer of the rising sun on her sword as it lay on the side table not far away, goading her. She stared down at her hands, wondering how her grandmother had done it. How had she, with her own two hands, laid the foundation for an entire kingdom?

The late queen had been notorious for her swordplay, more so—some said—than for her diplomacy. Mara's shoulders slumped and she sighed, finally bringing her gaze to her own reflection. In the mirror, high cheekbones were shadowed over. Her auburn hair was side-swept and braided, and her eyes glowed amber in the sunlight.

No one else. Her mother's words came unbidden from the depths of her memory. *Only you.*

Mara stood straighter with shoulders pulled back, attempting to reach her tallest stature. She pursed her lips, never losing her own eyes reflected in the mirror.

A knock came from the door.

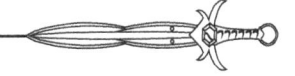

"Majesty," came the muffled voice of Petra, "they are waiting for you."

With a nod—a signal to herself that she was ready—Mara swirled fiercely around in her skirts, grabbed her sword, and left her room.

Petra was waiting for her just outside. "Majesty," she said again.

Her sandstone eyes were constantly studying Mara, attempting to read her and meet her needs before Mara ever needed to ask. A hand younger than Mara, Petra had come to the queen from the Training House. Selected at a young age based on disposition and intellect, the girl had grown into a highly perceptive young woman.

Petra's eyes fell to Mara's hands, which were deftly moving around her hips, wrapping the filigreed leather belt of the Sacred Sword.

"Your belt," Petra said. "Let me help you."

"No!" Mara recoiled from Petra's hands. "Only me."

"Just your belt, Your Majesty," Petra insisted.

Mara shook her head and finished buckling the belt herself. She did not like being touched, not really. She felt only a hint of regret for snapping at Petra. "They want to see the Sword Queen, grim and strong. They expect to see my mother. Well, I'll do them one better."

She left Petra in her wake. From within the scabbard on her belt, she felt the surge of power the Sword brought to the one who wielded it. It usually made her feel sick. A deep well of unrest would swell up in the pit of her stomach and she'd lose her appetite.

But today, she would use its power to her advantage. Today, she'd push the fear aside and embrace what was solely hers. She entered the throne room with her head held high and chin tilted slightly upward, mirroring the confidence she stoked within.

"Her Majesty, Mara of House Black. Protector of the Jeweled Realm. Upholder of the Golden Laws. Wearer of the Sacred Sword." The words, spoken by a court page, rang through the many-columned throne room.

They bounced off Mara's now hardened exterior.

A pair of gentlemen waited for her before the throne—gentlemen being used loosely. They'd hailed from the east, a kingdom small in size but great in armed soldiers.

Their customary beards were dirty and clung to their faces. Dirt caked their clothes from their ride, and they smelled even worse than they looked. Mara found herself pitying their women.

"Sword Queen," the shorter, older of the two growled out, "we've been waiting for hours."

Mara silently sank into her throne. A servant brought her vin, which she sipped as she stared coolly at the men. "I'm afraid I wasn't aware of your arrival until a few moments ago." She sipped again, dropping her eyes, avoiding their gazes. "I've instructed my household to only interrupt me for *important* things."

The older man ground his teeth and shuffled angrily from his left foot to his right. Mara knew he wanted to argue with her, probably even put his hands on her, but she also knew he wouldn't. Not with her Iron Guard standing sentry around them.

The younger man stepped forward. Despite his filthy appearance, brilliant blue eyes stared out at her from above his haggard beard. "We were under the impression the Sword Queen was most welcoming to her guests," he said.

It was a dare, a sideways insult, and she knew it. But she wouldn't take the bait.

"I'm afraid you are mistaken," she sipped from her glass.

The old man looked at the younger man, his hands displayed wide as if to say, *You see? I told you so.*

"Come, Your Grace," the old man said. "We'll find no help for us here."

Mara's eyebrows cocked up at the young man's formal title. She tried her best to hide the surprise she felt and keep it from displaying full force on her face. The young man nodded and looked back at Mara. While he looked at her, she studied him. From his hair—a forgettable shade of black—to his arched nose, to his ragged facial hair, to his throat. There, atop the layers of black bear hide and hung around his neck, was a twisted braid of silver complete with a bear's head biting a glimmering opal.

A royal seal.

Her eyes trolled back up to the man's own. Such an alarming shade of blue. Mara had trouble focusing on the hard exterior she was fighting so hard to build. Why did his eyes bother her so?

"You're the Prince of Ursa," Mara drawled. She leaned back in her throne as if amused, though, she was anything but. What she really wanted to do was return to her room. The arrival of a prince, so well hidden that her own Guard had had no idea, did not bode well.

"*A* prince," he corrected. "*The* Prince of Ursa remains at home. He sent me, his little brother, in his stead."

"This is Prince Boden, Your Majesty. Second in line to Ursa's throne," the older man added.

"Third, actually. My brother's wife is due any day with their firstborn." Boden smiled, and a red hue tinted his cheeks beneath his beard. Perhaps he realized he'd spoken too freely or too much.

Mara raised her glass. "A toast, then, to the future heir of Ursa." She took a large swallow, happy Boden's mission from the crown prince had not been a marriage proposal.

That was the last thing she needed.

She thrust her empty glass at a waiting servant. Standing, she gathered her skirts and descended the three steps toward the men. "Tell me, Prince Boden, third in line to the throne, what does your brother have you doing out here in his stead?"

Mara knew her words had grated against the old man's ears. He'd sensed the disrespect layered beneath each word. With a single step, he meant to position himself between Mara and Boden, but Boden held up his arm.

"It's alright, Mendel," he said. "She's fine."

Mara smirked.

"She mocked you, Your Majesty," Mendel hissed.

Boden nodded. "Yes, but I'm willing to bet it's because they're not used to royal siblings here. *Strength wields the Sword*—is that not your motto?"

He leaned in close to Mara, so close, in fact, that she could feel the heat from his body. He was taller than she'd realized, at least a hand taller than Mara herself. Smiling down at her, he seemed to be enjoying his view.

"But tell me"—his breath ghosted across her cheek—"where's the strength in sororicide?"

Mara held Boden's gaze. It was difficult for her to look away. The color of his eyes was so vivid. Mentally forming a wall around her stomach to keep from feeling sick, she dove deep into the blue before her. The color was that of a glacier-fed lake high in the mountains, meted with flakes of gold. Within them, she didn't sense danger, but she did sense something else. Something strange.

They reminded Mara of her father's, she finally decided. Though, his were not nearly that beautiful of a blue. His were of steel, like armor. Granite, like the mountain pass. But they were that same impassable solid. A doorway to the mind, impenetrable by anyone save for the select few allowed in.

Her father had never let her in.

Mara smiled, retreating a step. She accepted another glass of vin from her servant before turning back to Boden and Mendel. "My sister died valiantly, fighting for her right."

"To the throne?" Boden asked. "As you had claim to it, too?"

Mara swirled her vin, watching Boden from over the top of her glass. What was his game? Why had he traveled all the way to the Jeweled Realm? To taunt her? Surely the royal house of Ursa knew better than to send a bothersome man—no, boy—into the Sword Queen's palace.

If they didn't know better, she would make sure they did.

"The throne of the Jeweled Realm is sacred. Only those who pay the price and pass the test may claim it," Mara said.

"You mean the ones who kill their siblings?"

Mara rolled her eyes. "Did you come here to lecture me on tradition?" She placed her empty hand on the hilt of her sword. "Because I have an answer for you, if that's the case."

Boden watched her for a moment before bowing his head in acquiescence. He held up his hands in supplication and stepped away from Mara. "Of course, you're right. How rude of me. But we do have business. Important business."

Mara released her sword, relieved. Like most women of the House of Black, she'd begun training with swords early. She was good. The skill came naturally to the women of her family, as her grandmother had once told her. It was counted on, for those next in line to rule needed to possess the Sword lest it possessed them.

What they hadn't counted on was Mara's reluctance.

"Speak then," Mara said, returning to her throne.

Mendel eyed Boden warily. He stepped forward, offering her a hard stare. "It's best we speak somewhere else."

"Oh?" Mara returned her glass to the servant's tray. She tried—and failed—to avoid Boden's eyes. They told her to listen. "Fine. In the Round Room, then."

She motioned for her servants to run along and ready the room. Petra barked a few orders at some, telling them to bring more vin and some beer for the Ursans. Some table fruits, too.

Two Iron Guards led the way. They walked quickly despite their heavy armor. It clinked with every step they took, the sound echoing off the high, barreled ceiling of the great hallway. Above them, giant crystal chandeliers spun slowly, tossing their fractal patterns across every surface. The rainbow rays danced over Mara's dress as she passed. Mendel's beard. Boden's bearskin.

Mara watched the two Ursans stare at her world. The crystal reflected in their eyes, casting a look of bewitchment within. A bewitchment her kingdom was well known for. A bewitchment she was born from and bored of.

Mara cleared her throat. "Are chandeliers not common in Ursa? Here I thought you were a nation of civilized people."

"None of this size, I'm afraid," Boden replied. "We are a practical people."

Boden adjusted his bearskin cape and stood tall. He smiled at her, though she knew it wasn't a genuine smile. There was something dismissive about it. They walked on.

The Iron Guards stopped just outside a pair of tall wooden doors. Crafted from a single, giant walnut tree that once grew where the palace stood, Mara always admired the way the grays swirled into the blacks. Like fresh milk in her morning *café*.

Light spilled into the room from many windows. It seeped across the carpet like molten gold, allowing a southern view of the palace and the *ville* below. A wide thoroughfare cut through the buildings, eventually meeting the river Mousseaux before climbing over it on a stone bridge. Streets radiated off the thoroughfare like sunbeams. In the distance, Mara could see the *ville*'s walls, and if she looked hard enough, she could even see the arch that lay beyond that. Every visitor to the *ville* passed through the archway, built there by her grandmother to symbolize the Jeweled Realm's strength and power.

Petra ordered servants with her eyes, so skilled was she at commanding them. Two wooden chairs, their feet the carved claws of lions, were positioned opposite a red velvet highback. Mara sat in the red chair and motioned for Mendel and Boden to sit. The men hesitated but were ushered to their seats by Petra.

Boden and Mendel looked awkward in the richly colored surroundings. Their travel clothes were dull and dirty, and their boots left crusted mud wherever they walked. The east was a place of the earth. Raw. Hard. It was how the Ursans liked things. Boden was right in saying they were a practical people, but they liked to think this practicality made them humble when it also made them arrogant.

Mara waited for the men to be served. Petra stationed herself nearby, observing the servants, making sure they performed their duties to perfection. When a new servant nearly spilled a flagon of beer on Boden's lap, Petra snapped forward and grabbed the young girl by the arm.

"You embarrass us," she hissed in the ancient tongue.

"It's alright," Boden assured her. "No harm done."

Petra side-eyed him but released the girl. The small thing curtsied deep before backing into the hidden servant's door.

"Here, perfection is demanded," Petra said. "Your Majesty," she reluctantly added. Petra returned to her window, her eyes tracing the comings and goings of the servants.

Mendel shared a look of concern with Boden. His eyebrows rose into his hairline, as if saying, *Don't mess with that one.* All Mara could do was smile. Petra wielded her authority deftly, making the work and lives of all those who orbited the queen move like cogs in a machine.

"The Jeweled Realm has not crossed its army over kingdom lines in years." Mara blinked slowly, playing like she had patience. "So I'm curious to know what this meeting is about."

Boden's lips twitched, a weak attempt to cover his unease. "We appreciate the Jeweled Realm's armistice."

"Yeah, since the Red Queen got sick," Mendel added, "she could no longer lead her army to pillage and slaughter all she came acr—"

"My mother is dead," Mara spoke evenly over Mendel, "and I am not my mother. Though, I may yet prove to be far worse."

She watched his eyes dilate. Even if he didn't want to admit he was afraid of her, she knew he was. Or, rather, he feared the power of the Sword. His eyes drifted down to its shimmering hilt. Mara always admired the way the giant emerald decorating its pommel caught the sun. It was unreasonable for a gem to be so large, and yet it did not make the Sword any less deadly. It was obnoxious, which Mara liked. She stood a little taller, pleased with the man's fear.

Mara looked to Boden. "You came here to tell me something. Tell me so I may be rid of your disrespectful companion."

Boden dropped his gaze and fidgeted with his cuff. He cleared his throat. "A stranger came to the palace," he began. "A woman. She claimed to be a witch of the Waste. Skeletal thing. Twisted and dark."

Mara sank back in her chair, back held tall. She let her fingers delicately rub the velvet to calm her suddenly racing heart. It was a trick her mother had taught her, to utilize the textures around oneself to distract the nervous system so one could think. It was useful, too, when used against one's enemies.

"A woman of the Waste is nothing to fear. Even if she claims to be a witch."

"This one . . . proved powerful," Boden replied.

"Impossible," Mara spat.

"I saw it with my own eyes. She appears to command the elements. And she wants to join forces."

"Join forces? What for?" Mara held her chin high, forcing herself to look regal despite not feeling as such.

A witch of the Waste was a problem. The traumatized land—the barren gift left by the Black Rains—boasted home to several nomadic tribes. Whispers told of some sort of sorcery amongst certain groups. A mystical air to their existence. But they never traversed across the deep canyon to the east nor the fast-moving river to the west. They were animals caged. Mara liked them that way.

Boden cast a look at Mendel. The old man nodded his head, encouraging his prince to proceed. Boden sighed. "She speaks of a union of her forces with my father's."

"To what end?" Mara asked. "No amount of mysticism will save you from the Jeweled Realm's forces, if that is your endgame."

Boden stared at her. "The witch thinks she holds a winning hand."

Mara watched Boden, her eyes locked on his, waiting him out, daring him to be the first to look away. When he did, she smirked, took a glass of vin from beside her, and drank.

"So what?" she asked when she was through. "Is this an ultimatum? A warning?"

"No," Boden assured her. "The opposite, in fact. My father is afraid of the dark woman. He asked for your help in dispatching her."

Mara eased her glass down and sat a little straighter. She cocked her head, pretending she was mulling it over, when in reality she already knew what her answer to such a request would be.

No.

"Why would I do that?" she asked.

"Because—" Boden began, but stopped. He seemed to be having difficulty forming his next words.

Mara did her best to be patient, but it had never been her strongest trait. She ground down hard on her own teeth, trying to avoid interrupting the prince. "Spit it out," her voice was barely above a whisper. "Please," she added.

"The witch claims to be . . . your sister," Boden finally said.

Mara's left eye twitched, but she reached for her temple, hoping to hide it. "That's impossible. I killed her."

"She seemed quite certain. She was very convincing," Boden said.

Mara looked at him out of the corner of her eye. "The best liars are always the most convincing."

Boden shook his head, insistent. "She offered this to prove it."

He stood, and from his side pouch, produced a gold-plated necklace. He tossed it to Mara, but she made no move to catch it. It fell on the woven rug at her feet.

Mara took a deep breath as she stared at it. A flattened half-circle reflected the sun brightly. It hung from the chain with a giant emerald sitting in its center. Round rubies were inset within the links of chain like drops of blood.

The pendant was supposed to represent the arch—her grandmother's foundation. And the emerald was a seed of the new realm to come. A sigil of House Black.

Her sister's necklace.

Chapter Two

Mara sat stoic. She stared at her sister's necklace, but gave up no sign of worry or weakness. Instead, she stood, lifted the jewelry off the floor, and set it on the nearby table. Her stomach churned seeing it there next to her things. She had hoped she'd never see it—and in turn, her sister Iris—again.

It had been seven years since Iris's defeat. Mara thought the girl had learned her lesson, taken Mara's gracious gift of life, and left the Jeweled Realm, never to return. But the necklace blazed in the direct sun of the table like a beacon. Iris had not stayed away. She wanted back in. Mara's hand instinctively went to her sword, adjusting it on her hip.

Iris wanted the Sword.

"So I kill my sister, and in return, I gain what?" Mara faced Boden.

Boden grimaced. "Well, considering you were supposed to kill her in the first place . . . you get a chance to right your wrong?"

Mara tapped her fingers on the wooden tabletop. *Not good enough.*

"I'm not traveling all the way to Ursa when your father, who I assume, like all Ursans, is handy with an axe, could kill her himself. Are you telling me she's that terrifying?"

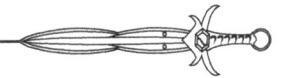

"You should've killed her." Mendel stood now, his chest puffed up with pride. "That's the point, isn't it? You aren't supposed to wear *that* unless she's dead." He thrust his thick finger at the Sword.

Mara couldn't look away. The man's brown eyes stared back at her, daring her to argue, but she couldn't. He was right.

Behind him, Petra stood silent, but Mara knew she was greedily observing the unfolding news that Princess Iris still lived. While Petra was loyal to her queen, she was also loyal to the empire. This included its many rules and laws of ritual, war, and the favorite maxim: *eat or be eaten.* Mara had done neither. A frown sat crooked on Petra's thin lips.

"You needn't travel to Ursa," Boden said. "We've arranged for a rendezvous with your . . . the witch."

"Now why would she agree to do a thing like that?" Mara narrowed her eyes.

"She thinks we're bringing you to her to hand over the realm," Mendel explained.

Mara nodded. "But really, you're bringing her to me."

"Look at that, Your Majesty," Mendel nudged Boden. "Beauty *and* brains. Now all that's left is to see if she really can use that sword of hers or if it's just for decoration."

Mara cleared her throat, silencing Mendel. There was nothing left for her to decide, then. She must agree. "I need time to think," she said. "Rooms have been prepared for you." She glanced at Petra to confirm, and Petra nodded. "You'll rest. We'll speak more about specifics at dinner."

Mara walked to the windows as the men were escorted out by a pair of Iron Guards. The blue brocade curtains were warm from the sun. Mara leaned her face into them, embracing the scent of dust while watching the lives of her people go on below.

For seven years, they thought her their rightful queen. For seven years, she lied.

A part of her felt lighter for the revelation of the truth. But the rest of her—having been raised in the Jeweled Realm and knowing the value of winning quickly—squashed that part.

"Is it true?" Petra's voice broke the silence.

Mara turned to see her standing by the table, almost in tears.

"Your words, by law, are truth," Petra said. "Speak them. Tell me she is dead and these men are liars, and I will believe you. I will slit their throats myself."

Mara let the brocade fall back against the window. She walked over to the table and picked up her sister's necklace. Feeling the cool gold on her skin made Iris's existence tangible.

She handed it to Petra. "This is her necklace." Mara sighed. "It's true. All of it."

Petra squeezed the chain in her hand until her knuckles turned white. Hot tears fought to fall from the corner of her eyes, but never did.

Mara placed a hand on Petra's wrist. "You have sworn an oath of loyalty to me," she reminded Petra. "You will speak of this to no one. Yes?"

Petra nodded. Barely.

"I *will* fix this. I will finish what I started."

Mara looked back out the window, her sight settling on the faraway arch. Her grandmother, the First Queen, had built it side by side with slaves won in battle. When they had finished, she freed them, telling them their sweat and blood was valuable to the Jeweled Realm. Like the finest sculpture, the citizens of the Jeweled Realm could shape themselves. With precision, they could master anything. Or anyone.

For the Jeweled Realm valued hard work above all else. For the realm, war was a machine and its people, the cogs. Mara knew it would have been easier if she'd done as instructed and killed Iris. It was expected. Law mandated it. But she couldn't.

Mara had never enjoyed being a cog.

She turned back to Petra, who still stared at her while trying to hide her anger, and forced a smile. "I want to rest. Wake me when it's time to change for dinner."

Petra offered Mara a strained smile. "As you wish, Your Majesty."

Mara plucked Iris's necklace from Petra's hands and shoved it in the hidden pocket of her outer skirt's seam. She walked with her fingers stroking the gold plate.

She'd nearly ripped it from Iris's neck that day. Such a stupid girl, wearing it beneath her armor.

Mara had been sixteen when the ritual was ordered. Early, perhaps, when compared to her mother's ritual at twenty-three, but the Red Queen had been sick, and an heir needed choosing. Iris had been barely fifteen, her *anniversaire* but a week prior. It hadn't mattered, though. The ritual had been ordered, and so it began.

They had both trained since infancy. Horsemanship began at three. Swordsmanship at five. Offensive techniques were always taught before defensive techniques. They learned to fight adeptly with both their strong and their weak hands. Diplomacy waited until one turned twelve.

Both were highly praised for their skill, though the Red Queen was enthused by Mara's left-handed strength.

"It comes naturally to you, and, therefore, your enemies will not expect such force," her mother said to her one day.

Iris had pouted, though, not for long. Their father tended to her ego, telling her that Mara's handedness was no feat because she did not have to work at it. Born left-handed, her strength was expected. Once her enemies noticed, they'd switch tactics.

Mara smiled, remembering. Iris had always listened to their father so intently. She'd believed his word was law. But she had never managed to best Mara, despite knowing her chosen hand.

Two Iron Guards followed Mara, as always, as she thought back on the way to her room. They stopped outside her door, where they made their post. With the heavy wood swinging closed, she released the breath she'd been holding.

Just like Petra, the guards were devout—zealously so—but their loyalty and obedience to Mara relied heavily on her status as queen. Her *legal* status.

She chose not to remove her sword. Instead, she paced. From one corner to the other, past the large glass doors that led to her balcony. Every time she passed the window, she marked the position of the sun. It sank too slowly for her liking, but Mara knew her power of influence did not extend to the sky.

The sooner she was done with the business of killing her sister, the better. She froze, staring at nothing, the display of her large bed before her blurring and twisting into obscurity.

Kill Iris.

It was a simple solution to choosing a monarch: let the heirs sort it out. The Jeweled Realm valued strength, cunning, and dominance in all aspects. So why not let the one who survived rule?

From an early age, Mara had seen the downside to this solution. In an empire where loyalty was expected, the system did not create loyal family members. But more than that, Mara didn't see any sense in killing those that didn't deserve it in some way.

A passing phase, her mother had called it. A sensibility rooted in her womanhood that would soon get weeded out and replaced with something much more useful.

But it was never weeded out.

Mara pulled herself from her spiraling thoughts. The room was darker. Shadows fell across the floor in sweeping slashes. Outside, the sun was sinking behind the top of the arch. Even the sounds of the *ville* were hushed as her people went home for their dinners. The Mousseaux rushed through on its way to the coast, never ceasing, never sleeping.

The stillness soothed her. Her worry momentarily slipped away, and a calm filled her stomach where her agitation liked to house itself. For a moment, she felt nothing. And it felt nice.

But a knock at the door startled her.

"Majesty," Petra's voice said, offering no hint of her earlier disappointment, "dinner is prepared."

"Are the guests seated?" Mara called.

A moment of silence, and then, "Yes."

Mara checked herself in her vanity mirror. She should have slept. Fatigue spilled from her amber eyes, culminating in blue slate below her lower lid. Her hair was falling out of its braid and her makeup—the thick kohl lines drawn across her lids—was smudged.

She opened her door and motioned for Petra to enter. "Fix me," she said, seating herself at her vanity. "I look disheveled."

Petra silently obeyed. Her hands reached for Mara's braid and undid it, all within a singular, practiced motion one might miss if they blinked. Mara kept her eyes open.

And on her steward.

Petra stared at her hands, at her work, not daring to look at Mara. This was new. By position, Petra was Mara's highest-ranking servant. It afforded her rights and privileges that some only dreamed of. Petra benefited from her proximity to the queen, managing her own private affairs in a sphere of affluence unreachable to her were she not Mara's steward.

Mara usually enjoyed the girl's company. She liked to think she nurtured a small friendship with Petra, knowing Petra's oath kept her loyal. They mutually benefited from each other, but Mara sensed Petra pulling away, putting up a wall.

"Are you alright?" Mara asked as Petra redrew the lines on her lids.

"Hush," Petra murmured. "You must be still, Your Majesty."

It was a small insolence, veiled well by words of respect. Mara said nothing more. She waited, eyes closed, as Petra moved from one eye to the other. Mara's hands habitually went to her sword, where they rested. Deep down, Mara thought she should be ready, should Petra decide to abandon her loyalties.

A loyalty founded on a lie, Mara reminded herself.

When Petra was through, Mara blinked several times to clear her vision. She studied Petra's work in the mirror. As usual, it was perfect.

"Well done." Mara stood, staring at her and Petra's reflection. "You've managed to make me presentable."

Petra stared at Mara's reflection, too, their eyes meeting in the mirror. Mara could see the pain there, the hurt she'd caused from her lies. "Thank you, Majesty." Petra's lips barely moved.

"But if you ever tell me to be silent again, I will have *you* silenced. Permanently. Am I clear?"

Petra nodded and stood back, hands clasped behind her while Mara left the room. She followed her queen like a ghost. Her footfalls were always silent. Her body, quiet. It was what they taught at the Training House. How they all were taught. Blend in. Be a part of the room, lest your presence insult your master.

But now Mara wondered if it was too much. Too easy to turn insult to injury should the need arise.

Or the will.

A shift change had occurred while she was in her room, and she was now being escorted by two different Iron Guards. Two men had replaced the two women. They were wide, like moving walls, and did not walk silently like Petra.

Their movements resonated around the hallway. Their armor shook and shifted.

It was so distracting that Mara couldn't think. They were nearly at the dining hall before she realized that wasn't where they were leading her.

"Where are we going?" Mara stopped in the middle of the hallway. She turned to Petra for an explanation.

"The eastern salon, Your Majesty. A more intimate room for intimate conversations." Petra explained.

She seemed rather cool about the entire ordeal. Mara had not asked her to move dinner to a different room. Of course, Mara *should* have asked her to. Petra was right. She was just doing her job. Mara forced herself to relax, releasing her hand from the pommel of the Sword.

"As it should be," Mara agreed. "Very well."

They continued walking, arriving at the windowed and gold-gilded doors of the salon. Mara could see Boden and Mendel already seated inside. The Iron Guard took their positions on either side of the archway while Petra glided past Mara and opened the door for her.

Boden and Mendel—talking feverishly—stopped immediately upon seeing Mara. She tried to smile at them, but it was forced and weak. Petra pulled a chair out for her next to Boden, then stepped between Mara and her seat.

"Your sword, Majesty," Petra said.

It was tradition to place the Sword in the center of the table during dinner. A mere moment of respite, her grandmother had ordained, from the burden of the Sword. A symbolic gesture suggesting that sometimes—even briefly—the Sword must be laid down.

"No." Mara stared evenly at Petra. "There isn't room on this small table. I'll wear it." Mara slumped herself into the seat before Petra could try and insist. She shoved the Sword to the side before adjusting it, scooting her own chair in.

"There, it's fine," she assured her steward, motioning for Petra to take her place in the corner.

The Sword would remain on her hip. If Iris wanted it so badly, she'd have to take it off Mara's dead body herself.

Mara cleared her throat, her signal that she was ready for dinner. Footmen appeared bearing silver trays and gold ewers. They plopped down hot breasts of chicken on plates, followed by scoops of steamed vegetables and roasted fingerling potatoes smothered in butter fresh from the royal *laiterie*. Knowing her well, a footman quickly presented her with a glass of the darkest red vin.

"To my guests," Mara raised her glass.

Boden and Mendel raised their drinks—large steins of fizzy malted beer—and tipped them toward Mara.

When the entire meal was served, Mara watched the footmen from the corner of her eye. The last to leave fussed with the trays on the buffet, but finally backed into the hidden doorway in the corner. The door snapped shut, disappearing into the wall.

"Finally," Mara said, washing her food down with some vin. "Now, tell me more of this rendezvous."

"Well," Boden didn't wash his food down, choosing to speak over it, "there's a dam to the northeast. It acts as a bridge between the Jeweled Realm and the Waste."

Mara nodded. "Roully Dam, by Valenbeuge. I know it."

"Good." Boden speared a thick potato with his knife. "We'll meet there. Atop the dam, the witch will have no means of escape. My men and I will guard the Jeweled Realm's side, and my father's escort will guard the east."

"You're certain you can beat her?" Mendel growled at Mara.

Mara took a bite of chicken, setting her face void of emotion. Perhaps she gave herself away with the slight uptick of her eyebrow, but she hoped Mendel didn't notice.

She swallowed and wiped the corner of her mouth with a silk napkin. "I'm certain."

"Perhaps you thought that last time," Mendel said.

Mara fixed her eyes on Mendel's. They really were the color of dried leaves in the fall. Brittle. And dead.

"The reason I stayed my hand last time no longer exists," Mara explained.

"And what reason was that?" Boden asked.

"Love, or something like it."

"Love?" Mendel questioned. He started to laugh, which then got him coughing. His face turned red. Leaning back in his chair, he stared at the chandelier and heaved for air between coughs. His hand beat on the table. Glassware shook and toyed with the idea of tipping over in the wake of his hysteria.

Boden looked from Mendel to Mara, his cheeks reddening beneath his beard. Mara narrowed her eyes and glared at Mendel.

"I believed my sister young and perhaps innocent in the sentimental way your religion views your youth," Mara spoke softly, forcing Mendel to quiet himself in order to hear her.

She sipped from her glass, pursing her lips at the vin's initial bitterness, thinking about Iris at the age of fourteen. The girl had been tall and thin. Breakable. But their father always spun it into something positive. *Lithe and quick* was his favorite.

Iris had worn her black hair chopped to shoulder length, the ends left violently blunt. She would always wear the upper section in a topknot and despised Mara's long auburn hair and penchant for plaits.

"I was young and thought our relationship mattered. I thought sparing her was a greater justice than killing her." Mara said, coming back to the present, to the table, to her guests.

"And now?" Mendel asked.

Mara studied her napkin. The way the golden thread of the embroidery twinkled from the chandelier reminded her of Iris's eyes that day, when Mara had held her sword still, when she hadn't brought it down on the girl's throat. When she'd let her live.

"I was wrong." Mara refused to look up from her napkin.

Mendel didn't respond. When Mara eventually dared a glance, she found him studying her, his eyes flitting across her face, trying to determine if she was genuine or not.

"There's nothing wrong with loving your sister." Boden's voice filled the void that consumed the room.

Mara glared at him.

Boden cleared his throat and attempted again. "In our religion, as you say, a child's innocence is a sacred thing. It's why our warriors must be grown before we accept them into the ranks."

Mara knew enough about Ursan religion to know it didn't sit well with her. Or her people. One creator, demanding obedience yet lovingly receiving any who call on him?

The Jeweled Realm shied away from deities. The world was hard enough without the oppressive wants and needs of an unseen, unknowable god. Needs of the people, though, were easily assessed. Protection, food, a place to carve out their own lives. And how to achieve these goals, too, was simple.

Power.

Thus, the Jeweled Realm functioned on the words of the Red Queen: *Strength wields the Sword.*

And the Sword controls the land.

Mara set her glass on the table a little too hard. The truth of it all was she couldn't explain what had stayed her hand that day. Mara had always found that there was something different within her. Different desires. Different dreams. She could play the part of heir to the throne well. Swords sat happily in her hand, pleased to do her bidding. Words, whether harsh or soothing, came easily to her in matters of diplomacy.

But all the killing . . .

She watched other children grow up with siblings to call on in their times of need. Sure, they fought, but they were still an entity united. But she was destined to kill her own sister?

It didn't seem fair. Not when her sister had been her closest friend. They'd spend hours riding together in the forest, chasing foxes, hunting for wild turkeys. And while they'd practiced swordplay together, Mara found it more fun than damning.

But seeds of division were sowed early. Each parent picked a favorite, Mara receiving their mother's affectionate gaze and Iris gaining their father's. The seed found root in Iris and fell fallow in Mara. She hated them for it, of course. Perhaps without their goading, she and Iris could have been friends. It all could have worked out. There need not have been any more bloodshed.

But this was the Jeweled Realm. There was always a need.

Boden and Mendel stared at her. Wine had spilled from her glass and soaked into the tablecloth, growing across the white fabric like a flooded river. Mara ignored it, instead setting her gaze on Boden.

"There is no such thing as innocence, Prince Boden, only weakness."

"Then who was the weak one when you let her go?" Boden asked, his tone serious.

"Aye, there's no strength in a draw, is there?" Mendel added.

Mara chewed the corner of her lip and stared at Mendel's face. She wasn't really looking at it, but rather looking past it, at how far he'd land if she hit him square in the jaw.

"Perhaps I should offer a demonstration?" Mara smiled. "Care to assist me, my lord?" She asked Mendel.

Mendel shook his head and carried on eating. Boden did his best to hide a bemused smile, but Mara caught it out of the corner of her eye.

"And you, Prince Boden? Would you like to assist me in showing Mendel the true ability of my swordplay?"

Boden choked on his beer. "No, Your Grace," he coughed. "Let's save that demonstration for the witch."

"Fine," Mara said. "We'll leave at the rise of the moon."

Mara, finished with her meal, waved to Petra. Petra nodded and rang the bell for the footmen. The hidden door swung open almost immediately.

"The queen is finished," Petra decreed.

Plates were cleared even before the men could finish their meals. They watched in something akin to horror as servants removed their dinner.

Ursa was not known for its abundance of food. Their livestock and crops were limited to things hardier in nature. The meat of their animals was stringy and tough. Their vegetables were mostly rootstock.

Mara did her best to hide her amusement. Footmen returned shortly, before the men could complain, with plates of delicate desserts. Pastries enveloping jammed fruit. Miniature cakes topped with iced roses. Smooth-surfaced tarts, brilliant and shiny as a mirror. And Mara's favorite, brightly hued cookies sandwiching a delicious, sugared cream.

She took a cookie and watched as the men couldn't settle on any one thing.

"They're all good, I assure you," she said, encouraging them to try some of each. "The Jeweled Realm enjoys dessert most of all."

Chapter Three

Mara wrapped a cloak around her shoulders in her dark and silent room. No one, not a single civilian of the *ville*, had the right to question what their queen was doing in the middle of the night. She could arrest and silence anyone she chose to. And yet she wondered why fear was sinking low in her stomach, like a stone.

She was tired of bloodshed. The thought of fighting Iris was already tugging at her. Her body was feeling exhausted even before the battle began. It settled deep in her chest, and no matter what she did, it wouldn't be shaken.

She sighed and pulled up her hood. Exhausted or not, she had to fight her sister. And exhausted or not, she knew she'd win. Mara was confident in that one aspect. For even though she sought a different course than most of the Jeweled Realm, she was still a daughter of the Red Queen. She would fight and she would kill if need be.

Iris would regret her return.

Petra was waiting for Mara outside her room. She silently followed Mara down to the stables, where Mendel and Boden were told to meet her.

"You'll remain here," Mara instructed her. "Await my return."

"Your Majesty," Petra argued, "I would rather travel with you."

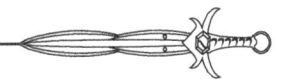

Mara looked the steward over, wondering how much of her words spoke truth. Petra certainly seemed eager to serve her queen, but how much of that was really just eagerness for the opportunity to watch the two heirs fight for the throne?

"No." Mara climbed onto her dark stallion. "You will remain."

"It will seem suspicious, Your Majesty, that your steward is not traveling with you." Petra switched tactics, appealing to Mara's now endangered image as queen. She quickly cast a side-long glance at the two men in their company.

"Let there be suspicion. I will address any troublemakers when I return." Mara guided her horse up next to Boden's. She nodded to signal she was ready.

"I stationed my men outside the *ville*'s walls. They'll join us there," he said.

Boden led the group down the cobblestone yard toward the stable gates. The moon still offered several more hours of its gentle light. Mara calculated how far they'd ride before sunup. How far before high noon. How far before dusk the next day. It would take more than a day's ride to reach Valenbeuge. They'd avoid entering the *ville* at all costs, not wanting to draw attention to the queen's reason for visiting the nearby dam. But by the next moonrise, they'd reach Roully Dam, and Iris would meet her fate.

The minutes ticked by slowly, and Mara felt her stomach continue to roil with anticipation along with something else. Was it guilt?

Boden's muffled voice rocked through Mara's thoughts. Their horses stomped across the large bridge stretching over the Mousseaux, sending echoes into the night.

"This bridge is an extraordinary feat," Boden repeated for her. "How was it done?"

Mara shrugged, annoyed at the talkative nature of the prince. "You'll have to ask the engineer. I believe the woman who drew it out for my grandmother still lives."

At the gates, several guards waited at attention. The palace had already notified them to let the travelers through. Mara hid amongst the two men, hoping to not draw attention to herself.

"The queen finished with you already?" A guard laughed, "On your way then. Take your filthy soldiers with you."

The guards shared jokes with each other as the three passed, none even taking a second look at Mara. Had they looked closer, they'd have noticed her gleaming saddle, decorated with gold and silver, or her fine cloak, embroidered with a garden of red and green, the house sigil on proud display on the back.

But they didn't look well, and Mara made a note to address the lax efforts of the guardsmen upon her return.

Outside the walls, the icy wind hit them. It cut across the stone face and whipped into their eyes, reminding them that winter was just around the corner. Boden's men joined from the shadows, and they all worked their way from the *ville*'s wall. A dark shadow—the arch blocking the moon—lay sharply across the ground. Mara rode in and out of it, the light momentarily welcoming and then bashful.

When they passed through the arch, Mara kept her eyes forward. She'd seen it so many times, been paraded to it on multiple occasions for different celebrations and holidays. It was beautiful, that was certain, but Mara had been force-fed her grandmother's ideologies since birth. The arch and all it represented reminded Mara that she seemed to be missing something that the other women of her family had. Some certain ideal.

Boden looked back at it as they passed through. He shook his head.

"The mere courage to build something so large," he said, "and with her own hands. That's what they say, right? The First Queen built the arch with her own two hands."

"Well, she had help," Mara answered, "and surely she did the least of the work."

Mara stared off to her right at the faraway tree line. The trees, an elegant dark green during the day, bled black in the moonlight. If Mara stared hard enough, she felt her vision shift, the darkness reaching forward for her. She shivered.

Several fields lay between the riders and the forest, but Mara was counting each step of her horse, feeling the distance shrink ever so slowly.

Boden clicked his heels to nudge his horse forward. His stallion caught up to Mara's and they walked side by side for a while, not speaking. He'd glance at her, but she did everything she could to avoid looking at him.

It wasn't just his eyes themselves that bothered her—it was the *way* he looked at her. Men generally gazed upon her with a mixture of fear and respect. While

Mara was certain those feelings were there just beneath the surface, there was also a curiosity within them that she was unaccustomed to. She felt Boden actually *saw* her.

Her.

Not her crown.

Or her sword.

He finally broke their silence. "When was the last time you left the *ville*?"

She glowered at him, her amber eyes reflecting the moonlight harshly. "I went hunting just this past fortnight," she growled, "and I rode around the wall for inspection last full moon."

Boden nodded. "Yes, but beyond that? When did you last visit your realm? Your empire is vast—the largest on the continent. Surely there is a need for a queen to visit her people."

"And what need would that be?" Mara sat up a little straighter and lifted her chin higher.

Boden rode silently for a moment before answering. "The need to be known. The need for a people to see their queen and know her."

Mara slumped in her saddle as her horse slowed. She could barely make out Boden's features in the inkiness of night. His bearskin cowl cast shadows on his already dark features, but his blue eyes fought the darkness and shimmered in the pale light of the moon.

"What do you mean by that?" An ember of anger lit within her, but she fought to keep it subdued.

"I only meant, if they have no connection to you, then what do they care who wins or loses?"

Her hands gripped tighter on the reins and her nails dug into her palms.

"Allegiance, Your Majesty, and loyalty are two very important things. Do you command it of your people?"

"What are you suggesting?" she asked.

Boden looked into her eyes, staring deeply. It unnerved Mara, but she dared not look away. "When you rule by a sword, they only care about the sword."

Mara was silent. He was right. They were words she herself mulled over time and time again, long before she was ever queen. Her mother had tried to quell her worry, and her father had assured her it wouldn't matter. He'd always been so certain Iris would reign supreme.

If only he could see them now.

Mara imagined him smiling, amused at her weakness, knowing all along she'd mess it up. That she'd ruin the empire—and her name in history. Her father had never been shy about his favoritism toward Iris.

Mara was born quickly after the Red Queen married the only son of the prestigious House of Ducasse. She'd nearly killed her mother in the birthing bed. She came out screaming and didn't stop crying for days. Her mother said it showed Mara had spirit.

Her father remained silent and stayed away. It didn't help that Mara grew into a replica of her mother: tall, tan, and muscular, amber-eyed with red-hued hair.

Mara knew he had wanted to see some semblance of himself in the future heir to the Jeweled Realm. But Mara possessed none and was thus disappointing.

Iris, born just over a year later, was all that her father had wanted. Dark-haired with milk-pale skin, she seemed made of moonlight. Just like her father. They even possessed the same penetrating eyes.

Mara glanced over at Boden, peeking at his face while he rode silently beside her. His eyes intrigued her, too. While they were brilliant and as terrifyingly colorful as her father's and sister's, there was something else there. A kindness or gentleness that neither Iris nor her father had ever yielded to.

"What of you Boden, Prince of Ursa?" she called to him, disturbing the cool, quiet night.

"Huh, what?" he asked, his eyes already heavy with sleep despite not even being out of the *ville*'s line of sight.

"You speak of me and my sister easily, but what of you? Your family. Your brother is the heir apparent. His woman is with child, pushing you further from the throne each day."

Boden sighed and turned toward her. "The Prince of Ursa is a better man than me."

Mara scoffed. "Don't tell me you wouldn't want to be king should you have the chance?"

Boden shrugged. "No, I wouldn't."

"You must be joking."

Mara guided her stallion closer to Boden's. Their knees nearly touched as their horses clipped along the road. She was suddenly aware of her heartbeat thudding in her chest. It was deafening in her own ears, though one glance at Boden showed he didn't notice.

"I'm a student of my religion, Your Majesty," he said, "and our god asks us to be of benefit from whatever place we are born to be in."

"A benefit? Do tell, how can a spare heir be a benefit to his kingdom? Besides using precious resources for his pleasure?" Mara asked.

Her horse stepped sideways to avoid a fallen branch and nudged Boden's. Mara recoiled her leg, but it was no use. They rammed into each other and were now the closest they'd yet been. Mara could smell the dried sweat off his bearskin, and something strangely sweet.

"A spare heir? That's a good one!" Boden chuckled. "Perhaps I felt the way you describe, once, when I was young and naïve. But I am a student of Saint Kalda. Do you know him?"

Mara shook her head, her lip curling in a frown at the thought of memorizing the facts of some man or woman of a god.

"Well," Boden said, ignoring Mara's attitude, "Saint Kalda was a nobody. Born poor. He worked as a smith by trade. But even from that simple profession, my god chose him to ascend, to guide the king during the War of Husa."

"The War of Husa, where kingdoms battled over the abundant source of fresh water found in Husa's numerous lakes? Didn't Ursa lose?"

Boden smiled. "Yes, we lost the claim to Husa and all of its lakes. But we survived."

"Ah, did your god send rain daily to fill your barrels with water?" Mara mocked.

"No, my god led Saint Kalda to a place in the city where he dug down and down, discovering a hidden well of water. It is now the centerpiece of the village's main square."

"Unknown water beneath the *ville*?" Mara didn't believe it.

"An aquifer, still supplying us with fresh water hundreds of years later."

Mara rode on in silence, considering Boden's tale. She knew little of Ursan theology. She knew they believed in one god, and their history was full of prophets who—one way or another—performed the bidding of this god to the benefit of believers.

"The Black Rains would have sunk into this aquifer, poisoning your water," Mara tossed out, despite knowing her logic was flawed. The Ursan people had survived, thrived, and Boden was a product of that right before her eyes. But she didn't enjoy giving in too easily.

"The Black Rains touched the Waste and nothing else. Everyone knows that."

Boden sounded as if he had heard Mara's argument before. His face was expressionless as he avoided looking at her. From the side she could see his strong jawline clench and unclench.

Mara contented herself with riding in silence. She thought of Petra back at the palace, and hoped the girl would keep her word. The rest of the servants could gossip whatever they liked about why the queen left with the Ursans, unaccompanied by any Jeweled Realm citizen, but Petra needed to keep her mouth shut. *If they know the truth when I return,* Mara thought, squeezing the pommel of her sword once, twice . . .

She'd know who to kill.

Chapter Four

They rested when they grew tired. More specifically, when Mara gave the order that she was tired.

She chose a small copse to camp within. They were nearly through the forest, named Renard, but she didn't tell Boden that even though she felt like proving to him she had seen her own kingdom and knew plenty about it. Giant trees towered over them, blocking the moonlight yet allowing it to occasionally seep in when the breeze rattled the branches.

Small beasts scurried away from their torches. More than a few fox eyes glowed in the illuminating cast of the fire. Mara smelled the wet moss of the forest floor and the sap from the pines. It reminded her of hunting with Iris.

"We'll stop here," she had said, and the Ursans obeyed.

She didn't want to admit to herself that she liked watching the foreigners follow her command, but it fluttered beneath her chest all the same. To command and be obeyed possessed its own kind of thrill.

A blood-red sunrise shot through the fingers of pines scattered around them by the time they made a fire. There were several of the ancient trees, though, none were close enough to touch each other like back in the forest proper. Tiny saplings of birch and willow fought for space in the remaining air. Birch brush filled the rest. Squirrels chattered nearby.

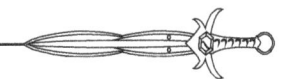

"Your Majesty," Mendel said, handing Mara a bread roll and hunk of cheese.

She nodded her thanks but said nothing. The bread was fresh from her palace kitchens, the cheese from a nearby *laiterie* what need did she have of speaking thanks to these men for her own people's food?

"The village is not far away," one man—Mara didn't care to remember any of their names—said to Mendel.

"Aye, we'll reach the dam by nightfall," he said.

"Are we to avoid the village completely, Your Majesty?" another man, the youngest in the group, asked Boden directly.

Boden chewed his food, his head tilted back while he stared at the sky. Mara admired the way his men looked at him. They were just as eager to please him as Mara's own people were to please her, but there was something different in their faces. They weren't afraid of Boden. They respected him.

"Yes," he said, bringing his gaze back to his men. "Our secrecy is of the utmost importance."

He looked at Mara and winked before carrying on eating. She was thankful he had not dragged her into their conversation. Words sometimes felt heavy, especially when Mara thought of all the words she'd need to explain why Iris lived.

But not for long.

The men—there were twelve—satisfied themselves with the bread and cheese. One man stirred a small cast-iron pot on the fire, brewing something the Ursans were eager to taste.

"Nah, get off, would you?" the man stirring the pot growled at a comrade trying to steal a taste.

He poured the steaming liquid into a tin camp can and gingerly offered it to Mara.

"Your Majesty." The man bowed while handing her the can.

She took the can in her hands. "What's this?"

"Ginger tea," the man replied, raising his eyes to meet hers, "an Ursan camp staple."

"Soothes rider's digestion." Mendel slapped his paunchy stomach.

The steam rose in curlicues toward Mara's face. It smelled wonderful. She had never heard of such a tea, though, she was not particularly curious about Ursan food either. As practical people, they kept their food practical, too.

Mara tipped the can back slowly, attempting to get a sip of the tea. Boden reached his arm out and touched her forearm.

"It is hot," he warned her.

It took Mara a moment to realize Boden meant the tea, for his hand was warm on her skin and she was immediately inundated with the feeling of his touch. Her cheeks burned. She pulled away from him, her anger ignited by his treatment. She wasn't a child. His touch was unwarranted. She lifted the can higher and received, as her reward, scalding hot tea on the tip of her tongue.

The pain seared through her mouth, but she held her lips tight and her face rigid. Trained in the art of deception, Mara knew how to hide her pain. She nodded her thanks to the Ursan man and held the warm can in her hands.

Boden smirked at her but said nothing more. He pulled from his pocket a small white stone. It crumbled in his fingers with the slightest pressure. He offered her some.

"For your tongue," he said. "It'll stop the pain."

Mara stared at him, trying at first to convince him he was wrong and she didn't need it. But a sting of pain rushed through her again when her tongue brushed the back of her teeth. She pinched the white powder out of his palm, avoiding touching him as much as possible, and placed it in her mouth.

"A mineral," she said as the powder coated her tongue and teeth.

"Aye, but harmless. It'll take the sting away."

"You Ursans are clever, I'll give you that," she said, wiping the residual powder away on her cloak.

The men chuckled.

"Are you not nervous, Your Majesty, traveling with a group of Ursan warriors?" the youngest Ursan dared ask her.

The rest went silent, wondering if Mara would answer. She looked at the man. He was short and thickly built, but his cheeks were ruddy and youthful. His beard was patchy, and his eyes carried a playful glimmer that Mara found distracting.

She glanced at Boden. His eyes glittered with amusement as he continued to eat. Through his beard the corners of his mouth ticked upward slightly.

"No," she finally said, turning back to the young man. "I'm not afraid."

"What if we're rogues?" he asked. "What if we attack?"

A nearby Ursan smacked the young man in the back of the head, but the man seemed unfazed. He stared happily up at Mara from his seat on the forest floor, pleased to have her attention.

Mara rolled her eyes. "Let's see, there are . . . " She made a big deal out of counting them all. Twelve warriors, Mendel, and Boden. "Fourteen Ursans. Hmmmm." She shrugged. "I'd give you five minutes."

"Five minutes?" the man asked.

"Before you're all dead." She smiled. "Six, if I'm feeling generous."

The young man lost his smile. Older, wiser men in the group laughed. Boden chuckled, too, though, he didn't seem quite as amused anymore. He watched Mara, his distracting eyes seeing past her hard exterior. The eagerness within them was back, and Mara shivered beneath their gaze.

"May we see it, Your Majesty?" asked the man who had handed her the tea.

Mara pursed her lips, thinking. All of them watched her intently like little boys waiting to see their first execution.

Why not, she thought. "It's not a toy," she reminded them.

It was the pride of the Jeweled Realm. The Sacred Sword had supposedly been smithed by the First Queen's father, forged at the cost of his life. He'd formed it and shaped it, sharpening its black blade to a vicious point, and handed it to his daughter before dying. The emerald was only added after the First Queen's dominance on the field—after she'd taken command of the local militia, followed by the overtaking of other small feudal colonies. Ultimately, she created one enormous army. One giant machine of death.

The Jeweled Realm was not forged in a day, and neither was the Sword she carried at her side.

Mara unsheathed it, the pear-shaped emerald in the hilt catching the light. Aside from the gem, the rest of the guard was simple. Golden metal, a few filigreed details, and rich black leather wraps finished the grip. A blackened blade, brilliant in its own sheen, blemished only by the engraving of the First Queen's name: Adra.

Overall, it wasn't the most magnificent looking blade on the continent, but the citizens of the Jeweled Realm bowed to it all the same.

The Ursans nodded their heads in appreciation. The black blade was a remnant of their ancestor's techniques. It was thought her great-grandfather had been born in Ursa, or his father, or his father's father.

The understated grip, made fanciful only by the giant gem, amused them.

"Should there not be more?" the young Ursan asked, finding his courage again. "I imagined the Sacred Sword would bear its blade weight in gems."

Mara clucked disappointedly at the young man. She stood, tossing the tin can into the air. The young man flinched, thinking Mara meant to hit him with it. Instead, she raised her sword, and in one swift movement, sliced right through the can.

Tea splashed across the young man, along with one half of the tin. The other half landed at Boden's feet.

Mara smirked before wiping her blade once with the tail of her cloak and sheathing it. She sat down and nodded her head at the young man.

"Sometimes pretty isn't necessary."

"I'll say," the man mumbled, wiping the tea from his face.

"Enough," Boden spoke over the group as he stood. "The Sword Queen needs to rest now. You should all rest as well."

He gestured for Mara to follow him. She hesitated, not liking being told what to do or where to go, but eventually stood and followed. They walked toward the horses not far away, where Boden's bearskin made a makeshift bed.

Boden pointed to the fur. "Here, rest. You'll need your strength for your sister."

"I'm not a child." Mara turned to face him. "I'll rest if I feel like it."

A hint of a smile moved across Boden's lips. "Funny, you sound like a child."

Mara's hand floated to her pommel, but she fought the movement, instead grabbing her belt. It would do no good to kill the Ursan prince now. Not with his men around. She could certainly dispatch all of them, but the effort she'd have to put into it after riding all night was too great a gamble.

Her rage must have shown in her eyes because Boden stepped back a stride and bowed his head. It was strange to watch a man like Boden give in to her so easily. He was a prince in his own right and built for war. There was some satisfaction to be found in it. And something equally annoying.

"As you wish, Your Grace," he said, "but you know I'm right."

He smiled warmly at her and she felt off-kilter. She ground her teeth together, resisting the shallow feelings she felt bubbling up toward the surface. Only a foolish woman gave in to an attractive man. "You are an insolent prince, you know?"

"I'm just trying to be helpful," Boden said. "Saint Kalda speaks of rest before war."

Mara rolled her eyes.

"He also speaks of tending to ourselves to maintain balance."

"Alright, alright," Mara groaned, "I'll rest. Just stop speaking about your stupid holy man."

"Saint," Boden corrected.

Mara surveyed the bearskin, contemplating how to recline comfortably enough to rest. Unfortunately, all she could think about was the days and days Boden had worn his bearskin. The weather it had repelled, the sweat it had absorbed. It was enough to make Mara's skin prickle.

It was then she noticed green spreading across the ground behind the skin. She kicked Boden's cowl aside to reveal a patch of fluffy moss big enough for Mara to lie on. Lowering herself onto the mossy bed, she reclined in her cloak and looked up at Boden.

"See? Resting." She smiled.

Boden picked up his bearskin. "As you say, Your Majesty."

He walked back to his group of men. Mara fought the sudden surge of loneliness. She crossed her arms over her chest and rolled away from the fire, from Boden. It wasn't like she needed him close. She barely knew him, after all. Warmth from the fire still reached her. The horses were near, their breathing in the dark its own type of lullaby. There was nothing within the woods that frightened her. But what about the other side, where Iris waited? Her hand worried over the metal of the Sacred Sword's pommel, thoughts of the fight to come drifting in and out of her mind.

The so-called magic Iris was said to possess sounded problematic, if only in a distracting sense. Mara knew Iris couldn't wield magic. She had barely understood the *maître d'armes* when he instructed the girls on the proper way to forge a weapon.

Mara suppressed a laugh. Rolling over, she folded her arms beneath her head and allowed her eyes to shut for only a moment.

Iris will see the error of her ways, Mara thought, and then she'll die.

Chapter Five

Mara jolted awake. Sunbeams waned across her face as the light began its fall below the horizon. She grabbed her cheek delicately, feeling the warmth left by the sun, like a kiss.

The Ursans' voices were low. She couldn't hear their words from where she lay, but the timbre of their sounds comforted her. It reminded her of being a child and sleeping in the room beside her parents, of hearing them talk—and sometimes argue—as she drifted to sleep.

She lay there a few moments longer, listening to the fire crackle. From her vantage point, she could make out the dim glow of the moon. It was full and sat on the edge of the pending darkness over a tall pine. The tree looked like a spear, ready to stab the moon.

Like a sword.

Mara stretched and stood. She wiped the pine needles and forest debris from her clothes and approached the Ursans. They growled a welcome to her, sounding less cheerful but no less friendlier than before.

"Here, eat." Boden handed Mara a chunk of meat and bread. "Fiske went hunting while you slept."

The youngest Ursan smiled and held up a blackened piece of meat on bone. "Forgiveness, Majesty, for hunting in the Jeweled Realm."

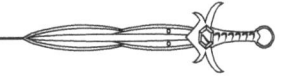

Mara took a small bite. It was sizzling hot but earthy and delicious.

"For now"—the corner of Mara's lips twitched—"I'll pardon you."

Mara welcomed the food. The thought of the fight with her sister was making her hungry, she knew, but she felt it deeper. A need, a desire, about to be satiated. She finished her food and asked for more.

Boden handed her another piece of the beast and watched her dig in. The way he looked at her was bothersome. Something *pleased* him, but Mara wasn't interested in pleasing anyone but herself.

"Where is she putting it?" one of the Ursans mumbled to another.

The last of the sun's rays finally drifted behind the trees. Within the sky, the bright blue of day bruised to blue-black, then just black, like ink in water. Stars popped out, winking at them while they prepared for the last leg of their journey.

Mara stared at the sky and swallowed her last bite. She remembered the stars the day she let Iris live. Not in any particular position, but just the way they glittered. They were like the tiniest diamonds, scattered on a black velvet cloth, waiting for her to choose. She remembered feeling she could reach up and pluck one from the heavens.

The darkness of that long-ago night had been suffocating. The summer air had been humid, and a young crescent moon had sat in audience for them. Though illuminating very little within the royal forest she had tracked her sister to, Mara had barely noticed. Lack of light never seemed to affect her fighting as much as it did Iris. Her sister had looked scared, genuinely terrified, which Mara found strange. Iris was, if nothing, confident. Perhaps too confident. Maybe she hadn't been ready to die that day.

Mara's eyes now traced the halo surrounding the moon, thinking of Iris's eyes the moment she'd realized Mara was giving her a second chance to live.

Perhaps now she would finally be ready to die.

Mara's horse seemed eager to return to the trail. The beast, like Mara, did not like lingering in one place for too long. Sounds from the forest left the animal on edge. Mara patted him gently as they wound their way through the trees.

The tiny saplings grew shorter and shorter. Soon, they gave way entirely to the birch brush. It was thick, with the reaching branches blocking their way on nearly every turn. Mendel took the lead and sliced through with his sword, clearing a straight path out.

Out of the tangle, the grass grew tall. It was cooler. A chilled breeze blew through them while they found their new path. The noise of the forest, branches breaking and cracking beneath the horses, gave way to the quiet hush of hooves whisking through grass.

Mara's cloak billowed around her. She tugged it tighter.

"Are you ready?" Boden asked, bringing his horse near hers.

"Yes," she assured him, guiding her horse over a small stream. "The rest was needed."

It was all the thanks he was going to get.

Mara kicked her horse, letting it run and stretch its legs. It galloped ahead, past a grumbling Mendel, and leapt over another small stream. She let the horse go where it wished for a while, not even glancing backward at the Ursans, not even caring.

Before long, a stomping of hooves arrived behind her. Boden appeared, his horse's eyes bright with joy from the run. He smiled at Mara, and she smiled weakly in return. She slowed her stallion, allowing Boden to keep the pace. More stomping, more horses' hooves, and the Ursans quickly surrounded her once more.

"Your Majesty should compete with that horse," Fiske said.

Mara wanted to laugh. She really did, but far off on the horizon she could see the spires of the church in Valenbeuge, low mountains looming nearby, the glint of a lake, and the dam.

Her destiny.

She let the dread she suddenly felt settle low inside her. Her mother always said it was alright to be a little scared, for fear often brought with it a ferocity. But Mara's throat tightened at the thought of seeing Iris again. She wanted it to be a happy meeting, deep down, but she knew it wouldn't be.

Not this time. Not ever.

The travel party soon found the road—a wide boulevard paved with stones too large for one man to lift. Ruts were worn into the road from the overuse of carts, displaying a double pathway toward Valenbeuge.

Mara ignored the city's rooftops, spying them from just above the city walls, and instead kept her sight on the ever-growing dam. The Ursans admired the paved road, though, some grumbled it was unnecessary.

"A dirt road is just as good, and twice as easy to make," one mumbled.

Above the dam, stars blinked. The moon drifted lazily above, but Mara felt its anticipation—her anticipation. The weight of the Sacred Sword hung off Mara's right hip. She felt the Sword, too, was eager. It was an odd thought, but one she was bred to understand from an early age.

Not every small girl was taught to sleep with a sword beneath her pillow. To spend the evenings examining, sharpening, and taking care of her weapon. Not every girl was meant to inherit such a prosperous land like the Jeweled Realm.

Mara's eyes drifted down to the pommel of the Sacred Sword. The emerald always looked cold and lifeless to her.

Not every girl laid claim to such a monstrous weapon.

They rode in silence. The Ursans seemed on edge, their eyes darting back and forth amidst the darkness. Boden sat straight in his saddle, stealing glances at Mara. She wanted to tell him to stop, but she knew it'd make no difference. The prince seemed to fuss over her. She frowned just thinking about it, though, there did seem to be a bubble of anticipation blooming deep in her stomach. Mara chalked it up to the greasy meat she had consumed.

The plain rolled away in front of them, decorated here and there by a small grouping of oak brush, but otherwise only grass. An hour passed with nothing happening and no one speaking. Then another.

Around the end of the third hour, a grass owl hooted. Mendel held up his fist, signaling a stop. He cupped his hands around his mouth and hooted in return. The owl replied. Mendel turned to Boden.

The prince nodded his head politely at Mara, as if begging his pardon for leaving her side, and sauntered his horse ahead to Mendel's. As he did so, a figure appeared from the nearby oak brush.

It seemed to Mara the figure had melted into being, though, that made little sense considering things didn't melt into shape, they melted into nothing. The being, be it specter or cloaked Ursan, approached. Its voice, deep and low, hailed a salutation to Boden.

"My lord, grace has brought you back," it said.

Boden bowed his head curtly. "Grace, and the Sword Queen." He looked back at Mara and motioned for her to come forward.

She hated being called like a dog, to come when Boden called, but she obeyed anyway, fighting the urge to sneer when she arrived at Boden's side. There was no reason to make faces, though. No one would see. The night was darkening. Clouds moved across the moon, shrouding the moonlight in gossamer.

The figure moved upon Mara's arrival. It took her a moment to realize the person was bowing.

"Your Majesty," the Ursan said with a voice full of thunder, "it's an honor to gaze upon your beauty."

Mara choked on her laugh. "Please. It's dark, and my beauty—though radiant—is all but impossible to see in this darkness. Spare me, and speak what it is you need so that we may pass."

The figure removed his hood, revealing a shaved head and bushy beard. Beneath this, Mara saw shimmering eyes—eyes that caught the moonlight despite the cloak of clouds.

Eyes like Boden's.

Her throat tightened as her blood rushed in her ears. "Forgive me," Mara said. "I was unaware I spoke to an Ursan prince."

The prince smiled, his eyes twinkling above his bearded cheeks. Every man bowed low from their saddle, save for Boden and Mara.

"I daresay my brother feels no need to introduce me." The prince pointed at Boden. "You've been gone for nearly a fortnight, and already you've forgotten your allegiance."

The prince laughed then and patted Boden's horse.

"Apologies, brother," Boden said.

Mara watched him, realizing Boden had no idea his brother would meet them here. His mouth wouldn't form the same easy smile his brother's seemed to be making, the same easy smile he'd offered her before at other times. Boden was stiff, unamused.

"This is Prince Gerik, heir to Ursa," Boden explained, not taking his eyes off his older brother. "Long may he reign."

Gerik nodded a thanks. "Long may House Solberg reign." He winked at Boden.

"Where is your guard?" Mara asked. "Surely an Ursan prince wouldn't traverse the Jeweled Realm unaccompanied."

Gerik rubbed his shaved head, nodding in agreement. "Certainly, Your Grace, but a group of Ursans would be cause for alarm, wouldn't it?"

Mara looked at Boden, who was sitting straight, still unnerved by his brother's presence. It was obvious this wasn't part of the plan. Or, at least, not part of what Boden had thought was the plan.

Forcing a smile, Mara looked back to Gerik. He studied her, his eyes finding their way to the Sacred Sword. Mara shifted in her saddle, hiding the Sword in the shadow of her cloak.

"Well, Prince Gerik, did you walk or ride?" she asked.

He gestured to a small group of trees on the next rise of the hill. "My horse is tied there."

Mara turned to the closest Ursan, who happened to be Fiske.

"Retrieve the prince's horse," she commanded.

Fiske didn't hesitate. He happily nodded and galloped quickly to the rise. Fiske disappeared into the darkness, his body blurring into the shadows.

She turned back to Gerik, who was still watching her. A smile was painted on his face, one that Mara found unsettling. She shifted in her saddle, the leather complaining in the cool of the night.

"What was so important that Your Grace rode all the way here to meet us, rather than wait at the dam?" Mara asked. She tried to make it sound like she was just making conversation. But she wasn't. She needed to hear his answer.

Gerik shrugged. "I just wanted to make sure the Sword Queen was present and accounted for. I wanted to make sure my baby brother did his job." Again, Gerik winked at Boden. Boden didn't return the gesture.

"And the witch," Boden broke the silence. "Is she there?"

Gerik nodded. "Of course. She awaits the arrival of the dear queen."

The way his words twisted from his lips made Mara frown. "She waits for her death, like a fool," Mara said.

Gerik held his breath, then released it with a laugh. He looked like he was about to speak, but Fiske returned with his horse—a tall black reaper of a creature. Gerik mounted his ride easily. He turned the stallion and cozied up next to Mara. "Shall we then, Your Grace?"

She didn't answer right away. There were many thoughts going off in Mara's head. Her mother's training, drilled into her since a toddler, was surfacing. It told her something was wrong. Something wasn't quite right.

But Gerik sat so close, and his smile was so charming. He paid close attention to her, making sure she, too, paid close attention to him. It was his men surrounding her. Men she had agreed to travel with to the dam.

The twin of the moon glimmered on the lake's surface now. Mara's eyes found the dam once again. Beyond the lake, dark walls rose up between two jagged spikes of the mountains, one side the Jeweled Realm, the other the Waste.

It did not look welcoming.

But the mere thought that Iris was nearby spurred Mara onward. Her mistake, her failure to kill her sister, could be righted in moments.

Gerik sat there, still smiling. Patient. Too patient.

"Yes, let's go," Mara finally said.

The prince's behavior was irksome. Were there more time, she might hold a blade to his throat to see what words he spoke under duress. What secrets he'd spill. But the moon continued to drift. She only had till sunrise, or risk citizens of Valenbeuge realizing Princess Iris still lived.

That their queen was a liar.

"Very good, Your Grace." Gerik steered his horse into a walk. "Very good."

Boden said nothing when Mara's horse trotted by. If anything, he looked like a small child being left out by their bigger sibling. His eyes pleaded something, but she turned toward the dam. She could still feel their heat on her back, a sensation that had begun to grow familiar. It bothered her how much she enjoyed it, but there was little time to muse over these feelings.

Her sister waited.

CHAPTER SIX

About halfway down the opposite side of the dam, water cascaded like a bed skirt. Far below, Mara could see the serpentine river glowing in the moonlight. On one bank, a shriveled forest, fields of stone, and nothing. On the other side, the Jeweled Realm. Lush forests carpeted the landscape where mountains receded into a deep-blue horizon.

The moon was sinking. Mara's time was running out.

At the top of the dam, Mara saw a figure. It stood in the center without companions. A group of warriors, dressed in the traditional furs of Ursa, stood watch on the far side.

"Your men stand at the ready?" Mara asked Gerik.

They looked at ease, perhaps even unaware that Mara approached. She already knew the answer to her question. Ursans were strong, but ill-practiced at obedience.

"Of course, Your Grace, of course," Gerik mused. He pointed to the figure in the center of the dam, cloaked in cloth and darkness. Even without seeing her face, Mara knew who it was. "And there is your witch."

Mara dismounted her horse at the edge of the dam. She checked her sword for no other reason than comfort. Her boot found the edge of stone that marked the start of the dam, but a hand pulled her back.

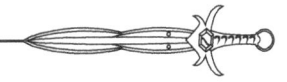

"Shall I follow, Your Grace, in case?" Boden's voice filled her ear.

His breath was warm on her neck, invading her space and pricking her anger. "In case of what?" she hissed. She ripped her arm from Boden's grip. A heat tingled beneath her skin in anticipation of the fight. The last thing she wanted right now was to be touched.

"It will be over before it starts," Mara said as she stared ahead at her sister.

Over and over, her boots struck the stone, the distance between herself and her sister shrinking. Iris didn't move. She stood motionless, waiting for Mara. Despite not seeing her face, Mara imagined her sister smiling.

But soon, Mara would be wiping it from her face.

Mara realized footsteps were following after her. Boden was walking cautiously behind. Gerik as well. Mara increased her speed, wanting to be through with the entire ordeal as quickly as possible. Wanting to be done with the Ursans as much as she wanted to be done with Iris.

When she was within a sword's length of Iris, she stopped. She said nothing, but she watched everything. Mara would counter any movement from Iris with her own. She wasn't about to lose solely from surprise.

Iris's arms moved upward. Mara's hand jumped to the pommel of her sword. A bubble of laughter flowed from within the dark hood, and Iris slowly removed it. It fell to her shoulders to reveal her face backlit by the moon.

Her dark hair, always kept short, was shorter still, nearly to her scalp. A scar ran above her ear and across the back of her head, a bright white through the fuzz of hair that once shined black. Smudged over her eyes was thick kohl, darkening them, creating the illusion of two giant holes in her head. A skull. A corpse.

"Iris," Mara said. The words came out as wisps in the cool night air. "What happened to you?"

Iris smiled. Or snarled. She had sharpened her canines into a rough bite akin to a mountain jaguar. The girl before Mara looked nothing like the sister she'd released years ago. This woman was a skeleton, a shroud over a frame, roughened by nature, by betrayal, by the Waste.

"Destiny, dear sister," Iris drawled. Even her voice was unfamiliar. Empty. Hollow. "My queen."

Mara tightened her grip on the Sword. Iris laughed once more, her sharp teeth on full display in the moon's light.

"I was wrong to let you live," Mara spoke over Iris's laughter. "I'll right that wrong now."

Mara, in one swift movement, pulled the Sacred Sword from its sheath and swung at Iris. It should have been a killing blow. On any other fighter, it would have been. Mara was fast.

But Iris was faster.

She held her arm up and blocked the Sword easily enough, catching it on a thick metal cuff around her wrist. She winked at Mara before kicking her backward.

Mara stumbled but righted herself easily. With a quick slice from her sword, she cut the corded neckline of her cloak, allowing it to fall to the ground. She would not let garments be her downfall in the fight against her sister.

"Wait a moment," Iris held up her hand, her voice almost sounding like her old self, like the sister Mara remembered. "I forgot. The Queen of the Jeweled Realm must best her sibling before staking claim to the Sacred Sword." Iris looked down, examining herself. She felt her thigh, her stomach, arms and face. A wicked glimmer grew in her eyes. "But I'm not dead . . . so then, you can't be queen." She lunged at Mara, her hands empty of any weapon, intending to disarm Mara of the Sword.

Mara sidestepped, avoided Iris's body, and swung the Sword down hard. She should have caught the backside of Iris, but instead she met stone. Iris's laughter rang around her, sending Mara spinning.

"You look pathetic." Iris stood on the nearby wall of the dam. "Like a child with its mother's blade."

Mara ran at Iris, frenzied agitation fueling her, nothing else. She should have thought through her next attack. She should have remembered her mother's words. *Always see your next move, and the move after that, and after that.* But Mara didn't want to plan her steps. She just wanted Iris to be silenced.

Iris was gone before Mara even reached the wall. The stone slammed hard against her thighs, but she ignored the blow. Breathing heavy like a warhorse, she turned and looked for her sister.

It made no sense. Iris's moves were too fast. The Ursans' words floated back to her mind: a witch, they'd said, assimilated into the nomads of the Waste. *Magic.* Mara shook her head, refusing the word. It wasn't real. It was impossible.

Iris laughed again, the sound drilling into Mara's mind like pain itself. "Shall we end it now, then?" she asked, walking in a circle around Mara. "Shall we finish what we started?"

Mara tried to focus on Iris, but her constant movement was distracting. Mara didn't know whether to watch her sister's feet, her hands, or her eyes. Truth be told, she felt dizzy. It wasn't normal. She wondered if the height of the dam was affecting her.

Gerik and Boden were yelling at each other, both still standing nearby. Mara strained to listen to them while she forced herself to watch Iris. Boden sounded angrier than Gerik. Gerik sounded amused.

"Why?" Boden yelled at his brother.

"Why not?" Gerik replied.

"It's dishonorable," Boden said. "Father wi—"

"Father agreed, idiot. Why else would I be here? Do you think he'd send his heir on a fool's errand?"

Mara's ears rang with the constant noise around her. Her feet shuffled sideways without her consent. Panic spread through her body. There was something wrong. "What did you do?" Mara drawled out.

Iris smirked. "Not me," she said, tipping her head toward Boden and Gerik. "Your Ursan friends helped."

Mara looked back at the brothers. Gerik offered his largest grin yet, pleased with the proceedings, while Boden watched, just as confused as she.

"You see, I'm not the only one who thinks you betrayed the Sacred Sword and your oath when you let me live and named yourself queen," Iris hissed.

Mara choked out a laugh. "And what do I care if the Ursans agree with you?" Her lips felt numb, and she was having trouble keeping saliva in her mouth. It trailed out of the corner of her lips as she spoke, landing with a drip on the tip of her boot.

Iris took a step toward Mara, and then another. She lowered her gaze, her eyes diving into a depth of darkness Mara had never seen before. It was like the kohl drank all signs of light, leaving nothing but a void, a space where eyes should have been. Iris looked like a monster. A demon.

A witch.

Perhaps if Mara hadn't been so mesmerized by the wickedness of her sister's eyes, she would have noticed Iris's hand slip into a pocket deep in her cloak. She would have seen Iris bring forth a handful of dark, glittering dust. But instead, she was lost in Iris's gaze, memories of long ago forcing themselves to the surface like bubbles in a lake.

She was not on the dam, but years into her past, helping a weeping Iris up off the garden bricks. Blood trickled down her knee, ruining her silk stockings. Mara assured her their mother wouldn't notice. Iris was then ripped away by their father, his eyes scowling down at Mara, scolding her for tripping up her younger sister.

Another memory surfaced, and she stood before her mother, a black bruise blooming around Mara's eye. Her mother's twisted smile was frightening as Mara explained why she and Iris had been fighting. Iris stood beside her, blood dripping from her nose and down her blouse.

Blood. There had always been so much blood.

Behind her, Mara heard yelling. The Ursan princes were still arguing. But Mara was too entranced to look, too ensnared in her sister's trap.

Iris brought her hand to her mouth, and she blew. The dust took to the air like a luminous cloud. Sparkling black particles caught the moonlight and erupted with light for a second, even less, and then drank it away. The cloud jetted toward Mara, and the queen could not move.

A body thrust itself against Mara, destabilizing her already weakening stance. The pain was enough to rip her gaze from Iris. She finally took in the shimmering dust. Finally realized she didn't know what it was, but still somehow knew it would harm her.

Her face collided with her attacker's shoulder. Iris vanished from Mara's vision only to be filled with bearskin. A familiar scent wrapped around her as they flew toward the nearby wall of the dam.

The force was too great to stop. Together, they tumbled over the wall and, together, they fell toward the flowing waterfall. Mara thought she heard Iris shriek, but the thunderous sound of the rushing water soon took over everything she could hear or feel. It rumbled in her head, her chest, and her hands.

Boden tried speaking to her. Mara wanted to laugh at him. Didn't he know they were falling to their deaths?

He was probably speaking to his Saint Kalda anyway.

Water broke through her thoughts and her clothes. It wouldn't be long now. The water flowed freely halfway down the dam. Mara didn't know what they'd find at the bottom, but she was certain of one thing.

So her hand tightened on the hilt of the Sacred Sword.

Chapter Seven

The sun bit hot-cold on Mara's high cheekbones. She sat up coughing so hard she puked. Around her, the forest buzzed alive with creatures and insects. Across the wide river was the face of a cliff, barren and dead.

At least she'd washed up on the right side of the river.

Her body wouldn't stand, but she could wait that out. Fatigue from trauma was something she'd trained for. The wisest warriors knew their limits and how to manage when they pushed past those limits.

Mara took stock of her situation. Boden was nowhere in sight. Mara tried to convince herself that this didn't bother her, but deep down, it did. Upriver, she couldn't see the dam, but the water curved away from her behind a mountain's long arm. Her hand went to her sword.

She felt nothing.

Her heart thudded in her chest. She forced herself up, crawling, digging around in the riverbank's mud. At the edge of the water, she thought she saw a glimmer of metal, but it turned out to be a piece of quartz. When she exhausted herself, she fell back into the mud, staring up at the gray-streaked sky.

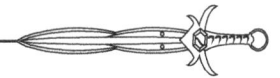

Green mountaintops reached for the clouds, but never quite got there. The river sang to her as it moved farther away from the capital than she had ever been. The dam was probably on the other side of the mountain, but what use was that to her? She didn't have the Sword. Iris was alive. The Ursans were helping her.

The Ursans.

Mara sat up. The anger she tried to pathetically reign in during her fight with Iris erupted, overflowing from inside her. Hot tears streamed down her cheeks. She kicked and screamed out.

"Rotting bears!" she screamed. "Filthy, stupid, bears!"

She threw her head back, allowing herself to fall, unaware of what lay directly behind her. Her head connected with a rock, and instantly she saw nothing.

This time when Mara awoke, she was being dragged on a makeshift litter. Long branches had been lashed together with rough rope. Mara bounced, jolted by a root exposed on the trail. She looked around, though her head ached severely.

"Who are you?" she demanded.

The dragging stopped. The figure hauling her lowered the litter. A woman, alone and aged in years, looked her over.

The woman appeared neither pleased nor upset. Her face was one of hard work, with deep-set wrinkles in her forehead, presumably from squinting at some needlecraft or handcraft. Her hair was tucked beneath her headscarf, but she appeared strong by the way she pulled Mara along on the litter.

"Oh, you're awake then?" the woman replied. Her accent was of the Jeweled Realm, but it was rough. Mara had a hard time understanding her. The woman stared, awaiting her response.

Mara searched for words but found it hard to speak any. What would she tell this woman? She was her queen? There was no way to prove that. Mara wore no artifact of the monarchy. She'd left her jewels at the palace, preferring to wear nothing decorative when fighting. Her hand groped for her sword, briefly forgetting what had happened before she passed out. When she found empty air, her fingers clenched into fists.

Without the Sword, she was nothing. No one. The sickness she felt consumed her. It grew from within her stomach to her tightened throat, and eventually it came out as vomit.

The woman rushed to Mara's side. "Whoa, easy now." She pulled at the apron she wore. It was much less delicate than the aprons of the palace servants. It was made of thicker, rougher fabric which scraped Mara's lips when the woman wiped at her face.

Mara pulled away, disgusted at herself and this strange woman.

The woman stared at Mara's vomit, nodding her head. "I see water there." She pointed to the foamy liquid. "You went in the river, didn't you?"

Mara said nothing.

"River's quick. Been more than enough drowned." She studied Mara some more before standing and wiping her hands on her apron. "Can you walk?"

Mara stood, wobbling on her legs. She grabbed a nearby birch for support. "Fair enough," Mara finally answered.

The woman's eyes narrowed. "That's a voice from a *ville*," she said.

Mara swallowed, hesitated, then nodded. "Valenbeuge."

The old woman smacked her lips, contemplating Mara's words. Finally, she smiled a gapped grin. It was then Mara realized she was missing a few teeth. "Well, you *ville* folk never show nature proper respect. How'd you fall? Showing off?"

Mara shook her head no. She shifted her eyes back toward the direction of the river, its violent sounds of rushing waters still filling her memory. She turned back to the woman. "I was with my brother. Have you seen him?"

"You mean floating by?" The woman laughed at her own cruel joke. "No, just your waterlogged body on the bank there."

A light breeze blew through the forest, raising hairs on Mara's arms. She wrapped them around her body, shivering.

The woman frowned. "You must be freezing. And here we are chatting. Come, come with me. I'll get you some dry clothes and warm food."

"That isn't necessary," Mara said, but the woman grabbed her arm and pulled her along anyway.

They left the makeshift litter behind, abandoned on the side of the trail, looking how Mara felt.

"Name is Gabi, by the by," the old woman said.

"I'm—" Mara choked, her mind reeling for a name, any name, except her own. "Mallory."

"Mallory . . . never met a Mallory before," Gabi mumbled to herself. "'Course, haven't met a woman from the river before either. Time for everything s'pose."

Gabi guided Mara down the trail. It was a wide, well-worn path, one Mara imagined Gabi traversed often. They passed by small spruce and birch, Gabi's hand reaching out and touching or caressing each in turn, almost methodically. Mara noticed the polished wood in these places, worn away by Gabi's touch.

"How long have you lived here, Gabi?" Mara did her best to keep up. The woman was much older than Mara, but she was quick.

"My whole life. Was born just over there in that thicket." Gabi pointed to a dense underbrush nearby.

Mara stared at the bush, imagining a woman trying to give birth in it.

"Just kidding. Might as well have been. Born farther down river a bit, moved out here after my husband died. Built a cabin. Take care of myself. Keep to myself."

Gabi kept on walking, not waiting for Mara. Mara took a deep breath and trekked onward, feeling more fatigued the farther they walked. Her strength sapped away from her with each step, melting from her body into the earth. She stopped to take a few more deep breaths. Gabi turned, possibly to speak to Mara, but double-backed when she saw Mara leaning against a tree.

"Sorry," Gabi said, "used to keeping my own pace."

Mara nodded, not needing an explanation. "I just need to catch my breath."

"It's just around the corner there, my cabin." Gabi gestured down the trail.

Mara studied the path. Her mind calculated how many steps it'd take her to reach the bend, how many more after that. She felt too tired to try. Her mind was dizzy with the effort. She shook her head. "I'll just stay here." She sank down the trunk of the tree.

"Oh, no you won't." Gabi grabbed her firmly by the arm. "No use sleeping out here. Bugs'll get you. And if not the bugs, the wolves."

It was enough motivation for Mara. She pushed up with her legs, ignored the weakness she felt, and walked arm in arm with Gabi down the path.

Gabi's cabin sat in a meadow surrounded by sentinels of wildflowers. A garden, guarded by a fence of small spruce trunks and a stone well house, sat to one side. Chickens scratched at the dirt then scattered when the two of them walked by.

The house was of rough-hewn beams interlocked and stacked together in a rudimentary cabin. The doorway leaned to one side, crooked in its framing, but easily opened with a nudge from Gabi.

Inside, Mara inhaled the scent of roasted vegetables and meat. The fire burned low in the hearth, but Gabi sat Mara down in a chair and rushed to stoke it. She had the flames bursting with just a few pokes of her stick.

"Fire, a fickle thing," Gabi said to herself. She turned back to Mara, and for a second, looked surprised to find her sitting there in her home. If Mara was being honest, she found it surprising, too.

The thatched roof was thick with beams holding it up. In the nearest corner, a brown stain decorated the thatching, suggesting a leak. Hard-packed dirt made up the floor. A bed, with a mattress of straw shoved in a sheet, sat in one corner. The chair Mara sat in paired with a table that took up another corner. The kitchen occupied a third. And in the fourth, a window let in enough light for several potted plants.

A far cry from the palace.

"Well, now, Mallory," Gabi said, hands on her hips, "let's get you fixed up."

Mara sighed, feeling nothing. The fall from the dam, the river's cold water, her loss at the one thing she considered herself talented at, drained her. She felt nothing of herself, save for a small fire that burned within. It was down to coals, embers really. Like the fire when they'd entered the cabin, it was in danger of going out.

She finally nodded, giving Gabi the permission she needed to fuss over her. There was nothing else to do.

She was lost.

Chapter Eight

Mara slept all day and through the night. When she finally awoke, the sky was saturated in reds and oranges, with deep purple fading away in the far-flung edges. A new day began, but with it, Mara brought the previous day's worries. She was nowhere closer to knowing what to do.

Gabi had offered Mara her bed while she'd opted to finish her chores—she had some work to do on the garden fence among her usual dailies—but it was not as if the bed were comfortable. Mara stretched out on the mattress, feeling every poke and prod of straw within. She let the irritation build until it was too much, then sat upright and scooted toward the bed's edge. The room was stuffy and filled with a hodgepodge of knick-knacks. Mara found Gabi asleep at the table, her head in her arms on the tabletop. Mara fought a laugh.

"What's funny?" Gabi stood and stretched, awoken by the noise of Mara stirring. The old woman made her way to the fire and the large pot that hung above.

"Nothing," Mara said. "Just didn't think I'd live to see another day."

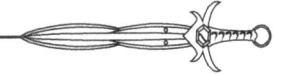

Gabi nodded while she stirred. She reached up to a high shelf, bringing down a sizable chunk of dried bread. A bowl was produced from another shelf, and she plopped the bread in before spooning a large ladle of soup on top. She placed it at the table and motioned for Mara to sit. "Eat," she instructed. "You might've lived another day, but you look like death."

Mara ignored the insult, knowing now would not be the time nor the place to assert her influence as queen. She sank into the chair and stared down at the bowl. The brothy soup swirled around the bread, an iceberg in the ocean. It reminded her of her travels north with her mother, of the rich furs they'd worn and the richer food they'd eaten. Of being a child and completely absorbed by the world around her.

She felt it welling up again, the sickness, but she picked up the battered spoon nearby and started eating, shoving the feeling down with every bite.

"See?" Gabi said. "You were hungry."

Mara emptied the bowl and handed it to the old woman. Gabi cleaned it off in a nearby tin filled with water, wiped it dry with her apron, and shoved it back on the shelf. The counter she leaned against was scrubbed pine, planks probably milled from the local trees, some maybe even from the very spot the cabin sat. She crossed her arms and stared at Mara.

"What'll it be then?" Gabi asked.

"Excuse me?" Mara leaned back in the chair, attempting to control her eyebrows, attempting to not let her annoyance show at being spoken to like that.

"Well, shall I get the *docteur* from the nearby village?"

"No," Mara said a little too quickly. The last thing she needed was a man poking and prodding her, asking her too many questions.

Gabi uncrossed her arms. She looked Mara over, examining her for what Mara hoped were wounds and not because she recognized her. "You don't seem too hurt." Gabi nodded. "Alright, if that's what you want."

"Yes," Mara said, slowly this time, trying to rein in her anxiety. "I'm fine. I feel fine, just . . . tired."

Gabi pointed to Mara. "And your clothes. I reckon you'd feel better with clean ones. I've got another shift around here somewhere." She dug around in a trunk at the foot of her bed. Mara tried to organize her thoughts, to choose words to phrase her desire to keep her own clothes. They were dirty, yes, and ripped in places, and they stank terribly. But they were hers. Mara knew their original luxury, their tremendous cost.

Clothes fit for a queen.

Mara stared down at her blouse. The white silk thread used to embroider the edges in swirls and filigrees was frayed. Once white, it now looked gray and brown. A pink cloud bloomed on her side, from blood she knew, but she didn't know whose or where it had come from.

Bare skin stared out at her thigh where her riding breeches were ripped. Her cheeks felt hot as the shame of her appearance took hold of her.

A queen shouldn't look like this.

And there on her belt, where the Sword should have been, was nothing. A simple reminder of her failure.

"Ah-ha!" Gabi pulled a shift from the chest and held it up for Mara to see. "Should fit you well enough. Can wash your clothes, too, and mend them, if you'd like."

Mara nodded. "I'd like that," she mumbled.

"Oh, now don't be like that." Gabi wrapped an arm around Mara's shoulders. "People fall all the time. The test is getting back up."

Gabi held the shift out for Mara, who took it reluctantly. She trudged to the corner of the room where she could have some semblance of privacy and changed.

"Pleased to have you stay, Mallory, as long as you need. When you're ready, we can get someone in the village to take you back."

The rushing waters of the dam still echoed in her mind. Her body felt off balance as she pulled her blouse up over her head, like she was falling once again.

"Take me back?"

"To Valenbeuge."

Mara fell onto the bed but managed to finally remove her blouse. *Valenbeuge.* Yes. *Mallory.* Right. She wasn't the queen of the Jeweled Realm anymore. She was a nobody. A girl from Valenbeuge who'd fallen into the river with her brother.

Boden.

"This village"—Mara pulled the shift over her head and let it fall, cascading down to her feet—"is it nearby?"

"Oh, an hour or so walk," Gabi replied.

"What's it like?"

"Nothing like Valenbeuge, if that's what you mean," Gabi chuckled. "Got a cluster of buildings down a main way. Some houses. A market. We're quite lucky to have the *docteur*—"

"I don't need a *docteur*. I'm fine," Mara said.

She laid her old clothes on the table. Gabi walked around her, fussing with the shift in places. Mara fought the urge to pull away. A common girl wouldn't be so proud.

"It suits you fine," Gabi said with a smile. She took up Mara's old clothes and placed them in a basket already piled with other things. Mara's heart sank at the thought of them being taken, almost like her own skin was being removed. Gabi picked up the hulking basket and winked at Mara.

"You rest today. I'll tend to these. Tomorrow, if you're feeling right, perhaps you can help around here." She left through the front door, humming a song unfamiliar to Mara.

Mara nodded, though she had no desire to help around the cabin. With the door shut, the room was silent, stuffy, and Mara had the feeling she was being squeezed tight. She looked down at the shift, fluttering it with her hands, and frowned.

The heat from earlier, the inexplicable warmth that had quickly turned sour and made her feel sick, returned. She rubbed her stomach, shushing herself.

"What a mess," she muttered.

Mara busied herself by looking around the room, hoping to find a distraction from the pain. On a nearby shelf sat a painted miniature of a mustachioed man, a medal pinned to his lapel, a joyful glint in his eye. Next to it, coiled like a snake, was a thick golden chain. Mara picked it up and a locket swung heavy from the shelf. It swayed back and forth like a pendulum. Engraved initials dug into the gold: G & P.

She shoved the necklace back where it had been, careful to re-coil the chain as it had sat before. Another painted miniature caught her eye on a different shelf. Mara stepped closer, peering past the other *bric-à-brac*.

The painted woman sat tall in a chair formed of gold and cushioned with blue velvet. Her hair fell in loose waves down her shoulders and back. Amber eyes penetrated the surface, as if the woman gazed at the viewer and not the other way around. Rose lips were upturned in a bemused expression on a bronzed face. Smug, some people might say.

It was Mara's mother.

The Red Queen shared her royal image around the Jeweled Realm. It was common practice for citizens to cherish their monarch's visage. In larger *villes*, it denoted a sense of patriotism and loyalty. In the smaller villages, in homes like Gabi's, it often verged on worship.

Mara settled her eyes on her mother's, admiring the strong face she saw. A face much like her own. It was like looking in a mirror.

Her heart thudded in her chest. Would Gabi eventually notice the similarities? Would she actually wonder why a girl from Valenbeuge held an accent of the interior? One look at the Red Queen and Mara would be enough to rouse suspicion in the kind old woman.

Ice filled her veins. The thought of being found out, of returning to the capital, choked her. She couldn't breathe. Iris was still out there. Soon, the entire realm would know Mara's secret.

But she was Mallory now. On the nearby table sat some gardening shears. Mara chanced one more look at her mother's miniature, at the luxurious long hair they both shared, and knew what she had to do.

There was little time to think. The shears were in her hands, then shredding through her hair in seconds. She watched the long locks of red-brown hair fall down like leaves in autumn. Her eyes welled with tears, but her mind forced her hand to continue. It was hard work. The shears, made for trimming delicate plants and not thick swaths of hair, fought her. But with each squeeze, Mara felt the sickness leave her. She felt lighter, less nauseous.

She felt free.

By the time Gabi returned, Mara's hair was shoulder-length, the ends uneven by her left-handed use of the shears. Gabi froze, the empty basket held aloft momentarily before she dropped it.

"What did you do?" she asked. She picked up the fallen strands of Mara's hair, rubbing her fingers together to feel their fine texture. "Needed a change?"

Mara nodded, slowly handing her shears back. "I'm afraid I've botched it," she said. "Will you fix it?"

Gabi nodded, brandishing the shears and gesturing toward a chair. Mara sank into the seat and listened as the blades sliced cleanly, almost thankfully, from use by their rightful master.

The silence in the cabin simmered. Mara wanted to fill it, but she didn't really want to hear Gabi carry on about nothing. Her eyes found the portrait again, the mustachioed man smiling benevolently at her. "Is that your husband?" Mara pointed.

The slicing of her hair stopped while Gabi gazed at the portrait. She smiled, nodded, and carried on with her work. "Yes, that's him."

"He was a soldier?"

"Mmmhmm. Rode with the Red Queen's legion, first cohort."

Mara wanted to turn and look at Gabi, to see if she was joking, but the woman was still holding firm to her hair. She focused on the photo instead. The man did not look special. Mustaches, as was all facial hair, were not tolerated for low-ranking warriors. Gabi's husband must have been at least a sergeant.

"An honor," Mara said. "He must have been something special."

Gabi tutted. "He was decent, as they say. I think the Red Queen wanted more to soothe the purlieu."

"Soothe?"

"War takes and takes. I'm sure there are those in Valenbeuge that know, that you've heard speak of it." Gabi sighed. She set the shears on the table, finished with her work. "The purlieu—the fringe—of the Jeweled Realm always gets it worse. The queens think we're disposable. That we're a limitless entity without complaint."

Gabi walked to the portrait of her husband and took it in her hands. She stroked his face with her thumb, a tear filling up one eye. "Phillipe was a good man. Honored, he was indeed, to be in the first cohort."

"But you don't seem happy about it." Mara felt the ends of her hair, no longer jagged and uneven, but straight and blunt. Images of Iris appeared in her mind, but she shoved them away and focused on Gabi.

"Aye, well"—Gabi set the portrait back on the shelf, straightening it and the rest of the *bric-à-brac*—"as I said, he was decent. No business being in the first cohort, though. But the Red Queen . . . she sought to honor some of our local warriors to . . . make us feel important. Special."

"You keep her portrait," Mara couldn't stop herself from saying, though she knew bringing any attention to her mother's face could bring scrutiny to her own.

"Yes," Gabi sat down opposite Mara, admiring the work she'd done on Mara's hair. "It accompanied the letter I got detailing my husband's death. I keep it as a reminder."

Mara's chest tightened at the old woman's words. Death wasn't new to her, but she had a hard time facing the mass amounts of it her mother had once created. "Of what?"

"Greed." Gabi's cheeks flushed red. "Is the realm wealthy and safe because of her? Sure. But it was greed that did it. She didn't care who died. I can see it in her gold eyes."

Gabi stared at Mara. Mara blinked several times, trying to find something else to turn her attention to. She looked at her mother's portrait, and then Phillipe's. Anything to hide a direct view of her own golden eyes.

"Ah, well, don't matter now, does it?" Gabi tapped her hand on the table authoritatively and pushed her chair back. "The Red Queen is dead, and her daughter sits upon the throne."

"And what do you say of her?" Mara had to know.

Gabi went to the tin basin, fiddling with dishes laying within. She shrugged as she took up a washcloth and wooden plate. "It's been seven years, and the Jeweled Realm hasn't raised up any more wars," she said.

"But we are conquerors, are we not? Strength wields the Sword," Mara insisted.

Gabi chuckled. "Maybe in Valenbeuge you believe that. In bigger *villes* where the days move fast and life faster still. But out here, in the wilderness"—she sat the plate and cloth down and turned to look at Mara—"nothing gets done unless I do it. There is no Us. No Strength. No Sword. Just me."

"So," Mara began, "you think the Sword Queen is . . . "

"Who cares." Gabi turned back to her work. "Whoever possesses the Sword rules the realm. Reckon I don't have much of a say in it anyway, do I?"

"So it doesn't matter who's queen." Mara stared at the table, following a fine line of pine through to a knot in the wood. It cycled around like a hurricane, like an eye.

"It doesn't matter," Gabi agreed.

Chapter Nine

Mara tossed and turned on the floor of the cabin. Gabi had offered to share the bed—a friendly gesture, no doubt—but Mara wasn't about to share a bed with anyone, let alone an old woman.

A peasant.

The cold snuck into her feet and up her legs. If she reached out her hand, she could feel a fading trickle of warmth emanating from the hearth. Wiggling over, she situated herself closer to the fireplace. A vague heat washed over her.

Sleep came to her lightly, settling like a misty rain in the spring. Before long, Gabi was knocking about, telling her to get up.

"Nights are getting colder, eh?" Gabi said, struggling to stoke the coals into a fire for breakfast.

Mara rubbed her arms, trying to create heat in them.

"You look like you've gotten your strength back. I'd like for you to help collect wood today. There's some cut in the forest a ways, just need to haul it back." Gabi didn't look at Mara but glanced at her out of the corner of her eye.

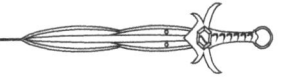

"Haul wood?" Mara asked. It wasn't that she couldn't. She was strong enough to do it. But she'd never done it before. Wood had always appeared in her hearth—along with a fire—almost magically, though, she knew someone had put it there. Someone had chopped it, hauled it, and stacked it neatly in a hidden alcove beside the hearth. Someone struck the flint, erupting flames to life and stoked them to make it roar. Mara had never worried about it. She'd never needed to. There had always been someone else.

There had always been a servant.

She decided it couldn't be any harder than shooting her bow on horseback or shield-bashing while dueling. What Mara needed was more time to think, and walking back and forth collecting wood seemed a great way to do that.

"Sure," Mara finally answered. "I feel better."

Gabi nodded. "Good. After we break fast then, yeah?"

Gabi offered Mara an oversized coat before she went to gather wood. "It was Phillipe's. I wear it, too, when the weather is colder. But you seem to need it today."

Mara did her best to keep her face normal, even offering Gabi a small smile. Though, the thought of wearing more of the old woman's clothes made her skin itch.

"Sure," Mara forced. "Thank you."

The wool of the coat scratched her chin and was long in the arms, but once outside, Mara was happy to have it. It smelled of pine and dust and wasn't altogether horrible. A chilly morning haze drifted around the cabin, and she hugged the coat tighter around herself. Gabi had pointed in the direction of the wood, telling her to pile the logs beside the cabin.

Leaves littered the forest floor. Seasons were changing. The world turned and turned again. Mara loved this time of year usually, when she was in the palace and could enjoy the bounty of her kingdom from luxury and comfort. She took a deep breath. At least the air was fresh.

Something skittered in the brush nearby, disturbing berries clinging to thin branches. Mara instinctively reached for her sword, only to realize it wasn't there. Again.

A brown rabbit poked its head out of the brush, its nose twitching in the breeze. Mara took another step. Leaves crunched beneath her feet. The rabbit scampered away, a blur of mottled fur rushing off into the distance.

"Wild hares," Gabi's voice called from behind her.

Mara's shoulders tensed at the initial surprise of Gabi's voice at her back, but she forced herself to relax, to appear calm. "Do you trap them?"

"Me? No. Some of the others." Gabi gestured to the forest, a place so vast and mysterious Mara wondered where these "others" were and how close they could possibly live. "The wood is there." Gabi pointed to a pile at the bottom of a nearby tree. "Hold your arms out, I'll stack."

Mara did as Gabi instructed, gritting her teeth the whole time lest she speak her true mind. The woman piled more and more wood into Mara's arms, waiting for her to tell her to stop. When she finally did, the old woman looked impressed.

"I knew you were strong," she said as she led Mara back to the cabin, a few small logs in her own arms, "but I didn't know how strong."

Mara breathed heavily. The bark bit at her wrists, exposed where she'd yanked up the jacket's long sleeves to better work. A tuft of stringy lichen billowed with Mara's steps, tickling her nose, threatening to force her to drop her load and itch.

"What is it you do to be such a strong young woman?"

A fog filled Mara's mind while she tried to think of something, anything, that would be believable to this old woman. Finally, she settled on what she thought she knew enough about. "My father is part-owner of a *vignoble*. He processes the vin. My brother and I toss barrels and such for shipments to the capital."

"Oh, the capital? You think the queen has drunk your father's vin?"

Mara choked on a laugh. "I guarantee it."

"Well, that explains your strength." They walked on for a few more moments, Gabi careful to point out roots and stones for Mara to avoid. "I'm sorry about your brother," Gabi said as Mara dropped the wood next to her cabin.

Mara watched Gabi stack logs for a moment before understanding and following suit. She said nothing of Boden. There was nothing to say. If she focused too intently on him, the strange feelings she tried so hard to ignore would bubble up, and she'd lose her composure. He'd come into her life and left just as swiftly. She had to focus on herself. Her survival.

Gabi stopped and stood up, putting her hands to her back to stretch. "It is a hard thing to lose someone. Were you close?"

"Not particularly," Mara muttered, still stacking wood. "You could say we had a common goal."

Gabi nodded. "There are eight children in my family. I'm in the middle. There are a few I feel that way about. A brother and sister, particularly."

Mara stood up, studying her stack of crooked logs, proud of her work. "Eight?" The families of the *villes* favored two children. A tidy number for a family structure. Occasionally, Mara met a family with three children. Once she'd met four, but the last was a set of twins and unintentional. "I've never met a family with so many." She wiped the sweat forming on her forehead away with the sleeve of Philippe's jacket, wincing at the itchy fibers against her skin.

"You still haven't." Gabi smiled. "You've only met one of us."

"What was it like?" Mara asked, her curiosity getting the better of her. "I only had my s—brother. It was either me or him. This or that. But eight?"

Gabi readjusted the Mara's wood stack, making the edges even and straight. She moved a log from one spot and plopped it in another arbitrarily.

"It was loud," Gabi said, still fixing Mara's sloppy work, "and busy. Like working in a popular shop in one of the *villes*. But I loved every moment."

Mara stared at Gabi's work. The wood she'd thrown down was now neatly stacked up and down, like small mountains. Where before the wood looked as if it might fall over with one small shove, it now had a strong and steady base.

"I can only imagine," Mara said. "Is it common? To have so many children in the purlieu?"

Gabi shrugged. "Common enough. There's work to be done, and more children help with that. More to take care of you when you're old, too."

Mara stared at the wood, not really seeing it, just thinking. Gabi watched her.

"Family is a treasured thing. The queens have us thinking it's not, what with making the heirs fight. And it's poisoned the bigger *villes*, too. Two children are common because, like you said, it's this or that. Whichever is best." Gabi shook her head. "Sad, if you ask me. Making enemies where there should only be love."

Mara wanted to argue with her. The seed of belief her mother had planted in her was still there, even if it hadn't taken strong root, even if it hadn't grown large and full. But there was another voice, a smaller, quieter voice—a voice of her own—that spoke. It told her Gabi was right. Gabi was speaking the words Mara had always thought deep down.

"Hallo?" a thunderous voice called from the far side of the cabin. Gabi looked at ease, but the sudden noise startled Mara. Her heart thumped in her chest.

"Sounds like Charles," Gabi said, wandering around the corner of the cabin.

Mara hesitated to follow. While she'd fooled Gabi, she didn't know how long she could go without someone questioning her more aggressively. All it would take was another who knew Valenbeuge well enough to ask who her father was and her lie would crumble. And then what? Revealing the truth would bring her exceptional shame. She needed to remain hidden from Iris.

She inhaled deeply and plunged herself around the corner of the cabin, following Gabi. When she rounded the front of the house, she saw the old woman standing in the garden with a tall man.

His silver hair trailed down his back in a braid, much like the one Mara favored when she had long hair. His laugh echoed off the cabin, deep and boisterous. Around his waist, he wore a belt of hares, dangling grotesquely.

Behind him, beyond the garden fence, there was a horse and a cart piled high with furs. The horse, a beautiful chestnut, reached through the garden gate, munching on Gabi's lemon balm.

The man spotted Mara. "Oh, Gabi, you didn't tell me you had a guest." He smiled.

Gabi beckoned Mara over. "Charles, this is Mallory. I found her over on the banks."

"The banks." Charles seemed impressed. "If only I could find a beautiful woman on the banks."

Mara felt her cheeks warm beneath a forming blush.

"Oh now, Charles, don't." Gabi swatted him. "Her brother was with her, too. Lost him as well."

Charles's face changed. What had been soft and joyful, sank and hardened. "I'm sorry," he said. "Lost a brother myself in that river, long ago."

"It was an accident," Mara got out. "I'm just happy to be alive."

Charles nodded. "The *ville* then—where you're from, with that accent."

Mara laughed nervously. "Yes."

"But not Valenbeuge. Even Valenbeuge has an offbeat edge to it. Yours is much more proper."

Her chest thundered with her heartbeat. She wondered if they could see it smashing in and out, each thud lasting a thousand times longer than it should, each one waiting like a sword above a neck. Would her ruse be over so soon?

"She spends time in the capital. Her father sells vin to the queen!" Gabi said.

Charles looked her up and down, hands on hips. Mara stood square, defiant, daring him to probe further. But thankfully, he didn't.

"I have spent little time in Valenbeuge. Not since I was a youth. You know that, Gabi."

"Aye." Gabi turned to Mara. "Charles sells to the furriers in Narlès. It's a *ville* on the other side of the mountain." Gabi pointed to the mountain that loomed nearby. It wasn't the mountain that separated them from Valenbeuge. That mountain was behind them, farther away and to the north. This mountain was wider at the base, greener, friendlier. Mara could make out the pass and see the well-worn trail travelers took. Narlès seemed to be much more familiar to the people of this forest. Mara was thankful they didn't know Valenbeuge well.

"I'm afraid I've never been," Mara said.

"Well, perhaps sometime then." Charles smiled.

"Enough, Charles," Gabi warned. "Leave the young lady alone. What is it you wanted?"

"I just wanted to check on my favorite. I'm heading to the *ville*, wanted to see if you needed a ride."

"Oh." Gabi glanced back at Mara. "Well, I have some vegetables I wanted to sell off, but with Mallory not feeling well, I didn't want to leave her."

"I'm fine, Gabi," Mara assured her.

"If it worries you so badly, Gabi, why doesn't Mallory come along?" Charles offered. He watched Mara. His eyes were blue, haloed with gold. Mara felt they were looking too deeply. She had the odd feeling Charles already knew her secret.

"I'd . . . I'd rather rest," she said. "After I do this for you, Gabi." She turned back to the woodpile.

"Are you sure you're up for hauling more wood?" Gabi called after her.

"Sure," Mara responded, reaching the corner—her freedom—and turning around it.

"I'll just grab my basket, Charles. Be but a moment," Mara heard Gabi say. The woman seemed giddy, almost excited about the prospect of riding in Charles's wagon to the *ville*. Perhaps they were sweethearts. Mara thought back to the way Charles had looked at her, not Gabi, and settled on Gabi being sweet on Charles and not the other way around.

Mara stared down at the woodpile. She did not feel remotely like building it higher, but knew if she didn't put some effort into hauling more wood, Gabi would ask her about it when she returned from the village.

"What's your brother's name?"

Mara jumped at the sound of Charles's voice. He stood at the corner, leaning against it, arms across his chest. His eyes twinkled with amusement when he saw he'd startled her.

"Sorry, what?" Mara took several deep breaths through her nose.

"Your brother? What was his name? I'll ask around the *ville* when we get there. Perhaps someone knows something."

"Oh, uh, Boden." Mara was too tired to lie. His name felt hollow in her mouth, like a wound. Like something was missing, but she couldn't figure out what. Did she miss him?

"Boden? Unusual. Is that Ursan?"

Mara laughed nervously. "Yeah, our parents . . . my father, he likes . . . Ursan history."

Charles's eyes narrowed, but Gabi's voice called to him from the front of the cabin. He nodded a farewell to Mara and disappeared back to his wagon and Gabi.

Mara sank onto the woodpile. She bit her lip, letting the pain calm her. With Gabi gone, Mara could finally think about what to do next. Her eyes settled on the path she'd walked earlier, to the base of the tree with a pile of chopped wood. She realized Charles must have cut it for Gabi. There was no way the woman had done it herself.

Initially, Mara thought she'd be safe with the old woman, but she was realizing there were more people to meet, more people to juggle. Lies would need telling, and she needed to consider her story now, not on the spot like with Charles.

Or else she might unravel the whole tale.

Chapter Ten

Mara had been living with Gabi long enough to find herself staring up at another full moon. Gabi had asked Mara if she'd like to find someone to take her back to Valenbeuge before the snow fell—making the trip impossible—but Mara had declined, feigning a fear of seeing her parents' faces when they realized their son was dead. And their daughter was to blame.

Gabi agreed it would be a hard thing for a child to do. And an even harder thing for a parent to hear. She didn't push Mara anymore, so long as Mara helped around the cabin and held conversation pleasantly enough when Gabi felt like talking. Which seemed often.

Charles returned to Gabi's cabin twice more. But Mara avoided him, trekking into the forest to hunt whenever she heard his horse and wagon approaching. She had gotten very good at listening, at hearing the sounds that were just barely sounds, the prelude of a noise before it solidified into something. Or someone.

She wouldn't really hunt. The desire to kill had drained from her the moment she washed ashore on the banks of the river. Instead, she'd walk and touch the trees and their dying leaves. A fading flowerhead would plead to her to be plucked. Eventually, she'd have enough forest debris to throw into the river where she'd watch them float away like the beautifully colored boats of the capital.

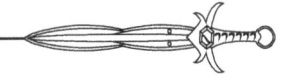

Charles was now back for another visit, and Mara was sitting on top of a hillock just inside the tree line. Brush grew thickly here, and she was hidden by the vast branches. She watched as Gabi and Charles talked and laughed.

But then, their friendly chatter transformed into heated whispers.

Mara did her best to hear, but their words fell far short of the hillock. However, her eyes caught what her ears could not. The joy that often filled Charles's chiseled features was gone, leaving instead a pale face lined with concern. He seemed to be urging Gabi to do something. Gabi seemed hard to convince. From within his pocket, he withdrew a folded piece of paper. After handing it to Gabi, he crossed his arms and waited. Gabi read the parchment, and, finally, seemed to relent. Charles's shoulders relaxed. Their conversation returned to normal, and Charles even laughed once before leaving.

As his wagon trundled away, Mara removed herself from the hillock. She wiped the forest floor debris from her riding pants—newly mended by Gabi—and returned to the cabin. Gabi was busying herself with some weeding in the garden.

"Was that Charles again?" Mara asked.

Gabi yelped in fright, shoving the folded piece of paper into her apron pocket. She patted her chest, soothing herself. "Oh, Mallory! You scared me," she laughed.

"Sorry." Mara knelt in the dirt next to the old woman. She started weeding, her hands knowing what to do after this much time at the cabin. "He visits often."

Gabi said nothing. She weeded beneath her lavender plant, engrossed with the tiny horsetails trying to encroach upon the purple flowers. When she finally felt satisfied she had removed every offender, she looked at Mara, only to find her still staring at her.

"Well," Gabi said, moving on to weed beneath another plant, "he's a lonely old man. Can you blame him?"

"I guess not," Mara reluctantly agreed.

"He's planning a trip to Valenbeuge soon, before snow flies." Gabi didn't look at Mara but kept her head tucked beneath her lavender. "Wanted to know if you're sure you aren't wanting to head home."

Mara sat back on her heels, her brows furrowed. "He said he hasn't been to Valenbeuge in years."

"Yes, well, his furs are in popular demand this year. Seems wolf and lynx are coming back into fashion." Gabi stood, dirt smudged across her face.

She was avoiding Mara's eyes. Something had changed. Charles knew something, and he had shared that knowledge with Gabi. Mara didn't want to believe it. The old woman had been kind to her so far. For weeks, she'd fed Mara, housed her, healed her. All that she had asked in return was help. And while Mara had been less than enthusiastic to perform the manual labor, she had learned to enjoy the calm that came with the work. There was a purpose to her body other than fighting.

"I have no desire to return, Gabi," Mara answered.

"Alright," Gabi conceded. "Alright."

The old woman moved on with her weeding. Mara stayed and helped until the sun fell below the tree line. They made their way inside to eat.

Sleep that night was fitful for Mara. She dreamed of skeletal faces lunging at her. Of moonless nights. The darkness was so heavy she couldn't shake it off. When she finally woke up, the blackness of the cabin convinced her she was still dreaming. It was only when Gabi coughed in her sleep that Mara realized she was awake.

She sat up slowly from her pallet on the floor, rubbing her eyes. Gabi laid asleep in her bed with her back to Mara. Gabi's apron was slung on the chair nearby. Mara wondered if the folded paper was still in it.

Slowly, silently, she crept toward the chair. Gabi stirred in her sleep, and Mara stopped. But the woman was just dreaming. Mara moved again, reaching for the apron and feeling the parchment within.

Carefully, she opened the foldings. It was a post from the palace. A realm-wide announcement, complete with a royal seal. It claimed the queen was missing after betraying the trust of her people. She was to be found and returned to the palace immediately. Beneath the words was a hand-drawn portrait of Mara. Her hair was still long, but her clothes matched the ones she'd worn that very day—the clothes Gabi had mended for her.

Gabi stirred in her sleep again, so Mara carefully refolded the paper and shoved it back into the pocket.

If Gabi had finally figured out who Mara was, there was nothing left for her here. She needed to leave. And soon.

She made her way to the corner where a sackcloth bag hung on a peg. Mara used it when she was gardening, but it would do for carrying supplies.

The bag was in her hand when she heard the bed shift behind her.

"What are you doing?" Gabi's raspy voice asked. She coughed again, stood, and slowly approached Mara.

"I was just . . . I couldn't sleep," Mara lied.

Gabi's eyes narrowed. She leaned toward the window, peering out at the approaching sunrise. The grays of the night sky were giving ground to pinks. Soon red and a delicious shade of orange would erupt. Soon, the day would begin.

Gabi frowned but nodded. "Almost sunrise anyway. I'll make the food if you want to get a head start with the garden."

"Sure," Mara said.

She ripped the bag from the peg and stumbled for her boots, forcing herself to walk and not run to the door. Gabi's back was to Mara as she stirred a pot. Mara took one more inhale of the cabin, one last taste of the life she had made within, before opening the door and allowing the outside to pull her away.

Chapter Eleven

In the garden, Mara had to pretend to work, at least for a moment. At her feet were the carrots, so she knelt and checked their greenery's base for the thick orange tops. She pulled one and then two, momentarily forgetting her worries. Something about working in the dirt seemed to send her mind blank. Not in a tiresome way, but restful. Almost like when she practiced with her sword on a training dummy.

Almost.

Her hands ached for something more, and filling them with vegetables was the best she could do. More carrots popped from the pregnant earth, and she shoved them into her bag. She'd need them for later if she were going to make her escape.

She checked the window, set deep within the wall above the kitchen tin where Gabi liked to wash dishes. Gabi was bent low over the water, scrubbing away at some stubborn stuck-on food.

Mara stood. Her body tensed, ready to take one step and then another and leave the garden—Gabi's cabin—behind forever. She snuck to the corner. Just beyond stretched the forest, draped in autumnal golds and reds. Once in the woods, it would be difficult for Gabi to follow her. Mara would have to find the river and keep to it, hoping it'd take her somewhere safer.

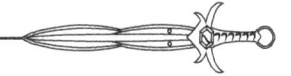

Gabi was intensely focused on the dishes. It was the opportunity Mara had been waiting for. She made her way along the edge of the cabin, her mind set to run once she turned the corner. Her pace quickened and her heart thudded in her chest as she took one last look toward Gabi to ensure she was thoroughly distracted. Mara's feet seemed to be propelled by the surge of nervous energy. Still staring back at Gabi as she turned the corner, she collided with something—no, someone—and fell hard on her back. A sharp pain pulsed from her head, and her ears rang.

"What . . ." she mumbled.

"Mara?"

The voice was familiar, but she couldn't place it. She lifted her arm, wanting to motion for more, more words, more voice to listen to and decipher. Instead, an arm reached out—a powerful arm—and hauled her easily to her feet.

"Kalda's Well, what's happened to you? You are thin . . . and your hair!"

Boden stood before her, his beard gone, only a short display of stubble where it had once grown thick and black. She marveled at the face beneath, in awe of how one man's features could be so hidden behind his own beard. His hair, on the other hand, had grown longer, and he'd tied it back with a leather strap. His clothes had changed. They seemed new. Clean. Unfortunately, he still had possession of his wretched bearskin.

"Bo . . . Boden?" Disbelief lined her voice.

"It's me." He smiled warmly at her. "I've been searching for you for ages."

"I've been here." Her head still ached, and her vision was a little fuzzy. "Here at Gabi's."

"Who is Gabi?" he asked.

"I am," came the old woman's voice. Gabi stood by the far corner of the cabin, a knife in one hand. Sunbeams, bursting from the rising sun, glinted off the blade. Mara instinctively reached for her sword before stopping. It was only a twitch. A muscle memory she had learned to hide over time while at Gabi's. Mara wanted to laugh. It was almost comical how the woman was holding the knife like it was nothing, while Mara knew full well she'd at least try to thrust it in this large man's chest should he try anything sneaky.

"Oh, hello, Gabi. My name is—"

"Boden. I'm old, not deaf," she said.

"Gabi, this is my brother," Mara inserted, offering Boden a look with her eyes, daring him to argue.

"Yes, yes, I am," he agreed hastily.

"Is that so now? After all this time? We thought you were dead, and you suddenly just appear?" Gabi stepped closer, knife still held high.

"Gabi, it is him. I assure you," Mara insisted.

"We'll see what story he tells." Gabi stopped short of Mara.

"Story?" he asked.

"How'd you survive the fall? Mallory here was near dead when I found her."

"Mallory?" Boden looked at Mara. "Yes, well, Mallory was always the worst swimmer. Bested her time and again when we'd race the quarry overflow."

"Quarry overflow?" Gabi repeated slowly.

"Uh, by the *vignoble*. There was a quarry. Made for the most excellent soil." Mara stomped on Boden's foot.

"*Agh*—yes," Boden said through gritted teeth. "The *vignoble*, where . . . where I hope our father works," he muttered.

"Owns," Mara said beneath her breath.

"Of course," he whispered, leaning on his good foot, "couldn't be a commoner, had to be a wealthy business whelp."

Gabi looked from Mara's face to Boden's. No doubt she saw little resemblance. Boden's angles were of a different sort than Mara's. His hair was black, like the cool night, while Mara's whispered of mahogany. Regardless, Gabi lowered the knife.

"But how'd you survive?" she asked again.

"Dragged myself out several leagues farther down. Caught myself on a log in the river first, pulled myself hand over hand to the edge. I was exhausted when I finally got out." He looked at Mara. "Passed out on the shore for who knows how long."

"Aye, this one, too." Gabi pointed the knife at Mara, then laughed nervously and hid the knife behind her back. "Apologies."

"Gabi," Mara said slowly, "my brother has been looking for me for a long time. I missed him terribly." The smile that formed on Boden's face when she spoke these words sank heavy in Mara's stomach. "Perhaps we could have a moment to ourselves?"

"Oh, of course, of course!" Gabi took a few steps backward. "I'll go pour some tea. You must be exhausted."

When Mara was certain Gabi was well beyond the chance of hearing, she turned and glared at Boden. "What took you so long?"

Boden smiled. With his beard gone, Mara was having a hard time focusing on anything else but his mouth. She tried to focus on the dimple now visible on his right cheek, but it only served to make his smile even more charming.

"You *missed* me?" he asked. "Well, doesn't that make all the endless days I spent searching worth it?"

Mara flushed, the heat rising up her neck, toward her cheeks. How could someone want to simultaneously choke and hug another person? She wished she never had to see him again, but was happy—no, relieved—that he was there. The emotions fought with themselves inside her, and it only served to make her angrier.

She scowled, the only face she could make convincingly without giving away her other feelings. "I did everything I could to survive."

"I see that." Boden reached his fingers toward Mara's shortened hair, but catching her eye, realized what he was going and stopped. "I like your hair like this."

Mara jutted out her chin and bile rose in the back of her throat. She hadn't wanted to do it. In a moment of frantic fear, she'd thought it the most prudent choice: change her appearance. Had Boden not done the same by shaving his beard? But her hair had been something she prided herself on. It had been like her mother's, who'd often reminded Mara that beauty and war could go hand in hand.

War *was* beautiful.

"I hate it," she spat, her eyes gleaming with the tears she would not allow to fall.

Boden stared at her, a realization falling across his face. He smiled again, only this time, it was small and calculated. This time, it was sincere. "We have to get you out of here."

"Obviously." Mara wiped viciously at her eyes, removing any evidence of the salty tears.

"Can we trust your friend?"

Mara thought back to the letter in Gabi's apron pocket. She remembered Charles's face and the way Gabi's shoulders slumped as she'd finally given in to his words.

"No," Mara said, "unfortunately not."

"Then we go now, while she's busy."

"But . . . " Mara's tumultuous insides—still fighting opposing feelings—soured into fear. She had no place anymore. The Sword was gone. Iris still lived to torment her. At least Gabi offered her a place to be. A place to exist and not worry about the heavy weight of tradition.

Boden's hand was on her forearm, pulling her toward the woods. She looked down at where their bodies touched. No one had touched her in over a moon's turn. With no steward to dress her, Mara had grown isolated and far lonelier than she thought possible. It amazed her that a single touch could both sear and soothe her skin at the same time.

"Come, I don't have a horse, but I have a canoe. We'll take it downriver, then we can make it the rest of the way to Narlès on foot."

"No." Mara dug her feet into the soil, the world suddenly becoming far too heavy for her. The mountains loomed on all sides, leaning toward her, suffocating her. "I can't Boden. What of Iris? There was a proclamation against me."

Mara sank to the ground, rocks grinding into her knees. She forced herself not to cry.

"Mara, we have to go," Boden whispered. "So what if Iris lives? We'll deal with her. But we can't if you're out here or dead."

"Dead or alive, no one cares," Mara said.

"I care." Boden's voice took on an edge of finality Mara found surprisingly like her mother's. "And if that's not enough, then we'll find other reasons. Just—please, Mara, stop acting like a child." He tugged on her arm again.

"You said it yourself." She wiped at her nose with the sleeve of her blouse and looked up at Boden. "Me or her, doesn't matter. It's the Sword they worship."

Boden stared at her, taking her in. His chest heaved with anxious breaths, but he inhaled through his nose, attempting to calm down. "I was wrong." He held his arms wide for Mara, displaying himself before the forest. "It matters. It matters to me."

He squatted down next to her and gingerly took her hands, staring deep into her eyes. Mara shivered, reveling in the ice-cool color.

"Iris will bring fire and ruin to the Jeweled Realm, and then she will drag every last kingdom down with her." Boden bit the corner of his lip and leaned in closer, so that Mara could only see his eyes and nothing more. "*You* are the only one that can stop her, Mara. Only you."

Only you.

Her mother's ghostly voice emanated in the back of Mara's mind. She allowed Boden to help her up, and she wiped away the pebbles still clinging to her knees.

"How can I beat her if I don't have the Sword, Boden?" The weight that hung from her neck finally bubbled up, and she watched his face to gauge his reaction.

His jaw tightened in pain before he released it, his face going slack. "You don't have it?" he asked.

"No." She shook her head, tears biting hot in the corner of her eyes. "It's gone."

She was nothing. It didn't matter. Go or stay. Trust or betray. Her eyes trailed back to Gabi's cabin. The weight of being the only one didn't feel quite so heavy when she was hidden in the woods, plucking carrots from the earth. But Gabi waited for her within, a war going on within herself, too.

"Mara." Boden's hand reached for hers. It was strange, the warm coarseness of it against her cold, blistered hand. He squeezed her fingers, jerking her back to reality, back to him. "It's okay," he said. "We'll figure something out. But we have to go now."

She nodded, allowing herself to be pulled along, like she had been so many times before. He guided her toward the woods. A path, one she had taken many times to hunt or pick berries, unfolded at their feet. They hurried along it for a time before Boden veered them away down a game trail.

Mara's heart raced. By now, Gabi would be pacing, wondering how long was too long to leave them alone. Wondering if her plans—Charles's plans—were going to work out. She'd probably stand at the kitchen tin washing and rewashing dishes like she always did when something bothered her.

Boden yanked Mara in another direction, down another game trail. The trail was receding, disappearing, becoming part of the forest again. Mara found it hard to discern any proper path.

"Where are we going?" she asked.

"It's just through the woods here," he said.

The feelings inside Mara—the ones that fought over Boden—stilled. For a brief moment, Mara felt only the anger and annoyance at his presence. At the way he sought to guide her. To tell her where to go and what to do. To rule her. She yanked her hand free. "I'm able to follow," she said. "I'm not a moron. I can keep a trail."

Boden seemed wounded. "It's just . . . the forest gets thick."

"I've lived here for a moon phase." She pushed past him. "I can find my way to the river."

She led the way, realizing how foolish she was being. There was no way she could lead them back to Boden's canoe, not without knowing where it was to begin with. And truthfully, she had only returned to the river once, within the safe companionship of Gabi. The old woman had encouraged her, but the sound of the rushing water had brought it all back, every terrible detail. Mara had puked in the thicket Gabi once pointed out as her birth spot.

A voice called for her through the woods. No, not for her, for *Mallory*. Gabi must have realized they were gone. Mara increased her speed, pulling Boden along by an invisible tether that seemed to have grown between them.

"It's just there." Boden pointed her in the right direction.

They moved faster, their footfalls breaking fallen branches and crumpling dried leaves. Gabi was yelling frequently, the name of Mallory filling the forest every few seconds, like birdsong.

"She really wants you to come back," Boden said.

He spotted the canoe and grabbed Mara's hand once again. He pulled her toward himself and shoved her through a dense wall of birch brush. With their bodies so close, Mara could smell Boden's sweat and that sweetness she couldn't quite place. But before her curiosity could muster up the courage to ask him, he shoved her forward and through, emerging into the sun-drenched bank of the river.

A canoe bobbed in the water, tied to a crooked spruce. An ermine, too distracted to notice them, ran the length of the canoe and back, enjoying its new toy.

"Scat," Boden growled, approaching the canoe and grasping for the oar.

The ermine skittered away, screeching at them as it retreated into the woods.

"Hop in." He held the canoe steady for Mara.

She looked over her shoulder, the voice of Gabi sounding so close. The old woman called for the girl, Mallory, and Mara almost answered. Mara struggled with understanding the vastly different personality of Mallory that she had taken on. She was a piece of Mara. A portion, taken on in a moment of need—no, desperation. And despite no longer needing Mallory, Mara couldn't help but feel a hint of grief. Gabi had been sweet. She had welcomed Mallory gently and kindly into her home.

Mara sighed. She ran to the canoe and hopped in, remaining still while Boden shoved it back into the current and jumped in behind her. Her stomach tensed. She clamped her lips tight together to avoid puking. Closing her eyes, she imagined she was on her horse, far away from the water. The sound of the rapids was a rainstorm. The nightmare of the dam wasn't real.

She opened her eyes in time to see Gabi appear through the dense underbrush. The concern evident on the old woman's face relaxed into relief. She waved to Mara at the last second, singing out a farewell.

"Until we meet again, Mara," the woman called warmly. Mara's veins turned to ice at the sound of her true name. She steeled her features and turned away, setting her sights downstream. It didn't matter what she was called or if she possessed the Sword or not.

Her time in the forest was over.

Chapter Twelve

A jolt in the canoe, a slip of her seat, and Mara woke too quickly. She inhaled sharply. The reflection of the sun off the river seared her eyes. Her forearm went up like a shield, and she tried to see where they were.

The mountain that had once loomed near Gabi's cabin slowly withdrew to their left. Covered in thick forest, the slopes were green in places with conifers, fading to orange where the birch grew thickest. A large outcrop of stone jutted out high up the slope.

Mara had to squint to see it, but there was a wooden watchtower projecting high into the sky.

"Boden," Mara said, still gazing up at it, "there's a tower, just there." She pointed to her discovery.

"Aye, and?" Boden kept paddling, not even looking at the tower. "It's a river that borders the Waste. You're their queen. Don't you want them on guard?"

Mara's hand dropped. She glared at Boden over her shoulder. "Yes."

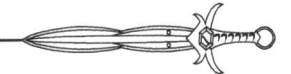

She let her eyes wander to the right, to the Waste. The sheer cliffs of before were gone, eroded to nothing but sand. Rough grass, sharp as razors, grew in patches near the river's banks. Thick mud would make the transition from river to land difficult, if not impossible, to traverse. Beyond was nothing but an orange haze. The wind whipped the sand up and into the light of the sun. If one were to wander into it, they'd receive nothing but dust. Dust in their eyes, their mouth, their clothes.

Mara settled her eyes downstream once more. Better to look ahead than at nothing. They'd been on the river for hours. The rising sun was turning downward again. There were still several hours of light left, but Mara didn't know how much longer her back could take the canoe's seat.

"They'll know me in Narlès," she finally said, filling the silence that sweltered between them. They were words she'd been ruminating on since they launched the canoe. She'd gone over them again and again in her mind until they felt smooth rolling off her tongue, though, their truth tasted bitter.

"Oh?" Boden pulled the oar through the water, steering them away from the center and closer to the bank on their left. "And why is that?"

"The proclamation," she said. "It showed my face. Everyone will be looking for me."

"Well, a missing queen isn't something to ignore."

Mara turned in her seat and scowled at Boden. She started to think he wasn't taking any of it seriously. "I can't be found," she snarled. "I don't have the Sword anymore. And Iris lives." Mara turned around to face forward again, crossing her arms with a huff. "I'm no queen."

Boden maneuvered the canoe closer to the bank, skillfully avoiding a fallen tree. "Well, if you're no queen, then Narlès won't notice."

"They'll find me," Mara muttered. She held her knees to her chest, breathing deeply, attempting to calm her worries. Her mother told her fear wasn't always a bad thing, but she was having a hard time finding a benefit to it.

"They'll find you wherever you go." Boden sighed as he prodded the tip of the canoe into the soft sand of the riverbank. He leaped gingerly from his seat, splashing his boots down into the water, all to haul Mara and the canoe safely onto the shore. With his hand extended, he offered her a smile. "To the ends of the continent, I imagine."

Mara stomped out her own smile, preferring to feign an eyeroll. She took his hand and stepped out of the canoe. "Thanks," she muttered.

The ground was springy with moss beneath her feet. A soft breeze brought the sweet, floral scent of nearby lilac. Mara picked a bloom and gently cradled it in her hands. It reminded her of the palace's extensive gardens. She'd played with Iris under the giant lilac bushes day in and day out during the summer when the plants grew and bloomed.

She'd had them ripped out the day after her coronation. It hurt too much to remember the love she had had for her sister. A love meant to be squashed, snuffed out, until all that remained were ashes. Mara might have let Iris live that fateful night, but it didn't change the fact that Iris was supposed to be dead. So Mara had killed her in her mind, removing anything and everything that reminded Mara she once loved her sister. That she once called Iris friend.

"We'll leave the continent." Boden's voice broke off her thoughts. She turned to look at him, her eyebrows pinched together in what she hoped was an obvious sign of her dissatisfaction with his answer. The bear's fur around his neck was filthier than before—if it were possible—adding to her displeasure. She wondered how he'd kept hold of it after falling from the dam. She wished he hadn't.

He stood with his hands on his hips, proud of his problem solving. Mara's lips twisted into a smirk.

"Why would I do that?" She again sniffed the bloom she'd plucked, enjoying the way the scent covered up the acrid smell of Boden's clothes.

"You just said they'd find you," he explained, "so we'll go where they won't look."

"I'm not leaving the Jeweled Realm." Mara dropped the bloom on the ground and turned her back to him, her eyes exploring the beginnings of the forest nearby.

"Mara."

It was only her name. There was no need for him to add anything else. His worry and concern were packed well within both syllables. But Mara didn't like the way her name came out of his mouth. It sounded better when people called her *Your Grace* or *Majesty*. It had the right degree of respect she deserved. But her name coming out of Boden's mouth sounded . . . too familiar. Mara had to fight herself. It wasn't the way he said her name, but the way she *liked* the way he said her name.

Mara rounded on Boden, making short work of the space between them. Their faces were so close she could feel his breath on her cheek and bask in the warmth of his body heat. But she ground her teeth together, clenching and unclenching her fists. She would remain in control of her own emotions.

She brought her finger to his face. "You forget yourself," she growled. "Don't call me Mara."

Boden studied her for a long time. His eyes, so perceptive, didn't look away. And neither did Mara. She wouldn't be the first to lower her gaze, to lose her point, so she frowned harder, glared fiercer. She'd drown the feelings deep down, where even she couldn't find them. Boden was a means back to her throne, nothing more.

To her surprise, Boden smiled. "There's the queen I know."

Mara narrowed her eyes, offering Boden her fiercest glare. There it was again—that familiarity that simultaneously irked her and thrilled her. Boden politely dropped his gaze, clearing his throat before glancing toward the forest's edge. Mara turned on her heel, returning to the trail, the back of her neck perpetuating an annoying heat. It was enough she'd spent a moon phase being called the wrong name, void of title, of place, or purpose. Now she was stuck with an Ursan, the spare heir no less, with his lack of Jeweled Realm decorum, *liking* the way he said her name.

She couldn't forget who she was. And she didn't need an Ursan forgetting who she was, either. Her hand found her belt—and its emptiness—and she paused mid-stride.

Or was Boden right? Perhaps adding space between Iris and herself would help.

"What is your command then, Your Grace?" Boden called, daring to enter the forest behind her. "If you'd be unsafe in Narlès, then where should we head?"

Her hand rested on a branch. She stared ahead at nothing, the forest blurring into itself until she saw double. The truth was she had no idea. Her feet wanted to move. Her body demanded action, but empty was her mind. Seeing Iris's face had confused her.

Mara had let her live long ago. Did she really want her dead now? No, but she wanted the problem to go away again. And in the Jeweled Realm, that meant only one thing: death. But with the Ursans on her sister's side, her options were shrinking.

The Ursans.

Mara turned to Boden, her face set in a frown. "How long had you known of your brother's betrayal?"

Boden laughed but choked it away upon seeing the anger flare in Mara's eyes. "About as long as you did."

Mara crossed her arms, unconvinced.

"Look"—Boden rubbed the back of his neck—"my brother and I were never . . . on the best of terms. He was born to lead. I was born to follow."

Her frown deepened. What a horrible fate. "You're not making a very strong case for yourself," she said.

"We're not close. I've spent the past several years either training on a battlefield or training in a temple. He's been holed up in the palace with my father."

"Scheming," Mara added.

Boden shrugged. "I cannot pretend to know what their purpose is. My father was always . . . " but his voice trailed away. He looked off into the forest, seeing something but not what was in front of him. A memory, engrained within his mind, blooming to life as a reminder.

"What?" Mara goaded him. "Your father was always what?"

Boden blinked, finally looking back to Mara. "Paranoid. The years spent fighting your mother and grandmother left scars. I suppose he's always had an eye for the Jeweled Realm, waiting for some way to ruin you."

Mara's throat tightened. It was rare for her to discuss the effects of her grandmother's conquests with a survivor. Rarer still for her to care. The people her grandmother had dominated either fell in line, assimilated, or perished. Despite the Ursans maintaining their own kingdom, whispers spoke of the Waste being their saving grace. Without it, the Jeweled Realm would have rolled the country. The Red Queen would have marched through it en masse, forcing the Ursan king to bend the knee.

"Your kingdom is not worth the resources it would cost to take it," Mara argued.

"Tell that to the people that call it home."

Mara shook her head. How could she, Queen of the Jeweled Realm, argue the principle of protecting one's land? The Realm thrived on its conquests, on its ever-expanding boundary. Or, at least, it once had.

"Your father is wrong, you know," she told him, "if he thinks Iris will offer him anything in return for his help."

Boden said nothing, but he didn't have to.

"She'll destroy Ursa," Mara continued. "She'll take it all."

He broke his silence. "I know, which is why we have to stop her."

Mara nodded, staring at those chilling blue eyes. Regardless of Prince Gerik's betrayal, or the other Ursans, Boden had done nothing but prove his allegiance since he'd arrived at the palace.

We have to stop her, he had said. *We.* The loneliness that had grown around Mara like a shell during her stay with Gabi began to thaw and crack, but Mara worried she'd be too exposed in Boden's icy gaze.

Perhaps she'd even freeze.

"Why are you helping me?" she asked.

They walked together through the woods, dodging branches and fallen trees alike. Mara didn't know if they were making their way toward Narlès or not, only that they had left the river behind. And she had no interest in seeing it again.

Boden shrugged.

"Oh, come on," Mara demanded. "No one helps anyone without a purpose. What's yours?" She suddenly realized she had a deep desire to know. A hunger. And if she didn't find out, she might be sick.

Boden stopped to adjust his fur. He wouldn't look at her, instead admiring the foliage around them. Finally, only when Mara stood with her arms crossed, did Boden relent. "Fine," he sighed. "There is a story of Saint Kalda."

Mara moaned. She turned from Boden and stalked away. A fallen tree blocked her path, but rather than return to Boden and his countless ramblings about his favorite saint, Mara took to climbing it. She was pleased to not hear him follow her. His voice faded into the noise of the forest, and for a moment, she felt singular. Herself. Mara.

A bird trilled nearby, flitting from branch to branch. Leaves rustled upon the branches beneath her feet. Even the river, a friend she'd rather forget, barely mumbled far behind them through the forest.

When her feet touched the ground on the other side, she smiled. It had been a small jaunt, a waste of time as her mother would call it, but she felt better already. Using her body to actually do something always felt better to Mara than just simply existing.

Boden appeared from around a nearby tree, having found an alternate route around the mass of fallen forest. He was out of breath, but carried on as if nothing had happened.

"Saint Kalda heard a maiden's cry within a nearby forest, so he entered, intending to find her. On his way, he faced many trials, each one more difficult than the last. When he finally found the maiden, it wasn't a maiden, but a noble spirit."

Mara rolled her eyes, but Boden was focused on his story and didn't notice.

"The spirit blessed Kalda and told him to return to the city as a great prophet, the mouthpiece of our god himself."

Boden studied Mara now, gauging her reaction. She did her best to not roll her eyes again, but she could think of nothing else to do with her eyes. Looking at Boden was out of the question, for as soon as she did, she'd start laughing.

"It's called the *Trial of the Seer*," Boden said.

"And let me guess," Mara began, "you think you're on your own trial, eh?" She leaped onto a log and jumped to the other side. Holding her arms out, she spun around to face him, her body on full display. "And I suppose I'm the maiden?"

Boden grimaced but nodded in agreement.

"Ah, but you're forgetting one thing, young prince." With each step Mara took toward Boden, branches cracked beneath her boot like breaking bones. When she was within inches of his face, she whispered, "I didn't call for your help."

They gazed at each other for a moment, each one's breath ghosting across the other's face. The corner of Mara's mouth curled upward. As did Boden's. He began to incrementally lean forward, and Mara saw her opportunity.

She turned sharply, knocking him back with her shoulder, and continued on into the forest. A smile spread across her face while she attempted to make out trails when none were present. Perhaps she saw a game trail, or perhaps it was nothing. She didn't care. She couldn't stand there with Boden discussing saints anymore. With his body so close to hers.

The forest floor gave way to shale. Roots fought their way across the hard surface, only to plunge into any crack they came across. The birch trees couldn't survive here. They'd given up several yards back, where the ground still yielded to their soft roots touch. But the spruce, with their long taproot, fought and wiggled their way into any place they landed. Mara reached the edge of the rock, a cliff face falling steep below her.

Boden arrived beside her, and they stared together. In the distance, the shale gave way to grass again, growing in tufts across rolling hills. The feet of the mountain sidled away, the pass to Narlès visible from its opposite side now. Below, nestled in the high valley, was the *ville*.

The sun set before them, filling the sky in oranges and bloody reds. Mara couldn't help but think of her blouse and the red that had decorated it when Gabi hauled her from the river's edge. She distracted herself from that thought by searching for a way to descend the cliff.

The rock offered a set of natural steps nearby, worn down by large game. Mara moved toward the stairway when Boden grabbed her by the wrist. She turned to face him, her eyes burning hot with his touch, once again igniting two opposing feelings inside her: to be touched by him and to be left alone.

"I am a simple man from a simple people," he said. "I do not pretend to know how my god works, but I was drawn to the Jeweled Realm. I was compelled to go."

"By your brother," Mara said.

"By you," he answered flatly. And before her anger—the quick fuse tied tightly to her emotions—could ignite, he continued, "a woman told to kill her own sister, but showed mercy instead. I'm here now, and you need help. I will help you, come what may."

Mara tried to pull away, but Boden's grasp was firm on her arm. She ground her teeth, hating the tightness of being held against her will. Slowly, she nodded. "Alright," she said. "Come what may."

He released her. She rubbed her arm where his strong fingers had encircled her wrist.

"I apologize, Your Majesty," he added. "I didn't mean to hurt you. I . . . would never mean to hurt you."

Mara rubbed profusely at her aching forearm, glaring at him. His eyes danced over her, seeing her, and she hated it. His touch was like a vice, and it had hurt. And yet, the voice she tried to squash kept rising up, telling her she wanted more.

"Call me Mara," she said before turning her back to him. "If I'm to be your maiden, then superlatives won't do."

Boden bowed his head, a small smile playing across his lips. "As you say, Mara."

Chapter Thirteen

The rocky path crumbled beneath their feet, providing little stability. Mara fell twice to her knees, Boden barely grasping her shoulder in time to stop her from falling to her death. His fur proved too hot for him, so he tossed it off halfway down.

"Not your beloved fur," Mara chided when it fell past her. She found herself looking forward to finally walking beside Boden without the grimy essence of his bearskin floating over them like a specter.

"I'll get another one," Boden huffed, slipping down the cliff and sending rocks toward Mara's head.

"Careful," she hissed. "We're nearly there."

Boden spoke unintelligibly, but Mara assumed they were curses. She wanted to ask what Saint Kalda believed about foul language, but her foot slipped its hold, and she decided it best to wait.

At the bottom, Mara collapsed to the grass. Her arms ached with the tension of holding herself up while descending the steep portions and her legs trembled with the constant flexing of climbing down so many steps and footholds. Boden fell down face-first beside her.

Together, they laid in the setting sun. Boden saw nothing, pressing his face instead into the cool earth. Mara watched the shadows grow. They spread long from the forest nearby, spearheading toward the cliff face.

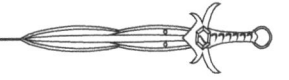

"We haven't long before nightfall," she told him. "We should hurry."

"We won't make it." Boden lifted his head off the ground. "I have flint in my pack. There is wood aplenty. Let's make a fire here and move out come the morn."

Mara wanted to argue for authority's sake but relented out of fatigue. "Fine, but we leave for Narlès at first light." She got up and set about searching for wood.

Soon, Boden fell into step beside her, grabbing broken branches and logs before she could reach them.

"I'm capable of hauling wood, Boden," she warned him.

"As you say," he apologized. He left her to retrieve the rest of the wood while he started the fire.

She trekked farther into the forest. The scattered trees were nearly naked from shedding their leaves, preparing for winter. It allowed the sun to penetrate to the forest floor. Mara admired the beauty of the paper-white birch that flourished there, deciding she preferred it to the mixed-up spruce and birch at the top of the cliff.

A rustle behind a tree startled her. She reached for her sword, only to find herself disappointed once again. She glanced over her shoulder, pinpointing Boden through the trees. He'd come if she called for him, but the question was: did she want him to? She turned back toward the noise, refusing to appear so weak as to require a man's protection. The skittering continued. Mara stepped backward slowly, keeping an eye on where the noise was coming from.

The fear of being without a weapon seized her. She reeled with multiple thoughts on how to protect herself should it attack her. It didn't matter to her that the creature making the noise was most likely a small rodent. Her brain had realized she possessed a weakness—she had no protection. And now, she would ruminate on it into oblivion. Could she swing a branch? Would a nearby rock yield enough weight to bash the creature's head in? Would she have time to defend herself?

It was enough to distract her from seeing the large root growing behind her. She lifted her foot to step backward once again and instead sat hard on the forest floor, her bounty of branches and logs falling with her.

"Mara?" Boden called.

She said nothing. A marmot, curious about the commotion as well, poked his head from behind a tree, right where the noise had been. Her cheeks blazed hot while she collected the wood she'd dropped.

"A beastly rodent," Mara muttered to herself. She stood and dusted off her riding pants. "It's not enough you don't have the Sacred Sword anymore, now you're a coward, too."

Boden arrived, axe withdrawn. He looked about, eyes tracking for anything dangerous.

"It's alright," she assured him. "I just tripped over a root."

"Oh," Boden sheathed his axe. "There are a lot of those out here. Better watch your step."

She eyed the creature warily and nodded. Her neck burned where she blushed, and her throat tightened with embarrassment. How could something so small have frightened her? Mara ground her teeth and spun on her heel, shoving past Boden and pushing away the fleeting spark she felt when her shoulder touched his.

The marmot chattered at Boden before diving back behind the tree. He watched the animal disappear before chasing after Mara. "Did that marmot scare you?" he teased.

"No," she lied.

She heard his footsteps following her, crashing through the dried leaves, but then they stopped. "Mara," Boden said more seriously, "you needn't worry. I'll keep you safe. I promise."

Mara stopped and peered at him over her shoulder. He was serious, standing square shouldered and head held high. But Mara had never been serious about a man in her life. She pushed forward, out of the forest, away from Boden. She had never required saving, either. She was the Queen of the Jeweled Realm.

All should tremble before her.

Boden had started a small fire. Its flames cracked and licked the air. Dropping her load, she slumped down next to it and rubbed her hands together, holding them close for warmth.

Boden said nothing more. He sat opposite her and fed the fire. With precision, he stacked the wood neatly within the hungry blaze, building up enough to keep the fire lit well past sunset. He chanced occasional looks at her, but her scowl turned him away.

Her life had tied itself into a knot that could not be undone. And when an ember flicked itself onto her fingertip, searing her with pain, she couldn't help but welcome the sensation. It drew her outward, a welcome distraction from the warring emotions within her. She looked at Boden, who was still distracted by the scarlet flames.

Mara sighed. "It did frighten me," she finally admitted. "I don't have a weapon. Without the Sacred Sword, I'm . . . helpless."

It was Boden's turn to scowl. "Surely there are other swords in the Jeweled Realm," he said. "Don't tell me you always use the Sacred Sword."

Mara shook her head. "Once it's attained, it's the bearer's sole weapon."

"You mean you don't have a dagger hidden in that boot? Or a"—his eyes trailed down to his axe—"a handy axe to toss about?"

Mara laughed. "No. No dagger. And certainly no axe."

Boden fell back off his feet onto a log he'd placed for sitting. He looked at Mara, thinking over her words.

"Without that sword, I'm weak," she told him. "Without it, I possess no protection."

"I said I'd keep you safe," he said. "I *want* to protect you."

His eyes were filled with such conviction, she was nearly prepared to give in. She *believed* him. But what was worse, his loyalty didn't rely on her possession of the Sacred Sword or the successful killing of Iris. No, Boden was giving it to her freely, and Mara wasn't used to such devotion.

"I need to be able to protect myself, Boden."

"Well then, we'll get you another sword. Tomorrow, in Narlès."

Mara stood. The frustration she felt pumping through her blood was enough to warm her. She didn't need the fire anymore to feel the heat.

"No," she argued. "I need my sword. *The* Sword. Without it, I am nothing. I cannot bear the thought of using another."

She spun away from Boden and the fire, her frustration building up in tears on the edge of her eyes. They threatened to fall, to break the illusion she held of herself as strong. As a queen. She swatted them away.

She would overcome her weakness.

"Then . . ." Boden's voice called to her, gently, concerned, "I'll teach you to use an axe."

And when Mara turned to scowl at his suggestion, his softened features softened her own.

"For now. Until we find the Sacred Sword. Or die trying."

Mara said nothing. His certainty was comforting.

Of course, she had trained with axes once, long ago. They were not a favored weapon among those of the Jeweled Realm. Larger blades were picked over the light, angled edge of the Ursan axe. But her had mother insisted she learn everything. And she had.

The *maître d'armes* had been a difficult man to impress. He was large and rough and had fought alongside her grandmother. When she threw the Ursan axe for the first time, it hit the target flat on the axe's eye and fell to the ground. The lightness of the weapon was something she never could get used to.

Her hand favored the weight of a sword.

"Fine. I'll use one of your axes. Until we find my sword."

"Of course," Boden bowed his head, a specter of a smile across his lips.

He unsheathed one axe and handed it to her handle first. She took the weapon into her hands and felt its coolness. It always amazed her how dead a thing could be, but how alive it could become in the heat of fighting.

"That one is Liv. She's a good slice when you throw her properly," Boden explained.

Mara stared at Boden, expecting him to burst into laughter at his joke. But he didn't. "You . . . name them?"

Boden frowned. "Every Ursan does. It's tradition. I don't see how it's any different from you calling your sword the Sacred Sword."

"That's a title," Mara scoffed. "I don't actually have a name for it."

She looked down at the axe, at Liv, tossing the handle from hand to hand.

"What's that one's name?" she asked, using Liv to point to Boden's second axe.

Boden withdrew the axe and held it in the firelight. "This one's Edda."

"Edda?" Mara couldn't stop her judgment from weaving itself into the tone of her voice.

"She was my grandmother's." Boden held it to his chest defensively.

Mara laughed. She sat down across from Boden and admired Liv. Her hand turned the blade over and over. Boden kept her sharp. The edge of the blade shimmered in the firelight, reflecting globules of light. Her handle was smooth from use.

She turned to the nearest tree and lined up her shot. When she threw Liv toward the tree, she felt confident. The release of tension in her shoulders—built up from not using a weapon—made her feel lighter. It felt good to wield something again, even if it wasn't the Sacred Sword.

The axe jammed against the tree by the handle and fell with a thump to the forest floor. Mara's shoulders sagged, but only momentarily. She sat up straight and tossed her hair out of her face.

"I haven't thrown an axe since I was a child," she said.

Boden nodded, his eyes giving away his amusement. "Yes, well, we can practice more tomorrow. Before we head into Narlès."

"Fine," Mara agreed.

She retrieved Liv and returned to her seat. The sun was well below the horizon now, leaving behind the last spills of color in a darkening sky. Mara lay down with her head propped up on her hands, staring at the stars.

Boden settled down near her, within arm's reach, though, he didn't dare touch her. She imagined it was because he had equipped her with a weapon. Perhaps he was lying there wondering if he'd live to regret it. The queens of the Jeweled Realm were known for their quick tempers. But he had looked right at her and admitted he *wanted* to protect her. She could still see the way his eyes had opened like a lake, cool and clear, when he'd said it.

With the fire flickering and popping and Boden's presence near—which was slowly becoming a comfort to Mara, to her distaste—it wasn't long before the day's events weighed her downward, tugging her toward sleep. Her eyelids were heavy, but she fought to keep them open a little longer. It had been a long time since she simply gazed at the night sky. At Gabi's she had been so exhausted from the day, she'd fall asleep inside the cabin soon after supping on dinner.

She had always imagined she could fall into it—the night—if only she could reach it. It was like an ocean with a million fireflies floating lazily above the water's surface. Everything coiled tight, functioning perfectly, until something dared to break the tension of the surface.

Mara realized she was holding her breath and didn't know why.

"We'll head south tomorrow, after stocking up in Narlès," she informed Boden.

"Oh? What's south, may I ask?"

Mara smiled, still staring upward at the stars. "An ocean."

Chapter Fourteen

Mara growled and cursed beneath her breath. Boden had spent well over an hour instructing her on the proper throwing technique of an axe, but she was no better for it.

"It's pointless!" She tossed the axe onto the ground. "I need my sword."

Boden picked Liv up and dusted her free of forest debris, stuck to the handle courtesy of the morning's dew. "No, you need to let your sword go. It's holding you back."

"How is it holding me back when I don't even have it?" Mara displayed her empty hands.

"It's just a sword, Mara."

Chills ran down her back at the sound of her name from his mouth. It was still unfamiliar to her ear, and she couldn't help but want to hear it again.

Mara rolled her eyes, attempting to cover up her reaction. "You don't get it."

"Then explain it." Boden returned Liv to Mara and crossed his arms. "I'm an excellent listener."

The Ursan prince seemed serious. No doubt he'd listen eagerly to every word from her lips. Mara was tired of throwing the axe anyway. She slouched down on a fallen tree.

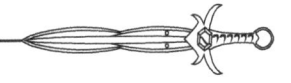

"The Sword is powerful," she said. "Simply wielding it . . . strengthens the wielder."

Boden frowned. "I don't understand."

"Forget it." Mara stood and stalked into the forest. It was not worth explaining to an outsider. Only those of the Jeweled Realm would admire the power that fitted itself around the Sword. "Let's go. Narlès is waiting."

She didn't look back to see if Boden followed. She knew he would. Instead, she focused on what laid ahead. Narlès. The *ville* wouldn't be safe, not really, not for long. No doubt the proclamation from Iris would have made it there. They would need to grab what they could for supplies and get out.

"Are you going to tell me what's south besides the ocean?" Boden asked, appearing beside her.

They walked silently for several yards. Their boots crushed forest debris, sending echoes through the trees.

"I don't know," Mara said. "I just have a feeling."

"A feeling?" Boden mused. "Like a . . . premonition?"

Mara sighed before pursing her lips in a frown. "I don't believe in your saints, or their powers. I just know there's nothing north save for more mountains and tiny kingdoms who dislike the Jeweled Realm as much as—" But she stopped herself short of saying what she really wanted: your father. "South, there is an ocean, and oceans are nothing if not possibilities."

Boden nodded. "Might I make a suggestion, then?" He leaped across a log and reached back to offer Mara his arm.

She wanted to reach for his hand, but a sourness peaked in her stomach, a discomfort arising from such familiarity. Instead, she chose to leap across of her own accord. She smirked at him as she breezed by. "Suggest away."

"There is an island people to the south—the Bastians," Boden said. "Perhaps they could be of some help."

Mara considered this. She'd learned of the Bastians long ago as part of her education on geography. *One must know the lay of the land in order to conquer it,* her mother had liked to say.

The Bastians occupied a large archipelago south of the mainland, splayed out in the turquoise ocean, like a brushstroke upon the sea. They were known for their maritime prowess, their agile warriors, and their penchant for keeping large jungle cats as pets.

"But why would they help me?" Mara asked.

Boden shrugged. "We won't know until we ask, will we?"

"Your optimism is welcome, but I grow weary of it at times," Mara joked. "Have you dealt with them before?" An important question. Bastians were not a welcoming people, preferring to keep to themselves. Mainlanders were—if Mara's memory served her correctly—seen as troublesome.

Boden ducked beneath a low-hanging branch. "There is trade between us, Ursa and Bastia, but I've never spoken with one personally."

Mara sighed. It wouldn't be enough. She shoved branches aside to reveal a meadow and opposite it, a dirt road. It zigged its way through the hills, finishing at Narlès on the horizon.

But it was a start.

"Fine," she said, entering the sun-soaked meadow. The warmth fell upon her skin, and she realized how hungry she had been for it in the cool, shaded forest. "We'll attempt to approach them. They do a little trading in our southern ports. We'll have to go to a coastal *ville* with a large harbor, where they may be trading."

Boden nodded, standing and soaking in the sun just as she did.

"Bouzy is large and formidable," she said. "The harbor there is the biggest on the southern coast. It should be suitable."

Boden tried the foreign name on his tongue. "Bouzy." He smiled. "I like the sound of it."

Mara groaned and carried on across the meadow. Was it possible to be glad he was there with her, but not glad he could speak?

Flowers drooped throughout the meadow, the last of summer's bloom, their color already faded. They reminded her of supplicating peasants, those conquered by her mother so long ago. With bent knees and bowed heads as they appealed for mercy.

How little they knew her mother.

Despite Mara only a being a toddler at the time, the images of her mother's devastating conquest still splashed vividly in her mind. She shook away the faces still painted there, and before her were flowers once again. She took a deep breath and pushed onward.

"Everything alright?" Boden asked as they reached the road.

"Fine," she assured him.

Boden watched her walk on, not attempting to keep her soldier's pace. "Wait," he called to her.

She stopped reluctantly, her heels digging into the dirt and her teeth grinding in her jaw. "What?" she growled.

Boden studied her, his hand thoughtfully rubbing his stubble. "You need a better disguise. A simple haircut is not enough."

"And what are you suggesting?" Mara crossed her arms. "A shaved scalp, perhaps? Like Iris?"

Boden smiled. "It wouldn't hide your beauty. No, we need to cover you up."

The way he said it so simply shocked Mara. It was suddenly hard for her to swallow as her cheeks flushed with a noticeable heat. Biting her tongue, she forced the sensations back, trying—with great difficulty—to master her own body and its sudden betrayal of feelings she didn't quite understand. She needed to focus. She watched, eyebrows furrowed, as Boden rummaged in his pack.

The pull to keep moving forward burned in her chest. Standing still never did her much good. She felt rooted, purposeless, like a failure. Which was why she always tried to stay busy. But constantly stopping with Boden's incessant desire to discuss things—and with such honesty—chafed her to no end.

"Well?" she pressed.

"This." Boden withdrew a simple muslin strip.

"And what am I supposed to do with that?" Mara frowned. "Wrap it around my face?"

"Sort of." Boden grinned. "It's my scarf. I wore it 'round my face when we crossed the Waste. The sandstorms get bad at times. But you can wear it around your face and hair."

"My hair?"

"Yes! Is it not custom for your women to cover their hair once the trees lose their leaves?"

Boden awaited her answer, though, she could tell he already knew he was right. And he was. Tradition held that women covered their head with a scarf once summer's heat subsided and the leaves fell from the trees. It guarded a woman's hair from unfriendly winds and cold. Mara seldom wore one in the palace. There was no need.

She snatched the muslin from him and studied it.

"This was on your face?"

Boden smirked. "I've washed it in a stream a time or two."

Mara doubted it, but she wound the length of cloth around her head and neck. She didn't quite know how to set it stylishly, like some ladies in the *ville* she'd seen before, but it likely wouldn't matter in Narlès. It was smaller, a border *ville*, amidst the mountains and forests. They'd have little use for fashionable trends there.

It smelled of minerals and something else, something of Boden. Mara exhaled, her hot breath camping over her lips. It was like a snake wrapped around her throat, preparing to suffocate her.

"That's good," Boden said. His hands reached up and straightened the edge of the muslin, laying it neatly around Mara's cheek. He smiled at her and leaned forward incrementally before realization filled his eyes and he pulled away.

She would have missed it had she not been staring right at him.

"Alright," he said, "now we're ready."

He brushed past her and headed further down the road. She stared at the back of his head, the ghost of his touch still lingering along her cheekbones.

"We don't have all day!" Boden called back to her, peering over his shoulders. Amusement was evident in his eyes, even from a distance.

She marched onward, intent on ignoring him. When she finally caught up to him, his smile was gone. Instead he focused on what was ahead, thinking. She watched him for a moment, not wanting to interrupt, before clearing her throat.

"Narlès should be just over the next hill," she said.

Boden sprang from his thoughts, a new smile filling his face as his eyes fell on Mara.

"Yes. I am thrilled to see another one of the Jeweled Realm's marvelous *villes*." He smiled too big.

"Liar." Mara looked away and kicked a rock. "Tell me true: you hate it here."

Boden shrugged. "Hate is an exceptionally exact word. Kalda teaches us not to use it."

Mara cast a distant look ahead, her expression unreadable. Kalda seemed simultaneously wise and exasperating in equal measure.

"It is not the journey I expected," Boden finally ceded.

"Because your brother betrayed you?"

Boden nodded. "Yes."

They walked on for several moments. Rocks ground beneath their feet with every step. Mara kicked a few loose stones, sending them skittering across the dirt into the opposite ditch. Birds whistled at them from every direction. If one listened too closely, they'd be at risk of being swallowed by the sound.

"I always wondered about my father," Boden said to fill the silence that tried to weave between them amidst the ambient music of the forest and road. "He'd attend worship. He knew all the answers to all the questions. But I just never could tell if he heeded Kalda's teachings or not . . . if he thought loyalty was a word better suited for fables and parables."

"And what about your brother?" Mara asked. "Did you suspect him?"

Boden shook his head. "That's just it. I never doubted him. How is that possible?" He looked at Mara for answers, though, she couldn't provide him with one.

Mara shrugged then knocked her shoulder into Boden's, attempting to lighten the load she saw he carried about Prince Gerik. "You said it yourself. You weren't on the best of terms."

"I should have seen it, though. Despite spending his days with our father, we'd still sit at the same table and break bread. But I never looked in his eyes and saw it."

Two wooden posts loomed ahead, marking the edge of Narlès. Mara felt her chest squeeze tighter with each step they drew nearer. To distract herself, she kept Boden talking, hoping his droning way of speaking would lull her into forgetting about her pain. "What does your Kalda say? About helping Iris?"

Boden sighed. "Kalda believed war was best reserved for defending oneself."

Mara laughed. Boden shook his head knowingly. The maxim directly opposed the Jeweled Realm's beliefs on what war could be and what benefits it brought with it.

"War for the sake of making war was never sanctioned," Boden explained further. "Kalda spoke of peace."

"Peace." The word filled her mouth in odd angles. "What a strange word."

"The Jeweled Realm has remained relatively peaceful for seven years," Boden argued. "Your reign has been nothing but peace, Mara."

She fought the flutter brought on by her name—again. Even if they were growing more familiar with each other, Boden still needed to see her as the queen she was. The Queen of the Jeweled Realm.

Warrior. Warbringer. Woman.

"Because peace has been useful to us," Mara said simply. She paused and fixed a guarded gaze at Boden. "And it's a moratorium. A pact my mother made. Temporary in its creation, easily broken."

"So . . . why haven't you broken it?"

Mara felt her heart sink. To answer that question would be to completely unveil herself, revealing all the hidden places within that made her different, odd. She wasn't ready to reveal that to anyone, let alone Boden. But the dam that separated them was beginning to crack. Her ruse of the unyielding Sword Queen needed to remain intact, though, if she were to ever reclaim the throne and her family's legacy.

But she was so tired of pretending.

She looked at Boden, who stared back at her eagerly. His anticipation spooked her. She'd never seen a man look at her that way, with such honesty. She could look into his eyes and see who he really was. In all her life, she'd only seen people—those of the Jeweled Realm—use their eyes to deceive. To lie. To hide behind.

Was that not what she did herself?

Her feet naturally withdrew her, and she turned away from him. She looked ahead at Narlès instead.

"There are many reasons," she said. "Ruling a powerful place such as the Jeweled Realm isn't easy."

"Certainly not." Boden dropped his eyes, appearing hurt that Mara wouldn't trust him with the truth.

An opportunity had been missed, and it fell heavily across both of them. He was the only one who had been honest with her. She knew. It would do her good to trust someone else. But her sister's face sneered at her from her darkest thoughts, and the look in Prince Gerik's eyes as the betrayal had unfolded. He had been so pleased. So eager to watch Mara die.

Trust no one, her grandmother had spoken once.

And so, she wouldn't.

Chapter Fifteen

Narlès unfolded before them. It filled the bowl of the mountain, neatly and orderly, protected by the peaks on all sides.

"A beautiful place," Boden marveled.

They neared a small house, its hedges clipped into perfect squares. Freshly painted shutters guarded each window, their green against the white shiplap pleasing to the eye.

"Yes," Mara agreed.

She, too, studied the *ville*. How it came to a ceasing halt as the rolling land of the bowl shifted to sharp shale. How the only way out, and in, was the pass they were on. Built and prospered on the back of precious stones, the *ville* boasted a healthy population despite its geographical location at the top of the mountain. To keep things healthy, Narlès made sure they could monitor visitors.

Closely.

Mara tucked her scarf tighter around her face, glancing at Boden. "It looks like a trap," she said, "a dead end."

"You wanted to come here," Boden said. "There's still time to change your mind. You can hide in the woods, and I can gather supplies."

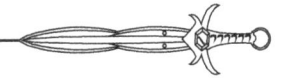

"No," Mara said quickly. She turned back toward the *ville* and started the low descent down the road. "A warrior wastes no time worrying." An Ursan adage she learned as a youth.

"You sound like my father," Boden moaned, his stride matching hers step by step.

The *ville* stirred with movement the deeper they walked. Women milled about in their gardens with their oversized hats, prepping the beds for winter. Children ran back and forth, their laughs echoing off nearby houses.

"Seems like a dream," Boden said. "Everyone is pleasant." He nodded his head politely to a man walking past.

Mara's palms were sweaty. She rubbed them on her riding pants. The mountain pass fell away behind them, and she could feel her exit shrinking. Militarily, marching into a dead end was a poor decision. Her mother would have been shaking her head, refusing the battleground, and finding somewhere else to go.

But Mara didn't have that option.

She tried to relax. Her shoulders ached from holding them at attention, so she took a deep breath and let them fall. Boden was right. The place was dreamlike. Picturesque. Beautiful. There had to be a way to remain aware of danger and enjoy the moment simultaneously.

Balance. As important to an individual as it was in a sword.

"Remember," Mara leaned into Boden. Without his bear hide, she could smell the sweat off his body, which wasn't entirely unpleasant. She pressed on, hoping to ignore the distracting odor of a man on a march. "We find the market. Then in and out."

Boden nodded. "As you say, Majesty." He offered her a quick, small bow, overemphasizing her title with his Ursan accent. A lopsided grin pasted itself across his lips, which she hated. Not because she realized he was joking with her, but because it only served to make him more handsome.

She crossed her arms and scowled. "This is no time for jokes, Boden. I'm Mallory. Remember that."

Boden, the corner of his lips still upturned in amusement, nodded before looking ahead at the nearing buildings. These, too, were white shiplap with small windows filled with thick glass. Smoke curled out of chimneys, reaching for the sky, filling the otherwise brilliant sunny day with a haze. The sharp scent of fires lit within hearths drifted by on the light breeze. A sign of approaching winter.

The closer they walked, the clearer the buildings became. None were stores, supplies or otherwise. Houses, as charming as they were simple, sat behind hedges and gardens. Mara chanced a smile at a little girl playing with her brother in the dirt. The girl smiled back.

Past the homes, they arrived at a four-way cross. Houses crowded three corners, but a large public building filled the fourth.

Windows interrupted evenly across its brilliant white walls. A single golden sign hung above the door: *Chapelier*. Displayed in the large windows were hats of many kinds, colors, and textures.

A man exited the building and crossed the street in front of them. A hat box was in his hand, and he seemed worried, muttering quickly to himself.

"Pardon, father," Mara called, formally addressing the man, "could you tell us where the market is?"

With the sun bright in the man's face, he held up a hand to peer at Mara. She knew her face would be shadowed, protected by the sheer light of the sun. After he blinked several times, the man straightened and gestured down the street.

"But first," he spoke, keeping them from heading on their way, "wouldn't you rather cover your hair with this fine hat?" He procured a hat from the box, a purple-billed thing with cascading violet flowers and black silk ribbon. "My newest and finest creation. Scarves are such an old habit. Why not a hat?"

"Oh, uh . . . " Mara's hand went to her scarf, her fingers feeling the fabric, anxiety tickling her fingertips. "It is a lovely hat, but I much prefer my scarf."

The man wilted. "Surely you'd like it as soon as you tried it."

"No, thank you." Mara moved toward Boden, her body suddenly instinctively seeking his protection.

The man ignored her words. He reached for her scarf and pulled it down a fraction. A lock of her auburn hair tumbled out, but Boden quickly ripped the man's arm from Mara.

"The lady said no, father," Boden growled at him.

Doubled over in the pain of Boden's grip, the man whined out an apology. But Mara couldn't help but notice the way he was looking at her. He peered from Mara to Boden, examining.

Mara grabbed Boden's forearm and pushed him down the road. "Farewell, father," she called to the man.

"What was that about?" Boden asked once they were down the street and around the corner. "Who grabs a woman like that?"

"He's a modiste, probably not the only one in Narlès. He's likely desperate for a sale. Frankly, I applaud his efforts. To be successful, one must make their success."

Boden rolled his eyes. "Where did you hear that?"

"My grandmother." Mara wasn't even looking at him now, instead discerning which street they were meant to take.

She heard the rumbling of many voices and a few stray notes from someone playing music. Certain it was the market, Mara followed the sound down the street. Boden followed, which pleased Mara.

The noises grew louder, and more people emerged out of doorways and alleys, like shadows grown in the afternoon sun. Some dressed finely—those from the rich families of the *ville* who owned the mining companies and ran the bank, the *couturières*, the diplomats. Others were more simply dressed—the grocer, the gardener, the miners and their families.

Like a funnel, the street led them toward the market. Booths popped up, food displayed beautifully and strategically in each one. Mara could sense Boden's hunger. She could feel his body tense when he spied the spoils of her kingdom laid out on rich display.

His voice arrived in her ear, whispering, "Let's grab some food while we're here."

"You managed to hold on to little coin when you fell in the river," Mara answered him, her eyes locked on to a stall that appeared promising. "It's best if we purchase what we agreed upon first. We can always hunt."

His body drooped.

"There will be other *boulangeries*," she assured him as they passed a sweet-smelling stall of baked goods. Mini cakes dressed in brilliant fruits sat next to pastries draped in golden crusts. They reminded her of her last meal at the palace, before her trek to find Iris began. Her heart pained for home, for the monotony of her old life.

But it had all been a lie and she, the creator.

Iris's words came back to her. *You can't be queen.* Mara bit her lip. The absence of the Sacred Sword on her hip felt like a void in her body. Like a lack of being.

Like a hole in space and time.

She couldn't be queen. It was true. Not without the Sword.

She hurried past the food, the scents turning bitter with the memories they carried.

They passed a forge. A man, biceps bigger than most people's thighs, swung a hammer. The *ting ting ting* of the hammer striking hot metal rang through the market, echoing against the surrounding buildings. It was music to Mara. She stopped to watch him. With each strike, red sparks erupted from the connection. It was the sweetest kiss Mara could imagine.

A woman appeared, a leather apron draped over her thick build. She smiled at Mara before beginning her own project. A sword, shorter than Mara's, sat half-finished on the woman's anvil.

"Fancy one?" Boden asked her, his head tilting toward one of the many swords the blacksmiths had on display.

"I told you," Mara said, still not tearing her eyes from the smiths and their work, "there is only one sword for me."

Boden frowned. He turned to stare down the street, the full sight of booths encompassing everything around them. But it wasn't just the booths that overwhelmed the senses with their bones of wood and muscle of goods, their skin of cloth draped to protect from the sun. It was also the sheer amount of people. They were coming from everywhere, filling the packed-dirt street, bringing with them more noise, more texture, more vibrancy.

Mara felt herself pull within. She never liked crowds. Where her mother's reign had been marked by boisterous parties celebrating yet another triumph, hers had yet to yield itself to such a cause. Birthdays were marked by small dinners. Solstices by hunting. No one complained. Parties were expensive.

And the queen's will was unquestionable.

She yearned for it then—her power. The way giving a simple command could gain her whatever she desired. The mere thought and casual glance would bring forth the supplies they needed. The food they wanted. The sweets Boden craved.

Mara watched him. He was observing the people with a glint of thrill in his sharp eyes. He'd nod politely to passersby. The men might nod, the women might giggle. Children watched him intently, whispering amongst themselves. It wasn't often an Ursan appeared in their midst.

It wasn't often Ursans were seen in the Jeweled Realm at all.

Mara was starting to regret their plan. Eyes were everywhere, watching them. Lips were moving diligently, speaking low to someone's listening ear. Why did they think they'd go unnoticed?

"You should have hidden your axes," Mara whispered to Boden.

He looked repulsed. "An Ursan never hides their weapons."

"Well, surely word of the missing queen has reached this place. And, with it, news she might be traveling with an Ursan."

Boden shrugged. "Danger plagues our journey, despite our choices. I've shaved my face, appearing less like an Ursan and more like a handsome stranger. I figured I might be a distraction."

"From what?" Mara chose to ignore Boden's arrogant statement about his appearance.

"From you."

She glared at him and crossed her arms, defending herself from his words. "I am well hidden. You are not."

"You are a strange woman in this town, with golden eyes—much like the queen—and a fluid grace of movement only royalty would possess."

Mara's mouth hung open. No one had ever described her in such a way. They were the observant words of someone who had spent considerable time watching her. Her head shook in disagreement, her mind a tumultuous mixture of thoughts and feelings, none helpful at that current moment.

A small crowd of children approached. One bumped into her, shoving her toward Boden. His arms instinctually wrapped around Mara protectively. Horrified by the way her body was tempted to melt into his embrace, she shoved herself away.

"Pardons, mother," the boy—brown of hair and eyes—mumbled.

Mara glared at the boy. It was the only thing she could do to abstain from unleashing her fury, which had been ignited by the confusion at Boden's words.

Anger was a fear response. Her grandmother had insisted it was her fear of being beaten and killed that planted the seed for her anger, which bloomed into rage, which reseeded an entire kingdom. It was a welcome response in her household. Which was why—as Mara found herself frightened by what was happening to her—she let the anger within her grow.

Her mouth curled into a frown while she wiped Boden's sweat from her blouse. Were she in the palace, Petra would have already snatched the boy and sent him away. To where, Mara never knew. She never asked what became of those who disappeared.

Boden seemed pleased by their bodies' meeting. A smile painted his face, and he moved to say something, but Mara would hear none of his jokes.

"Don't." She held up her hand. "Let's just get what we need."

Boden nodded, sealing his lips. He patted his belt out of habit, but his hand froze. His eyes grew larger than Mara had seen them, their blue so clear and vivid.

"What?" she asked.

"The money." He examined his belt wildly, discovering there was no coin cloth to be found. "It's gone. Those wretches stole it!"

Mara sought the mass of children in the crowd, following their exit route from when they'd run into the pair. But she could see none of them. Yet down the street, to the left, was the entrance to an alleyway. No doubt the thieves would find the quickest and cleanest escape.

"Come on." She grabbed Boden's arm and tugged.

"Where are we going?"

"To get our money back."

Chapter Sixteen

The market crowd grew thick and pressed against them. Mara shoved her way through, guiding Boden. Women glared at her but winked at Boden, who returned their winks with a charming smile. Mara yanked his arm again, a sudden rush of jealousy coming alive within her. Boden jerked his head back to Mara.

"Keep up," Mara growled. "We'll lose them."

"How do you know they're even there?" Boden picked up speed, his body propelling Mara forward.

At the end of the alley, a cat hissed at them before darting beneath a nearby stall. Stacked crates ran halfway down the alley and farther still were doors on either side. Mara stalked slowly, eyes darting, looking for signs of the children.

A giant crash came from behind. Mara turned, reaching for a weapon that wasn't there, only to find Boden stuck in an avalanche of crates.

"Sorry," he said.

Mara scowled and turned back to her search. She tried the door to her left, but it did not budge. As she reached for another door, children exploded out of it and flooded the alleyway.

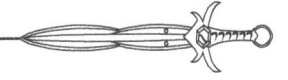

They bolted deeper down the alley, whooping and screaming. Mara knew if they reached the end and made the turn, they were as good as gone. No doubt the alley forked soon after the turn, spider webbing amongst the buildings. Once she lost them, they'd easily disappear like smoke, vanishing with her money and only chance of getting supplies.

She reached for anything—a child's shirt wafting amidst their quick getaway, a dragging scarf, wind-whipped hair. They all maneuvered past, laughing at her. It reverberated painfully in her ears.

But she noticed one child, the smallest girl, jostled about by her comrades. Mara read the group's movements, like a grass lion stalking a herd of deer, and snatched the girl. Mara's hands grasped the girl's wrists, and she whirled her around to face her.

"Our money," Mara growled. She ignored the girl's angry eyes. Such fear-filled rage had no effect on Mara. She had peered into the eyes of evil, and they belonged to her sister.

"I don't have it, miss." The girl squirmed. "Rox gives me nothing."

"I don't believe you." Mara squeezed the girl's shoulder tighter, watching her wince. She hated admitting it was the most powerful she'd felt since losing her sword. *Only a weak warrior harmed children,* her grandmother would say. *But sometimes necessary,* her mother would add.

"Honest, mother. I'm the littlest, see?" The girl tried to tug her shoulder away but was met with another pinched grip of Mara's hand. She flinched but spoke through the pain, gritting her teeth, "I . . . can get it back for you, though."

"Oh?" Mara narrowed her eyes.

"Mar . . . Mallory, enough," Boden said, his hand finding Mara's elbow. She's just a child."

"They were all children—the ones who stole your gold," Mara said.

Boden pulled her back, unforgiving with his own grip. His strength had a way of surprising her, reminding her that beneath Boden's kind smile was a warrior. Mara released the street cretin. The girl fell back down to her feet. She winced while rubbing her shoulder.

"Get the coin then," Mara commanded. "Bring it back here. I'll give you until the sun hits its zenith."

With a dirty hand to her forehead, the girl peered at the sky, estimating the time she had to retrieve their goods. "That isn't very long."

Mara shrugged. "You stole from the wrong people."

The girl glared at Mara but said nothing more. She turned and left, her body receding down the alley in the same direction as the other children, slinking like a caught cat.

"And what makes you think she'll return after such treatment?" Boden said as he watched her go.

Mara held up her left hand. Within it dangled a filthy gold chain, a dirty emerald the size of a pea dangling from a faceted pendant.

"It's the only thing of value she had on her." Mara stared at the end of the alley. "She'll be back for it, and she'll have to bring our coin to get it."

"And if she doesn't?"

"We'll use the pendant to get what we need."

Boden extended his hand toward the gem, cradling it in his palm. "A bit too luxurious for a child," he said.

Mara dropped it into Boden's hand. "Narlès feeds off gemstones. They fill the surrounding mountains. Everyone knows the best gems come from here." Mara walked back toward the end of the alley, allowing the sounds of the market to engulf them once again.

"Doesn't explain how she'd end up with a gem this size."

"Doesn't matter," Mara said.

"Probably stolen," Boden sighed. "Now what?"

"We wait." Mara seated herself on a crate in position to see either end of the alley. She didn't say a word to Boden, allowing him to draw his own conclusions.

He seemed to resign and fumbled around for a place in the shade. A small crate was suitable for propping up his feet. Boden leaned back and closed his eyes.

Mara allowed the sun to fall on her face. The scarf soaked in the warmth and mixed with her breathing, irritating her. She'd give anything to take the disguise off. Even with eyes closed, the sun pierced through her eyelids, illuminating her vision, making her feel uneasy. She opened her eyes, deciding it would be wiser to keep an eye on their surroundings anyway.

Shoppers strolled past them, all headed toward the market and its bountiful wares. A pair of girls, perhaps sisters, walked past giggling. Mara watched them for a time. They inspected a *parfumeur*'s booth before moving on to a jeweler.

Eventually, she closed her eyes again, letting the warmth of the sun lull her.

What is Iris doing at this moment? she wondered. *And who in the Jeweled Realm is helping her?* Her reappearance and Mara's disappearance were more than enough to deem Iris fit for queendom. But without the Sword, would the kingdom accept her?

Mara jolted. She'd been dozing. Something tapped her boot. When she opened her eyes, the world glazed over, impossible to see.

"I'm back," the girl whispered from the darkness of the alley nearby. "I got your stupid coin. You got my necklace?"

Mara smirked, blinking to clear her vision. "Yes."

The girl retreated down the alley, out of the sun and any prying eyes within the market's crowd. Mara made to quickly follow, but remembered Boden slept nearby.

He gently snored, curled within his jerkin behind some stacked crates. The sun had turned in the sky and was now working its way past Boden's protective barrier of shade. Sunlight fell across his face in a harsh line, highlighting his growing stubble and sharp jawline. His ear had turned a lovely shade of pink. He looked an awful lot like a street cretin. A handsome one, but a cretin, nevertheless.

She nudged him on her way past him, gesturing with her head toward the alley. "The girl's back," she said.

Boden jumped up and followed closely behind Mara. He followed so tightly she could feel the heat emanating off his leathers.

Once in the alley, tucked around the corner and shielded from the probing sun, Mara smiled at the girl. The way she scrutinized them with half-closed eyes made her look fierce. Regal, even. Mara admired that. The girl's hand was on one hip and her other held Boden's coins. All fear was gone from her face. Instead, a mixture of annoyance and arrogance filled it.

"Where's my gem?" she asked.

Boden moved to retrieve the jewelry, but Mara slammed her forearm across his chest, stopping him.

"You'll get it when I count the coin," she said to the girl.

The girl smirked. "How about you get the coin when I get my gem?"

Mara nodded. "Fine," she said. "We'll just take the gem and go."

"Wait!" The girl counted out loud each coin as fast as she could.

"It's all there," she said, shoving it toward Mara. "Here."

Mara ripped the coins from her hand. She squeezed them tightly. Only then did she nod the go-ahead for Boden to give the girl back her necklace.

"That's a big stone for such a little girl," Boden said while fishing out the jewelry from his pocket.

"Shows what you know," the girl sniffed. "This is Narlès. Everyone's got gems."

"Then why's this one so special?" He handed back the necklace.

The girl pulled it over her head, covering the stone in her clasped hand. "What's it to you?" She looked from Boden to Mara and back to Boden.

Mara had to admit, she admired the girl's tenacity. She didn't know what the child had done to retrieve their coin, but she noticed her bruised knuckles and a trickle of a red stain leading from her lip down her chin.

"What's your name?" Mara asked.

The girl frowned. She stood clasping her gem, eyebrows furrowed at Mara's question. Almost as if she were disappointed.

"You don't care what my name is," she finally said. "I'm no one."

Mara nodded. "Then I owe no one my thanks." She waved the hand holding the coins at the girl before turning to leave.

She caught the girl's eyes rolling, but fought the urge to strike her. *No one rolls their eyes at the queen,* Mara thought. But with hands empty of the Sacred Sword, she was slowly realizing she held little power over what others thought or did.

"I suggest keeping a closer watch on your coin, mother," the girl called after them. "In case you lose it again and I'm not around to fetch it!"

Mara ignored her, dragging Boden along in her wake. Once out of the alley and back in the market proper, the heavy smell of other people's bodies wrapped around them.

"Here." Mara thrust the money back to Boden. "Try not to lose it again."

The market had grown more crowded. They could no longer approach the blacksmith stall, for the crowd had grown so thick there with people watching the master smithies at work. It was a good thing Mara had no intention of replacing her sword. She'd never reach the smithy to even ask.

Farther down the street, the market opened into a square. A tall tower stood at the corner of a large building overlooking the market stalls, boasting the face of a large clock. A fountain occupied the middle—Mara's grandmother carved in stone, water flowing from her extended hand.

Booths and stalls filled every surface of the square. Orderly walkways were formed out of planks, often reduced down to one plank wide, wedged between booths. People called louder and louder, boasting their wares, peddling their goods, stealing the attention of would-be buyers.

"Where do we start?" Boden's voice rang behind her.

Mara gazed over the chaos, wondering the same thing. "We find the *maroquinier* first. They'll have leather packs and a possible jerkin for me." She gazed back at Boden. "And then perhaps some food."

Boden smiled at that last word. "Lead the way."

She centered herself before stepping into the chaotic space of the market. The planks beneath her feet were firm after years spent being pounded beneath the boots of Narlès. Some planks were old, ancient even, eroded to near pulp. Mara did her best to avoid these places, though sometimes it forced her to step down into the muck that had built up beneath the walkway.

They passed another smithy, this one worked by an old and weathered man. He had a hunched back and a leather-like face. His hands shook as he dipped the red-hot metal in water.

Fall vegetables filled the next several stalls. Gourds of many shapes and colors piled high into baskets, while some were emptied and carved with faces. Thick tubers overflowed into the next bin which was filled with tightly balled leafy greens.

"We must find one of those pastry booths," Boden said casually as they passed the vegetables.

Mara laughed. "Potatoes keep longer than cakes on a journey."

"Ah, yes, but a man marches on his stomach! A stomach of cakes is happier than a stomach of taters."

"Mmm, but I'm not concerned for your happiness." Mara stopped to look at Boden. "But perhaps we could find the ingredients for that Ursan camp tea. It seemed . . . beneficial."

She carried on walking, ignoring his further requests for pastries. *Boulangeries* were notoriously overpriced anyway and would gouge the little coin they had. At the palace, she had a pastry chef on staff who was gifted at creating all of the Jeweled Realm's colorful desserts. But out in the rest of the realm, one would have to suffer or spend all their coin on cakes.

A booth at the end of the row caught Mara's eye. Green linen draped across the top, marking the booth as a furrier's. Spotted furs of mountain cats. The brilliant red of foxes. Perhaps there'd be a black bear mantle with fur a slippery shade of night. She aimed them toward it, wanting to see Boden's reaction when he saw the furs of her kingdom displayed before him, bestowing her with his pleasant smile. It was a smile she had before only associated with small children amazed by the world, but she was quickly learning that Boden, too, found delight in even the simplest of things.

They were but two stalls away when Mara saw him—a man, taller than normal, his hair in a silver braid. She couldn't make out his words, but she heard the way his voice bounced off the surrounding structures. It was rolling and pleasant and loud.

It was Charles.

Chapter Seventeen

Mara froze. Charles seemed distracted by the sale of his furs. He hadn't seen them. Yet. She backed away, treading on Boden's foot. "Ow!" he groaned before knocking into a display of honey.

Jars filled with golden honey fell to the ground like stars. Several broke, erupting their delicious nectar onto nearby boots and ladies' shoes. Those that didn't break rolled down the planks, some lodging beneath the walkway through large gaps in the wood, others tumbling off under tables and dresses.

"Now you've done it!" the beekeeper yelled at Boden. "Ursan filth!"

Several heads turned and stared. Quiet whispers went up amongst the crowd. Mara checked Charles, who was still chatting happily with the furrier. But his back was to them. The furrier's was not, and he saw the crowd's attention turn from the goods of the stalls toward Mara and Boden. He gestured with his hand to Charles, who turned slowly to see what the confusion was about.

Mara searched for somewhere, anywhere, to hide. Her eyes landed on a thick wooden post, a large sheet of paper tacked to it. A depiction of her face sat idle in the middle. The eyes disturbed her. They were black and void, making her look like a monster. Beneath it were the words: CROWN TRAITOR. MAY BE TRAVELING WITH AN URSAN MALE. ARREST ON SIGHT.

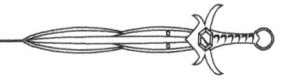

Others were now looking at the drawing, their eyes drifting back toward Mara. She tightened the scarf around her face. It was enough, she kept telling herself. They couldn't see her face, couldn't tell the shade of amber that saturated her eyes. But she glanced back at Boden.

Edda and Liv were tucked neatly into his belt. His earth-toned jerkin, made of some sort of Ursan creature's hide, was caked in mud and grime. His facial hair—despite his recent effort to shave his beard and appear less Ursan—had been growing in quickly and thickly. He was clearly Ursan. There was no hiding that fact.

"Mallory?" Charles called over the heads of the crowd.

Mara shoved Boden through the honey stall.

"You can't come through here!" the beekeeper yelled at them. He pushed Boden backward.

"She must, father." Boden grabbed the man's hand and dropped a few gold coins into it. "Sorry for your trouble." Mara noticed the gentleness in Boden's eyes when he offered the coins. Then it was gone in a blink, hidden beneath the fierce mask he wore whenever he sensed Mara was in danger.

Mara moved past Boden to lead the way, zigzagging through the spaces between the stalls. The rage-filled voices of the owners had risen into a toneless buzz by the time they emerged on the far side of the square. An alleyway with steep downward stairs appeared to their left. Mara motioned for Boden to follow.

They were halfway down before they heard his voice. It seemed to have lost some of its friendliness between Gabi's home and Narlès—between the chase amongst the market stalls and their attempted escape.

Mara!" Charles barked.

She stopped. Her name was frigid coming from Charles's mouth. The queen within her wanted to continue down the stairwell to whatever hellish squalor it led to, but no one had ever spoken to her like that. Not even her father had raised his voice to her, an heir to the Sacred Sword.

He stood on the top step, his eyes dark beneath his brows. Slowly, he descended toward them.

"That's far enough." Boden stepped between Charles and Mara.

Charles smirked. "An Ursan."

"Yes," Boden answered, "last time I checked." He withdrew Edda and held her at the ready by his side.

Charles eyed the weapon but looked at Mara. "You betrayed Gabi's trust. Anyone who betrays Gabi betrays me."

Mara's eyebrow arched. "Betrayed Gabi? Had she known who I was, she would have turned me in immediately."

"Fitting for a crown traitor," Charles replied.

So she had been right. Charles had spoken to Gabi about turning her in. The paper in the market depicting her face would have already spread across the realm. Their escape south was looking grimmer by the moment.

Mara ground her teeth. "You will not speak to me that way."

"Oh? Were you queen, I'd agree. But you're not, are you? Traitor," Charles sneered.

"That's enough!" Boden snapped.

Charles's eyes settled on Boden. He descended another step. And then another. "Ursans have never understood the comfort and safety that comes from a devout following of order. Order wrought by the Sword, wielded by a worthy queen."

Boden lifted Edda. "It's just a sword," Boden said. "No sword can rule a kingdom."

Charles smiled. "You reveal your ignorance then, Ursan. The Sacred Sword is precious. The one who wields it is the queen. She"—he gestured to Mara—"does not deserve it. While her sister still lives, she cannot be queen."

The silence within herself was drowning her. More and more she found she couldn't feel the words to defend herself anymore. They wouldn't bubble up her chest and out her mouth. Instead, they floundered in her throat, catching and suffocating her. Instead, the voice within her mind that told her it was true—all true—whispered its dark words. Words that shrank her, that made her feel like an imposter. Words that cut deeper than any sword.

Because, ultimately, they were right. They were all right.

But she wouldn't stand there any longer and let men speak as if she wasn't there.

"Neither can Iris," she called, finally breaking her silence, every syllable empowering her to push forward. "She's probably ensconced herself in the palace by now, hasn't she?" Mara stepped up, settling herself next to Boden, feeling braver still with his presence beside her. "She has claimed the throne by default. But if the Sword is truth, then the truth still stands: if I am alive, then she can't be queen."

Charles nodded in agreement. "I'm sure we can fix that problem, though, can't we? And then my new queen—the rightful queen—will reward me."

From a sheath on his belt he produced a skinning knife, its short, wide curve of a blade glinting razor sharp in the alleyway. He lunged for her, but Boden was faster. He knocked Charles's arm down with the butt of Edda before launching his shoulder into Charles's stomach, knocking him into a nearby window, its panes grimy from years of wet weather and wind blowing dirt from the mines. His head broke through. Charles cried out in pain as trickles of brilliant-looking blood dripped onto the stone steps. Boden kicked him harder, shoving him further into the window.

"Let's go!" He turned and grabbed Mara by the arm, dragging her down the remaining steps, slipping several times as they went.

"Slow down, Boden. Slow down!" Mara tried to free herself from him, but his grip was firm.

His fear was palpable, rising off his skin in a wild heat. Mara felt it beneath her own skin, and her heart thudded in her chest in response. It wasn't *his* life he was fearful for. It was hers.

His strides were long, and Mara fought to remain on her feet as they rounded a bend in the staircase. The stairs seemed never-ending. Boden only slowed when they reached the bottom step, and the streets unfurled before them in dark ribbons.

"Where to now?" he asked, each syllable clipped between breaths.

"I don't know," Mara said, looking around at the utterly new, darkened world the endless stairs had brought them to.

In either direction, the streets turned from filtered gray to inky black. Old lanterns sat lopsided on top of iron posts, some leaning so far over they risked lighting anything nearby on fire—if any of them were actually lit. There was only one, off in the distance, that glowed. Mara pointed it out to Boden.

"There," she said. "We have to keep going. He'll be on us soon."

The distant sounds of glass cracking and falling resonated down the stairwell. They could hear Charles yelling from up the many steps and around the corner of the building, his cries of pain and anger filling the air. Multiple footfalls echoed off the stairway's brick walls.

"More are coming," Boden said.

They moved forward into the darkness. Mara felt like she was being absorbed, overtaken by some monstrous creature, now and forevermore a part of it.

"I almost feel we are underground," Boden whispered after a few moments of walking in the dark.

Mara knew it was a trick of the eye, but it seemed the lantern was not growing closer, but drifting farther away. She bit her lip and increased their steps.

"That's because we are. There is limited space for a *ville* on top of a mountain," Mara told him. "The only answer is to build down."

Yells grew louder behind them, though Mara could not make out anyone following them. The darkness beneath the city was so complete. Mara wondered if any light filtered its way down there. What could survive in such a dark environment?

She needn't wait long to find out. A hiss came at them from the nearby darkness. Boden jumped in front of Mara, separating her from the unknown creature.

"Here," a small voice said, "in the window."

Mara shoved Boden away. "It's someone," she climbed some exposed brick to peer through the window, noticeable only by the way the pane reflected the far-off lantern light.

A candle glimmered dully within. It cast little light in the room, just a faint glow of warm orange, much more a suggestion of light than light itself. A body stood near the candle. It was impossible to make out any fine details, but Mara was certain it was too small to be anything but a child.

"Don't stand gawping, mother," the child said. "Climb in before they see you."

It was the street girl from before. Mara smiled into the dark, briefly wondering if she was sending herself to further doom by attempting to escape their current doom.

"Come on," Mara whispered back to Boden. "Follow me."

The window was small and square. Mara pushed through to her hips. She assumed her sword would catch, but was quickly reminded of its absence. With nothing to stop her, Mara continued to slide through the window, the drop higher than expected. She instinctively put her hands out to catch herself as she fell to the floor, then felt her left wrist bend inward and pop upon impact. She inhaled sharply, cradling her hand before crawling away to allow Boden to enter.

She sat in the dark next to the street girl, watching the large Ursan shimmy through the window. Boden paused several times to catch his breath, all while the noises of their pursuers grew louder outside.

"You need to hurry," the girl said. "Don't warriors move faster?"

In the candle's glow, it was easy to see Boden glaring. Mara wanted to laugh, but pain shot through her wrist with every movement and kept her humor chained. With one last shove, Boden fell through the window, landing flatly on his back on the packed-dirt floor.

The girl leaped past him gracefully, using a nearby chair to reach up and silently shut the window. She snuffed out the candle just as the noise from outside seemed to reach its peak.

Their pursuers were near. They were outside. And they were angry.

Chapter Eighteen

The grumbled voices of their pursuers faded. Apparently, they didn't want to spend any longer in the depths of Narlès than Mara did. When their footfalls disappeared, the girl relit the candle and placed it by Mara.

"It'll be impossible to get out now," Boden muttered to Mara. When he noticed she was cradling her hand, he frowned. "What happened to your arm?"

He reached for her wrist, but she pulled it away. "I fell on it," she said. "It'll be fine." The thought of anyone touching it—even Boden—made her stomach roll with anticipated pain. She held her arm tightly against her body, searching for the shape of the street girl.

The room was so dark they felt isolated, alone. A velvet voice, one accustomed to speaking words in the depths of darkness, startled them.

"I reckon not with the sound I heard it make," the girl said.

"I said it'll be fine," Mara repeated, her heart pounding in her chest.

"If you say so, mother."

They watched the small shape of the girl's body turn and moved toward the far wall, tangling with the shadows.

"Follow me," she said.

"To where?" Boden asked.

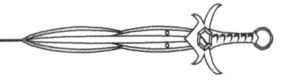

Neither of them moved. Mara, for lack of stamina. The fall—the pain in her wrist—had shocked her. She needed more time to think. More time to come up with an alternative plan. But the pain raced through her arm like a ballista, searing up her shoulder and neck into her head, preventing her from thinking.

"There's more than one way out of Narlès, if you know where to look," the girl's words drifted in the dark.

"How do we know we can trust you?" Mara exhaled between bouts of pain.

The girl stepped closer, her face illuminated by the candle. The red stain on her chin was still there, along with another from her nose. She had been fighting again. Recently.

"You weren't the first to take my necklace," the girl said, eyes unwavering as they settled on Mara's, "but you were the first to give it back."

Mara understood. Though she grew up privileged, coddled in the palace with every whim greeted with enthusiasm, she knew the way of the *villes'* alleyways. It was clear this girl did nothing unless she really wanted to.

"What's your name?" Mara asked her.

"Éliane."

Mara nodded. "Alright, Éliane, lead the way."

The girl smiled briefly, a fleeting warmth on a cold and angular face, before turning and rejoining the shadows. Mara reached for the candle with her uninjured hand, but Boden's hand gently clasped her fingers, stopping her.

"Are you sure?" he asked her. He looked scared. His eyes, the pupils so large they hid the blue, shone in the candlelight. Within them, Mara could see his worry, and it made her stomach lurch. She wasn't accustomed to such fear. Especially for her. There was little to fear in the capitol, locked in her palace, where her servants were obedient to a fault. Petra made sure of that. But to see that worry storm up in Boden's eyes and not know what to do with it? Knowing exactly what it meant but being too afraid to realize it? To speak it into existence?

She pushed him away and retrieved the candle. "What other choice do we have?" She disappeared into the darkness, once again one with the shadows.

Éliane waited in a small hall, her body a shade lighter than the darkness surrounding her. It was the only way Mara could see her.

"Your eyes will adjust soon enough, mother," Éliane said, turning to continue leading them further into the depths of the home. "Until then, I can be your eyes."

"Do you live here?" Mara asked, nearly skinning her shin on a chair.

Éliane laughed. "I live where I want."

"So no." Boden grunted as he ran into the chair Mara had avoided. "Whose house is this then?"

"Listen, I agreed to help you. That doesn't make us friends," Éliane said.

They walked on in silence, slinking through narrow hallways and thin doors. Mara had known of the *ville* beneath a *ville*, but she never thought she'd ever see it.

Late in her grandmother's reign, desperate for space, miners had done what they did best and dug down to build for their families. They'd used old mining shafts to carve out homes, some with great efficiency and skill and others with a less refined touch. Most were carved over, again and again, to suit the tastes of the newest owners.

With the installation of street lanterns, one could almost imagine they were merely in the darkness of night. But no moon ever shone there in the depths of the mountain. No light, save for what people could create for themselves.

"How far down does the *ville* go?" she asked Éliane. But Éliane continued moving forward as if she hadn't heard Mara. It was clear the girl would not be bothered to speak until she was ready, and not before.

The cool air melted into muggy, stale air. They had moved into a small room again. A low fire burned in a fireplace. A sleeping old man snored in a chair.

Éliane didn't seem bothered by the occupants of the homes they stalked through. Some nodded their hellos, others ignored her completely. The three of them were like ghosts, drifting through a dark and forgotten place.

They walked for nearly half an hour before Éliane broke the silence. "Stories say that the giant emerald of the Sacred Sword was mined in the depths of the mountain."

"Yes, it came from Narlès," Mara said.

Éliane stopped. A dimly lit lantern cast its dull light through a filthy window. But it was enough for Mara to see the girl's face. "Is it as large as they say?" she asked.

Mara pursed her lips and stared down her nose at the girl, but Éliane refused to look away from the Sword Queen. Instead, she crossed her arms and scowled at Mara, awaiting her response. This girl was defiant—and clever. Both were desirable traits for a young woman of the Jeweled Realm. Mara relaxed her shoulders and sighed. It was foolish to think that she could remain hidden and unknown forever. "What do they say?" she asked.

The emerald was the largest gem ever found. Not just in the Jeweled Realm, but on the continent. Its fame extended beyond the borders, with the people of the Waste claiming the jewel was the seed of the earth itself. But Mara knew better.

A gem half the size of her fist, its faceted faces reflected the light in many directions. Many assumed the gem was perfect, but having seen it up close, Mara knew it possessed an inclusion, an inky black streak deep within its depths.

"They say it took five men to dig it out," Éliane said, "and five more to clean it of the stone that held it. And once brought to the surface, it was wrapped and packed for the capital. No one ever saw it again."

"Well, I can assure you, it sits honorably in the hilt of the Sacred Sword."

Éliane's eyes followed a path to Mara's belt, or where her belt should have been. Where the *Sword* should have been.

"How did you lose it? Was it stolen?" Éliane asked. There was no judgment in her voice. No disappointment.

Mara inhaled sharply, the fact still a stinging nettle in her heart. She took a deep breath, and tried to smile when she answered, "I fell off Roully Dam."

"If you know who we are, why are you helping us?" Boden asked. "You could turn us in and collect a reward."

Éliane held Mara's gaze. It was like they knew each other, in a way. Like they were the same. Two of a kind. Strong, though beaten. Stubborn in the face of opposition. Resilient.

"I told you," Éliane began, "you were the first to give my necklace back. The others, I had to fight for it."

"How many others have there been?" Boden asked.

Éliane shrugged. "I don't keep count. Here, we will rest."

They were in a room, or what Mara thought was a room. A coolness sliced through it, like there was a draft rushing in from an open window. Sparks ignited within a small hearth and went out, only to reignite again. Éliane lit a fire, and it was then that Mara could see where they were.

A low, square chamber, windowless and moist. The walls were moss-covered stone, glistening with water. Everything smelled earthy, and Mara thought she smelled sage. A narrow door stood open behind them, but besides that, there was nowhere else to go. A dead end.

The hearth looked wet, but Éliane persisted in stoking the fire. Beside the hearth was a settee. It listed to one side, missing two of the four carved bear heads that acted as feet. It was there Éliane suggested they sit.

"You need to rest," she insisted again. "I'll return."

The girl attempted to leave them as unceremoniously as she had joined them, but Boden grabbed her sleeve. "You're not leaving us here," he said.

Éliane ripped her arm from the Ursan, her strength surprising him.

"You came to Narlès for supplies, right? I'll get them. Give me your coin."

"Forget it," Boden said immediately. "I don't care what your queen says, I don't trust you."

"Give her the coin, Boden." Mara slumped down on the settee. "You won't need it if we're dead anyway."

Boden ground his teeth but thrust the sack of coins at the girl. "As you wish," he mumbled.

Éliane took the money without another word, disappearing out the doorway. Mara watched her go, feeling an unusual easiness.

"What if she doesn't come back?" Boden sank down on the settee next to Mara. His weight shifted the chair, throwing Mara toward him. Their bodies touched, her side pressed firmly against his. The heat from his skin nearly burned. Combined with the muggy warm air in the room, Mara practically felt as if she were melting. He smiled down at her, his dimple fighting through his scruff. Mara pushed herself away, afraid of the warmth she felt rising up her neck.

"What does it matter?" she said, pretending to be intrigued by the faded pattern of the settee.

"She's escorted us down into the depths. Who knows where we are, and she could just leave us here. Did you think of that? Just leave us to starve."

"She has nothing to gain from that. If you want, we could try to find our own way." Mara gazed at the door. It shifted slightly on its own accord, adjusting to the pressure in the room. Another door somewhere opened and closed. Cause and effect. Like the whole *ville* beneath a *ville* was a living, breathing creature. Alive of its own volition.

"No," Boden said quickly, "not yet. I'll give the girl some time. But if she doesn't come back . . . Mara, we'll have to leave."

"Fine," Mara said. "Let's give her a chance."

"Fine."

Time passed strangely in the room. There was no clock. There were no windows. Mara watched the fire slowly fade to embers. Boden did his best to keep it alive, thrusting discarded chunks of moist wooden furniture he found within its hungry flames. He couldn't build it any bigger for the hearth wept water.

Eventually, Boden fell asleep leaning against the far side of the settee. His breathing was loud but rhythmic. It gave Mara something to count, to distract herself with, while they waited for Éliane. She watched his chest rise and fall in the dim dancing light of the fire and his pulse beat in the artery of his neck. For a very brief moment, while she was certain Boden was deep asleep, she dared to reach out and touch him. She let the soft pad of her finger trace the muscle of his forearm, stopping at a freckle just below his elbow. His arm twitched, and she yanked her hand away.

Love is a grave, her mother's words came rising to the surface of her mind, *and dead queens cannot wield swords.*

Mara leaned back on the settee, taking several deep breaths. Everything smelled earthy. She watched as dust floated up into the air, wafted by her movements, and cascaded toward the fire before being thrust back out into the air to land somewhere else.

She wondered how many people had been through that room. How many lives it had seen. By the looks of it, many. It had a way of appearing old and lived in despite being well beneath the surface.

Something bumped in the hallway outside the room. Mara's heart raced, but she forced herself to calm. She had been running for too long, she realized. Her courage was hiding from her.

Quietly, she slipped Boden's axe, Liv, from his belt. Her left hand fumbled, nearly dropping it. Pain pierced through the wrist like bone ripping from bone. It refused to lift the weapon, so she shifted it to her right. Crouched behind the settee, she waited to see what creature would present itself from the darkness. The door swung open slowly, creaking and groaning, to reveal a pile of leather.

Mara stood. It wasn't a creature, but Éliane. She dumped the leather—which turned out to be two bags and a jerkin—onto the floor.

"There's food in the bags," the girl said. "Mostly dried. It'll last longer."

Mara smiled. She picked up the leather jerkin, feeling the quality. It was smooth, oiled, and the darkest of green.

"Where did you get such a piece?" Mara asked. "We didn't have enough coin to afford this quality."

Éliane shrugged. "The queen of the Jeweled Realm shouldn't wear such common garb. But since you must, I got the best I could."

Mara looked down at the jerkin. Her fingertips were white from squeezing the leather. It was soft and blemish free. Beautiful in a way Mara didn't know leather could be. She looked up at Éliane. "Thank you," she said.

Éliane threw off the compliment like she had thrown off every other kindness toward her. She grabbed a pack and tossed it to Boden, who had stirred awake upon hearing Mara's voice.

"I heard Ursans prefer simple foods," she said, gesturing to the pack. "I hope you like horse jerky."

Boden frowned. "Not particularly." He dug through the bag, pulling up various food staples, flint and tinder, and a canteen.

"He'd have preferred cakes and macarons," Mara said.

Éliane rolled her eyes. She held up Mara's pack. "There are supplies from a *docteur* in here. You'll want to splint your wrist before you go."

Mara glanced down at her left wrist, already hot from swelling, and held it behind her back. "I'm fine," she insisted.

Éliane narrowed her eyes in what Mara could only assume was disbelief. She removed the parcel of aid items, wrapped in a linen cloth, and tossed Mara's pack onto the settee. "Before he died, my father was a *docteur*. I know what I see, mother."

Mara stared the girl down, but Éliane was unmoved. Her dark eyes refused to look away, refused to blink. Finally, Mara sighed and sank down onto the settee. "Fine." She held out her wrist. "If it'll help."

Éliane unwrapped the package and went to work feeling Mara's wrist. When Mara flinched, the pain so sudden she hissed at the girl through her teeth, Éliane smirked.

"You're lucky," she murmured, "it's not broken." Éliane set sturdy wooden splints on either side of Mara's wrist. She wrapped Mara's hand tightly with the linen and tied the end off. "Leave it for a few days, then take the splints away. Tie it up by your heart if you can."

She picked up two flower heads that had tumbled from the package. Both flowers were orange, though, one leaned toward yellow and was slightly wilted. Éliane thrust them toward Mara.

"That's kind of you," Mara said, "but I think flowers are a bit much."

Éliane flicked her eyes upward and sighed, shaking her head. "*Capucine.* They help with inflammation. They're a bit past their prime, but they're all I could find for your pain. *Manage the swelling, manage the pain.* It's what my father always said."

Reluctantly, Mara took the flowers. They were soft in her fingers, to the point of nearly disintegrating.

She eyed Éliane. "What do I do with them?"

"Eat them." The girl busied herself with cleaning up the medical supplies.

Mara glanced at Boden. He looked amused, his arms folded behind his head. She shoved both flowers into her mouth without a second thought. A hint of a spicy savory-ness came first, followed by a muted blandness.

The flowers were indeed well past their prime.

"Alright," Mara said, trying to remove the taste from her tongue, "what now?"

"It's time to leave," Éliane said.

Mara dressed in her jerkin, careful not to use her left hand. Éliane assisted her when she required it. Mara admired the fit of the leather. It was perfect. Éliane repacked Mara's sack and helped her put it on her back. Boden watched them, looking ridiculously large and uncomfortable in such a small room. The muggy air was making his skin glisten with sweat. Mara tried to hold in a laugh.

"What?" he asked.

"You look pleasant," she said.

Boden moaned and stalked past her, Éliane leading the way. They left the fire as it was to gutter out and die, leaving a scent of smoke as the only sign someone had occupied the room.

The narrow door gave way to a narrow hallway. Éliane turned left and drove them deeper into darkness. Mara found it hard to adjust to the depth of black after being in the fire-lit room, but, eventually, she could see well enough to not trip over the various *bric-à-brac* left in the homes.

A thunderous roar was coming from ahead of them. The farther they walked, the louder it grew. The floor vibrated. Mara reached her hand out to feel a wall, realizing it was rough stone.

"What's that sound?" she asked.

"Where in the depths are we?" Boden grumbled. He held his hand to the wall beside Mara but pulled it back. "It's wet." He rubbed his fingers together. "The walls are wet."

"We're near the river," Éliane said. "It plummets out the south side of the mountain. It's the only other way out."

Mara stiffened. *Not more water.* She could sense Boden watching her, so she turned and followed Éliane. *It's our only choice,* she reminded herself. She'd survived a fall once. She hoped she could survive it again.

Boden could be heard muttering a prayer beneath his breath, raising Saint Kalda's name to his lips.

"Your saint liked water," Mara reminded him, attempting to take her mind off what laid before them. "Surely we'll be fine."

"A well and a waterfall are two different sorts of things," Boden answered.

"It's here," Éliane called. Her body had disappeared around a bend in the tunnel. A dim light spilled from somewhere, casting her shadow behind her. "You must hurry. I'm not the only one that knows of these falls. They'll be here soon."

Around the corner, a thunderous tremble filled the tunnel. It vibrated Mara's ears and her mind. She had a hard time focusing on anything but the sudden sunlight and the sound of the waterfall.

Nearby, the falls gushed. The mountainside, black shale with some granite boulders, fell sharply beneath it. Black spruce grew where it could, grasping crevices up the mountainside, but all were small and stunted. Nothing survived in the path of the fall.

Several yards wide and the bluest blue she'd ever seen, Mara felt small in the falls' presence. The roar of it crushed her. It echoed off the mountainside like a bellowing giant. She was suddenly a child again. And afraid.

"There is a ladder." Éliane pointed to the edge of the falls.

Tucked beneath the edge was a rope ladder. It descended the sharp face of rocks and was sopping wet from the spray. At certain junctures where the rock face was wide enough, the rope transitioned to ancient wooden stairs. These stairs pulled away from the face of the cliff, teasing of falling. Eventually, the stairs transitioned to more rope. But long before it reached the ground, the rope gave way to nothing.

Mara traced the path downward, imagining their likelihood of survival. She thought jumping off the falls would be more successful than taking the ladder.

"Did you think I meant for you to jump?" Éliane was amused. "The ladder is good. Don't let it deceive you."

"I'm not deceived," Boden said, peering over the edge. "*That* is a death wish."

"I'm afraid you haven't a choice," Éliane said. She pointed to the mountainside at the cliff that ran above the falls. Specks were moving. "They'll follow a goat trail down." She guided her finger downward toward the falls, toward the tunnel in which they stood. "I took you a faster way, but they'll be here quickly."

Mara looked at Boden. The Ursan breathed heavily, perhaps also having memories of falling off Roully Dam. He set his jaw and nodded to her encouragingly. She took in the ladder again, its wet rope lashing against the side of the cliff. They'd be soaked before they reached the ground.

If they reached the ground. But this was their only chance.

"Let's go," she said to Boden. She extended her foot gingerly onto the cliff's ledge, her eyes tracing the way to the rope ladder.

"Mother"—Éliane's hand reached out and grasped Mara's elbow—"may you carry what you kill."

An old Jeweled Realm idiom, one said to be coined by her grandmother, the words instantly brought back a memory of Mara's mother. Mara was four, taken to hunt with the Red Queen in the royal wood. She had managed to kill a turkey after several attempts with her bow. She'd watched, horrified, as the creature convulsed and writhed on the forest floor, blood sprinkling across tree trunks and ferns. The Red Queen made Mara carry the bird all the way back to the palace—despite her tears and grief—while spouting off the First Queen's words. Words meant to suggest one carry the physical and emotional toll of the kill as their burden for success.

Mara blinked back tears. She didn't know why she felt so vulnerable. Why did she feel like this was a final goodbye?

She nodded at Éliane and stepped onto the ledge.

Chapter Nineteen

It did not take long for the waterfall's spray to soak Mara through. Her new jerkin, though oiled and meant to repel water, was never meant to keep one completely dry. Tendrils of dripping hair stuck to her neck and cheeks. Only when she reached the bottom of the rope ladder and planted her feet on the stairs did she pull her hair from her face, cursing beneath her breath.

"Should have cut more off," Boden joked, jumping from the ladder to the stairs. He shook his head like a dog, spraying her with water. Water shed from him much like the falls sloughed from the mountainside. He reached up and squeezed the ends of Mara's hair, smiling at her as he did so, before gently removing one last tendril of hair from her face and tucking it behind her ear.

Mara steeled herself, shoring up her emotions to focus on their getaway. She searched for their pursuers but could not see them. They were above the falls by now, tracking across its perilous edge in attempts to reach the cave Éliane had brought them through. She couldn't see the girl anymore either.

Boden adjusted his pack. The bag dripped with water but was well oiled. Mara hoped the contents of the bag were still dry. He began the descent of the stairs first. The wood creaked beneath his weight. Wind whipped past, biting at their cheeks, but they pushed onward, making quick work of the stairwell.

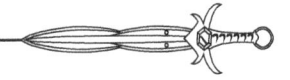

The second rope ladder was drier than the first, but its fibers cut and bit through their hands. Mara gritted her teeth, forcing herself to move ever downward, following Boden as he cursed with each rung.

"Does Kalda not mind your foul tongue?" Mara called down to him, attempting to distract herself from the constant pain of the rope.

Boden ignored her, though, a particularly fierce piece of rope caused him to cry out louder than before.

"Kalda would understand," he finally answered her as they neared the end, "should he meet such a nasty ladder."

At the bottom of the ladder, Boden hesitated. There were no stairs after this rope. He searched on either side for a foothold in the rock to begin the climb to the bottom.

"Careful," Mara called to him. "The shale is weak. It may break, and you'd slip."

Boden nodded.

She looked upward for those that followed, but saw no one. They must have disappeared into the cave. Boden found a suitable path and called her to follow.

But Mara couldn't tear her eyes from the mouth of the cave. A fear seeded itself into her heart about Éliane. She hoped the girl had found a good place to hide.

A small rockslide cascaded down the mountain from beneath Boden's feet, and he yelled as his legs dangled freely in the air. He clung to the wall with white fingertips, his shoulders beginning to shake with fatigue. When the mountain stilled itself, he slowly continued his descent. Mara followed, mimicking Boden's every handhold and footstep.

It was difficult to focus on her own hands, her own feet, while Boden struggled to descend the cliff beneath her. She tried to count her breaths to distract herself from the fear creeping up from the pit of her stomach, but it was no use. With every tumble of rock and sharp exhale from Boden, Mara imagined him slipping to his death. It was only when the ground neared did her mind relax. She forcefully exhaled as her feet firmly touched the ground beside Boden's.

She looked at him, and they both started laughing. It was a tense laugh. One reserved for surviving the odds. One hopefully used few times in a life.

They said nothing. Both knew no words would be enough to describe the relief and fear they felt simultaneously.

For the last time, she checked the mountain. Shale shards shot up like teeth on either side of the waterfall. She couldn't see the rope ladder from where they were. It was well hidden beneath the falls and between the shale. It seemed no one had followed.

"Maybe they gave up," Boden said as he followed her gaze.

"Or maybe they're after Éliane." Mara shared a long look with Boden. His pale eyes didn't hide his thoughts beneath.

"She'll be fine," he said softly. "Let's march."

They descended the gentle slope into the forest. The shale shards grew smaller, though no less slippery, before giving way to moss and finally forest floor. The stunted black spruce grew taller, straighter, and soon birch appeared.

A muskiness filled the breeze, emanating from high-bush cranberries. Mara gathered a handful, tossing them into her mouth. Her cheeks squeezed tightly at the tartness of the berries. Boden did the same.

Leaves crunched beneath their feet. They'd entered a lower elevation where the spruce gave way to the birch and the cool air of fall forced the trees to release their summer garb. A few leaves remained on the birch, but soon they'd be naked. Left to meet the pending winter, undressed and unencumbered.

"It seems to be cooler than I remember," Boden's foot crunched in an iced-over puddle.

"A cold snap," Mara said. "A false winter. It'll warm up again. Thankfully, we'll be out of here before real winter starts."

Boden nodded. "Ursans prefer winter. Things are simpler then."

Mara smiled to herself. Of course they liked the cold best, when the landscape was erased, left to a stolid white. Everything was easier on the eye. In the winter, Ursans reduced chores to the simplest of commandments: survive. Boden was good at surviving. He had already proven that to her time and time again.

"It will take many days to reach Bouzy," Mara said. "Unless we find some horses." She missed the days of her queendom, of speaking a word and it being obeyed unapologetically. An utterance, and she'd have a horse. Another word more, and they'd have everything they needed for the journey.

In truth, she missed Petra. She wondered how the girl was faring with Iris. If her sister had made it to the capitol, which Mara knew would have been her goal, then Petra would have come face to face with the princess.

Mara remembered the black of Iris's eyes. The way they seemed to see right through her. Iris would see Petra's value. She'd see that turning the girl against Mara would be beneficial in more ways than one. Once Petra was on her side, the others would turn. She hoped Petra would remain loyal.

But Mara had her doubts.

They walked on for miles, barely saying anything. A word might be uttered, usually by Boden, as he walked through a spider's web cast between two trees or tripped over a branch. Mara would curse when a fly attempted to bother her. She'd slap at the insect brutally, only to miss.

The sun tracked westward across the sky, turning shadows like a clock. When it kissed the horizon, Mara said, "We should rest. Though, I'd rather not."

Boden smiled, "Kalda says 'rest before war.'"

Mara smiled unevenly. "I seem to remember that lesson from before."

"And did it help?" Boden asked while stacking branches into a pile for a fire.

Mara froze, remembering the dam, the moment before her own personal war began. Iris had been strong. Unreasonably strong. But something tugged at the back of Mara's mind. Mara had been *afraid*. Seeing Iris like that had thrown her off her focus. That never happened to her.

Could Iris truly be superior?

The thought seared fire beneath her skin. She was the queen of the Jeweled Realm. She wasn't afraid. Or were those her mother's words surfacing?

"No fire," Mara barked at Boden, the anger she felt toward herself aimed outward instead. "We aren't that far from the mountain. Someone will see."

The mountain leered at them from their backs, already sinking into the shadows of the evening. Its peak, where Narlès sat snuggled, was bathing in the last rays of light before the sun disappeared completely. Like a jewel on a crown, it glittered.

"As you say," Boden said. "But we'll never be completely out of danger. You know that, right?"

Mara nodded.

"So we'll have to have a fire eventually."

"But not tonight," she said, smiling as sweetly as she could.

"Not tonight," he agreed, smiling in return.

She piled moss into a bed between the root collars of a tree. It smelled sweet and earthy, reminding her of her childhood, reminding her of a time when Iris's eyes weren't black, but blue. When Iris seemed reasonable. When everything was simpler.

"Tell me of your brother," Mara called to Boden, who was preparing his own bed next to her. She had grown accustomed to his nearness—his body's warmth and presence. She relied on it, she realized, to anchor herself in the chaotic sea of emotions she found herself adrift in as of late.

"Why?" Boden asked. "So you can dream of him? Not a chance."

Mara choked on her laugh. "No. But I want to hear of childhoods in other places. Places . . ." but she didn't feel like finishing her sentence.

"That don't promote hatred of one's sibling?"

"Yes."

Boden sighed. He sat back on his bed, head against the tree. Mara found him most handsome like this—with his face dressed in the fading light of the sun. A deep red faded to orange behind him, highlighting the burgundy hidden in his growing dark beard.

"He was a good brother. Hard, sometimes. He always bested me at everything. Axes. Games. Women." Boden rubbed his head, reminding Mara of Gerik. "But he seemed . . . good. Always a kind word after besting me. Always encouraging me. He alone found my studies at the temple worthwhile, not our father."

Mara propped her head up on her elbow. This was why the Jeweled Realm sought to eliminate royal siblings: divisiveness.

"I loved him," Boden said. "I *do* love him."

"Despite his betrayal?" Mara asked. Her throat knotted itself up at the thought of such a belief: to forgive no matter what.

From Mara's perspective, Gerik showed his feelings for his brother when he withdrew his axes upon Roully Dam—when he forced his little brother to leap to his death or perish by his own hands. How was that love?

Boden shrugged, settling down in his bed. "What is love but forgiveness? I've spent my lifetime with Gerik. A lifetime of happy moments strung out like a necklace, perforated maybe occasionally with sadness. Anger. But nothing outweighed happiness. What is one more moment to that chain?"

Mara was speechless. In the Jeweled Realm, Gerik's actions were enough to sanction a head hunt. For once betrayed, blood must be spilled before satisfaction would be reached.

"Those are Kalda's words," she said. "Surely you don't believe them."

Boden laughed. "Am I not his student?"

They lay in their mossy beds, close enough to be comforted by each other's presence. They both stared at the night sky, thinking different things. Mara couldn't seem to understand Boden's easy acceptance of his brother's betrayal and even easier forgiveness of it. Would Boden not be arrested should he return home? Would Gerik not find him guilty of supporting a crown traitor to their newfound ally, Iris?

But such was the way of the continent. With the Black Rains came division. A lost language was not the only thing the rains had consumed. Left to go their separate ways, the people's philosophies changed as well. Ursa to rebuild something resembling their past and the Jeweled Realm to construct an unbeatable machine. It didn't matter what the realm had lost in the process. It didn't matter if one's family suffered, so long as the realm reigned supreme.

Mara saw the cracks in this ideology, even if her mother hadn't.

She spoke into the quiet night, "Were there games that you played? With your brother?"

Boden was silent for a moment, thinking. "Seek-and-find was a favorite," he said. "Warlord was another—a board game based on battle tactics."

Mara thought back to her childhood, to Iris giggling in the dark as they played their own version of seek-and-find. "We'd make food," Mara said. "Not actual food. We'd take dirt from the garden once the gardeners finished watering and squish them into pies."

"Mud pies," Boden sighed. "I loved making mud pies."

Mara laughed. "Are they made in Ursa?"

"Are mud pies not universal?" he asked. "I should think they are. What child doesn't play in the mud? Even future queens, it seems."

Mara didn't reply. Instead, she rolled away from Boden. *A string of moments*, he had said, *like a necklace*. Mara liked that description. She imagined a pearl necklace she owned, one given to her by her grandmother, with its large, black sea pearls gleaming next to one another. Each one identical but also unique, for within was something—a grain of sand, an oyster irritant of some sort—making each its own.

Her eyes fluttered. The forest grew blurry as she fought the urge to sleep. She needed to think more. She needed to figure out what to do once they reached Bouzy, but it did no good. Even queens needed to sleep.

"Goodnight, Mara," Boden murmured as he, too, drifted off to sleep.

Mara didn't respond, though, she smiled to herself into the night.

She awoke with the sun. It gently laid morning rays upon her face, warming her cheek, telling her it was time to rise.

She swatted away the leaves that had fallen on her during the night and sat up. Boden was already awake, rummaging through his bag.

"Everything in order?" she asked him.

He looked startled. He hadn't noticed she was awake.

"Yes, fine," he said, continuing to rummage. "Just seeing what there was to eat."

Boden, having reached the bottom of the pack, slumped back. He withdrew a linen bag of apples. Reluctantly, he grabbed one and took a large bite. The crisp snap of the fruit's flesh cut through the cool morning air.

"No cakes, I take it?" Mara asked, reaching for her own pack.

Boden grunted. He tossed her an apple and thrust the extras back into his bag. He stood and stretched, the apple stuck in his mouth like a roasted pig. He squinted into the sunlight that fell across them, an unnatural furrow settling across his brow. Mara found she much preferred when Boden smiled, though, he was no less handsome when he didn't. His eyes met hers and her heart skipped. She shoved her thoughts away lest Boden found some way to read her mind.

He gestured down the mountain. "We should reach the river lands today," he said. "Perhaps we'll find horses there."

Mara nodded, distracting herself with her own apple. The tension between them felt like the surface of that apple: taut, and ready to snap at the smallest, sharpest, bite.

"Though, we don't have the money to buy them," Boden said.

Mara laughed a bit too easily. Her confused feelings made her feel uncertain and off balance. Navigating their escape wasn't doable while she fumbled with them. Better to put them away, for a while—or perhaps permanently—until a better time arose. "I am queen of this realm," she said. "All horses are my horses."

Boden shrugged. "As you say." His eyes lingered where her sword should have been, but he said nothing more. Instead, he loped off into the forest.

"As you say," Mara mocked him.

She realized he was her only help in her bid to retrieve her throne. She realized that without him, she was utterly alone. But there was a portion of her, raised by the sharp criticisms and hard hand of her mother, that preferred utter obedience and fearful silence rather than Boden's cheery, enthusiastic disposition. He respected her, but he didn't fear her. Mara's mother always suggested the latter was better than the former, and Mara was starting to wonder if the confusion she felt within was part and parcel with this notion. That respect built up understanding, and with understanding, closeness. And queens of the Jeweled Realm were not used to letting anyone close. Ever.

When Boden returned, he seemed more awake. He handed Edda to Mara. She studied the axe, admiring the sharpness of its bite.

"But this was your grandmother's." She attempted to hand it back to him. The polished handle made it clear it was Boden's favored axe. It gleamed where his hand—and his grandmother's—had found purchase while being used.

"Perhaps you'll have better luck with her than you did with Liv," he tilted his head toward a nearby tree.

A large knot protruded from the trunk, bulbous and drooping. Mara eyed it before taking Edda and throwing. It struck the knot near the bottom. A sloppy throw, the *maître d'armes* would have said. But it was her best throw yet, and Boden clapped.

"I would barely have injured them." Mara retrieved the axe.

"A killing blow is not the only blow," Boden argued.

"Maybe in Ursa," Mara said. "But in the Jeweled Realm, when you draw your weapon, it's to kill."

Boden stared at her. He scratched his beard, fighting himself against saying something. Mara waited, wondering what Ursan or Kaldan knowledge would spew from his lips this time. But nothing came. Instead, he gestured to the knot. "Again."

She threw Edda several more times, each one striking the knot, but never perfectly. The blade would bite into the wood, sticking firmly to the trunk, the handle quivering. But often it was from the edge. Once, it even missed the knot entirely, settling in the trunk a few feet too high.

"Edda suits you," Boden said after this last throw. He retrieved the axe for Mara, for it had struck too high for her to reach. "She flies easily from your hand."

Mara took Edda back, squeezing the handle. "It does feel different," she said.

Boden pointed to the handle. "The wood. My grandmother carved it herself. It is stronger but lighter than Liv. A special wood, from Ursa."

They spent the rest of the morning practicing melee with the axes. Boden was as thorough as the palace *maître d'armes*, if not more patient. Under the gentle correction of Boden, Mara excelled at this aspect of fighting. Though, she often attempted moves that were more suited for swords.

Her sword.

At one point, she had meant to parry his attack, but met his axe's bit at the handle, where her fingers were nearly sacrificed to her practice session. He showed her how to anticipate and block incoming attacks, deflecting them safely aside so she could then step within striking distance with Edda.

"These are not long edges," Boden instructed her, his breath heavy after they'd been at it for so long. "You cannot treat them like your sword." His hand wrapped around her wrist, guiding it upward against a pretend attacker. The motion brought him so close she could feel his breath ghost along her cheek. They locked eyes briefly before both pulled away.

"I see why Ursans favor two axes." Mara sat on the forest floor to rest.

Boden sat on a fallen tree, still avoiding Mara's gaze. "Yes," he said, "two are much better than one. But we must make do."

He wiped sweat from his forehead. It glittered in the bright light of the midday sun. She patted her forehead, her hair moist on her scalp. She was sweating, too.

"I feel better now," she said, "with the axe." She held up Edda like a prize, more pleased now with the way it sat in her hand than she had been before.

"Good," Boden said. "Then can we move on?" An impatience had arisen in his face. His jaw was held tightly as he ground his teeth.

Mara nodded, wondering if the sudden hostility was because he was fighting his feelings as well.

The walk down the alpine slopes was not incredibly steep. They descended through the maze of birch. High-bush cranberries continued to emerge, their musky scent hinting of their nearness. They came across a meadow filled with giant lupine. The deep-purple banners were embellished by the brightest white. Mara watched a bumblebee buzz from flower to flower.

At the foot of the mountain, the moss-strewn ground gave way to grass. The trees receded to ill-defined forests, leaving the open river plains to unroll before them. Valenbeuge was tucked amidst the mountains to their left, hidden by the mountain's long arm. If they were lucky, they'd cross the plain unimpeded.

If they were lucky.

Chapter Twenty

The autumn sky displayed blue for the third day in a row. It was good fortune, Mara thought, to have such marvelous fall weather. But she knew how quickly the weather would change, how fast the seasons would take hold of the countryside and not let go. The unusual warmth and sun would make way for wind and rain.

Temperatures dropped in the evening, and tonight, they were forced to make a fire for a second time. They shivered together while the wood smoked and then finally ignited.

Mara rubbed her hands together, squatting by the fire. The sun was still casting a beautiful glow over them, but it wouldn't last long. They had followed the long spine of the Diamond Highlands to the western plains. Soon the sun would hide behind them, playing seek-and-find for an hour or so before yielding completely to the night.

To Mara's pleasure, they had neither seen nor heard anyone else since leaving Narlès. Boden had spotted farms and homesteads early, allowing them to circle wide. And while horses had eluded them, Mara found the walking somewhat enjoyable. Her boots looked worse for wear, but her legs felt strong.

"Would you enjoy another apple, Prince Boden?" Mara joked, handing him the last apple from her pack.

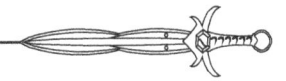

Boden scowled and withdrew a piece of horse jerky from his own pack. "I'm fine."

Mara chuckled, settling down for the evening. With her apple in hand and the stars peeking out on the horizon, she leaned against a tree. It was satisfying in its simplicity, this life she found herself currently living. If she managed to push Iris from her mind, push the danger until it was just a grain of sand in the back, she could relax. She could see the beauty around her. She could forget the imposed mask forced upon her and just be who she wanted. The woman Boden saw when his vivid eyes looked at her.

She wasn't certain she could be the woman he thought she was. A woman who could change the course of the Jeweled Realm, forever. She wasn't sure she wanted to be either. But there was something about the way he saw her—not *through* her—that made her feel more like herself than she had in a long time.

It was in the mountains, at the start of the descent from Narlès, that she first felt it fall away. Like a mask that had been left on for too long. Her face felt fresh, her skin like her own, but new.

Boden was staring at her over the fire.

"What?" she asked.

He shook his head. "Nothing, just glad you're smiling."

"Smiling?"

"Well, there is still a queen-hunt going on in the Jeweled Realm," he said. "For you. But I'm glad you haven't let it bother you. *A positive mind is a focused mind,* Kalda says."

"Is that why you are always so cheerful?"

"I try"—Boden poked at the fire with a stick—"but I am no saint. We all fail sometimes. We all have our own distractions." He stared at her evenly then.

Mara avoided his gaze, choosing instead to watch the flames dance. The red sidled with the orange, swaying like two lovers dancing. It snapped and popped, flicking embers into the sky. Her eyes blurred, distorting the fire, as she thought of her own failures.

"Do you *want* to kill her?" Boden interrupted her thoughts after a moment.

"What?" Mara jumped. So deep was she that she'd forgotten Boden was there.

"Even now, I sense your hesitation. Is killing Iris something you even want to do?"

Mara couldn't speak. A knot had grown within her throat, threatening to choke her should she try to utter anything. People asked her what she wanted all the time. Her servants. Petra. They all lived to serve her every whim. Her every want.

But there were some things she wasn't allowed to want. Not as the queen of the Jeweled Realm. Not as the heir apparent, with a mother who'd required her daughter to despise her sister enough to kill her. Not when Mara's own life was on the line. The thing Boden was asking wasn't something Mara was ever allowed to consider. She had found a way, of course. A sneaky, lying way to get what she'd wanted. But it hadn't solved anything. Mara was right back where she'd started with the same question and the same answer already written for her: she *had* to kill Iris.

Mara hoped she wasn't mistaken in thinking Boden's eyes hinted there was another way. If he believed it, she could, too. But her mother's voice was too deeply ingrained in her mind, and she shook her head and shivered with the anger rising beneath her skin.

Boden's blue eyes were unwavering. "You are different from them. From your family. The Red Queen didn't hesitate to kill your aunt, I've heard. Hunted her down and threaded an arrow through her heart like a stag."

Mara kicked dirt into the fire. Her throat would not relax. There was nothing she could say. Her childishness wanted to defend her mother and tell him that she had hurt as much as Mara had when she pulled the bow on her own sister, but she knew it wasn't true. Her mother had once regaled Mara of her trial, mentioning how thrilled she had been for the day to have finally come.

"And the First Queen, they say she ripped her sister from the throne herself before using the Sacred Sword to . . ." Boden stopped.

Tears silently streamed down Mara's cheeks. They glistened in the firelight, leaving glittering trails where they cascaded down her face. She didn't make a sound, didn't cry out or scream. She had trained herself to never raise her voice for any reason. *Make them lean in to hear you*, her mother had said. *Make them choose to listen.*

"My grandmother's sister thought to steal the throne while my grandmother was away fighting for it. Fighting for what she had created." Mara wiped tears away, keeping her voice low and level. "And my aunt . . . sought to poison my mother before their trial even began."

It was frowned upon, the act of war before the war began, but no one had sought to punish Mara's aunt. They'd all shrugged and said the heirs would sort it out. And so Mara's mother had—with an arrow to her sister's heart.

"And what did Iris do?" Boden asked.

"What?"

"Well, deception seems to be the seed of derision here. I make no claims as to whom is to blame, but someone sowed those seeds. And they yielded. Your grandmother and mother yielded to it. Your grandaunt and your aunt. So, what did Iris do to sow the seed in you?"

Mara slowly shook her head. "Nothing."

"Nothing?" Boden sat up. "And you say you loved her."

"Yes," Mara said.

"Then why did you do it?"

"The trial?" Mara frowned. "It is tradition."

"You didn't want to."

"Does it matter?" Mara argued. "If I wanted to be queen, I needed to earn the right to bear the Sacred Sword."

"But you didn't," Boden whispered. "You still haven't."

Mara's eyes burned hot from her tears and the fire's smoke. She forced the pain down and instead focused intently on the fire. He was right. She hadn't earned it, and she wondered if she was even worthy to try again. She wondered if she *wanted* to.

"Mara," Boden stood and approached her. He sank down in front of her and gently grasped her face in his hands. He dropped his voice to a gentle whisper. "I'm not saying this to shame you. I'm saying this so you can see . . . you're not like them. You are a different sort of queen."

"And what kind of queen is that?" Her voice was raspy from holding back more tears.

He pulled her face toward his, and for a moment she thought he aimed to kiss her. She held her breath, preparing for the moment when their lips would touch, but they didn't. He rested his forehead against hers and sighed.

"One that can change the course of her realm. For the better." He pulled away and held her gaze again. The crisp, cool blue of Boden's eyes was soothing. It was like placing tansy ointment on her spirit. Mara wanted nothing more than to sit and study their endless color, but voices crept through the wood, and her heart leaped into her throat.

Boden's head whipped toward the sound.

"They will see the fire," Mara said. She moved to kick dirt on it, to extinguish the light and hope they could dissolve into the darkening wood, but Boden reached out and gripped her arm.

"They've already seen it," he said. "It'll look suspicious."

"What now?"

Mara's blood raced. Her heart pumped so hard she knew Boden could hear it from where he stood. A dizzying scent of wormwood spread around them. She hadn't noticed it before. Perhaps it was merely a memory. Her mother had favored the fragrance, finding it both sharp and intimidating. Mara's head spun and her stomach sank. Boden looked at her, trying to appear confident. But his eyes could not fool her.

"They will know me," she said. "They will *know*."

"No," Boden whispered as the travelers grew closer. They continued to call out toward them, but their words were unintelligible. "It will be fine. Just stay calm."

Mara wanted to argue with him. She wanted to tell him Kalda was wrong and that a positive mind wasn't always a focused one. That these people could be dangerous, or worse—recognize her. But Boden moved away before she could get any of these thoughts out. He raised his arm and hailed the strangers.

"Hallo!" he called to them.

"Hello!" one called back.

There were four of them. Their bodies emerged from the shadowed forest to stand amongst the trees of Mara and Boden's camp. Mara felt like specters had suddenly solidified before her. Three men and a woman, all adorned with traditional traveling garb. None menacing. All happy, cheeks ruddy and red with pleasant youth.

"We don't mean to disturb," one man, the apparent leader of the group, said. His hair was brown and floppy over his ears and thatched over the top of his head. He had eyes that were smiling even if his mouth wasn't. He reminded Mara of a boy she'd once known, long ago.

Though, that boy was dead. Killed by his own brother.

"There's nothing to disturb," Boden said. "We're just settling in for the night."

The man nodded. His eyes fell on Mara, and he smiled. She waited. Her muscles coiled tight, preparing to fight. She didn't look at Edda, but her body felt the weapon against her thigh, hidden in the shadows cast by firelight. The air was cool against her cheeks, reminding her she'd forgotten to wrap her face in her scarf.

"We hope to trudge a bit farther before stopping for the night, but if you don't mind, we'd like to warm up by your fire." The man flashed his perfect pearly teeth at Mara again.

He seemed sweet. Kind. The woman of their group was tucked in behind his shoulder, almost like she had reason to be afraid. His hand went to hers and he squeezed it.

Mara returned his smile with a weak one of her own. She hoped it was convincing. She had been told often enough her smiles were more intimidating than comforting. More snarl than soothe, carrying with them a sense of ill-ease.

If they only knew.

"I don't see why not," Boden said.

The man gestured for his companions to sit. They gathered around the fire, squatting in the pine needles and fallen leaves. Relief filled their faces as the warmth reached for them.

"I'm Henri," the young man said. "This is Bayard, Loic, and his sister, Lucie." He gave a little squeeze to Lucie, who was still tucked into his side.

"I'm Duncan, and this is Bella." Boden tilted his head toward Mara.

It amazed Mara at how beautifully the lie slipped from his tongue. Though, she'd have to remind him later that Kalda taught not to lie. She wanted to laugh.

"A pleasure," Henri said. "Might we ask what leads your travels?"

Boden smiled. "You first. Tradition of camp."

Henri bowed his head. Newcomers always spoke first. It was the price they paid for accepting the warmth of the fire. A Jeweled Realm rule begun by her grandmother, it was meant to sound pleasant and welcoming. In reality, it was used to force out truths and lies. Her grandmother had been an exceptionally paranoid warlord. Discerning who was your friend and who was your foe was integral to building a realm.

It was Lucie who spoke. "We're traveling to a wedding." Her words were timid, muffled by Henri's body, before reaching them across the fire. Henri even looked surprised by her voice.

"Yes," he added. "Childhood friends."

"A bit late in the season," Mara said. "So close to the equinox."

Henri shrugged. "Late, but not forbidden."

Weddings were, by royal decree, held specifically between the spring and fall equinoxes. Royal weddings, when they occurred, always happened on the summer solstice. The rest of the realm could hold their jubilations on any other day, so long as the fall equinox had not passed. Her mother had made it so, noting that no one wanted to spend time at a wedding without sunshine.

But Henri's words were not as smooth as Boden's had been, and Mara's body would not relax. Boden noticed and placed a comforting hand on her knee. Mara found the touch distracting. She couldn't focus on the fine details of the moment, on whether or not these people were friend or foe. She shook her knee, displacing Boden's hand.

Henri watched the interaction. A small smile ticked up the corner of his lips. "And now you?"

"We're traveling home," Boden said.

"Ah, home will guide us, will it not?" Henri's companions nodded in agreement. "And where is home?" He picked up a stick and poked at their fire, his eyes flirting upward toward Mara. She ground her teeth, doing her best not to frown at him. The man placed her on edge.

"Liroux," Mara spoke, her tongue rolling the name off with her high-born accent. The *ville* of Liroux was much farther south than Bouzy, in the middle of the Golden Foot, the peninsula Bouzy acted as gatekeeper for. It was far enough away that Mara hoped the travelers did not know it well.

"Liroux?" Henri seemed interested. "Quite a trip you're on."

"Yes." Boden stood and feigned a yawn. "And we have much left to go. We'd like to sleep."

Henri stared at Boden, hardly blinking. He finally stood and smiled, clapping Boden on the arm. It was meant to be friendly, but Mara could see Boden's neck muscles grow taut with annoyance.

"Of course," Henri agreed. "We've warmed ourselves thoroughly. You have invigorated us for our own journey."

Mara couldn't shake the feeling she was watching an actor, like the ones who performed at the palace during the week of Frivolity, when the entire *ville* was ensconced in decorations, carnivals grew in every square, and plays were performed nightly for the queen. She did not recognize this particular man as an actor, but the way he spoke reminded her of one.

"Goodnight, beautiful Bella." Henri extended his hand to hers.

She didn't want to give it to him, but Boden was standing behind him, urging her with his eyes to do whatever she had to do to get them to leave. Placing her hand in his, she felt how cold she was. His was warm, strong, like an archer's hand. Mara withdrew her hand quickly, nodding her goodbye.

"It was a pleasure, Henri," she whispered.

He smiled. Again, seamless teeth flashed at her, and then he was gone. The others walked after him. They nodded their goodbyes, but otherwise remained silent. It took time for the sound of their feet crunching through leaves to fade. Mara found herself holding her breath, listening, waiting for their noise to be gone for good, signaling they were safe.

"Well, that wasn't so bad," Boden said.

"You were worried! I could see it in your face!" Mara said.

"Was not." Boden kicked at some leaves. They scattered in the air like confetti. "I told you it would be fine." He walked away in the opposite direction. "I'm going to find more wood."

Mara watched him go, but her gaze kept returning to the direction the travelers had left. Something was not sitting well within her. Her stomach still churned. She took a few deep breaths in an attempt to calm herself, but it didn't work. Instead, she lay down, her eyes tracing the wooden grain along Edda's handle.

Though not the Sacred Sword, the weapon was starting to provide her with some comfort. While her skill with it remained less than stellar, having a sharp edge at her disposal made her feel safer. Her hand squeezed the handle, feeling the cold wood against her palm.

She didn't expect to stay safe for long.

Chapter Twenty-One

Mara awoke to dancing trees. The sound of the wind fought through the branches like voices. Wood creaked within the trunks, screaming almost, laughing nearly. She wondered what they were saying. Autumn always brought more wind, and with it, the cold.

She pulled her jerkin tight, popping up the collar around her neck. Boden was already working on a morning fire. He stoked the coals from the night to bring it back to life.

There were many words that wanted to spill from her lips, but she watched Boden in silence. His brow was furrowed, his eyes narrowed. He was clearly thinking about something, some thought carried over from the night before. Mara herself had a bad habit of ruminating on things. She knew what it looked like on others, too.

She cleared her throat. Boden glanced up at her but carried on with his task.

"No sign of last night's visitors?" she asked.

"No."

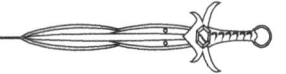

"Good." She stared off in the direction they had gone. Birch layered on birch, twisting the forest into a maze of black and white lines. Several brilliant orange leaves broke through the monotony of green, hinting at the coming fall, contrasting beautifully with the trees. But Mara didn't notice that. She searched for a sign—a fleck of an odd color, something of the travelers to emerge.

"They're not there." Boden never took his eyes off the fire. "We're fine."

Mara huffed. It wasn't that she wanted to be right. She was glad she had been wrong about the travelers. But she still couldn't settle the sour feeling in her stomach.

Boden broke camp while Mara sat on a boulder. She studied the Diamond Highlands. The long green spine extended before them, eventually settling into the river plains. Just north of the Golden Foot, just shy of Bouzy. If they followed it, they'd have no problem getting to the coastal *ville*, no problem reaching a ship.

If nothing stood in their way.

"Ready?" Boden asked, approaching with his back full of both packs.

"I'll take mine," Mara said.

He shuffled the pack over to her and wiped his forehead. Boden already appeared exhausted, and the day had just begun.

"Are you alright?" she asked as their feet started the journey through the forest.

"Fine," he heaved between breaths. "I just think I need a proper rest. Forest floors never suited me."

Mara chuckled. "But you're a soldier."

"Aye, and we had tents with camp beds. I've never campaigned without one."

"Well, this is no campaign." Mara stomped down on a Horridus stalk. Once broken open, the stalk emitted its noxious smell. Mara's nose curled, and she kept walking. "This is a restoration mission."

"Restoration?" Boden stomped on the Horridus some more.

The plants boasted sharp spines on the underside of their large leaves and woody upper stalks. Sometimes used for medicinal purposes, most people eradicated them from their property. The sting they offered to anyone who traipsed upon them was too great a risk. As a child, Mara liked to stomp them down, pretending to be her grandmother subjecting a kingdom to her will.

"You are helping to restore me to my throne," Mara said. "A feat Kalda would find worthy, I imagine." She beamed at Boden, daring him to argue. He stared at her, but eventually broke down and returned her smile.

"Perhaps," he said, "Kalda would smile upon our venture. I am unsure."

The sun stained the sky orange and lemon. Clouds, a haze of yellow, crawled across the sky. A crisp fall morning. Twigs snapped in a different tone than the day before. Mara could make out a faint wisp of breath when she exhaled.

"Shouldn't it be growing warmer? We are headed south," Boden complained.

He pulled the wolf fur around his neck. Éliane had read the Ursan right and found a fur for his pack. A black-footed fox fur awaited Mara in her own pack, but she hesitated on wearing it. She'd never liked furs.

"The weather shifts once we reach the Foot. Warm weather from the Steel Sea gets trapped there. You'll see," she explained.

She had been an excellent student. While her mother held her captive in the palace, practicing with the *maître d'armes* and studying with the *enseignante*, Mara had dreamed of traveling. An ancient map hung in her childhood room, its corners ripped, and one small section burned during an unsupervised experiment with a candle. Mara loved it. She'd spend hours lying on the floor, feet propped up on the wall, studying the mountains, the lakes, the coast.

If her mother never let her body leave, at least her mind could wander. At least she'd know the lay of her land by memory.

In truth she had traveled, a few times, to certain key *villes* her mother dragged her along to. But when her mother grew sick and reluctantly signed an armistice, all travel stopped. They remained in the capitol, almost imprisoned in the palace. Mara and Iris only ventured out when they were older and could ride and hunt or when their mother deigned to soak up the forests near the chateau.

When Mara and Iris were still friends.

Mara stopped walking. Boden looked back at her over his shoulder, scowling.

"What is it?"

"I remember," she said.

"Remember? Remember what?" Boden turned and stomped back through the Horridus.

"There is a chateau—a hunting lodge my family had," Mara explained. "It isn't special. Not overly grand. But it is on the way. We could . . . we could stay there tonight."

Boden was still scowling. "Will we not be found?"

Mara shook her head. "It has been abandoned for years. After I was crowned, and I banished Iris, I couldn't bring myself to go there without her. I had it shut up permanently."

"Perhaps someone else has gotten there already then, and calls it home?"

Mara shrugged. "Do you want to sleep on the forest floor again?"

Boden gazed at the Highlands, thinking. He rubbed his scruff, but slowly nodded. "Fine, if you think it's safe."

"It'll be fine." She pushed past him. "Come on, this way."

They changed course, angling closer to the rolling sides of the highlands.

She remembered how the chateau sucked in tight to the slope, its back gardens a gentle upward climb before jutting stone reached skyward. Tall poplar trees—the tallest Mara had ever seen—perched atop the cliff, signifying the start of the highlands. Like a massive green wall, they blocked the rising sun. But come evening, the brilliant glow of a fading sunset filled the mass of windows on the face of the chateau.

Mara longed for it, reminiscing about the way she'd sit around the fireplace in the evening, sipping her vin, sharing stories of the day's hunt with Iris.

Iris was competitive, even then. She'd always claim to have seen the largest stag or killed the most turkeys. But she was also warm, attentive. A friend.

They were but seven and eight when their mother showed them the chateau. It boasted a garden overflowing with hydrangeas, tamed wild roses, and ancient lilacs. A diverted stream crossed the front lawn where does and their fawn would often drink in the evenings. It was their mother's favorite place. In the high summer, the smell of flowers wafted through the portcullis porch into the giant doorways of the hallway, proper salon, and dining hall, bringing the outside in.

But Mara had loved the winters there, when snow coated the garden, leaving only empty branches like bones. They kept doors shut and fires roaring, belching their warmth into the library where she'd sit and gaze out at the falling flakes, each one a wonder. In the mornings, she'd find fresh tracks of hare and winter fox.

Her skin prickled at the memory of it all. It had been there that she'd first told her mother she didn't want to fight Iris for the throne. It had been there her mother had slapped her—the first and only time she'd raised a hand against her daughter. Mara held her hand to her cheek as if she could feel the memory. Her skin had hardened that day. Dreams had shrunk. Eyes that once looked outward at the world had fallen inward. She'd turned her focus toward the one thing her mother wanted.

Victory.

Mara balled her hands into fists. She had wanted the throne. Always. But never through the ways of the Jeweled Realm. She still didn't know if that made her weak or righteous. Her eyes glanced at Boden, who hummed to himself while thrashing through the underbrush.

"What's that you're humming?" she asked, distracting herself from her spiraling thoughts.

"Oh, uh . . . nothing. Just a song my mother would sing."

"An Ursan lullaby?"

"Not really. I mean, Ursan mothers sing it, but it's not a lullaby. More of a warning."

"A warning? Of what?"

"To stay the path until the journey is over, or . . . die."

Mara rolled her eyes. "Rather dark for a children's song, don't you think?"

Boden stepped over a fallen log. "Children should be brought up knowing the dangers of this world. It keeps them earnest and aware."

Mara stepped over the log as well, following Boden's trek. They had entered a dense portion of the forest. Birch brush grew rampant, as did the Horridus. Its pungent odor flooded into the light breeze passing by, ruining the crisp scent of fall Mara generally enjoyed.

Stay the path until the journey is over. Mara repeated the words inside her head, ruminating on them. She knew the course her mother had set before her. She had had little of a choice. The Red Queen had demanded her oldest daughter outperform her youngest. It is what she had done herself, so long ago, by sinking the arrow into her little sister's heart.

After Iris was long gone, they'd presented Mara before her mother. She'd lain dying in her grand bed, the unseen and unknown sickness killing her from the inside out. It had been a week of watching her mother and her shallow breaths, rarely coherent. A week of holding her hand.

To think she might have missed it, had she lost to Iris.

But if there were truths to speak, this was one: she hadn't stayed the path. She'd been meant to kill Iris, and she hadn't. The Sword had wavered in her hand. Iris had asked her to stop. And she had.

So was Mara meant to die?

Gravel crunched beneath their feet, rousing Mara from her deep thoughts. Before them laid a drive of crushed white stone. It led the way to the chateau, bordering the entire front of the two-story building. Weeds erupted in clumps throughout the gravel. No gardener remained to keep them at bay. No one was left to maintain the shape and appearance of the chateau's façade. Even the stream, carving its way around the chateau, ran dry, abandoning it to the forest.

"Is that it?" Boden asked.

Mara nodded. She crept past him but stopped. It had been so long since she gazed upon it, since she last sat beyond the windows and stared out at the world. She retreated, choosing instead to hide beside Boden, peering at it like one might look at a stranger.

"It's beautiful," Boden's words drifted down from his sweetly smiling face.

"It was," Mara said, concerned for the fuzziness that grew within her stomach, "once. Now it seems like a lonely place."

"We shall revive it"—Boden turned his smile down toward her—"at least for this night."

The gravel drive improved their speed. Without the birch brush to fight, they rounded the hill and were soon within the shadow of the chateau.

Large and symmetrical, the building was built of white stone that had been hauled from the top of the Diamond Highlands. Black paint flecked off in chunks from the tall, peeling front doors to fly adrift in the breeze. Blue shutters—sun-bleached and faded—framed each window on both floors. A steep pitched roof made the tall building even taller. Dormers decorated in what were once white-and-gilded-gold shutters were now water-stained and grayed.

Mara reached out a hand to stroke the stone. It was smooth, worn down first by master craftsmen and later by the weather. The nearby window was cracked, broken in the upper corner. Mara noticed no signs that someone occupied the place.

Boden tried the door, but it was locked.

"Perhaps around the garden way," Mara suggested. "There are large portico doorways. We should be able to shove one open." She led the way, disappearing around a giant lilac that dominated the corner of the chateau. Once pruned and kept within a defined shape, the bush had clawed its way up the chateau, growing so tall it leaned away from the building, cascading its purple flowers over them like a bower. Beyond that was a gravel path, once again interrupted by invading weeds.

They walked along the side path. Sheer curtains were drawn across the chateau's windows. Mara remembered hiding amidst them, their fabric so soft she'd rub her face with it, inhaling the muted smell of dust and flowers.

Her mother's favorite room, the evening salon, was beyond the first window. She'd meet with friends there, or imbibe in the local vin with Mara's father. Situated in the front of the chateau, it received the best light from the evening sun. A simple, white marble fireplace filled one wall. And despite being covered by drop cloths, Mara could remember each piece of furniture: a velvet chaise, deep purple like winter vin; a wingback armchair, embroidered with gold and silver thread; an ancient wooden table, four tiny carved humans holding up the surface.

All luxurious. All stolen from her mother's conquests.

The room beyond the next window was empty. Mara remembered it as a dining hall. The chandelier hung lopsided, coated in dust. None of the crystals sought to twinkle in the light that leaked through the curtains. Where once the table stood, a naked rug was half rolled up. In the corner, a broken vase.

The last room was the day room. Mara remembered spending many mornings within, trapped with the *enseignante* and Iris, wanting nothing more than to be released into the wilds of the gardens and forest outside. The large oak table that once occupied the center of the room was moved, shoved up against the far wall. A wooden cabinet, where the *enseignante* would keep books and supplies, was broken and leaned heavily toward one side. A portrait of their grandmother, so vast it took up most of the wall itself, was slashed and a red frown had been painted over the First Queen's beautiful olive-skinned face.

"It seems we aren't the first visitors." Boden's words bounced off the glass while peering through the window.

"Yes." Mara peered in as well. "Even so, the damage was done long ago. Probably the first winter we did not return."

"How close is the nearest *ville?*" he asked, following her to the rear of the chateau.

An arched arbor, once white but now gray, greeted them. It sagged beneath the weight of a bursting hydrangea, daring them to enter. Boden went first, glancing up at the large clumps of purple-blue flowers. He shoved a sagging branch bedecked in blooms aside and stepped through, holding it aside for Mara. She reached up and gently stroked the flower as she went by.

On the far side of the arbor, Boden peered around the corner of the building. His eyes widened in wonder as the wild garden unfolded before them. "It's safe to say the gardener hasn't been here in a while."

Overgrowth spilled out of the cement containers and worked its way between white stone bricks. Leaves stopped up the fountains with murky water. Statues that once flaunted themselves proudly were now overdressed in vines. It was all in various stages of life and decay. The smell was heavy in the garden.

"Where to now?" Boden asked.

Mara continued into the overgrowth. It was darker than she remembered. The bushes, once so tame and almost genial, reached skyward ominously. Allowed to grow unchecked, the flowering trees and shrubs seemed crazed with power. No mortal could chop them down, shape them back to how they'd been. No, they now grew where they chose.

Where a bench once sat, Mara found Horridus. It thrust its woody stalk up, proudly displaying itself next to the hydrangeas and the lilacs. There should have been a forked path, but Mara couldn't make it out. The portcullis porch stared at them from behind the greenery. Vines traced their way up the arches and cascaded downward like wild curtains, filling the void of archways. Rabbit trails were their only guide, and those were not generous.

"Well, we'll never make it through that." Boden studied the porch.

"Yes, we will." Mara withdrew Edda. "We just need some help."

Mara sliced at the plants, their wooden arms yielding to the sharp edge of the axe. Nothing withstood the likes of Edda. The overgrowth wilted, bowing down to Mara as she moved closer and closer to the porch.

"You know," Boden followed Mara, his own axe withdrawn but limp in his hand. "I didn't give you Edda for gardening."

Mara laughed. Feeling the axe slice through the air, striking something, anything, relieved the tension that had crept up her arms and into her neck. The chateau had once been her favorite place, but now it seemed to be a tomb. Thoughts of the dead—and those who should have been—leached from its windows and filled her with a sense of foreboding that she needed to release with Edda's blade.

"Here." Boden's voice interrupted her thoughts as his body pressed upon her, intruding her space. "Let me help." He tried and failed to swipe at a hydrangea, its blooms dancing lazily in the wind, as if mocking him.

"You know, I do not always require you to jump to my defense, Boden. I am perfectly capable of doing some things myself." She shoved onward into the overgrowth, suddenly far too aware of how close together they stood. Of how warm her cheeks had grown.

Instead, she focused on what was in front of her. The branches fell easily to Edda, and Mara found herself smiling at their quick deaths. Her arm only grew tired as they neared the portcullis, where she finally relented and allowed Boden to take the lead. Her mother would have been disappointed by that.

Once on the portcullis porch, she pointed them toward a set of large glass doors. They were as tall as the wall itself, were narrow, and opened into the hallway between the back rooms. One remained perfectly intact, but the other was shattered. The glass on the ground glittered beneath the vines, a pretty invitation to reach for it and bleed.

"Shall we?" Mara asked.

Boden smiled at Mara, amused, before nodding. He took the first step across the threshold. She watched his back as he took several steps inside without her. Only a fool entered an unknown room first. Mara wondered what made Boden so brave. Or so stupid.

The hallway smelled of wet earth. Rain-soaked wallpaper bubbled in places and curled in others. Mara, distracted by the ghosts of memories filling her mind, tripped on a broken chair. Boden threw out his arm and held her up, keeping her on her feet. Her heart fluttered for a moment, but she shoved the feeling away like a bug beneath a boot.

"It seems abandoned," Boden said. "But let's be cautious."

"I told you." Mara released herself from Boden's grasp, attempting to hide the blush that she could feel blooming on her cheeks. "We will be fine. The closest *ville* is leagues away. The forest surrounding the chateau is reserved for royal hunting, regardless if the chateau is used or not. No one may enter here."

"And yet someone has."

They had reached the doorway to the dayroom. The red, frowning face glared down at them where her grandmother's handsome features should have been.

The First Queen was the mother of the Jeweled Realm. Her own hands had founded the kingdom. Her own blood had bled on the battlefield for it. Mara didn't understand why someone would desecrate her face in this way. Why would someone show any sort of displeasure toward the first matriarch?

Her confusion must have shown on her face, for Boden placed a hand on her shoulder. "It's impossible for a ruler to be loved by everyone."

Mara turned away from Boden, forcing herself to blink back the tears that came unwanted to her eyes. She didn't know why they'd appeared there so suddenly. She didn't know why her emotions felt so close to the surface.

"There's a usable fireplace here," Boden called after her, overlooking her behavior. "I'll clear it, and we can make a fire for the night."

"Fine," she called back down the hall to him.

She reached the door to the dayroom. It seemed darker from the inside. She approached the round table, her eyes searching for what she was looking for. And there, etched in the wood like it had been done yesterday, was Iris's carving.

There was Iris, sword in hand, and Mara, also sword in hand. Both dueled, their swords crossing evenly in the middle. Mara's finger traced the shape of her sister's head and body, following the line to Iris's sword and making the way to her own head and body. She traced the smiles on both their faces.

Mara smiled.

Chapter Twenty-Two

Boden did his best to filter the smoke filling the evening salon out the cracked window. He had cleaned the fireplace thoroughly, but there was no use if he couldn't clear the chimney. Finally, after several attempts, the chimney breathed, releasing years of collected leaves and birds' nests, allowing smoke to rise. Boden burnt the debris within the flames, and soon the room was warm and bathed in the gentle glow of the fire.

Mara had never been allowed in the evening salon. It had been a place for her mother. A place for adults. She had yet to prove herself the heir to the realm, to prove she belonged there. She and Iris would sit in their rooms late at night and pretend to be their parents, carrying on with a ridiculously mundane and boring conversation.

She stroked the mantle of the fireplace. The cool marble felt even colder against her fingers. She studied the room, wondering all the while what her mother had found so appealing about it.

The evening salon was layered in whites: white plaster bedecked white wainscot from floor to plafond; a white coffered ceiling displayed white rosettes within; an off-white rug overlaid a scrubbed pine floor. The only thing colorful in the entire room was the seating.

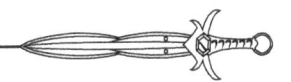

Mara bent down before the hearth to warm her fingers. The room reminded her of her mother. Cold. Hard.

"Kalda smiles upon us," Boden called from the opposite side of the room.

There, framed with blue pine, was a giant map of the Jeweled Realm and those lands immediately surrounding it. No doubt he'd notice her mother's scribbled handwriting on the edges, denoting weakness in borderlands, strengths in others. How she'd circle natural resources, sometimes two or three times, emphasizing the importance of keeping or taking more and more.

"Bouzy is not far," he said. "Two days' walk, maybe three."

His finger found the chateau, a scarlet dot upon the map, and dragged it along the path southward toward the Golden Foot and Bouzy. The Diamond Highlands would give way to the hillside just south of the chateau. These hills would eventually give way to farmland. The Golden Foot was known for its wheat, thus its name. Their perilous journey across her realm was nearing its end.

Now if only they could survive maneuvering through Bouzy.

"How certain are you that the Bastians will hear me out?" She stood, rubbing her hands to spread their warmth.

"I'm not." Boden still studied the map, his eyes settling on the east.

Ursa should have been there, but the map didn't go that far. Instead, it stopped at the Waste. Few objects were marked there. An X marked a pair of nomadic outposts. A giant mountain visible from the edge of the Jeweled Realm, its peak penetrating deep into cloud cover. Nothing else. Nothing beyond.

Mara felt sick. The anticipation filled her like a weight, like water forced down the throat of those sentenced to death, left to drown in the river. Despite trying to warm them, her fingers still felt cold. Her hands shook.

"But I am certain what awaits you with Iris." Boden arrived by the fire next to her. "And I'd rather take my chances with the Bastians."

He smiled down at her but frowned upon noticing her shaking. He grasped her hands in his and a look of realization flooded his face. "You're freezing." He tucked her hands within his jerkin beneath his arm.

His body was warm, and Mara immediately felt the relief creep up her fingers. She closed her eyes and let the heat of the fire and Boden wash over her.

"You're nervous, too, aren't you?" Boden murmured.

With her eyes closed, she didn't have to look into his knowing eyes. The blue that seemed never-ending, like the sky. Perpetual and permanent, like time itself.

"I am the Sword Queen," Mara answered, creeping closer to Boden—for warmth, she told herself—her eyes still shut. "I am not allowed to be nervous."

"Your name is *Mara*."

He said it so forcefully that she had to open her eyes. She stared upward, his face only a handbreadth away, and saw the conviction settled there.

"The Sword Queen is only a title. A facet of you, perhaps, but it isn't all of you. It doesn't have to be."

"Boden—" Mara began, but his lips pressed softly against her own, staying her words.

Again she fought with herself. On the outside, her lips pressed gently back into Boden's, as if afraid too much force would ruin the moment, but on the inside, her stomach roiled. Her mother's sneering face filled her mind with her poor decisions.

At all her failures.

Thunder rumbled at them from atop the highlands. Boden jerked away, spooked by the noise, and ran to the window, grasping to shut it. "I didn't see any rainclouds," he grunted, pulling hard on the window frame.

There was a crack of wood, and the pane slipped toward the ground but stopped, wedged within the frame.

"It's alright," Mara assured him. She quickly straightened her shoulders and held her chin high, suppressing her feelings once again. "Rainstorms are common this time of year. They sneak across the highlands. This window won't let much in. The clouds come from the other side." And when Boden hesitated, she added, "Leave it."

It was the first time she had used her queen voice in several weeks—confirmed by the look of confusion on Boden's face. The commanding tone seemed distant, unfamiliar. Since falling off the dam, she had felt herself fading. All the decorative vestiges that made her queen were gone. The facets—as Boden had said—were ground down, and something new was emerging. Some new shape.

"I saw rabbit tracks in the garden," she said. "Perhaps I can catch one for dinner."

She turned and made her way toward the door.

"Mara," he called, but she didn't stop.

In the hall, she unsheathed Edda. The sky rumbled once more, shaking the chateau. The storm was moving closer.

Mara stopped on the porch. She could vividly remember the sunny days she and Iris would spend lying around on the outdoor chaises, discussing some forgotten topic. They would sharpen their weapons, much to the annoyance of the *gouvernante*. They'd even sip vin there—before officially being allowed to drink it—in the darkening evenings.

But their mother or father would invariably arrive, ushering one of them along, away for some other purpose. It got worse when Mara turned twelve. They separated her and Iris's lessons. She began sitting with her mother, discussing diplomacy and warcraft.

Iris never told Mara what she discussed with their father. Probably the same sorts of things Mara did with their mother. But from the age of twelve onward, when Iris returned from meeting with their father, she was different. Like a cave closed off, lacking light, cold.

With a sharp inhale, Mara brought herself back to the present, grounding herself in it before stepping off the porch into the night. The clouds were a bruise in the sky, a darkness that promised rain. From the top of the highland, the poplars greeted the storm. A wind picked through the garden, rattling the lilacs nearby. Mara quieted her mind. The time of Iris was long ago. It was over.

She was as good as dead.

The rabbit tracks picked up near the center of the garden where the fountain once trickled. It had been a gift from her grandfather. A quiet man, once married, he'd used his hands to build rather than fight. He'd balanced the First Queen well, though, some had thought him too weak.

He'd sculpted the statue that stood in the center of the fountain himself. It was of the First Queen's father, the man who'd smithed the Sacred Sword. He was smiling, hands extended, beholding a sculpted version of the Sword. Only, it wasn't there. The hilt remained in her great-grandfather's hand, but the blade was gone, broken and eroded over the years.

Mara sympathized. She placed a hand on the man's empty one, consoling herself and him.

"I'll find it," she whispered to herself. "I will."

The hair on the back of her neck prickled. There was rustling behind her, somewhere in a twisted bush. She twisted and threw, trusting Edda would find her mark. A squeal rang out, so sharp against the quiet rustle of the wind in the leaves that it startled Mara.

Edda pinned the rabbit to the ground. It kicked once, twice, before going limp. Blood gurgled up from the wound, but its eyes locked forward, blind to life forevermore. Mara wrenched Edda free, pleased at her improving skill. Raising Edda once more, she lopped off the rabbit's head.

Mara allowed herself to relax as she sheathed Edda. They would be eating fresh food. It would warm their bellies, and a night on the chaises would rest their bodies. Though, she tried not to think too closely about Boden's body. Her lips still tingled with the ghost of his lips, but she shoved the thought downward where it would perhaps wither, or—if she were lucky—die.

She was halfway back to the porch when she heard it: the nicker of a horse. Her feet froze, heart thudding in her chest. Training told her she should reach for her weapon, but fear froze her mid-stride, rabbit held tightly in her hand. Her breathing was hard, and she couldn't hear over it. She cursed herself and held her breath. There was no more noise. The horse, if it had truly been a horse, was gone.

Fear urged her to run to the porch, but she forced herself to walk. Perhaps it had all been a trick of the wind. It had picked up more, blowing steadily and was no longer a gentle breeze warning of a storm. *A shake of anything could sound like a horse,* she lied to herself. It had sounded distant. Like it had come in with the wind, echoing off the forest.

It was nothing, she told herself when she got inside. She wouldn't even mention it to Boden.

He awaited her on the chaise, feet propped up on the end. The fire was roaring now. He smiled wide when he saw her catch. "Perfect." He took the rabbit from her. "I'll prepare it."

While he made quick work of the rabbit, Mara stared out the window. The world outside flickered every once in a while as lightning added itself to the thunder. It was still far away, by her count, settled above the highlands. But she knew it would descend soon, crashing over the cliffs and onto the chateau.

It always did.

She cleaned Edda and waited for Boden to be done roasting the rabbit. It turned on a makeshift spit Boden had constructed from reclaimed materials; the legs of a broken chair cradled the long dowel of a curtain rod. Boden turned the spit cautiously, careful not to burn his hands.

He'd eye her warily every once in a while, but never spoke.

"What is it?" she drawled from the wingback chair, grown annoyed by his looks.

"Nothing." He tended to the rabbit. "You just look like you've seen a ghost."

She thrust Edda back in her sheath and stood so violently the wingback chair threatened to topple over. "I'm fine," she said. "Just hungry."

"Well, good," Boden replied, "because dinner is served."

He used his knife to slice chunks of meat onto some plates he'd found. They were blue with gold veining. The finest in the chateau. Mara only remembered using them once, when her father's father had visited. She had to smile as she watched Boden plop the sizzling meat onto the finery with his knife. He handed it to her and turned to his own plate. Her mother would be furious at the use of her war prizes, shared with an Ursan no less.

Sizzling fat ran down Mara's wrist and arm as she took bite after bite, savoring the gamey taste of the rabbit. It had been days since she'd had a full meal. The jerky Éliane packed for them had been tough and over-dried. Mara had been grateful for it at the time, but with the blistering-hot meat in her mouth, she could give into how hungry she'd been.

Together, they made quick work of the rabbit. With nothing left but bones and sinew, Mara vanished to the kitchens in search of some forgotten vin. There was a cellar, she remembered that much, where her mother kept the more expensive bottles. It would have been well-hidden from vagabonds and thieves.

Her mouth watered at the thought of such vins. The dark reds of Valon and Liroux, full-bodied and harsh when first tried at the ripe age of ten, would now be bold and earthy to her matured palate. Sweet rosés and white vins of the northern towns of Vatou and Montnoît would also be there. Her mother had only favored those occasionally, when certain diplomats joined them for state dinners.

Mara imagined Boden would enjoy the dark reds, though, she had witnessed more than one man admit to preferring the sweeter over the bitter. Perhaps she'd grab a bottle of both, and if he preferred none, then the more for her.

Beneath the scrubbed wooden table amid the center of the kitchen was a hidden doorway. Mara effortlessly shoved the table aside and pulled up on the inconspicuous latch. The passage opened downward, displaying a circling staircase. Carved into the stone were shelves for wine. Round and round the staircase went, at least for another floor or two that she knew of. But Mara had honestly never ventured that far beneath the chateau. She'd only ever had time to grab the closest bottle before she and Iris snuck beyond the confines of the chateau.

Life had moved forward, like it always did, and left the wine cellar perfectly intact. Bottle neck after bottle neck peered out at her from their shelves. She wandered down a complete rotation, pulling random bottles as she went. Some possessed a dry, brittle cork, owing mostly to lack of a wax sealant. She placed those bottles back.

Halfway down the stairs, with light limited from above, she pulled a bottle of red vin. Wiping away the thick layer of dust, she saw it hailed from Valon. A dark red, then. The wax appeared thoroughly sealed.

She moved to return to the surface, breaching like a sea creature, but stopped. Something moved beneath her. Or so she thought. She knelt, peering through the gap in the risers. Nothing could be seen but shadow and void, black cast on black. Again, she held her breath, realizing she breathed too hard, but heard nothing.

Deep within her, something twitched. A nervousness. A warning. She swallowed hard and stepped gingerly up one step. Still nothing. She lingered, but nothing moved in the depths of the cellar.

In the kitchen, she pushed the wooden table back over the trapdoor. It wasn't heavy, and she was uncertain if it would hold should someone try to push through the door, but it was better than nothing.

Back in the evening salon, Boden dozed. She hesitated to tell him about the wine cellar, just like she hadn't told him about the horse. There was no reason not to tell him, but something within her choked her words. They were safe, she convinced herself—no need to appear spooked.

Do not display weakness. These were her mother's words, embroidered into her mind, unable to be restitched, unable to be undone. They were as much a part of her as her eye color or hair. And regardless of how she felt about Boden or how much she disagreed with her mother's ways or principles, she was a daughter of the Jeweled Realm.

She must obey.

Boden stirred when she slumped into the wingback chair. She held the vin in one hand, staring at the black liquid behind the green glass. Outside, the branches of the giant hydrangea beat against the chateau. The wind had risen. A blinding flash ripped across the sky from directly above the roof, followed almost immediately by a thunderous explosion.

Mara glanced at Boden, who watched her intently.

"About earlier, Mara . . . " he began.

She held up the bottle of vin, as if to silence him. "If you're not drinking, we aren't talking." Her eyes settled on him, and she hoped they appeared as fierce as intended.

Boden said nothing at first, furrowing his brow and frowning before finally giving in. He reached for the bottle and snatched it away from Mara, running Liv down the bottle's neck and in one clean slice, lopping the top off. He drank deeply before thrusting the bottle back to her. He watched her take her own sip, his eyes tracing the shape her lips made when she sipped from the broken glass.

She handed the bottle back to him and motioned for him to make room for her on the chaise. When he scooted down, she sank next to him, the chaise creaking with complaint. The vin had invigorated her, feeding the part of her mind dominated by maxims and memories of her mother. She felt warm beneath her collar, and emboldened.

Boden took another long, slow swig of vin. When he was finished, she pulled his face down and kissed him forcefully and firmly. When she pulled away slightly, it pleased her to see his confounded face.

"The next time you think to kiss me," she whispered so close to his lips they tickled, "don't."

She pulled away, distancing herself by a handsbreadth, and leaned back against the chaise. His eyebrows quirked up as a wave of confusion passed over his features. She smirked. Deep down, it felt cruel, but Mara knew if she didn't control her feelings, they would ultimately control her. Boden was a liability. A distraction keeping her from focusing on what she really needed to do: kill her sister.

Boden's jaw tightened. A frown began to form at the corner of his mouth, but he seemed to regain some control over his face and kept it from forming. "As you wish," he said.

The fire popped and sizzled with the arrival of rain. She could hear it outside, thrumming against the windows. But the warmth soothed her. She sank further into the chaise and allowed herself to relax.

She closed her eyes. She didn't know if Boden did the same or if he slept. But sleep came over her, and with it, the storm.

Chapter Twenty-Three

At some point in the night, the storm ceased. It was within this quiet that Mara roused. Perhaps her body was used to the noise, and without it, couldn't sleep. Or perhaps the waning fire and its lack of heat had awoken her.

Or, more likely, it was the sound of feet on broken glass.

Mara's eyes ripped open. She remained completely still, breathing slowly through her nose. Boden's body was slack beside her, asleep. His arm had fallen too close to her, her skin burning where they touched.

The room, despite being so vividly white, was dark. Storm clouds covered the moon, reducing visibility to almost nothing. A faint glow from the fire was all she had to see by.

Luckily for her, it was enough.

The bodies moved within the hallway, attempting to be silent, attempting to remain undetected. She assumed they thought she was still sleeping. Her hand slowly moved to Edda. The intruders were near the doorway now, lingering in the frame, whispering. Mara could only hope that Edda would yield herself to her once again, like she had done with the rabbit.

Mara allowed herself only a second of pain, only a tick of her heart to steep with regret over the lack of the Sacred Sword. Edda would have to do. Mara was prepared to die trying to prove it.

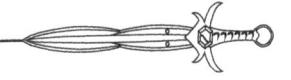

The first figure stepped into the room. Shadow blended with shadow, but not well enough. Mara could make out their torso. She could see where her throw needed to land.

She inhaled sharply. In one motion, she withdrew Edda and stood. Boden stirred.

Mara threw Edda and struck her target true. The figure howled in pain, grasping at the axe now buried deep within their chest. The other figures moved into the room now, their faces still disguised by the darkness, but Mara could make out four of them.

Three—Mara corrected—as the first figure fell to their knees and onto their face.

A sharp sting lanced through Mara's right shoulder as an arrow sliced past her. The shot was too wide and barely scraped her exposed arm.

Boden erupted from the chaise. Mara wasted no time, unsheathing Liv—and simultaneously disarming Boden—she turned in time to meet the second figure.

Up close, she could see a woman's face, vaguely familiar, though in the moment her adrenaline would not let her mind wander to faces of her past. Instead, she kicked the woman hard and slashed down with Liv, opening the woman's ear. The woman screamed and dropped her blade. Mara ducked beneath another arrow—the archer proving to be a terrible shot—and snatched the woman's dagger.

She kicked the woman again and threw the dagger at the archer. It dug deep into the throat, releasing a torrent of blood onto the off-white carpet. Bow and archer crumpled.

Boden yelled at Mara, demanding his weapon. She tossed Liv to him, and he struck down the one-eared woman as she tried to claw her way back to Mara. Only one figure remained shrouded in the darkness.

The man spoke. "Impressive."

This voice, too, struck Mara as familiar. She stepped closer, trying to see who the man was.

"Mara," Boden growled in warning. He stepped protectively between her and the mysterious figure.

"Listen to your Ursan dog, Your Majesty," the voice said.

"I don't heed orders from anyone, let alone faceless cretins," Mara answered.

The cretin laughed. "You'll heed orders soon enough, when your rightful queen orders you to die."

Mara snarled at the man. He lunged for her, but Boden kicked the man backward before swinging Liv angrily upward, clipping the man squarely beneath the jaw. The man stumbled, but Boden wasn't finished. With a warrior's precision, Boden buried the axe in the man's stomach, felling him to his knees.

Blood spilled from his smiling lips, and he bubbled out his last words. "Strength wields the Sword."

The man fell to his side, his face now illuminated by the dim light of the fire, eyes ever staring at Mara.

It was Henri.

Mara turned to Boden. She couldn't breathe. Her head spun in multiple directions and her skin felt cold. Boden's warm hands were on her arms then, guiding her back to the chaise. The walls she had so neatly constructed came tumbling down in the crimson tide filling her mother's evening salon.

"Don't worry," Boden said in her ear. "I'll get rid of them."

She sat and stared at the floor, carpet and wood blurring, seeing nothing. Unaware of Boden's movements, or if he even spoke to her, Mara remained still for what seemed like hours. The sun hinted at the horizon before Boden finally roused her enough to look at him.

"Are you alright?" he asked. He knelt in front of her, hands on hers.

"Fine," she said with numb lips. "I'm fine."

But in truth, all she could think about were Henri's words. If she didn't wield the Sword, was she strong enough to defeat Iris? Her sister's eyes replaced Henri's in her mind and her stomach shrank. She would need more than axes to defeat her sister. Her gaze fell to Edda, placed on the table by Boden.

"There will be more." Mara studied the weapon, still flecked with blood. "They won't stop until they've found me."

"So we'll go." Boden began gathering their packs.

"How can you do this?" Mara accepted her pack from Boden, but did not place it upon her back.

"Do what?"

"Risk your life for mine?"

Boden stopped his gathering. He stood, his eyes fixed on Mara. She rarely saw him this serious. His face was etched of granite, his brows furrowed.

"I told you," he said, "I think you can lead the Jeweled Realm down a different path. Your sister will bring war back to the continent. Many will die. And for what? Her pride?"

Mara dropped her eyes. "I am Mara of House Black. We are masters of warcraft. What makes you so certain I won't bring war upon the continent?"

Boden sighed. He violently shoved his fur deep within his pack. "I grow tired of this game, Mara."

"What game?"

He stood up straight, looking angry now. "The one you play in which you are anything like them. Like you are some shadow of your mother." He tightened the drawstring upon the pack, cinching it closed, securing the items within. "You are *not* your mother. You are not your grandmother. You can tell a different story, one with a different ending."

Mara's throat felt tight. She was choking, though she couldn't say on what. "And what ending would that be?" she asked, speaking through the lump. She breathed heavily through her nose. Her blood coursed within her, almost deafening her to Boden's words.

"One in which sister need not kill sister," he said, approaching her. "One in which *love* wields the Sword, not strength." His hand cupped her cheek then, gently, delicately. He leaned in to kiss her, but—perhaps remembering her words from the night before—stopped short.

Mara swallowed down the lump that threatened to choke her. "I see," she whispered. She could feel the heat of his body and his breath on her cheek. She looked up into his eyes. "I am a daughter of the Red Queen. My realm must come before all else." She wiped the beading sweat off her forehead and continued. "Should there come a need for war on the continent, I must bring it, Boden. Iris or no Iris. I cannot . . . I cannot love you."

She turned away from him, digging her nails into her palms, using the sharp sting to ground her anger lest she explode with it. The hardest part was realizing she didn't know who she was angrier with: Boden or herself.

"I understand," he said. "I misjudged you."

"Yes." She watched droplets of a light rain cascade down the windows, leaving their misshapen tracks. "You have."

"Then"—Boden fumbled with his pack before swinging it around his shoulder and onto his back—"consider my help a service to Kalda." His eyes hid his feelings. He had shored them up like the walls of the chateau, just like Mara.

Boden kicked out the fire. Smoke fumed up into his face. He coughed once, twice, before turning back to Mara. She bowed her head to him, curt and sharp. They were at an understanding, then. They began the walk out of the chateau.

She hated hearing the sentiment in his voice. The one that those in the Jeweled Realm mocked outsiders for. A sense of oneness and love, without power? Impossible.

But what she hated more was that deep down, she wanted it, too. Or something like it. She wanted the fighting to end, the violence to not be status quo. She wanted her responsibilities to make sense, and not just be for the sake of tradition.

Her eyes snuck toward Boden. His large feet stomped through the chateau, echoing off the walls strangely. Outside, he squished through the dirt and mud and overgrown greenery. Their steps were the only noise penetrating the chateau's sleepy silence.

A short distance into the woods, Mara heard horses again. But these horses didn't sound energetic from riding, they sounded lethargic. They sounded bored.

She followed the noise, ignoring whether Boden followed, and found them in a small meadow. Four horses, each one flicking their tail, attempting to busy themselves with the dying clover within the grass. None were pleased with their holdings.

"Their mounts," Boden's voice came from behind.

Mara smiled as she approached the nearest one and stroked it down the nose. It whickered and leaned its head against hers. She patted its neck, whispering gentle words into its ear. When she was certain she'd pacified the beast, she reached for the reins and hauled herself up onto the saddle.

Boden frowned at her, still upset over their heated exchange in the chateau, but all she could do was smile and say, "We shall make excellent time now."

Chapter Twenty-Four

"What do you know of the nomads of the Waste?" Mara asked nearly an hour later.

Their silence had carried them through the forest, along the spine of the highlands, and down their slow descent into the flatlands. Ahead she could see the land roll downward like waves, falling to sea level where it met the Golden Foot and, eventually, the ocean.

"They are a hard people. I suppose that's necessary to survive there," Boden said, his words clipped.

"Well, everyone knows that," Mara spat.

Boden stopped his horse. The animal was a large, speckled gray thing with an off-white mane. It had disliked Boden at first but seemed to succumb to the large man's control.

Mara could tell Boden was fighting the desire to glare at her. His anger at her rejection still simmered there beneath his skin. She wondered if she were to touch him, if she'd feel that anger, hot like an ember.

"They are straightforward and direct, focusing nothing on trifles and everything on survival. Loyal to their own, they'd die for one another. It's probably their only endearing trait."

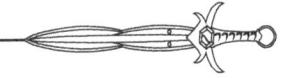

"I see." Mara mused, admiring the fields before them. Knee-high grass waved, orange and dying, preparing itself for winter. Farther away, she could see the change from orange to gold. The farmers would thresh soon, collecting their harvests. "How would my sister have ingratiated herself with them?"

Boden sat back in the saddle and removed his waterskin. He drank deeply and ignored her. Finally, he pulled away, water trickling down his chin. He settled his gaze on her and wiped the water away. "They wouldn't follow her easily, that much is certain. She's indebted them to her somehow. Or else given them enough reason to fear her."

"How likely is that?"

Boden shrugged. "She seems to possess a skill in their sorcery. Perhaps it spooks them. She isn't of their blood, but she wields their powers so easily."

"Yes . . . her power." Mara kicked the grass from atop her horse, her riding boots barely touching the tops. "You've seen her wield it?"

"I've seen her conjure fire, fill a sun-bright room with darkness, purify filthy water." Boden sighed, still thinking. "Perhaps there are other things I've not seen her do. There are whispers, just like there are whispers of the nomads."

Whispers did Mara little good. It perplexed her to think that Iris could control such things. They were sisters, after all. Were they not the same? Mara looked down at her hands, covered in leather, gripping the reins, and wondered if she, too, could control the same power.

It was true the Sacred Sword boasted its own secret power. The bearer gained a confidence not known unless holding the hilt. A soothing calm would rush over them as they prepared for battle. Victory was assured.

But Mara had never seen anything conjured from nothing. Her grandmother had stomped out the ancient magic people once practiced when she conquered the land. Nothing would be worshiped, save the Sword. Magic wasn't real. It didn't work.

Save for the Sword.

"How will I defeat her if I don't have the Sword?" The words Mara had meant to keep inside fell out forcefully before she could bite her tongue.

"I'm sure you'll find a way." Boden seemed uninterested in talking any further. He kicked his silver horse onward, galloping past Mara, striking out across the hills. She followed at a trot while considering her options, trying to ignore his insolence.

Perhaps it wouldn't matter if she died. Her eyes settled on the clouds. The white behemoths pulled through the air, leaving their streaks of wisps behind. A patch of blue would peek out in places before eventually being swallowed by the clouds again. What would her mother say, she wondered. She tugged the reins of her horse and caught up with Boden. Her thoughts weighed her down, causing the body aches brought on by riding to set in faster.

She knew what her mother would say. She always knew.

Strength wields the Sword.

But could strength come from something else? Why was the Sword the only thing her grandmother had found strength in? Wielding the Sword looked an awful lot like hiding behind it, and Mara couldn't quite decide what she thought was worse. Or what would help her better control the prosperous Jeweled Realm.

The Jeweled Realm, with its manicured *villes* and forest villages alike, spread out across the continent to take up nearly half of it. It was a lot to control. And each place different from the next.

Bouzy occupied one of the many arms of the Mousseaux's delta. It forked and forked and forked again. The largest distributary was wide enough and deep enough for even the largest of ships to dock. And so that is where the port city made its roots. The land surrounding the port was swampy, but mineral-rich thanks to the dredging of the Mousseaux. Farms surrounded Bouzy, all attributing to the goods that were shipped out via the port and occasionally over land in wagons.

Further still, grapevines covered the hillsides. Vignerons tended these day and night to ensure a prosperous harvest. Mara could see them tending to their plants now. She wanted to stop and beg for a taste but knew better.

Only queens could do such things.

They rode their horses along the stoned path that wound through the vineyards, over hillsides, and descended toward Bouzy and its foreboding walls. A breeze blew gently, picking up the sweet smell of grapes—some overripe—and the bitter mix of disturbed earth. The smell was fleeting, but always returned with a new brush of wind. The fields of wheat stood proudly on the opposite side of the road, waving beneath the breeze, their dancing audible and calming. Mara desperately wished to pause a moment and take in her kingdom, but ahead was a group of three vignerons.

A woman, her face also shrouded with a scarf of fall, waved at them. "Sister, brother, are you heading to Bouzy?"

Her eyes were that of faded blue, skin sun-soaked as if she'd spent too much time in the vineyards. Wrinkles decorated the corner of her eyes, but Mara could sense the woman smiling beneath her covering. *Too old to be a sister,* Mara thought with a smile of her own.

"That is none of your concern, mother," Boden said, angling his horse around the trio that blocked their way.

Mara absently let her horse wander too close to the woman. Her hand shot out and grabbed Mara's horse by the halter. Her arm, too, betrayed her profession, speckled with sun spots and scars. "Please," she pleaded, "I have important news that must reach the Lord of the Ville."

"What's so urgent you request help from strangers?" Mara pulled her scarf tighter. She glanced over at Boden, who moved his horse closer to hear the woman's reply.

"The queen's banquet," the woman said. "We're tasked with providing the vin, but I'm afraid we won't have enough of what the queen wants. We have to speak with Lord DeBouzy."

Mara did her best to hide the twitch in her eyebrow, the one that liked to betray her displeasure. She pulled her scarf down slightly, holding her lips and chin firm, and offered the woman a wide, cold smile. "Of course, the queen's banquet. What an honor for you," she said.

"If we survive," the woman sighed. "I'd hate to displease the young queen so quickly since ascending the throne."

"No one wants that," Mara agreed. She looked at Boden, considering, and before he could answer, she said, "Hop on behind my brother. We'll take you to the *ville*."

"Oh, thank you, sister," the woman said.

Boden's face was slack. He said nothing and offered no sign of displeasure. Instead, he reached down and hauled the old woman up, sitting her squarely behind him. "Comfortable, mother?" he asked.

"Oh, yes." She wrapped her aging arms around his waist.

He glanced at Mara then, but stiffened his jaw and kicked the horse into a canter.

"Thank you, sister!" the two vignerons left on the road called after them.

If Boden spoke to the old woman during the ride, Mara could not tell. She rode in silence, listening to the horses' hooves bite into the dirt wedged between the stones, the sound dying shortly after being born with nothing nearby to bounce their echo.

The sun was high in the sky, heating the top of her head. She wanted to remove the scarf but knew she couldn't. The people of the northern Jeweled Realm, like Narlès and Valenbeuge, followed social customs when it suited them. But for the people of the south, like Bouzy and Valon, it might as well have been law. If she were to remove her scarf, she'd not only reveal herself, but the old woman would berate her for displaying her hair after the autumnal equinox. She inhaled deeply, staring ahead at Bouzy, marking the slowly shrinking distance between them.

When they neared the walls, Boden slowed their pace. Large stones bigger than their horses sat stacked neatly atop one another, row after row, to form the menacing walls. Mara had learned that they were hauled from a northern quarry, the wall taking several years to complete. She extended a hand and brushed the stone, its warmth feeding into her own skin.

"We haven't the time, sister," the old woman called to Mara. "Your reminiscing about home will have to wait. This is urgent."

"Of course, mother," Mara said through thin lips.

As they approached the large gates, she reined her horse next to Boden's. Formed of alternating black pine and oak, the doors stood as tall as the wall and twice the width of a carriage. Inside, four horses were assigned to each door, their handlers whipping them in order to haul the doors open or closed.

A knot formed in Mara's throat again. An annoying development that was becoming a fixture when she grew nervous. Her hand gently stroked her neck, attempting to calm herself.

Two guards appeared, dressed in black. They hailed Boden, urging his horse to stop.

"What business do you have in Bouzy?" a guard asked.

"What business is it of yours?" Mara replied as she stopped her horse next to Boden's.

The guard peered through his helmet at Mara, but she had already wrapped her face tightly once again within the scarf. "The queen's business," he said. "We must search everyone until the Liar Queen is arrested."

Mara did her best not to glare at the guard. He spoke of treason. Once, she could have had him killed right there and then. Once, she might have even done it herself. But she knew which queen she was to him.

"Abe," the old woman said, "I've known you since your mother pushed you out. I nursed you, for a time, when she was sick. So I mean this when I say: if you don't let us through this gate this moment, I'll rip your helmet off and beat you with it myself."

Abe stared at the vigneron. He swallowed hard but released Boden's horse. "I heard you're supplying the queen's banquet with wine, Mother Denise."

"Indeed." Denise nodded. "And I need to speak to Lord DeBouzy about it. Now, will you let us through? Or, when I'm arrested for displeasing the queen, will I throw your name in as well for obstruction?"

Abe stepped back, as did his fellow guard. "I would never dare. Did you hear of the girl in Narlès, Mother Denise?" Abe asked.

Boden kicked his horse, but she was being stubborn and refused to move. It occupied itself with a sprig of grass erupting from the stones of the road and refused to budge until it was thoroughly satisfied.

"Hung her, didn't they?" Denise replied. "Caught her helping the Liar Queen." The old woman locked eyes with Mara. "If you ask me, the sooner she's caught, the better for all of us."

Mara found it hard to swallow again. She inhaled deeply, slowly, relaxing her face. *Éliane. The girl knew what she was getting into,* Mara thought, but she felt a sense of guilt settle over her shoulders.

Boden's horse finally heeded his commands and started to walk. A look of relief washed over his face, mixed with something else. Mara wondered if it had to do with Éliane.

"Enjoy your day, sister, brother, Mother Denise." Abe bowed his head curtly when they passed.

Denise patted Boden on the shoulder. "He's a good boy, but he lets that armor get to his head. Now, take me to the market square, and I can make my way from there."

"As you say, mother," Boden said.

Mara tracked along slowly behind Boden. It had been many years since she had been to Bouzy. She had been a toddler, really. There were no specific moments she could remember, just fleeting feelings. The sound of the gulls over the crashing waves. The smell of the salt and fish from the docks. A cacophony of sounds while Jeweled Realm merchants tried to communicate with foreign-tongued traders.

Buildings were stacked tightly with no room for alleyways. The streets of Bouzy had been laid out thoughtfully, circling the port in rings, each ring connected by two separate spokes. But what had not been considered was where people would go when the space between the walls ran out. With no more room, the buildings went up. Homes were built on top of homes. Towering higher than some trees, the buildings blocked out the cascading sun.

The most densely populated part of Bouzy was Green Park. A misnomer, since there hadn't been a park or green belt in several decades. It was cheap to build within Green Park, though, land was scarce. Families built on top of families, sometimes four or five times, as high as they could get away with before the buildings came crashing down. When one of these tall human hives fell, it usually took out more than one other, resulting in homelessness and death for many.

Sunshine didn't penetrate to street level there—the buildings blocked it out. But if they were going to get to the docks, their best option would be to go through Green Park and stick to the shadows.

"There," Denise's voice cut through her scarf. She pointed through an archway protecting a large central square.

Boden guided the horse beneath the arch. Carved stars cut across the white surface while ivy fought its way up to the faux heavens. Within the square, the sun beat down on them once again. Wooden stalls filled every nook and cranny. Merchants stood outside, calling off their goods for the day.

Denise slid off Boden's horse and patted his leg. "Thank you, brother," she said. "You've certainly saved me. And perhaps the queen's banquet!" Denise turned and bowed her head to Mara. "Sister," she said. And then she melted in with the crowd, making her way across the square to the large central avenue that led to Lord DeBouzy's manor.

Boden watched the old woman disappear before looking over his shoulder at Mara. He offered her a smile, the first one since their argument at the chateau. Only this was not an expression of kindness. It was worry and guilt.

It was fear.

Mara didn't want to admit she felt similar. Instead, she pushed her shoulders back the way her mother had shown her and turned her horse upon the path. "Shall we?" she asked, leading Boden beneath the archway once again and toward Green Park. "We've a ways to go before the docks."

She didn't look back. She couldn't.

Chapter Twenty-Five

Green Park was saturated with smells: wet dirt, acrid smoke, night soil. Some scents were left to the imagination, strange and unnatural as they were. Occupants of the hives burned their trash in the small dirt plots that made up the shared yards. They used the same fires to cook their food.

It was not the prettiest part of the Jeweled Realm, which was why Mara felt her shoulders tense the farther they rode. She could feel Boden behind her, watching, observing. Judging.

Had she been a good queen, perhaps she would have improved these people's conditions. But she never did. She never cared. Now, forced with their dirty faces looking up at her on her healthy horse, she felt exposed. The people watched them pass, their eyes like coals, burning right through her. Children squatted on steps, bickering over this or that. Old women stood close together, knitting and whispering the gossip of the *ville*, perhaps even the kingdom. Men were nowhere in sight. Either inside or working, they relegated the difficult tasks of child-rearing and trash-burning to the women.

Darkness descended upon them. Buildings reached for the sun on foundations not meant to hold such weight. Boden kicked his horse into a faster trot, moving up beside Mara.

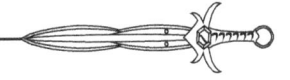

"This place is . . . lovely," he whispered.

Mara pursed her lips and nodded. "Green Park is old. The seed of the *ville* itself. It makes sense that the buildings would be this dilapidated."

"Perhaps, but what makes little sense is why your people shove in here like the fish we Ursans pack tightly in jars."

Mara said nothing. Boden's judgment was layered between his words, though, Mara wondered how much of it was due to Green Park's condition and how much was from her refusal of Boden himself. She watched him out of the corner of her eye as they rode past the fresh ruins of a hive, smoke still stirring from within. He adjusted himself in his saddle and averted his eyes from an old woman that sat in the rubble, wailing. She cried uncontrollably, calling for a girl who wouldn't come.

The collapse of the old woman's hive had trickled onto the hive next door, breaking through the roof and tearing down the top two floors. A mysterious liquid leaked from these floors down onto the remaining homes, where no one seemed to be, its constant drip deafening in Mara's ears.

More smoke drifted from above, the heavy scent of burning meat coming with it. Mara tightened her scarf around her mouth. Women glared at her from the shadows of drooping stoops.

"A queen cannot fix everything," she said to Boden.

They were in the inner ring of Bouzy now. Green Park festered around them, the scents and sights of decay and death on every side. Mara kept her gaze forward on the road, on the spoke that would take them to the innermost ring and then to the docks.

"Perhaps you're right," Boden mumbled. He steered his horse around a body lying prone on the street.

She had hidden in the palace after her coronation, insulating herself against any blowback, any hint of Iris's existence. And for a time, it had worked. She'd commanded her realm from her high perch in the palace deftly and—she'd thought—sufficiently. But the look on those people's faces told her otherwise. She ignored their gazes now, like she had done since becoming queen, and instead focused on what was ahead.

Down several flights of steps, the docks loomed. Timber grew from the water, boxing in the giant wooden ships that came and went daily. Beyond it, the glittering inky-blue sea waited for the ships to return, like a suitor awaiting their beloved.

Here, she could hear the gulls crying and the waves rocking against the wooden hulls. This was the Bouzy she remembered.

They dismounted their horses at the top of the steps and guided them down by their reins. People of the street eyed the animals greedily, but Mara pulled her horse forward, never stopping long enough for anyone to come near.

At the bottom of the stairs, the stone road turned to wooden slats. A walkway jutted forth into the water. Fishermen and women shouted the day's catch, some even holding up large fish. Farther down, the walkway forked, running to the left and right a considerable distance each way, filling the harbor with space for docking ships.

"There." Boden pointed over her shoulder toward a towering ship in the distance.

Docked farthest away from them, its white sails were emblazoned with a snarling black panther—a Bastian ship. They would have to maneuver between market stalls to reach it, and the horses would prove impossible to keep.

"Tie them up there"—Mara nodded toward a nearby post—"and whoever finds them can do what they will with them."

Boden reluctantly tied his horse next to Mara's. He retrieved his pack and offered the horse a gentle pat between the eyes. "You were a good horse," he said, placing his forehead to the animal's.

Mara rolled her eyes. "It's just a horse."

Boden gestured with his head toward a group of children sitting idly on the steps nearby. The urchins watched them tie up their horses and retrieve their bags. "They know we won't be back," he said. "And the brittle strips of horse jerky still remain in my teeth, constantly reminding me how dear it is to your people."

One child stood, watching for the pair to turn their backs. Mara bit her lip. It was just a horse. She turned and plunged into the crowd upon the pier, forcing herself to forget the animal. It had proven its usefulness. Now it was time to move forward.

Boden walked shoulder to shoulder with Mara. Not intentionally, but the business of the port forced them to walk closely. The market stalls were overflowing with fish, jugs of vin and spirits, and foreign trinkets whose purposes were unknown. Several displayed foreign textiles—luxurious silks and buttery chiffon—alongside more common cottons, linen, and wool.

Mara had to shout to Boden over the noise. "The port is booming."

"Aye, but for what purpose?"

She shrugged. Perhaps because the Jeweled Realm was prosperous. But her thoughts drifted back to the children on the steps eyeing her horse and the woman wailing for the lost girl in the rubble of her home.

"The queen favors black silk." A merchant pulled Mara by the arm into his stall. "Perhaps this will do for your tribute."

Mara ripped her arm from the merchant's grasp. "Tribute?"

"Yes." The merchant pulled a sample from a stack and held it before Mara. "The Queen's Demand? All must pay an acceptable tribute, according to their standings, or face punishment."

Mara took the silk and rubbed a thumb across the fabric, the surface cool upon her skin. "An acceptable tribute?" She admired the sheen across the smooth black. Once, she would have paid well for such a silk.

"Yes!" The merchant seemed to have lost his patience. "Where have you been, under a rock?"

"We've no need for second-rate textiles." Boden smiled at the merchant as he wrapped an arm around Mara's waist. "We've got bigger ideas."

"Oh?" the merchant sneered, ripping the silk back from Mara's hand.

Boden pulled Mara back into the flow of the pier's crowd, pushing her toward the Bastian ship. He kept his arm around her shoulders protectively, pushing them through the throng. "A tribute? Your sister is out of her mind," Boden huffed in her ear.

Mara nodded, her voice temporarily missing with the warmth of Boden's arm around her waist. Part of her wanted to lean into it but another wanted to rip herself away, remembering the decision she had made the night before. She needed to focus. She was amongst her people, yes, but they might as well have been her enemies. She focused on Iris and her demand for a tribute, as if she were a god herself.

It was then they noticed the guards. They were stationed at every crossing, where the dock parted and moved in another direction. Mara searched over her shoulder and saw that they had indeed passed several already. None seemed to notice them, though, they were all looking for something.

Or someone.

She suddenly grew self-conscious. Her hands sought any display of hair escaping from her scarf. The confidence in her clothes—the one's Éliane had packed for her—waned. Despite her ensemble no longer matching that of a queen, Mara felt exposed. Scratchy cotton, dyed an off-blue, had replaced the cool white linen of her blouse. Her black riding pants were now brown and no longer embroidered with black pansies—a status symbol. All that remained were her boots, caked in dirt and debris from their journey.

"Stop fidgeting," Boden growled at her. "You make yourself more obvious that way."

Mara didn't argue. She went numb instead. Boden gripped her tighter and guided her past the closest guard. Eyes watched them from behind the helmet, but if the guard suspected them, he did not show it. Once past, Boden released Mara. The mass of people was suffocating. She felt her eyesight lessen. The world narrowed into a pinprick. Her knees grew weak.

Boden's arm was around her again, this time around the small of her back. "What's wrong with you?" he hissed. "I wouldn't have thought the Sword Queen a coward."

Mara wanted to laugh, but her throat was weak. Instead, it came out as a sort of lazy giggle. "I'm not afraid," she said. "I'm just out of place."

"Now you sound like a lunatic," he muttered.

She wanted him to call her Mara again, but she didn't dare voice her desire. Perhaps she'd give herself away with her high-born accent.

Boden guided them through the throng of market goers, his arm never leaving her. She wanted to shove him away, but what she had told Boden was true. She felt out of place. No longer where she belonged. No longer herself. Besides, his arm was warm through the fabric of her blouse. It was solid and kept her centered through the moving mass of bodies on the pier. Without it there on the small of her back, she thought she might float away. Boden grounded her, and she clung to that feeling like a child to their mother.

They took one more turn and were finally on the long walkway leading toward the Bastian ship.

It was massive. Three tall masts shot up from the deck, their square sails whipping in the breeze. Two levels of cannons stared at them from beneath the deck. Colored glass decorated the windows of the multi-storied captain's quarters. A figurehead of a woman, dark of skin and hair and wearing a headdress of jewels, welcomed them as they neared.

A Bastian woman sat on a crate nearby, sharpening her knives. Her skin was that of many years spent on the water, sun-kissed and salt-licked. The loose garments of sailors adorned her fit body, billowing with the movement of the wind. Like every Bastian, her hair was black as the night itself.

"Stop." She held up a browned hand. "What business have you here?" Her voice was much deeper than Mara expected. Dark eyes looked them over from beneath the brim of her leather hat. A long white feather, tucked within the hat's band, seemed out of place amidst the sea-stained scene.

"We seek passage aboard this ship," Boden said, taking the lead after feeling Mara stiffen at the gruff voice of the woman.

She wanted to demand passage, but the voice inside her wouldn't take control. It was so small and so far away that she wondered if it was even hers.

"We take no Jewels with us on our passage. Rules." Mara wondered if that was the Bastian term for citizens of the Jeweled Realm. The woman studied them, her eyes settling on Mara's covered face. "What's wrong with this one?" she asked.

"Nothing," Boden said as he nudged Mara, attempting to force her to relax her stiff body. "She's just . . . we just need to get out of here."

"Out of the Jeweled Realm?" The woman stood, tucking away the knife she had been sharpening. She appeared interested now. "Only criminals would want to leave such a prosperous place."

"No, out of Bouzy," Boden said. "The fastest way is by ship."

The woman frowned, disappointed at not discovering two Jeweled Realm criminals. "Well, not on this ship." She gestured to the behemoth. "Like I said, we take no Jewels with us. Ever."

She turned her back on them then, the scarlet sash she wore vibrant against her skin. Boden glanced at Mara. Panic settled in his eyes. Instinct struck her then, shaking itself from its hibernation, and she reached for the woman's shoulder. She gripped hard and turned the woman around.

Instantly, the Bastian had her knife at Mara's throat. Mara breathed slowly, knowing the result of her action would dance with the woman's wrath. Boden stepped forward, but the woman shook her head, warning him.

"What's the commotion?" another Bastian, a tall woman with aged white hair cascading from her head, called down from the ship's railing.

"Nothing, Captain Osanna. Just two Jewels, lost."

The woman pressed her knife tight against Mara's skin. Mara did her best not to flinch. Dealing with pain was something she'd trained for, though, it didn't come easily. She looked into the Bastian's eyes. They were pools of darkness, but with a ripple of gold around the iris. It was like staring down into a pond in the middle of a moonless night. It was like letting the sky unfold, unencumbered before her.

"We're not lost," Mara said quietly, swallowing hard against the knife pressed through her scarf. "We need your help."

Mara switched her gaze to the captain on board the ship. Leaning against the banister, Captain Osanna listened to the words shared between her crewman and Mara.

"As Bastians, you have no interest in the politics of the Jeweled Realm, save for the riches the queen can drain into your pockets." Mara spoke loudly so the captain would hear her.

Captain Osanna coughed a short laugh. "Ain't that the truth." Several crew members gathered around their captain and laughed along.

Mara swallowed again, bracing herself for the words about to rush from her lips. There was a part of her that thought it a bad idea. A part that knew once she spoke the words—the truth of who she really was—the game would be over.

Her life would be over.

But there was another part of her that reached for freedom. A part of her that yearned for sunshine and air. For the truth to be spoken and the shadows of lies to be cast away forever. She clung to those truths now, hoping they'd buoy her upward and out of the pit.

"We seek refuge aboard your ship, for passage to your island, to . . . " she hesitated, realizing she didn't know how she planned on reclaiming her throne, only knowing that she must. " . . . to coordinate an effort to reclaim my throne."

Captain Osanna stood straighter, her hand on the banister now. "*Your* throne?"

"When I am reseated upon the throne," Mara continued, ignoring the mumbling now going on amidst the group of Bastians, "I will reward you and your queen handsomely. Whatever you ask. Whatever it takes." She stood motionless then, allowing the captain to fully take her in. The Bastian holding a knife to her throat looked from Mara to her captain, confused at the turn of events and unsure of what to do. Boden held his breath, and Mara could feel his stillness.

Finally, Captain Osanna smiled. She bowed her head curtly and then motioned to the knife wielder to let Mara go. "Best get you aboard, Your Majesty," she said.

With the knife removed from her throat, Mara swallowed and relaxed her shoulders. A sense of relief washed over her. They approached the gangplank. Their travels, their survival at the chateau, all seemed worth it then. They'd soon leave the Jeweled Realm, and she'd be able to breathe once again.

And then, maybe a plan would come to her.

But a voice hailed them from behind. Mara stopped with one foot on the gangplank, Boden hesitating behind her. A guard of Bouzy stood at the end of the dock. The golden medal dangling from his chest marked him as a captain. Not a nobody. "Everything alright, Osanna?" he called up to the woman.

Osanna smirked. Her eyebrows twitched as she painted an amused expression across her face. There was a clear heat between the pair, and Captain Osanna seemed agitated by it. "Fine, Captain Porcher." Osanna offered her fakest smile. "Just business."

Captain Porcher drifted his gaze over Mara and Boden. He seemed to linger over Mara, his eyes narrowing. "Bastians don't normally take Jewels onto their ships, do they? Some sort of unwritten law you have?"

Osanna's smile dissolved. "What I do on my ship is my business, Porcher." She motioned with her head for the knife-wielding Bastian to push Mara and Boden up the gangplank and onto the ship. Mara obeyed, but felt her chest tighten when she stepped down onto the deck rather than the imminent relief she expected.

"This woman is a premier cartographer." Osanna grasped Mara by the elbow. "And her assistant"—she gestured to Boden—"are guests upon my ship."

Porcher nodded. "Then why's Aleen got her blade out? Seems a strange way to escort esteemed guests onto a ship."

The knife wielder, Aleen, hid her knife, its existence disappearing like a wave rolled under. She displayed her empty hands to Porcher.

"I repeat," Osanna said, "what I do on my ship is my business. Now, I'm late for disembarking. You know timeliness is holy to me, Porcher."

"Aye, I remember," he replied.

But he didn't move. He stared up into Mara's eyes, searching. Her throat tightened, threatening to suffocate her, but she didn't move or look away. She would weather this storm. She would prove she wasn't afraid.

Osanna waited no longer. She shouted orders to the crew standing around her, who immediately moved into motion. They hoisted sails and untethered ropes. Bastian voices, their words melodically filling the breeze, rang from all sides.

"Returning home, Osanna? Or calling on another port?" Porcher called to Osanna.

The captain glared at the man. Her eyebrows were set and her lips pursed. She sighed before answering. "Like you care, Porcher." She turned her back on him.

With a whip of her head, she instructed Aleen to escort Mara and Boden behind her. Mara gladly followed, but felt Porcher's eyes on her the entire way.

"Do not worry," Aleen told them as they followed Osanna. "The captain reserves a special hate for Porcher. You are unlikely to receive the same."

"What did he do?" Boden asked.

"The less you know, the better," Aleen said, "But I tell you this for free..." Boden and Mara leaned in close to hear Aleen's advice. "Do not humiliate a Bastian woman."

Chapter Twenty-Six

They waited inside Captain Osanna's quarters. The stained windows, from the inside, bled vibrant colors across the scrubbed wooden floor. Blues and purples gave way to reds and whites. A purple panther lurked within a field of red flowers in the glass.

An ornately carved desk sat in the center, held aloft with legs ending in four carved claws. Two leather chairs, aged but luxurious, sat opposite the desk.

Mara looked at Boden, wanting to say something but not knowing what. Her feet were no longer planted on the soil of her realm. Throughout all her travels, she had never, not once, left the actual earth that bore her. She felt like the ship itself, untethered and loose in the waves.

But would Boden understand that? His eyes were still guarded, and Mara suddenly found herself desperately wanting him to smile at her, just once, like he had before.

When Osanna finally entered the cabin, the ship had turned and made headway through the narrow entrance of the port. It rolled and shifted with the waves but moved swiftly and deftly. Osanna slumped into a chair behind her desk and stared up at them. Up close, fine wrinkles decorated around her eyes and lips. Dark freckles hung on a deep brown forehead. A tattoo on her neck was indistinguishable, blurred by time.

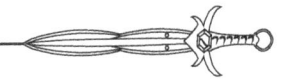

"Cartographer. That's certainly a new title for me," Mara said, hoping to ease the tension in the cabin.

Aleen stood nearby, knife out once more, flipping it in her hand. Another crew member burst into the room, and Aleen barked at the man in Bastian. He backed away quickly, muttering what must have been an apology.

"I suppose you're more accustomed to *Your Majesty*, Mara of House Black," Osanna said.

Osanna leaned back in her chair, a sense of ease appearing to flood over her the farther from the docks the ship moved. It was clear by looking at her she was one with the water. She had probably spent her whole life on it, more a fish than a panther. Of the sea and not the land.

But the sea was unpredictable. More so than land could be. Mara wondered if they had made a mistake.

"Thank you. For saving us," Mara said. "And I give you my word, your queen will have whatever she asks for once I retrieve my throne."

"Yes," Osanna said, "that pesky problem."

She reached for something on her desk and withdrew a sheet of paper. A wanted poster. Mara's face was neatly block pressed on it next to Boden's.

"*Wanted: Liar Queen and Ursan Traitor*," she read.

Boden choked on a laugh. "I betrayed no one."

"Your Kalda will be the judge of that, I wager," Osanna said. She placed the paper back on her desk. "Have you any idea how much your life is worth if I turn you in?" she asked Mara.

Mara shrugged. "I imagine my sister had a hard time assigning any value to my life, but necessity dictates she offers something worth people's time."

Osanna nodded. "So I can either trust a deposed queen or trust an undead one."

She stared at Mara then, her foot tapping out a rhythm Mara didn't know. If Osanna was hoping Mara would give her an answer, would drop to her knees and plead, she'd be waiting a long time.

"Well," Osanna finally said, "I know too well what Queen Hali will request." She stood and walked to the stained-glass window, peering between panther paws and grass. "Your sister has placed an embargo on all Bastian goods sold to anyone outside the Jeweled Realm."

Boden leaped to his feet. "But the Ursans trade heavily with Bastia. Without it, we are left only with what we can scrounge from the earth."

"A fact I'm sure she is aware of." Osanna looked at Boden over her shoulder. "It bodes ill for Bastia, too. Your continent is not our only source of trade. We panthers travel to faraway seas, to lands you could only dream of." She walked to a nearby cellarette. The wood was a handsome red. Large golden hinges held two doors shut. Atop were glass bottles of various liquids, secured from the rolling waves by golden girding. Osanna retrieved one of these bottles and a copper mug from behind the doors and poured herself a drink. "Unfortunately, your continent acts as gatekeeper to our travels. The ocean to the west is unmanageable and dangerous. It is said not a single ship has crossed it since creation." She sipped her drink and leaned against her desk. "So we travel east, past the Jeweled Realm's coastal lands, past the Waste, and past Ursa, trading as we go. For your sister to stop us . . . it would be the ruin of our people."

"Another fact I'm sure she's aware of," Mara said.

Osanna locked eyes with Mara again. They were a deep chestnut with flecks of gold. Warm and inviting. Mara felt she could trust this woman, though, she didn't know fully why. She had done so little trusting over the course of her life. Instead, she inflicted fear to promote obedience.

But she could never call it trust.

That was until Boden. She glanced at him now, seated again, his jaw grinding away. The wanted poster labeled him an Ursan traitor, but he had betrayed no one. It was he who had been betrayed.

"Can you not overpower her?" Mara asked. "Bastians are known for their naval ability. Set fire to her fleet."

Osanna shot back the rest of her drink, slamming the mug on her desk. A swell of the ocean threw the ship sideways, but the furniture was bolted down. The mug, however, slid along the desk, stopping just short of the edge. Osanna stared at it, frowning.

"We tried. Iris equipped her fleet with some sort of demonic fire. Once they sling it across the sky, it shatters and spreads, sticking to our ships. Nothing puts it out, nothing gets it off. We've lost several warships. Queen Hali deemed it unprofitable to continue."

Demonic fire? Mara could only imagine what that looked like. Outside the window, the waves fell and rose with the ship. The coastline drifted farther and farther away, Bouzy growing smaller and smaller.

Perhaps Iris *was* a demon.

"The fire is nothing more than a parlor trick," Osanna said, seeing Mara's worried stare. "Regardless, it is impossible to remove the substance, whatever it is." She sighed. "Bastia does not believe in your sister's powers, but we do believe she holds something over the people of the Waste, and now the Jeweled Realm. And soon, she may take aim at the Isles. And that, Queen Hali will never let her do."

"So, what?" Mara pulled her gaze back to the woman with the warm eyes. "What would Queen Hali request in return for her help?"

Osanna returned to her chair. She interlaced her fingers and set a smile on her face. "Remove the embargo. Ensure our trade routes."

"That's it?"

Osanna shrugged. "I am not the queen, but I can assure you, Queen Hali is fair. She will see the preservation of our way of life as a fair trade for your retention of the throne."

Mara nodded. "Fine," she said. "Take me to your queen."

Osanna smiled again. "Bastians understand little of the Jeweled Realm, besides your ports. We know how you choose your queens. We know you favor . . . a certain ferocity over generosity."

"You can trust me," Mara said without hesitation. "I may be the product of my mother, but that doesn't make me my mother." She glanced at Boden, who was staring out the window. The words she had spoken to Boden in the chateau felt heavy in her chest. It was true, all of it, but so were the words she spoke to Osanna.

Hours later, Mara sat alone on deck. She leaned over the banister, watching the horizon appear and disappear with the roll of the ocean. Her stomach lurched, and she retched over the side. It was a wonder there was anything left for her to vomit, having sat near the banister and released her food several times already.

Aleen approached her, a pitying look on her face. She cradled a small cloth in her hand. Sitting next to Mara, she unwrapped it, displaying a hunk of bread.

"Sea bread," she said, suggesting Mara take a piece. "A Bastian staple on voyages. It settles the stomach." When Mara hesitated, she added, "It tastes like your butter bread. Better even, if I say so." She smiled, but Mara couldn't return it.

Mara's hand shook as she retrieved the small piece Aleen extended to her. At her lips, the salty scent brought on another spasm of her stomach. She stood and retched water into the wind. Aleen produced another cloth from her pocket and handed it to Mara instead.

"The young ones are much the same," she assured Mara. "When they first start on the ships, they all spend time hugging the railing."

"I am not young," Mara said between heaves. She took several deep breaths, attempting to soothe her stomach. It seemed to work, so she sat slowly on the step next to Aleen. "Rumor is you start your children at ten on the ships." She coughed but held down any more vomit. "A hard life for a youth, is it not?"

Aleen smiled crookedly, amused. Up close, Mara realized the woman was not much older than she. Gone was her hat with the white feather nearly moving on its own in the wind. Her hair was plaited. Six of the plaits hung off her head and down her back, like snakes. Colored thread weaved within the strands, vivid in the sea of black. "Is warcraft and weapons at five not a hard life, Jeweled Queen?"

Mara shrugged, wiping spit off her chin. "Fair enough."

"What is it you work so hard to do?" Aleen asked. "To rule, or to conquer?"

"Are they not the same thing?" Mara said.

Aleen laughed—a sweet sound—before stopping when she realized Mara was serious. "There is a difference, Jeweled One. And perhaps once you learn it, the Shipwright will see fit to bring you back to your throne."

"The Shipwright?" Mara asked.

"Our creator," Aleen said, pointing to some vague space amongst the sky. "Our god."

"Ah"—Mara leaned back on the step—"you would have me pray, like Boden to his Kalda?"

Aleen batted her words away. "The Ursans focus too much on Kalda. His works were great, yes, but they spoke for a greater one."

Mara frowned. "I was unaware the Bastians were religious. I have to say, I'm a bit disappointed. Is not the sea your mother?"

Aleen laughed, fully this time, tipping her head back and throwing the sound to the wind. Mara felt tension release from all the vomiting. It was nice to hear laughter once again, so free and musical. Mara admired the woman.

When Aleen finally stopped, she watched the rise and fall of the waves. "Aye, our mother, sure. Cold. Unrelenting."

"Sounds like mine," Mara said.

Aleen shot her a small smile. "The Shipwright breathed life into humans. The ocean, though womanly, is not seen as our mother, not really." She sighed and leaned back, nudging Mara as she did so. "Who can claim the ocean, anyway? So wild. So powerful. No, the ocean is herself. No one does she own, and no one owns her."

"Sounds dangerous."

"The most dangerous." Aleen winked. "It is why most Bastians don't attempt a life at sea. Only the strongest manage it. The rest remain in the Isles. A useful life, but not dangerously so."

"And your queen?" Mara asked. "Does she traverse the ocean so easily?"

"Queen Hali?" Aleen sat forward, a serious note in her voice. "She has not left the palace for many years."

"Why?"

Aleen swallowed, not looking Mara in the face. "When Queen Hali birthed the crown prince, his twin sister was stillborn. The queen was wounded by the loss. Both in body and in soul. She remains at the palace, guardian of the princess's memory on this earth."

Mara nodded, though, she didn't know why. It was a confirmation of sorts, this information from Aleen, that the Bastian queen was human. Possibly even weak. Mara could handle the manipulation of a weak woman, but that tiny voice was back again, telling her it wasn't true. Telling her that her mother had lied to her when she told her what weakness really was so long ago.

About what made a woman strong.

"And the crown prince?" Mara asked.

"He travels on her behalf, engaging with the people, doing for her what she cannot do."

"What she *won't* do," Mara corrected.

Aleen shrugged. "Two sides of the same sword, Jeweled One. Could you not rule your kingdom without this sword you call sacred?"

"No," Mara said. "The Sword is powerful. It is power itself. With it, the wielder commands a certain strength and authority. They are unbeatable."

"And yet you lost. On a dam, I hear." Aleen played with the end of one of her plaits, an amused glimmer in her eyes. "Did I not say water was dangerous?" She stood and stretched, her lean body glimmering with sea salt where her clothes exposed her skin. She leaned against the banister and admired the swelling blue ocean. "You could rule without it, if you chose to. But you don't. You believe the Sword wields some amazing power, but you do not stop to consider that perhaps it is the one who wields it with the power."

Mara scowled. A heat spread across her skin, prickling where she had just been cold from the ocean spray. Her mouth moved to speak the dark words spreading in her chest, but Captain Osanna appeared on the steps.

"Don't you have work to do, Aleen?" Osanna asked.

"Of course, Captain." Aleen tipped her head at the woman before vanishing down the steps.

Osanna watched Mara shuffle from foot to foot, attempting to get a grip on her temper. Mara turned away from the old woman, crossed her arms, and stared at the horizon. A trick, one sailor had told her, to conquer her seasickness.

"Something bothering you?" Osanna said, arriving next to her, studying the same horizon. "Aleen can be . . . forward at times."

"She said nothing I haven't heard before," Mara replied.

Boden had said almost the same thing, back in the high forests of the mountains. Or near enough to it. But they were wrong. Weren't they? Mara furrowed her brow, attempting to think back, to physically remember the Sword's heavy hilt in her hand, to feel the pulsing power deep within her bones when she held it.

"The Ursan prince informed me you have lost your Sacred Sword?"

The captain read her like a book. Mara forced her face to relax, tired of being so easily read. She would have to remind Boden later that he'd sworn allegiance to her, which meant he should keep his mouth shut.

"Yes," she said, "as I fought my sister on Roully Dam."

"Water can be dangerous," Osanna echoed Aleen's words.

They stood silently together, letting the calls of the ship's crew and the waves of the ocean converse. Land was but a thin line on the horizon now. Gulls no longer followed the ship, weaving between the masts. Osanna had informed them it was at least seven suns before they'd reach the Isles, then another two to maneuver between the many islands and reach the large port of Colendos. This would be the noise of Mara's days, from waking until falling asleep in her hammock beneath deck, next to Boden.

"Might I ask, Jeweled Queen, why you let your sister live?"

Mara sighed. She grew so tired of answering that question. "I don't know." Her hands balled themselves into fists, but she didn't know what to do with them. Had she her sword, she would have wrapped her hands around it and cut something down until she felt the heat of anger abate and the wave of agitation relent. But with nothing, she inhaled deeply and exhaled, forcing her hands to relax. "I did not wish to kill her," she finally admitted, feeling once again like a slight weight lifted from her chest.

Osanna nodded. "To kill a sister would be a terrible thing."

"Do you have any?" Mara asked.

With a smirk, Osanna said, "I call one sister. Queen Hali."

Mara shifted away from Osanna. She took the old woman in once again, trying to find any sort of regal air to her. But there was none. The woman was meant for the sea and had been one with it for a long time.

Osanna did not look at Mara. Instead, she gazed at the horizon, letting Mara stare all she wanted. "We are a beginning and end," Osanna continued, still watching the sun reach for the horizon, "between us, four brothers."

"Four?"

"Loud and bothersome, each one." She winked at Mara. "But also kind and brave. And dead."

Mara didn't know what to say, so she kept her mouth tightly shut lest something insensitive spewed out. Brave did not necessarily mean they'd been good warriors. She waited for Osanna to continue, wanting to hear more about the Bastian royal family.

"A war between the Isles broke out when we were young." Osanna continued. "They all joined our parents on the ships leaving for battle. And they never returned."

"With your parents?" Mara asked. "How old were you?"

Osanna picked at a splinter of wood on the banister. "Twelve. Hali was twenty. Already a woman and perfectly capable of ruling the Isles."

"But was she *ready*?"

Osanna finally brought her gold-flecked eyes to Mara's. Within them was a wealth of knowledge. *She's seen things no other has,* Mara thought. And with it, learned so much that Mara never would.

"Who is ever ready for the throne, Jeweled Queen? Were you? Even after your performance, even after feigning the death of your sister, were you ready? Or, perhaps, you *had* killed her, like intended. Would that have made you *more* ready?"

"I-I suppose I wasn't ready," Mara stuttered, the words falling out before she could stop them. "I don't deserve it. I think about it all the time. I didn't do it—I didn't kill her. I didn't earn the Sacred Sword. I don't deserve to be queen."

Osanna's hand clasped Mara's elbow. She leaned in and whispered, "Sometimes, those that rule are held there by an unjust chain. It takes strength to break it. But I think you will, Jeweled One." She released Mara and straightened her jacket. "My sister punished herself for my niece's death. You punish yourself for your sister's life." Osanna turned to go but stopped on the bottom step. She looked over her shoulder with a smile before adding, "The world is full of people who do not deserve what they have, Jeweled One. A throne. A kingdom. Loyalty. I suggest you do your best to deserve it, whatever it is you end up with."

Osanna's words sunk into Mara's chest, and she grew heavy with thought. She sat on the deck until the sun was nearly gone, watching its body sink beneath the horizon, shooting sharp slices of scarlet in the sky as its last dying act. She found Boden below deck, lying in a hammock and eating an apple.

When he saw her, he sliced off a piece and offered it to her. "Here," he said, "you should eat."

Mara took it, their fingers brushing together briefly before Boden withdrew his hand. She nibbled at the fruit and studied him. A lantern hung on the nearby post, illuminating his face darkly. His eyes were still closed off, as if he were preoccupied with deeper thoughts than Mara.

"Are you alright?" he asked her, his voice cutting through the shadows, reverberating on her chest.

Mara smiled. "I was going to ask you the same thing."

Boden began to roll his eyes but stopped, instead setting his jaw rigid as he cut off another piece of apple and offered it to her. "I'm fine."

Mara held the apple slice in her hand but didn't eat it. She sank into the hammock opposite Boden, watching his features dance in the lantern's glow. His beard was growing back, hiding his dimple. Mara found herself admitting she liked the beard more. While she hadn't liked them at first, she had grown accustomed to Boden's Ursan features: the beard, the sharply cut jaw, and those penetrating eyes.

"Boden," Mara said, staring down at her fingers as she fiddled with the apple slice, her fingers growing sticky with its juice, "about the chateau . . ."

"Don't, Mara," Boden nearly growled.

Mara flicked her eyes up to his, and even in the dim light of the lantern, she could see the heaviness Boden carried, hidden beneath his skin. The weight of the second born, perhaps, but also the weight of a good man. A man who did what was right, no matter the cost, no matter the difficulty. Because he wanted to. Because he chose to.

"I just wanted to . . ." the word stuck in her throat, having never required its use before, "apologize."

"You don't have to," he spoke over the apple in his mouth. Boden swallowed hard and stared at the apple in his hand, thinking. When he finally looked up at her, his eyes were open, and Mara felt seen once again. "I know you, Mara. You don't . . ." he hesitated, like the words were difficult to wrench from his mouth, "you don't have to apologize to me. Ever."

Mara smiled and felt the uncontrollable pull then. She launched forward, knocking Boden's knife away as she kissed him deeply. He dropped the apple and grabbed her arms to pull her closer, but Mara pushed herself away as suddenly as she had attacked him.

"No," she said. "Just the one. We must remain focused." She delicately wiped the touch of Boden's lips from her mouth and slouched back into her hammock.

She watched his face dissolve into a disappointed amusement before nodding. "As you wish, Sword Queen." He retrieved his knife and apple.

"My name is Mara," she said as she rolled away from him, still smiling.

Chapter Twenty-Seven

The darkness was thick below deck. As Mara hung in her hammock and Boden slept nearby, she felt like she'd fallen into the night sky itself. If she stared hard enough, her stomach would lurch at the uneasiness of not knowing where one was in space. A sudden shift of the ship in a wave would send her head reeling. She finally closed her eyes, breathing in and out through her nose, reliving the brief moment her lips met Boden's in every excruciating detail.

Eventually, Mara slept.

A crack of thunder woke her, but she was already in the air when her eyes blinked open and she was thrown from her hammock. A gaping hole in the ship's side stared at her. Fire illuminated everything, stinging her eyes with light and smoke.

"Mara!" Boden coughed, his arms swinging into the chaotic light to find her.

"Here!" she called out, only to be cut short by another deafening crack. This time, she watched as the wooden hull of the ship exploded farther down. The Bastians that had occupied those hammocks were already gone, manning their battle stations.

Boden gripped her wrist and pulled her into his arms. "We've got to get up top," he yelled.

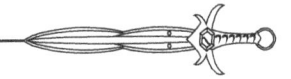

She allowed him to pull her toward the stairs leading upward to the deck, fresh air, and the night sky. They were intact, though, the hull burned nearby. Boden shoved Mara up the steps ahead of him, grabbing other Bastians behind him and thrusting them forward as well.

"Boden!" Mara called, the rush of the ship's crew ushering her farther away from him.

"Jeweled One!" Aleen yelled upon seeing Mara. She reached Mara as Boden did, each gripping one of her arms.

"What's going on?" Boden asked.

The ship shook from the Bastians' cannon fire. The crew members were yelling far below on the cannon decks, loading and firing the giant guns.

"Porcher followed us," Aleen spat. "He did not hail us, but opened fire once the moon was dressed in darkness." She pointed with her knife to the glowing moon, dulled behind thick gray clouds.

"Bastard," Boden growled. "He must have figured out who you are, Mara."

"Well, he messed with the wrong captain," Aleen laughed madly. "I told you he humiliated Osanna. Bastian women do not forget easily. Or forgive."

Osanna appeared above them, leaning over the banister of the quarterdeck, barking orders. A flame within her had been lit, and the woman's eyes appeared to glow. It was surely the reflection of the fire slowly engulfing the ship, but fear filled Mara then. A base fear. A fear that made one want their mother.

This should have been her fight, but now the Bastians' ship was listing to one side while they continued to fire on one of Mara's realm's own ships. She watched the ship of the line, her own crest decorating its sails, turn broadside again, prepared to send another volley of fire.

"Get the Jeweled Queen to a boat," Osanna called down to Aleen. "She must escape."

Aleen called back in obedience and then tightened her grip on Mara's arm. "To the boats," she said. "We'll get you as far away as we can."

"I can't leave." Mara tried to free herself, but Aleen's grip was certain.

"You must." Aleen's good-natured smile was gone. In its stead was a serious face carved of darkness. "The only way to ensure Porcher's failure is to ensure your survival."

"But, Osanna . . . " Mara tried to pull away again, but now Boden was pulling her other arm and hauling her in the direction Aleen directed them toward.

"The captain will be fine," Aleen assured her, dragging her past crowds of Bastians, all obediently following Osanna's howling commands.

Mara turned to Boden, hoping her eyes would plead her case, but he shook his head.

"It can't end this way," he said. "We have to get you out of here."

A shock of wood erupted nearby, sending splinters down on them like hail. The mast creaked and groaned, tipping toward them. Aleen yelled and shoved Mara out of the way. Mara landed on her knees, pain shrieking through her legs, before Boden hauled her to her feet.

The mast crashed to the deck and ripped off the nearby banister. Several Bastians fell into the churning sea, its waves hungrily greeting them.

Aleen appeared from a gap beneath the damaged mast, shaken but not hurt. "Keep going, Jeweled One," she said, a smile daring to cross her lips as she joined Mara's side again You've many days left to live."

They reached the rear of the ship where pulleys were already in play. Aleen barked at the crew, who replied in unison and lowered the lifeboat toward the waves.

"Osanna told them to get you on the boat," Aleen said.

She pointed down the back of the great ship, where a ladder was built into the wooden slats. Mara looked over the edge, her stomach shifting with a sudden jolt of the ship. Porcher continued to assault the Bastians, striking again and again with cannon and fire. And yet Mara could not bring her feet to start the descent to her only chance of survival.

"This isn't your war," she said to Aleen. "Tell Osanna to stop. Don't do this."

"Do what, Jeweled One? Fight?" Aleen held out her arms, displaying the chaos around her. "We are Bastians! To fight is in our blood. From the sea we came, to the sea we return." And when Mara held back her tears, Aleen placed a gentle hand on her shoulder. "Death is nothing to fear, my jewel, for it comes for us all. But . . . now is not your time."

Aleen nodded to Boden, who bowed his head in return. He placed both hands around Mara and thrust her toward the ladder. The tears broke then, spilling over her lower lids and splashing down her cheeks, yet she did not cry out. She let them fall, silently, as she descended the ladder and settled into the seat of the bobbing lifeboat. When Boden sat across from her, he grabbed both oars. Only then did he look at her face and see her pain. Mara could tell he wanted to say something, but there were no words to heal her.

She looked up while Boden rowed them away, listening to the groaning sounds of the ship as she slowly sank. Voices, foreign in accent and tongue, continued to fill the darkening sky. Fire licked at everything.

For her.

Porcher had only attacked because he'd realized who Mara was. Osanna had only agreed to bring them aboard because she'd known who Mara was.

Mara. The cause for so much death.

She turned away, her eyes attempting to dissect the darkness growing over the waves, trying to discern water from sky. By sparing one life, she had sentenced so many more to death.

The screams continued long after the ship sank.

In the morning, gulls cried. Their noise awoke Mara, who didn't know she had fallen asleep. The night had been so absolute, so black, she hadn't realized her own eyes had closed. Boden lay slack next to her, still asleep. Around them, the water glittered with the morning sun. All that was left of Osanna's ship was a trickle of black smoke on the horizon, smeared across the beautiful morning.

"Boden." Mara nudged him. "Boden, wake up." Her voice was hoarse from breathing in the smoke of Porcher's fire attacks. She smacked her lips, attempting to moisten her dry mouth, but nothing seemed to help. "Boden!" She slapped him on the arm.

The Ursan stirred. He rolled over and glanced at her, his eyes still veiled in sleep. "What?"

"We survived." She looked around, but spied no trailing ship, no Porcher on their heels. "For now," she added.

Boden grunted with his efforts to sit upright. He stretched and yawned and looked around himself. "But where are we?"

Mara shrugged. She started digging around in the sacks at their feet, supplies tossed in haphazardly by the Bastians. Her hands felt the smooth leather of a waterskin. When it was free of the bag, she yanked the stopper away and lifted the mouth to her lips. It was the coolest, sweetest kiss she'd ever received.

When she finished, she thrust the skin at Boden, but he shook his head no. "We should save it. Who knows how long we'll be out here?"

"Drink," she commanded, "at least once. You've inhaled too much smoke. Your throat is bound to burn as mine does."

He stared at her and only relented when she refused to put the waterskin away. Water trickled down his beard like diamonds. Mara wiped them away, sucking the moisture from her fingers, refusing to waste a single drop.

Once watered, they surveyed their surroundings, which were nothing but blue. Clouds moved like cows in the sky, slow and meandering. Mara could feel no wind and wondered if they were even drifting.

"I almost wished we'd stayed on the ship," Boden finally sighed. "At least we'd know definitively if we were dead or alive."

Something far to their left caught Mara's eyes. She shushed Boden, who glared at her but obeyed.

"What is it?" he whispered.

With her hand held above her brow, deflecting the sun's rays from her eyes, Mara peered at the object. "It's something," she said, "wreckage perhaps, from Osanna's ship."

"What should we do?"

Mara glanced at the oars tucked neatly inside the lifeboat. She looked back at Boden. "I suggest you row."

Boden said nothing as he hauled the heavy wooden oars from inside the hull and set them in the oarlocks. His row was slow but steady. Mara kept her eyes on the wreckage, never looking away. Her eyes watered with the effort, and soon her vision grew blurry. She hastily wiped the tears away before refocusing on the flotsam.

The closer they came, the surer Mara was that it was a large piece of Osanna's ship floating idly in the waves, and the closer they came, the surer she was that there was someone on it. "Boden," she said, "there's someone there. I see someone! Hurry!"

Boden increased his speed as ordered, but only just so. Mara attempted to keep her patience, but her stomach floated in her like the waves upon the sea. *Dead or alive,* she wondered. *Dead or alive?*

Finally, they rowed within earshot.

"Hello?" she called to the body. "Are you alright?"

Slowly, the head raised off the wood of the floating hull. She thought she saw lips trying to move, but she could not understand.

"Faster," she encouraged Boden. "I think they're alive."

"For how long?" Boden muttered, trying his best to increase his already slowing speed.

When they reached the debris, Boden slammed the oars down and leaned back in his seat, exhausted. Mara reached for the survivor, an older Bastian woman she vaguely remembered seeing onboard.

"Are you alright?" Mara whispered, carefully taking the woman's arm.

The woman's eyes—warm earth on a fall day—opened. "Gone," she whispered. "All gone."

Mara tried not to frown. "I know," she said. "I'm sorry."

Together, Boden and Mara hauled the woman into their lifeboat without tipping. It was a miracle, Boden said, and expounded upon the grace of Kalda. Mara shushed him and tried offering the woman water.

"We need shade," the woman said, "or heatstroke will kill us long before dehydration."

She instructed them on how to set up the lifeboat's tent—a cover equipped on all Bastian boats for just such occasions. Once up, a cloth canopy shaded most of the boat, save for the bow.

"Now, water," she sighed.

When she had had her fill, she handed the waterskin back to Mara. The skin was nearly empty.

"There should be three more beneath that seat," the woman said to Mara, pointing to Boden's bench. "There are always four in a lifeboat. Osanna was a stickler for rules."

"And did you see her?" Mara asked. "Osanna? Before the ship sank?"

The woman nodded slowly, staring off into the waves. Mara knew she was reliving the night, as she herself had done repeatedly since waking.

"She told me to jump," the woman said, still staring out at the ocean. "She told me to save myself. So I did."

"She was an excellent captain," Boden assured the woman.

She finally pulled her eyes from the waves and looked at him. "Yes, Ursan prince, and she died for you and your Jeweled One. So we best not make it in vain."

The woman swiveled in her seat—her turn to study their surroundings. She examined the sky and the sun and finally set her gaze just over her left shoulder. "That way, Ursan. We need to row that way."

Boden followed her gaze. "And just how far do you expect me to row?"

The woman shrugged. "As long as it takes?"

Boden scowled, but Mara swatted his arm. "Pick up the oars," she said, using her queenly voice. "We can't just sit here."

Grumbling Ursan words beneath his breath, Boden picked up the oars and rowed, turning the boat in the direction the Bastian woman had indicated.

"What is your name?" Mara asked her.

The woman looked at Mara out of the corner of her eye. "Xida."

"I saw you on the ship, but only briefly."

"I am the cook . . . or was the cook. Doesn't matter now, does it? From the sea we came, to the sea we return."

Mara nodded, though, she didn't know why. "She is owned by no one," Mara whispered the words of Aleen, remembering the way her lips had formed the words so perfectly, "and no one does she own."

Xida turned to face Mara fully, impressed with her words. "A student of Aleen, I see. She prided herself on her words. A poet, I imagine, she wanted to be. Not a quartermaster. Not on a ship."

"She said the water was dangerous."

Xida chuckled. "The most dangerous."

"And that only the strongest survive."

Xida acknowledged Mara's memory of Aleen's words with a nod before handing Mara a medal. Perhaps it had once hung from a ribbon, for a frayed fragment was all that remained. Stamped on the surface was a roaring panther, foot firmly planted on a skull. Mara turned it over to find something written in Bastian.

"Osanna handed me that before I jumped. She told me to give it to her sister. But I think you better be the one to do it."

Chapter Twenty-Eight

They floated for nearly three days. The waterskins were close to empty, and Mara couldn't stomach the idea of eating another piece of the dry, flat crust Bastians dared call bread. But Xida didn't seem worried. In fact, she seemed distracted. She searched the horizon line continuously, barely able to maintain conversation.

"What are you looking for?" Mara finally asked, her patience run thin by the unceasing movement of the ocean.

"A ship." Xida didn't even look at Mara. "I've navigated us into a trade line. A Bastian ship should be by."

Mara sat up a little straighter. "A trade line?"

Boden moaned, perhaps to demonstrate his hope in a passing ship, but he leaned back on his bench exhausted. While they had all taken turns rowing, Boden insisted on doing most of the work. His hands bled from erupted blisters, chapped and cracked from the relentless wind that constantly whipped at them.

"He'll need a doctor," Xida whispered to Mara. "His hands will become infected should we not get them clean soon."

Mara reached for Boden's sweat-covered forehead to feel for the signs of an early fever. He closed his eyes sleepily at her touch. She turned to Xida. "As you say."

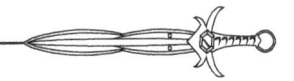

When the sun was high, Mara began to lose hope. Perhaps they had missed the ship, or perhaps Xida was wrong, and they were nowhere near the trade line. But Xida continued to search the horizon. She had instructed Boden earlier in the day to rest, that floating within the line would be fine and she would wake him should they need to maneuver into the pathway of a ship.

He gently snored. Dark circles beneath his eyes aged him. Mara no longer saw the youngest Ursan prince. She shivered. How could life age one so quickly?

Xida sat up. She leaned into her hand and peered toward the glare of sun over the water. "There." She pointed.

"Where?" Mara tried and failed to see what the woman saw. "I see nothing."

Xida muttered in Bastian. "You've not lived on the ocean. Your eyes are unaccustomed to her," she added.

Mara frowned at the suggestion that she was lacking in any shape or form and sighed as she squinted into the sun. The glare of light was too strong for her. She blinked away bright flashes, still unable to make out anything.

Xida laughed at her. "Easy, Jeweled One, just wait. You'll see it soon enough."

Time did not pass quickly enough for Mara, but eventually—yes, she could see it. A dark speck upon the horizon. It drew closer, incrementally, until finally it became a discernible ship.

Mara shook Boden to wake him. "A ship, Boden! There's a ship!"

But he only murmured and wouldn't rouse.

Xida looked over him, brows furrowed as she fumbled her hand against his forehead. "The fever's taken. We need to get him aboard as soon as possible."

Mara counted her breaths. It was the only way to pass the time, or else she'd stare at Boden and count *his* breaths, and she didn't know if she'd end up counting his last one. Her hand reached for his and held it tightly. Xida watched without saying a word.

The sun had started to sink for the day by the time the ship was close enough to hail. Xida yelled across the waves and received a reply immediately in Bastian.

"Thank the Shipwright." A faint smile broke over Xida's face. "There was a chance it was pirates." Mara stared wide-eyed at the woman. "What? I wasn't going to worry you, Jeweled One, with things we cannot control. Not when you worry over the Ursan. I knew someone would come along and find us. It was better than dying adrift."

Mara turned from Xida. Why had pirates never crossed her mind? There was so little she knew, she realized, as she settled her sights on Boden. She wanted to rouse him, to shake him until he opened his eyes. She suddenly realized how much she missed their color.

"Will he live?" she asked Xida, her voice barely audible over the waves and continued yelling of the sailors on the nearby ship.

Xida sighed. "If he's meant to, he will."

"I do not believe in your god," Mara said. "You can speak to me plainly. In terms of medicine and odds of survival, will he live?"

The Bastian ship was nearly upon them. Mara could make out distinct faces, all shadows beneath their dark hair, but faces nevertheless.

Xida cast her eyes from her nearing people and back to Mara. She smiled. "Odds of survival? Why, so you can start peeling your soul from him now? So that the sting of death won't hurt as much?" Xida shook her head. "You are a child. A queen, aye, but a child. Your *docteurs* treat ailments and injuries with poultices and herbal mixtures taught by Bastian doctors long ago, before the Jeweled Realm laid waste to such relationships. We studied corpses long before your queens started making them. *Bastians*. We understand more—much more—than you, Jeweled One. So hear my words when I say: *he will live if he is meant to.*"

Mara turned away from the old woman. She wouldn't be spoken to that way were she still home. Were she still queen. Her fingers tightened reflexively around Boden's, hoping he'd return a squeeze of his own, but he didn't. He lay across the bench, his breaths shallow.

The ship was lowering its own lifeboat now, Bastians yelling back and forth with Xida. She returned a call and smiled back at Mara. "They'll tow us toward their ship," she said. "Then we'll climb aboard."

"And what of Boden?" Mara asked.

Xida studied him before turning away. "They'll haul him up with a pulley in the boat."

The Bastian lifeboat cuddled up next to their own, and the pearly smile of a Bastian sailor greeted Mara. "I must be the first to tell the captain what we've found: a jewel fit for a crown," he said.

Mara didn't mean to return his smile, but it came unbidden. She felt the flush of her cheeks, more frustration than embarrassment. Her claim to the throne didn't concern her, not in that moment. Only Boden. Only his breathing, making sure he still exhaled and inhaled. Making sure he lived to see his efforts pay off.

"He needs help," Mara told the smiling man. "We must get him aboard quickly."

The man looked down at Boden and his smile faltered. "The physician will know what to do."

He turned and bark orders at the others in the lifeboat. They replied simultaneously, their words like a song. At once, they tied on the drifting lifeboat and started rowing back toward the ship. Xida exchanged words with the smiling man, looking at Mara and Boden.

"Do you know this man?" Mara asked Xida. The man was distracted, ordering his sailors on how to contact the ship, yelling words up to those that waited above them on the deck. They tossed down some ropes connected to the ship's giant pulleys, and waited.

"He is the son of an old friend. His mother and I were young sailors together once, many moons ago," Xida said.

"Where is his mother then?" Mara asked.

"She's dead." Xida did not seem bothered by this.

"Oh."

Xida caught sight of the frown spreading across Mara's face. She reached with a crêpe-papered hand to Mara's knee and patted it. "Death comes for us all, Jeweled One."

Mara dozed aboard the ship. Dubbed *Cat's Paw*, the frigate was larger and roomier than Osanna's. There were not one, but three luxurious cabins to be occupied by the captain and any esteemed guests. A smaller—but no less plush—cabin housed the first mate, quartermaster, and two physicians.

The physicians took turns watching Boden, muttering to each other in passing, their foreign words numbing to Mara's mind. She sat in a low-slung leather chair. Her head was too tall for the back, so she leaned it against the wooden wall of the cabin. Shrouded in shadows, she felt invisible.

Since arriving on board, she had spoken little. Xida acted as translator for her and had ushered her inside the cabin. The smiling man, who Mara now knew was named Jase, had carried an unconscious Boden in behind them like a groom carries a bride. It had been no small feat, but Jase was thicker than any man Mara had ever seen. He'd entered the cabin, always smiling, even as he carried the heavy Ursan.

"You tell him it was I who hauled his useless body in here," Jase had teased before leaving Boden in the feather bed, still sleeping.

Her eyes traced Boden's face as she silently begged for him to open his eyes. To peer at her with his piercing blue gaze. She didn't know what she'd do without him, suddenly feeling as adrift as the Bastians' ship in the sea. Her worry grew sour in her stomach, so she looked away, instead settling her gaze on Boden's axes. They were laid neatly side by side on the nearby table. Mara admired their simplicity, knowing how deadly they really were in the right hands—in Boden's hands. And yet he had so willingly offered her one, giving up Edda so Mara could protect herself. To fight without the Sacred Sword.

His unwavering belief in her tasted bitter in the back of her throat. She swallowed the bile that rose there. Glancing back at Boden, she wondered if she'd ever be the queen he thought she could be.

The sound of footsteps stirred Mara from her thoughts. She had hoped Jase would return, but instead, it was Xida who entered, followed by the captain. This captain was nothing like Osanna. Etched onto her shaved head were tattoos of swirls and water-like forms, dancing and intermingling across her brow. Heavy earrings formed of metal teardrops hung down to her shoulders. A scar wound its way from her ear to her chin. She was a vivid example of a sea-worn woman. A traverser of the sea. A student of the world.

As if the captain could read Mara's thoughts, she grinned at her. "What a plain woman, to call herself a queen."

Mara's voice caught in her throat. She looked at Xida, who laughed silently then said, "Jeweled One, this is Captain Katyra."

Mara dipped her head, though, her neck seemed to falter. She didn't smile but cast her eyes back to Boden.

"Your Ursan will live," Katyra informed her. "The physicians have spoken. He will need to convalesce in Colendos, however."

"Colendos?"

"The capital?" Katyra said.

"Right." But Mara wasn't really listening. She knelt beside Boden, listening to his soft breaths and counting the times his chest rose and fell.

Katyra whispered to Xida in Bastian. Xida responded in Mara's tongue, sensing her growing anxiety of being unmoored by language. "She's fine," Xida said loud enough for Mara to hear. "The Jeweled One just needs food. *And sleep.*"

Mara heard the underlying suggestion in Xida's words. She was too tired to argue, too tired to stand up for herself. She returned to the leather seat and leaned her head against the wall again. "When will we arrive in Colendos?" she asked, eyes droopy with exhaustion.

"Three rises of the sun," Katyra said. "No more, no less."

Mara closed her eyes. The sounds of the Bastians screaming as Captain Porcher relentlessly attacked Osanna's ship sang over any other thought Mara tried to form. The sound of the water sloshing against the hull made her stomach lurch, flooding over her fire-filled thoughts and instead bringing forth memories of Roully Dam. Of the thunderous sound of water and her burning lungs as she tried to breathe. Her left hand twitched with the growing tenseness that had developed since taking off Éliane's splint. She opened her eyes and looked at Boden, at his soft, sleeping face and the sallowness it had taken on at the onset of his illness.

She had given all of herself to the throne, as her mother had insisted, as tradition demanded, but Mara felt the bruise left by the weight of it. She wanted nothing more than to heal. To rise from the mess she had made—that her mother had made—and right every wrong.

It would have to be enough. There was nothing left for her to give. Iris had taken it from her. She was nothing.

Chapter Twenty-Nine

Colendos rose before her like a tree from the earth. Built into the side of a mountainous island, the city traveled upward, climbing the slope, stopping at the base of the giant sandstone palace. Painted buildings in colorful hues of yellow, blue, and pink huddled close together. Gardens overflowed from verandas and rooftops, drooping over the sides of walls, adding floral notes to the salty air.

They had come up to the island from behind. Steep cliffs had met them there, defending the rear of the capital. They had then spent the morning traveling around the island, small villages and stilted houses watching them like sentinels as they drifted past. Small fishing vessels had watched the ship loom by. Suntanned fishermen surveying with intrigue, their catch overflowing from rattan baskets.

Now, as they rounded the corner and entered the crescent-moon bay, Mara saw the vastness of Colendos. The city encircled the bay in its entirety, like a shawl on a woman's shoulders. Mara watched the open ocean behind them retreat, and she wondered when she'd see it again.

Xida stood next to her on the bow of the ship. The old woman said nothing as the great city stared back at them, unabashed in its glory. She watched Mara and waited for her to speak first.

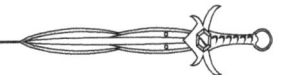

"It's more beautiful than I thought it'd be," Mara finally said, knowing the woman wanted to hear her say it.

Sunlight reflected off giant golden domes. Several were scattered throughout the city. All were monolithic and perfectly round.

"The temples," Xida explained, seeing Mara study them. "The domes mark them. They are each a place fit for the Shipwright."

Mara found it hard to swallow. She didn't know why her feelings suddenly seemed too big for her. All she knew was that she felt untethered from the Jeweled Realm. The faces that looked back at her now were unfamiliar, albeit friendly. The words were foreign. Even the shift of the boat in the water was alien to her. She was being shaped anew by these experiences, and did not know who she'd be on the other side. Boden was all that kept her anchored to her land, to her throne, to whom she thought she was. But before her lay a different road. It wound its way up the steep mountain, leading her directly into the mouth of the Bastian queen.

"I'll warn you now, Jeweled One," Xida said in a hushed tone, "Bastia will appear like a dream to you. Giant flowers overflow from balcony gardens, saturating the air with their intoxicating scents. Skyway streets suspend from rooftops, removing the need to ever touch the ground. People are friendly, perhaps too friendly in your eyes, and hug and kiss like everyone is an old friend. And then, of course, there are the giant cats."

"Ah, yes," Mara sighed, "I wondered when we'd get to that." She could see the harbor now. Its wooden walkways thrusted out into the bay with many ships already docked and moored. Sailors were moving about, cargo was being hauled to and from, and—yes, she could see them—several large jungle cats loped after their owners.

"Not everyone claims one," Xida explained, "but enough do. They are harmless."

Mara scoffed.

"They *are* harmless," Xida emphasized. "They attack only if provoked. They are true to their companion, and naturally obey them exclusively. You should be fine." They watched a pair of spotted cats follow a sailor with a rattan basket upon her head, long silver fish hanging over the side. "The queen's cat, on the other hand, is an overprotective creature. Should Queen Hali become upset . . . there's no telling what her leopard will do."

"Great," Mara said. "Am I walking to my death then? It is I who must tell her that Osanna is dead. You and Katyra made that very clear."

And they had. Katyra had waved Mara's words away when Mara told them of her last moments on the ship, of seeing Osanna order her sailors to fire and fire again, refusing to give any ground to Porcher.

"You must tell the queen," Katrya had said. "You were the last to see Osanna alive."

"Xida was," Mara had argued.

Katyra had frowned. "You would make an old woman bear your bad news for you? No. You will tell her. It is for you. The Shipwright has decided."

But staring out at the harbor drawing closer, of the large cats prowling, made Mara realize the loss Queen Hali would feel. Perhaps she'd meet her death not by the hands of Iris, but by the jaws of a protective, giant cat. What little joy Iris would find in that.

Xida patted the top of Mara's hand, the one that rested on the banister, and sighed. "Trials strengthen us," she said.

"I don't know how an angry leopard is supposed to strengthen me."

Xida shrugged.

The ship lurched as the crew tossed thick ropes overboard to waiting men on the docks. They hailed them in joyous greetings, singing an unknown song as they tugged on the swaying ship. A black cat and another spotted one lay together in the shade, appearing bored while they watched their masters work.

Mara's shoulders tensed.

Xida glanced at her and laughed. "Easy, Jeweled One," she murmured. "What I've told you is true. You'll be fine as long as you tread carefully."

"I never liked the word *careful*," Mara said.

Xida nudged her before turning and descending back to the main deck. Mara hesitated, her eyes still stuck on the giant cats. The spotted cat looked her way, but quickly found something else more amusing to watch. The black cat, however, caught her eyes and wouldn't look away. It still stared when

Mara finally released her hands from the banister—she hadn't known she'd been squeezing it so tightly—and turned to follow Xida.

They hauled Boden from his quarters, awake but still pale. The simmer of color in his eyes was dull, but Mara was happy to see them.

"Feeling better?" she asked him quietly, her hand now habitually reaching for his forehead.

"A little," he said, his voice hoarse. "If these physicians don't kill me first."

He said the words as loud as he could, glaring at the nearest physician. She was a tall woman with gray hair cascading down her back. Broad shoulders held up her red cloak, designating her status as the ship's chief physician. The younger physician, wearing the white and red cloak of a novice, laughed.

"Ma Saleema saved your life," the young physician said through a very thick accent.

"Felt like she was torturing me before my inevitable death."

"Because you are ignorant Ursan," Ma Saleema growled.

Boden was about to argue, but Mara spoke over him. "I am grateful for your knowledge and your help." Mara smiled at the physician before curtly bowing her head.

Ma Saleema frowned but bowed her head in return. "Anything for the Jeweled One, esteemed guest of my queen."

"We'll see about that," Mara mumbled, turning to watch the gangplank lower onto the dock. It landed with a thud that seemed to bounce off the nearby ships. The large cats' ears bent back with the sound, adding to their intimidating visage. Xida appeared by Mara's side, a traveling cloak of light cotton over her shoulders. A woven hat covered her salt-and-pepper hair.

"I'll escort you to the palace, but will go no farther," she said.

"And Boden?"

"He will be brought to the palace shortly. Ma Saleema insists his travel be slow and steady, lest it be too much for him."

Mara didn't like Xida's words. Without Boden, Mara considered Colendos might swallow her whole. Perhaps she'd disappear entirely, the world never seeing the Liar Queen again.

Her body felt uneven as she stepped off the gangplank and onto the pier. Having spent days on a moving ship, stepping onto firm ground suddenly made her feel sick. She waited for the moment that people would turn toward her, notice her, and try to speak to her. But it never came.

All eyes were on Xida instead. They smiled at her and patted her shoulder. Some even spoke soft words to her. She held back tears as she shook her head knowingly and hugged a young man.

"My nephew," she spoke weakly over his shoulder to Mara. "He thought I was dead."

"How did they know about the attack?" Mara looked around to see the concerned look on everyone's faces. She turned back to Xida, who wiped her eyes as she dislodged herself from her nephew.

"A message was sent. The ships keep doves on board for that reason."

Mara had seen them caged below deck, but assumed they were some Bastian delicacy. "So perhaps Queen Hali already knows about Osanna."

Xida pursed her lips. "You still have to tell her, Jeweled One. Words from a bird are nothing compared to words from a foreign queen."

Mara's shoulders slumped as she fell into step within Xida's shadow. The woman nodded and smiled at the people they passed. Some extended callused hands to grip her kindly on the arm or shoulder. Others removed their hats, woven of dried vines and flowers Mara had never seen before, and tipped their heads in respect. But few looked at Mara.

The two large cats were near. They sat up, both, and appeared eager to gaze upon Xida and Mara. Xida cooed at them, extending her hand to the large black cat.

"My nephew's cat, Lohi," she explained. "She's been his companion since he was a child, wandering without shoes on the beaches with his mother, collecting the black-shelled abalones."

Mara held her breath. Lohi glanced at her but seemed less interested in Mara. She allowed Xida to run her hand along her head and down her neck. The cat's neck wove around Xida's arm to her leg.

When Xida had had her fill of the cat, she pressed on. Mara quickly followed, finally releasing her held breath once she rejoined Xida's side. Xida laughed at her.

"How are the cats attained?" Mara asked. She tripped over a thick roped net, but regained her composure quickly. Several Bastians nearby snickered at her, but otherwise kept at their work.

"Attained?" A smile ghosted across Xida's lips. "Bastian cats are not attained. *They* choose *you*. Some Bastians wait their entire lives, praying to the Shipwright, for a cat to choose them."

"I don't understand," Mara said. She watched a cat snatch a live fish from the large wooden barrels some sailors had hauled onto the docks. It was smaller than the other two cats, obviously an adolescent. It played with the fish, watching it flop around, its keen eyes bouncing with the fish's iridescent body. When a Bastian approached, the cat's ears folded back in obeisance, running its head against the sailor's leg.

"Kittens are sometimes found curled up in bassinets with infants, choosing their partner at birth, but that is not usual. Once, a man was paddling his canoe in the tides, only to be overcome by an exhausted panther. He hauled the creature into his boat, and from then on, the cat remained forever by his side. For my grandmother, she found her companion after capsizing off the coast of a remote island. She managed to swim to the beach but had lain there expecting to die. A leopard arrived, bringing her an egg it had scrounged from some seabird's nest. Together, they survived for nearly a fortnight before she was rescued. The cat joined her, and she was never alone again."

"Do you have one?" Mara stepped over the next net she saw, saving herself from another embarrassing stumble.

Xida stared at her feet, before looking up at Mara. "No. I've never been chosen." And when Mara looked briefly concerned, she added, "It's just as well. The cats are not allowed on the ships."

Xida led the way onward, several of *Cat's Paw*'s sailors walking in their wake. But after they passed the port's end, they peeled away. Some dispersed and took up talk with other sailors. Others made it off the wooden dock and into the nearby tavern. And still some started the ascent up the stone road with them, only to drift away down winding alleys toward the brightly colored villas. Xida called a goodbye to these Bastians but continued to keep her head down and climb. Mara could do nothing but keep up.

The road leveled out momentarily. They were now in a large, cobbled square. A pavilion sat squat in the middle, its roof steep and bedecked with red terracotta. Bastians sat together, mingling in its shade. Their laughter echoed off the roof and reached for Mara's ears.

Trees lined the square—tall white things with delicate pink flowers. Their fragrance drifted down onto them, floating around the square and saturating everything. Mara reached up and plucked a flower from a nearby branch. Its many petals seemed to glisten in the sun.

"We carry on, Jeweled One," Xida called to her.

Mara looked ahead to the old woman, offering her a small smile. The first one in this new and peculiar land, she realized. Xida had told her the place would seem strange.

Across the square was the start of many steps. Mara couldn't count them. There were too many. But to the left was a tight spiral staircase, weaved of gold, that rounded its way to the top of a building. When she followed the gold, her eyes eventually found the skyway streets.

"Will we not take them?" Mara caught up to Xida at the base of the steps.

"No," Xida said, huffing after the first few steps. "Visitors to the palace must take the stairs."

Mara's eyes traced the steps, made of wide and smooth granite. They went up and up, ending at the large gold filigree gates of the palace. "For effect, I suppose," Mara frowned.

Xida exhaled slowly. "Wouldn't . . . you?" she asked between breaths. "It seems a . . . queenly thing to do." She paused on the stairs to catch her breath.

Mara waited with her and smirked. "Perhaps."

"And what of your grandmother's giant arch everyone enters through? Is it not the same? Look what we've made. Look what we've done. Tremble at our power."

"Should I be trembling?"

Xida raised a shoulder and said nothing more.

The villas along the stairs were even more glamorous than the ones at the bottom of the hill. These were tiled in large, luminous stones. They shimmered in pinks and blues. Slatted windows all sat open, allowing the evening breeze to pass through. Verandas were filled with Bastians, laughing, drinking, eating.

From their beautiful dark skin hung linens in royal tones: midnight blue, plum, and red wine. Glass beads wrapped around and around the women's necks, while the men wore beards tight and clipped. Some saw Xida and called out a greeting. Xida returned them but kept trudging upward.

When they finally reached the palace gates, Mara stopped to gaze upon Colendos. The capital unfurled like a woman's skirts, moving with the land beneath it, rising and falling as the island dictated.

Skyway streets jutted out across the rooftops like a spider's web, connecting far-flung reaches with a path directly to the palace. It reached the step below them, finishing its journey with two tall golden posts holding up ornate lanterns.

It was so extravagant. So luxurious. Why had she thought the Jeweled Realm was all there was?

"Come." Xida's gentle hand was on her elbow. "The queen awaits."

Chapter Thirty

Pillars of light filled the throne room. They fell from rooftop windows, illuminating pieces of a large floor mosaic. Mara couldn't quite make out what it depicted from her angle, but she eyed the gallery that encircled the throne room above and wondered if she'd ever get the chance to stand there and gaze down on the mosaic, decoding its secret.

Ahead sat two tall thrones. Queen Hali occupied one, the other remained empty. Mara forced a smile on her face, summoning the last remnant of queenliness she thought she still possessed, and approached the queen.

But her feet stopped when her eyes fell upon Queen Hali's cat. It was black as the darkest night, but the cat's eyes shone gold in a sunbeam. It sat upright at the base of the steps, poised just like a queen, studying her.

"Go on," Xida whispered, her hand shoving Mara forward. The panther never moved. Mara considered it could have been a statue.

"Who stands before Queen Hali?" the royal steward asked.

He stood just to the right of the cat. Mara noted he didn't seem bothered by the animal, nor did he seem aware of the power a giant feline like that could contain.

"Xida of House Alexos. Cook upon the *Queen's Eye*, captained by Osanna of the Royal House Leos."

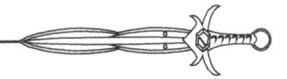

Queen Hali tightened her neck, tensed to hear the rest of Xida's words, perhaps hoping to hear of Osanna's fate, but Xida bowed and gestured to Mara.

"I bring Mara of House Black, Queen of the Jeweled Realm, displaced by her sister, a witch of the Waste."

Hali smirked but regained her composure. "That's the second time I've heard someone take claim to the Jeweled Realm."

Words stuck in Mara's throat. Where her courage had blossomed, it now wilted and died. Before her stood a woman that looked like a queen. Hali's hair, silver with age, was woven like the baskets Mara saw upon the dock, piled high upon her head. A golden halo crown exploded from her hived hair, green gems dangling from the largest spike. Smudged gold paint ran across both eyes in one continuous line, matching the gold of her lips.

When she stood, it was with elevated grace. Her motions were that of a dancer, fluid and slow, purposeful with little useless movement. She wasn't particularly tall. In fact, Mara found her quite miniature for a grown woman. But it didn't matter—she still filled the entire room.

Hali descended a step, her long shimmering gown dragging behind her, pulling at a slit in her dress and exposing her leg. She flicked her eyes at a nearby steward, who immediately responded as if he could read her mind. The man presented her with a letter, the House of Black coat of arms stamped in wax upon the bottom.

Queen Hali cleared her throat. "*Gracious Greetings to Hali, Queen of the Bastians. It is with great worry that I write to you, requesting assistance in the return of Mara of House Black, my sister and traitor to the throne. She was last seen boarding one of your ships. I can only assume she will head to Colendos. Should she arrive, I would ask that you return her promptly to me. Highest Regards, Iris of House Black. Protector of the Jeweled Realm. Upholder of the Golden Laws. Sorceress of the Waste.*"

Mara couldn't stop her eyebrow from twitching at the last title. Iris had wasted no time spreading the good news.

"Oh, there's more," Hali said, the corners of her mouth tilted upward in amusement. "*I will view any other action regarding my sister as an immediate act of war.*"

Hali handed the letter back to the steward, staring at Mara. She took another step down and then another. Her dress continued to drag behind her like a glittering waterfall. The opulence of the cloth itself hurt Mara's eyes, and she realized she had been too long gone from a proper palace.

"You can relax, little jewel," Hali cooed at her. "I have no intention of listening to your sister. We do not obey the words of faraway tyrants, no matter how insidious they may be."

Once, Mara might have balked at such pity, seeing it as weakness. But now, with not even the Sacred Sword to buoy her strength, she recognized how little she had.

"You are most gracious, Majesty." Mara tipped her head hesitantly, never having bowed to another sovereign before.

Hali stared at Mara a moment longer before returning to her throne. She sat tall, her halo sparkling in the sunbeams falling from the roof, emphasizing her glamor. *She's like a jewel herself,* Mara thought. A product of the earth from which her kingdom grew. A sun to shine light upon her own people.

"You were aboard my sister's ship," Hali said, her nose flaring while she attempted to remain calm. "Did you see her during the attack?"

Mara nodded, but her throat felt swollen. She swallowed hard. Hali stared down at her like she was nothing. Like she was no one. It irked Mara to be looked at that way. The Bastians on the pier had been the same. None had had eyes for her, only Xida. Here in the Isles, she was no one. "I did," she finally managed to eke out. "Prior to being ushered off the ship."

"She remained then?"

Mara again nodded. From her pocket, she pulled out the medal with the panther signet. Staring at it now, in the lighted splendor of the palace, Mara noted how worn it was. How dirty and scratched. She thrust it forward, only to have the steward relinquish it from her and deliver it to his queen.

"Of course she stayed," Hali said, more to herself than to Mara. The queen stared down at the medal cradled within her hands. Rings adorned each finger, one a long golden spike. Hali tapped this finger against the medal, thinking. "She would've had reason to let you aboard," she said, still not looking up. "If she knowingly made herself an enemy of the Jeweled Realm . . . I'd like to think it was for a worthy purpose."

"My sister knows no reason, Your Grace," Mara spoke barely above a whisper. "The Waste has turned her mad. If she says she will bring war—"

Hali held up her hand, silencing Mara. "As I've said, little jewel, I do not fear tyrants of a far off land. Your sister's ships may thwart us for a time, but the Bastians are of the ocean. She is not." Hali tapped her fingers on the arm of her throne. "But Osanna feared that my choice to do nothing was in error. She wanted to fight. And yet . . . she's brought me you."

Mara swallowed hard again. Hali's gaze was that of molten gold. It saw through Mara's façade—the face Mara had once thought was queenly—and saw what she really was: weak.

Her lower lip quivered, and she found it difficult to control her face. It wanted to contort and twist, releasing the pain she felt inside. Releasing the tears. The situation's complication felt heavy in her chest. It choked her. And for what? For her to remain seated on a throne?

"She asked me to lift the embargo on your ships," Mara said.

"Really? And how were you to do that without the power to do so?" Hali asked.

Mara cleared her throat. "She said you might . . . you'd help me reclaim the throne. In doing so, I'd remove the embargo."

Hali tapped again on the arm of her throne to a beat of some unknown song. She twisted her lips in thought. It was amazing how youthful she appeared. How much younger than Osanna she seemed. And yet, Osanna herself had said the queen was older. More than a hand older, Mara remembered. Time seemed to have left Hali alone, to age more slowly, to remain beautiful while others withered.

"No," Hali's lips finally formed.

Mara's heart stopped. It was several moments before she heard her pulse return in her ears like some unearthly drum. "What?"

Hali stood, the medal disappearing into some hidden pocket of her skirt. "I said no. I won't send my people to your aid. To die. Not for simply lifting an embargo that could be easily remedied by simply waiting it out."

The queen moved to leave, retrieving the arm of a nearby steward. Hali's black panther stood but continued to stare at Mara. Her knees quivered. Her heart, thumping just a moment ago, now seemed to flutter.

The great doors behind her opened. Mara turned, knowing it was Boden finally being delivered on his deathbed. The tears were filling her eyes now, blurring everything. The bed was visible, but Boden's body was a mixture of shadows.

Mara turned back to Hali and dropped hard to her knees. The tile floor echoed with the thud as she fell forward with her tears. "Please," a voice Mara never knew she had ripped from her throat. "Please, Your Majesty."

She felt like a child. She sounded like a child. A child alone and afraid, begging for someone to show her the right way.

Hali stopped her movement. She looked down at Mara with an unreadable face. Whether she pitied her or was appalled, Mara couldn't tell. But when Hali's gaze drifted to Boden, her face instantly softened. Her own jaw quivered. "Is that the Ursan pledged to you?" Hali released the steward's arm, and, grasping her dress, descended the steps. Her panther joined her, and she rested her hand delicately on its head.

Mara wiped the tears from her face. "Yes. His brother, the crown prince, and his father, the king, colluded with my sister to kill me."

Hali stopped short of her. The panther froze next to its companion, eyes never leaving Mara. Hali seemed to think again. This time, she nodded to her steward. "Take the Ursan. Have my physicians see him immediately. And"—she looked down at Mara, filthy and crying—"take the Jeweled Queen to clean up. Prepare her some clean clothes. We shall sup on my veranda at sundown."

Chapter Thirty-One

Blue glass plates and glassware decorated the wooden table. Fruit overflowed from a dazzling bowl crafted by a master glassblower. Flowers grew thickly on the vine that wove its way around the veranda's banister and filled the air with fragrant scents and the buzzing of insects.

Mara took her seat and waited.

It did not take long for the queen to arrive. She was ushered in by a man, dressed eloquently in fine linen, rambling on in her ear in Bastian. Hali's panther loped directly behind her, fading into Hali's shadow. Hali herself seemed bored, and as soon as she spotted Mara, she batted the man away.

"Court gossip," she informed Mara as she sat across from her. "I'm afraid I've never had the ear for it. But, of course, I hired someone else who does. Unfortunately, I still have to listen to it from *him* from time to time."

Mara said nothing. After cleaning herself up in the room provided for her, she had stared in the mirror for a long time. She hadn't recognized the woman staring back. She had lost weight, and where her face had once been round was now rigid and sharp. Her eyes appeared tired and dull. It seemed her transformation was not only mental, but physical as well. Petra would be hard-pressed to know her queen—her false queen—from that of a stranger.

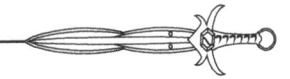

Mara didn't even recognize herself in the hungry, wolfish woman that peered back at her.

"Do you worry for your Ursan prince?" Hali accepted a glass overflowing with vibrant red liquid, and she suggested the servant offer some to Mara. "My physicians informed me he will make a full recovery. You needn't worry about him. You can see him, if you'd like, after we dine."

Hali waited for a response, but Mara only nodded, sipping at her drink. The juice was sweet, very sweet, and tasted like the fruit of some tree. Her hand shook as she attempted to set the glass down. Hali watched her.

The panther settled down on a pile of cushions in the veranda's corner. A gilded bowl sat next to it, filled with sparkling water. It ignored the drink, instead laying its head on its paws, observing Mara.

"Thank you, Your Grace," Mara said, watching the cat from the corner of her eye. "I would like that."

Hali stared at Mara over her plate. Servants arrived and dished food out. Cold salads with small flowers decorating the tops sat next to entire fish. Plopped into the middle of the table was a steaming, many-legged creature, its hard shell a bright red. More bowls of fruit were brought along with a pitcher of vin.

A servant dished food onto Mara's plate. She studied it, not knowing where to begin.

"You never asked me why I changed my mind," Hali said. She reached across the table and, with her own fork and knife, showed Mara how to open up the fish to remove its delicate meat. Mara took a small bite. It melted in her mouth, tasting of lemon and the sea.

"I assume you have your reasons," Mara said between drinks of vin. It was dry and earthy, and for a brief moment, Mara could imagine herself at some random table in the palace. For a moment, she almost felt home.

"*Reason*. Just one," Hali said, disturbing Mara's thoughts.

Mara set her glass down. It was becoming apparent that Hali enjoyed dragging out the space between moments, making her audience wait until she was ready to unfurl her mind on her own whim. The island queen kept her own time, it seemed, and it churned with the crash of the waves. Mara forced a patient smile across her lips to conceal her grinding teeth, and waited. Because she *did* want to know why Hali extended her generosity to a worthless, lying, would-be queen of a far-off place.

"There is something I could use your help with. You and your Ursan."

Mara's hand tightened around her glass at the mention of Boden and her smile began to slip. Had he not been through enough? Mara sipped at her vin, hiding her frown. "Boden will be doing nothing but recuperating the strength he's lost, Your Grace."

She hoped her words conveyed her message: *leave him alone.*

"Yes"—Hali mirrored her, sipping at her vin—"I agree. Allow me to be exact: I need *your* help. The help of the Sword Queen."

Mara stared at Hali, swallowing hard at the bile that rose in the back of her throat. Hali was her only chance at regaining her throne, but Mara wondered if it was even worth it anymore—if she wished to answer to the Sword Queen again.

"Then tell me what it is, before I lose all desire to see my throne again." She tried to say it jokingly, to lighten the mood and the heavy thoughts that weighed at her temples, but knew she partially meant it. Would it be a crime to never return to the Jeweled Realm again?

Hali smiled. She leaned back in her chair and appeared to relax, but Mara could see in the rigid lines of her jaw that she was still intent on having her way.

"The Bastian Isles only take up a portion of the archipelago, known to those that live in it as the Lion. There are several other tribes that make up the rest."

Hali watched Mara take this in. Mara didn't know what good the information would do her. Her memory of her own continent was convoluted at best, especially since she felt her head was full of fuzz.

Knowledge of the archipelago was spotty. Outsiders were not officially allowed there, as Osanna had reminded Mara before allowing them on board. Mara knew little else about the peoples that called the islands home.

Few cared, in the Jeweled Realm, of anything but themselves.

Hali took a deep breath before continuing. "Tradition dictates that disagreements be settled by hand-to-hand combat."

Mara nodded. A simple way to settle disagreements.

"Here in the Isles, life is sacred. To send hundreds to die for the sake of some argument between leaders would be frivolous."

"So there's been a disagreement?" Mara was trying her best to think through the fog that filled her head. For weeks, she'd been succumbing to it, letting it leach into her and take over, leaving little of the Mara that once was. But now she felt the need to listen. To wake up and hear what this foreign queen was telling her.

If not for herself, then at least for Boden.

"There has." Hali sipped her vin. "Both leaders will now select their champion to fight. To the death."

Mara's eyebrow twitched, intrigued. She reached for her own vin and sipped from the glass thoughtfully. "The champion that wins, wins the argument for whom they fight?"

Hali nodded. She watched Mara closely. Mara felt an unknown itch beneath her skin. She had never enjoyed being stared at so intently. It reminded her of her mother. It reminded her that as queen, she was always being watched.

She looked at the panther, who now sat upright. A bowl had been served to the cat while they ate. Nothing was left in it save for a pool of blood at the bottom. Its tongue licked its lips, savoring the last of its meal.

"And you want me to be your champion?"

"That's correct." Hali smiled.

Mara choked on her own laughter. "I don't know if you've noticed, Your Grace, but I cannot be your Sword Queen, as I have no weapon. I lost my Sacred Sword on Roully Dam."

"Water can be dangerous," Hali whispered.

The words echoed across her days spent with the Bastians. She saw Aleen's face. Osanna's. "How can you love the water if you fear it so?" Mara asked.

Hali furrowed her forehead, delicate lines weaving across her smooth skin. "Is it not possible to love and fear something at the same time? Do you jewels choose one way or the other?"

Mara thought of Iris. The Iris of her youth—the one she'd let go—and the Iris she'd met on Roully Dam. They were the same person, but she found she loved one and feared the other.

"To fear something is to respect it," Hali continued, looking at her panther. "And is that not a type of love?"

A servant arrived with dessert. Frozen fruit purée topped with small dark bits of sweetness. Sweetbreads dripped with honey. Small tarts filled to overflowing with sugared fruit. But Mara found her stomach ached for her own food. The food of the continent.

She shoved the plate away and stood. "I will speak with Boden now," she said, a sliver of bravery growing from the heat she felt in her belly. "And then I will give you your answer."

The panther jumped up, slinking to Hali's side. Its ears slid back with a menacing glare, but Mara did her best to hold her ground.

Hali bowed her head slightly. "As you say, Jeweled One." She clapped her hands, and a steward appeared. She instructed the woman in the fluid tones of Bastian, who gently took Mara by the arm and escorted her to the door.

"You'll find us in the sanctuary, when you're finished," Hali called after her, gazing absently into her glass of vin while petting her panther. "We await your agreement."

Chapter Thirty-Two

Layered curtains of linen billowed gently in the breeze from the open window. They kept Boden's room dark to keep it cool. It smelled of incense. There was a pot burning in the corner, its smoke curling upward and trailing before dissipating into the air completely.

It was a different scene altogether than the Jeweled Realm, where *docteurs* demanded light and then more light. Meticulously cleaned rooms resulted in a strict lack of any scent. They worked in pairs, always, and anyone else was excused from the room.

And yet before her sat at least seven Bastians, all wearing physician's cloaks. Two stood whispering near Boden, though, by their tone, the conversation seemed light and amusing. Another two worked at grinding something with a pestle and mortar, laughing at some joke as they did so. The other three seemed to be doing nothing but gossiping. They sat idly at the base of Boden's stuffed mattress, each taking turns speaking.

Mara's Bastian escort cleared her throat. She spoke, and the physicians stood. They all bowed their heads and made their way from the room.

"Shouldn't one of them stay?" Mara asked as they all exited.

"Would the Jeweled One like that?" the woman asked. "I thought the Jeweled Realm treated illness as an individual experience? To suffer alone is strength?"

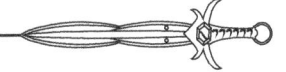

Mara knew the woman was poking fun at her. She ignored her words, thick with the Bastian accent, and instead focused on Boden. He sat propped up on many silk pillows, each one a different shape and color. His eyes fluttered open when he heard her voice.

He smiled. "Mara."

She sat next to him and held his hand. The movement was so practiced, it felt natural. Her fingers entwined with his and she rubbed his palm gently with her thumb. She looked at him, tracing his face with her eyes, wanting to briefly live only in that moment. There would be plenty of time later to think. There always was, usually in the dark of night, when most slept and Mara didn't.

Couldn't.

"You look better," she said.

He tried to smile again. "You mean I'm breathing."

"Yes, well, breathing is better than not. For a time, I doubted."

"Doubted? That doesn't sound like the Sword Queen I know."

Mara groaned. She turned to ask the queen's steward to fetch some water but realized the woman had left. Vanished on light feet, like all Bastians.

"What's wrong?" Boden tried to shove himself upright further to sit eye to eye with her, but winced with pain and wilted back into the pillows.

"Your infection has made you quite sick," Mara said.

"The physicians said the body aches will go away soon. I'll be back to normal before you know it."

But Mara wasn't convinced.

"Tell me what's wrong," Boden said. "I won't ask again."

Mara side-eyed him, not enjoying his tone, but remembering she was no queen. Not anymore. He squeezed her hand encouragingly. "Queen Hali will only help me if I help her first."

Boden nodded. "Sounds reasonable. What does she want you to do?"

Mara sighed and stood, pulling her hand from Boden's. While reaching for him seemed so natural, she still fought the feeling of relief she found within his grasp. She wasn't used to the comfort of another's skin on hers. "Single combat. Winner claims victory for their respected patron."

"And the loser?"

Mara couldn't help but laugh. "They die."

"So, to the death?" Mara thought she saw a flash of panic on Boden's face before his features folded in thought.

Mara shoved a handful of linen away from the window and stared out at the courtyard below. A shallow reflection pool filled the majority, collecting fallen petals from the many flowering trees around the courtyard. They danced in the breeze, scattering flowers with each gust. It reminded her of snow.

Far off, the ocean roared against the cliffs, its rhythmic sound crashing and retreating night and day. Mixed in were the cries of the gulls. Occasionally, the wind blew, bringing with it the scent of salt and sea. *It's enchanting*, Mara thought, *this difference in place.* But she still wanted to go home.

"You'll do it, won't you?" Boden's voice came from the darkness of the room.

Mara let the curtains fall back, extinguishing the light. Her eyes had been blinded by the daylight outside and needed to adjust, so she closed them while considering Boden's words.

"Are you so eager to see me die?" she finally asked.

Now Boden laughed. "I have no doubt you'll win."

"Oh? You forget, I don't have my sword. I refuse to fight without it."

"I forget nothing," Boden whispered.

She opened her eyes to see him staring down at his hands, gouged and scabbed over with the blisters from rowing. Xida had begged him to stop, but Mara had remained silent. If Boden wished to row himself to death before they died of dehydration, so be it. And he nearly had—for her. He would have given himself over to the sea if it meant her safety.

Mara still struggled to justify such devotion. No one in the Jeweled Realm died willingly for another.

"You fought with my axes at the chateau," Boden said.

It was true, she *had* used the axes, but what she'd never told him was how much she'd hated how they felt. How dead the axes were in her hand, and yet how similar. How deftly she had maneuvered their blades to do exactly what she wanted. How easy it all had been. How unextraordinary.

They had eventually felt just like the Sword. And that scared her. Because if the Sword meant nothing, if it wasn't special, then what did that make her?

If there truly was no power within the Sword, then everyone outside of the Jeweled Realm was right: the Sword meant nothing.

"You will fight," Boden interrupted her thoughts, "and you will win."

"And what if I don't?" Her eyebrow raised incrementally, questioning Boden's tone.

"Fighting for Queen Hali is the only way you'll see the Jeweled Realm again, Mara."

She turned away, closed her eyes again for just a moment, and imagined not opening them again. But she felt Boden staring at the back of her, felt his eyes peering past the invisible armor she tried to wear at all times. She gave in.

"And what if I don't want to be queen anymore?" She looked at him from her perch by the window, gauging his reaction, weighing each movement of his eyes.

But Boden must have learned a thing or two from her in their time together, for instead of unfolding before her, revealing his thoughts as he would have done before, he solidified. His eyes shored up, hardened, and reminded her more of her father than ever before.

"Don't be stupid," he said. "You would never leave Iris to rule the Jeweled Realm."

"Wouldn't I? I dared to disobey custom to sit myself on the throne. Why wouldn't I abandon it the moment it became dangerous?"

"Because you care."

His words were final. She could see it in the way his gaze never shifted from hers. Boden could see past her façade. Mara didn't know what made her angrier—that Boden could see who she truly was, or that it actually felt good to be seen.

"I don't want to die, Boden." The words fell flat in the room. Boden maneuvered himself to the edge of the mattress and threw his legs over to the floor, his penetrating gaze unwavering. The blankets were still arranged haphazardly across his lap, but there was little left to Mara's imagination. She felt the heat creep up her neck and to her cheeks, but Boden didn't seem to notice. His eyes were still focused and serious.

"As if I'd let you," he said. He reached for his clothes, folded neatly on a silk-covered ottoman. Atop them sat Edda and Liv. "You'll fight, because it's who you are."

"I am not the Sword Queen anymore." She tore her eyes from Boden's body. "Perhaps I never was."

Boden began fussing with his clothes, so she averted her eyes toward the sunlight fighting through the edge of the curtain.

She soon felt his presence and found him standing behind her, only partially dressed. His body drooped, as if it cost him all his effort to hold himself up. Mara wanted to scold him and usher him back to bed, but he spoke before her, his booming voice demanding she listen.

"Forget Hali and what she wants, Mara. Don't do it for her. You don't have to be the Sword Queen anymore." He half-smiled down at her, grabbing her hips and pulling her closer. "Do it for me."

"For you?" Mara murmured through her own smile. "You're assuming a lot, Prince Boden, third in line to the Ursan throne, if you think I want to do anything for *you*." He wrapped one arm around her back, hugging her tightly to his own body. With his free hand he grasped her cheek and tilted her head up to stare into her eyes. "What would give you such a ridiculous idea like that?" she asked. Her heart was in her throat, and she could barely breathe. She tried not to blink, worried she'd miss a single moment looking in Boden's bright eyes. They were luminous in the Bastian sun penetrating the linen curtains and falling across his face like fire.

"Because I love you," he said. "And I think you love me."

He waited for Mara to answer, but she pursed her lips and refused to reply. Boden wouldn't be deterred, however, and carried on.

"Kalda says that there will come a time in one's life when they lose their will. Their purpose. And it is that moment one must decide to do something for someone else. To put others first. So"—his hand drifted down to her neck where he gently stroked her pulse—"I'm asking you to do this for me. Fight for Hali. Win. Then we can get off this horribly hot island and back to where we belong. Where *you* belong."

He kissed her then, and this time, she let him. Because he was right, she did love him, and it thrilled her and terrified her in equal measure.

The sanctuary was at the end of a long breezeway. Carved pillars, twining ivy etched around each one, held up an open roof. Giant yellow flowers creeped across on their foliage, adding shade where there would have been none. To one side stood the start of the mountain's steep edge. Sharp black shale jutted from the cliff wall, along with the most stunted of trees. But on the other side, the slope fell away, the city with it, allowing Mara the perfect view of Colendos.

From her vantage point, she could see the way the skyway streets circumvented the island, working in a perfect pattern to join one place to another. She noticed the harbor was not an abstract creation, but built as a setting sun. It reminded Mara of Hali's crown, with some spokes longer than others.

And across the bay, an equally beautiful building. Pink sandstone held up a golden roof. It glowed in the sun, like it had sucked in all the light of the day and would glimmer until midnight.

But from within the sanctuary, a voice called, and Mara dragged herself away from the beautiful scene.

Inside, she found walls pockmarked with multicolored glass. The sun shot through viciously, leaving brightly lit columns on the far wall. The temple itself was a round room surrounded by another round wall, a double ring. Mara walked around the hall of the outer ring, catching glimpses of the sunset beyond the sharp, skinny windows placed every so often amidst the many smaller, round windows.

An archway appeared, cut through the wall itself. Two steps went down into the floor of the temple, where nothing sat except a plush carpet on top of tile. And Queen Hali.

The queen knelt, her hands idle in her lap, her head bowed. She muttered to herself, but upon Mara's entrance, she ceased.

"You've come so soon," Hali's voice drifted up. She wore a black lace veil over her face attached to a golden circlet draped across her forehead and tucked into the hive of her hair. Gone was the glorious sun-beamed crown. All the jewels that had adorned her fingers were gone, too. Instead, Hali looked laboriously plain, save for the veil.

She patted the rug next to her. "Sit."

"I do not bow to any gods, island queen," Mara said.

Hali chuckled. "I don't recall asking you to pray with me. Sit, and we will talk. You'll find the sanctuary is an incredibly... private place to discuss things of importance."

Mara hesitated. There were no guards, no stewards, no one. She did not even spy Hali's giant cat. As far as Mara could tell, they were the only two in the sanctuary at all. She sighed as she obeyed, drifting to Hali's side and sinking slowly to her knees. They ached from earlier when she'd dropped so suddenly to beg Hali for help, and she wondered if she had damaged them.

"So," Hali said on an exhale, "you will fight."

"What makes you say that?"

Mara didn't know what to look at. Hali's covered face was unsettling. The walls of the sanctuary boasted no ornament. The inside ring was flat and painted white. Her eyes drifted upward, finally taking in the golden domed ceiling. A giant chandelier formed of coral floated above them, illuminating the room in a soft glow. Mara had seen nothing like it before, in size or in form, and felt herself forgetting to breathe.

Hali chuckled to herself. "You are easier to read than you think, Jeweled One. And... you wear the Ursan's axes."

Mara dropped her eyes to Edda and Liv, tucked neatly into the belt of her dress where Boden had secured them.

"Yes, well"—she adjusted them and sat up a little straighter—"Boden insisted."

Hali laughed again. "You like this Ursan."

Mara felt the hairs on her neck rise defensively. "He pledged his obedience. What queen doesn't like obedience?"

Hali rested a hand on Mara's forearm. Goosebumps ran up Mara's arm from the coolness of Hali's skin. The touch was kind, careful. "You love him," Hali said. It was not a question.

"Yes."

Hali pulled her arm away and nodded encouragingly. "Good. Ursans are simple. You would do well to find a partner who can keep things simple."

Hali tipped her head upward, allowing the glow of the coral chandelier to fall over her veil. While the details of her face remained hidden, Mara could make out the features. The brow bone, the gentle slope of the nose. She followed Hali's gaze and looked up again, mesmerized by the chandelier.

"Osanna died bringing you to me," Hali said, still staring upward. "So I must know. And you must speak to me truly."

Mara felt dizzy from looking up, so she dropped her head and blinked hard. She suddenly smelled incense, a salty scent she hadn't noticed before. It choked her, but she nodded.

Hali slowly turned her head to look at Mara. The darkness cast over Hali's already dark complexion startled her. It was bewitching. Almost terrifying, in a beautiful way.

"Why did you let your sister live?"

Mara sighed. She was getting tired of trying to answer that question. But she felt Hali's gaze, and she knew she had to answer this time.

Truthfully.

"I didn't want to," Mara confessed. "I didn't . . . I couldn't see the point. Why did my sister have to die? Why was that the best way to choose an heir?"

Hali stared, unmoved. "To choose an heir is no simple task."

"It could be. If only one child is born." Mara said it before considering Hali, before remembering she had lost a child already, leaving her with only one heir.

Only one choice.

Mara's mouth moved quickly, searching for some words to apologize, to plead for forgiveness. But they wouldn't come.

Hali sighed and turned away. "Only one," she seemed to mumble to herself. *"One."*

She slowly rose from the floor, using Mara's shoulder to push herself up. She walked to her left, where Mara noticed a single tree. It grew twisted from a hole in the floor, dirt bared beneath. It was no taller than Hali. Leaves of shiny green sprung from branches that wound around but always sought upwards. Small white flowers bloomed, amongst the leaves. Hali extended her hand to caress one.

Her panther appeared, emerging from a dark alcove Mara had also missed upon entering the room. Mara could imagine her mother's eyeroll at another indiscretion, another lack of attention to her surroundings.

"The day my daughter died was the day I chose my son as heir. Natan is a good man . . . a good choice. But I was not *given* a choice." Hali turned to look at Mara, still on her knees on the floor. The panther rubbed around Hali's legs, nuzzling her hand to comfort her.

"The Shipwright brings change. They alone created the ocean in a constant state of movement. Nothing is more powerful at changing the surface than the waves. I will not fight what the Shipwright works into this world."

"But I did," Mara whispered, though, she had not intended to speak so softly. She did not care for Hali's god, nor the lessons she was attempting to help Mara understand. But something about the sanctuary, about being beneath the colossal golden dome with that giant chandelier, made her feel small. Something about the way the giant cat's eyes fell upon her, searching, made her shrink.

Hali smiled, slow and wide. She walked back toward Mara, extending her hand to help her off the floor. "No, my little jewel," Hali cooed as Mara rose to stand face-to-face with the queen. "The Shipwright does not create a weapon without the intent to use it."

Mara looked away, too afraid to stare Hali in the eyes. Hali grabbed her face and pulled her back to attention.

"Your sister shaped herself, in the deserts of the Waste. But you?" Hali grasped Mara's hands and held them up for her to see. "The Shipwright shaped you with blood and tears and, yes, even love." Hali let go. She stepped backward and crossed her arms, staring intently at Mara. "Most are meant for shaping, little jewel. The waves crash over us again and again, forming us into who we are. But some"—she tipped Mara's chin up—"some are the waves themselves."

Chapter Thirty-Three

The sand beneath Mara's feet stuck to the bottom of her boots. She shifted her weight, testing them, wondering if it would be best to remove them.

It had been decided between the two monarchs where their champions would fight. Queen Hali, queen of the larger kingdom, insisted the fight should occur during the morning. Warlord Tachti, patron of the second champion, insisted on the beach.

Hali had seen no problem with this, considering the Bastians' worship of the Shipwright. She found the water to be a good omen. Mara had her doubts.

"Water is dangerous—is that not what Bastians say?" she had asked while Hali's royal tailors outfitted her with fine leather pants and a linen shirt.

Hali had waved her worries away then and continued to ignore them now as she stood next to Mara on the beach. "It is a beautiful day for a fight, yes?" Hali inhaled the salty breeze washing in from the ocean.

Hali's hair was styled, the dreads twisted and plaited down her back, save for a few on each side. They hung down from her temples and seemed to have a mind of their own as they swayed with the wind. Gold wire wrapped each end tightly, held in place by a polished garnet.

Solara, Hali's panther, sat beside her. She wore a collar of gold and garnet herself, and her golden eyes traced the faces of the opposing crowd, just as Hali's did.

Boden stood behind Mara, his breathing still slightly labored from his illness, but he was unwavering on his feet. While the physicians had spent every day with him rebuilding his strength, Mara had spent every night with him, wrapped in his arms, head resting on his chest. She'd come into the habit of putting herself to sleep by counting his breaths, each inhale and exhale a small certainty of his devotion. He was getting better. Growing stronger.

He would live, and so Mara decided she would, too.

For the past nine sunrises, she had studied the way of the island fighters, spending time in the Bastian training grounds during the day. They were fast, intelligent warriors. Her hands squeezed themselves into fists in anticipation. She would have to be the best she'd ever been. She would have to kill. Or be killed.

"Remember," Hali whispered to Mara as Warlord Tachti's champion separated himself from the crowd, "he is quick, but you are quicker."

Mara nodded, taking long deep breaths, preparing herself to step forward.

"He is strong, but you are smarter," Hali continued.

Mara moved to take her first step toward her opponent, but Hali grabbed her arm, startling Mara with her sudden, vicious grip.

Hali turned Mara to face her. "And he may die today, but you won't, because you are meant for more. You are the waves."

Mara nodded, frightened by the look in Hali's eyes. They were storm-filled and fanatical. Mara had yet to see them so dark.

Boden appeared, gently prying the queen's hand from Mara's arm. "She's ready, Your Majesty," he assured Hali.

He offered no encouraging words to her himself. Instead, he squeezed her shoulder, as if trying to pass on the courage he couldn't voice. His confidence in her was so absolute. Mara took one last deep breath before turning back to the man she'd have to kill.

Or die trying.

The man stood a head taller than Mara. His shoulders were broad and sunbaked. Pale scars stood out starkly on his tanned skin where his leather armor didn't cover. He wore what Mara had been told was a traditional warrior's skirt. Woven of leather strips, it shielded from the thin, curved swords favored by the island peoples. His chest plate was leather as well, oiled and aged. Small round stones, their centers hollowed out, looped across, adding to the integrity of the armor.

Mara wore similar gear, though, she'd found the skirt bulky and opted for pants. Her linen shirt, worn beneath her chest plate, was already drenched in sweat. She pushed her sweaty hair out of her face and stepped forward. Hali stepped with her, along with Solara. They walked together across the beach to meet with Tachti and his warrior.

Tachti rambled on in his thunderous voice, though, his words were purely Bastian. Hali replied, seemingly unamused. Tachti's champion studied Mara, smirking.

Hali sighed.

"What?" Mara asked, feeling adrift in the strange language of Bastia.

"He asked if you were going to cover your pretty face, lest he ruin it for your burial," Hali said.

Mara looked at Tachti, who only beamed at his joke. She returned his smile. "Tell him we burn our dead in the Jeweled Realm. And if I were him, I'd be hoping there will be enough of my champion left to bury."

Hali laughed. She spoke the Bastian words, translating for Mara. Tachti listened intently and then furrowed his brow. He spat on the beach and muttered to his champion. He punched the man in the shoulder once, then backed away toward his people.

Hali bowed her head curtly to the champion and then turned to Mara. She smiled and nodded, then silently padded back to her own waiting party, Solara ever in tow. The cat rubbed around Mara's legs once before going. Mara wanted to watch her go. She wanted to see the cat slink after Hali, like her shadow, but she was unaccustomed to battles in the Isles. As soon as Hali was clear, Tachti's warrior yelled. His war cry startled Mara, and he used the moment to attack.

He leaped at her with his slim blade raised. Despite its thinness, the edge was like a razor. The sun reflected sharply from it, catching Mara's eyes and blinding her.

She barely stumbled backward in time. The tip caught the top of her right hand on the downswing, easily cutting through the leather gloves she wore. A scarlet line shot through the open leather. Mara looked up in time to see the champion swing again, this time bringing his sword into an upward swing. She turned and spun away, missing the blade entirely.

The champion smiled. Mara removed Edda and Liv from her belt and steadied her feet. "Strength wields the Sword," she muttered to herself, holding up the axes in the defensive position Boden had taught her.

This time, when the champion lunged, Mara was ready. She used her right axe to parry his attack, thrusting his sword tip down into the sand nearly to the hilt. With her left hand still gripping the axe, she reached out and punched him square in the nose. Blood trickled ruby down his lips. The warrior wiped it away, glancing at the blood on his hand, before wrenching his sword free.

Again, he moved with lightning speed, spinning around, swinging the blade at Mara's face. She ducked and stepped away to distance herself. The warrior was fast. Hali had warned her of this, speaking of Tachti's tactics as one of speed over stamina. They were taught to kill quickly, lest they tire before their enemy.

Mara spun and spun again, keeping away from the warrior, letting him swing his blade hard however he chose. At first he seemed amused, but, eventually, he grew annoyed. He bared his teeth and growled at her. Then he spat at her. She avoided the spit, spinning and smacking the warrior across the back as hard as she could with the cheek of Edda.

He fell forward but recovered his balance. Coughing from the impact of Edda's kiss, he backed away. Foreign words flooded his tongue, but Mara ignored it all. She focused on his feet, the position of his hands, his weapon. She paid attention to where he was looking and tried to figure out his next move so that she could outmaneuver him.

Fighting is like playing at Cavaliers, her mother would say, comparing actual warfare to a child's game played on a board of checkered spaces. The person who thinks far enough ahead wins.

Her body took control of the axes. She felt her arms reach and lunge, finally putting on an attack of her own. The champion was ready for her, deflecting her axes with his sword easily enough.

He attempted his own offensive, all while sparring with Mara. He knocked Liv upward and thrusted. Mara took one step backward and managed to barely avoid the blade slicing open her cheek. It slid past her eyes, offering her a moment of her own reflection. She'd have to do it then, and quickly, before the warrior moved and she lost her nerve.

Using her right arm, she countered, throwing the champion's arm upward. She stepped toward his instep and spun, bringing down her left hand—her strong hand—hard on his exposed knee. Edda cracked against bone, and he sent up a howl of pain.

She stepped back and let him fall forward, then brought Liv's sharpened edge down on his head.

As she walked away, the whispers of the crowd fell silent. Solara met her first, rubbing her head against her bloodied hand, but Mara stared at Hali. The queen blinked slowly, her mouth parting ever so slightly. She lifted her chin, eyes narrowed as if recalculating something in her mind. For a heartbeat, surprise seemed to flicker in her gaze, but it was quickly masked by a curt smile.

"Is something wrong, Your Grace?" Mara asked.

Hali shook her head as she stared over Mara's shoulder at the man lying prone on the beach.

Boden caught Mara's gaze and offered her a small smile. "Edda and Liv like it in your hands," he said.

Mara held up the axes, now dressed in blood, and smiled back at Boden. "Perhaps they do."

"Perhaps it was never the Sword, but the wielder of the Sword," he offered.

Mara's smile melted away. She turned to look at the defeated warrior. His blood stained the beach a dark brown. Tachti had rushed forward to check his champion, but Mara already knew.

If he wasn't dead, he would be soon.

She turned back to Boden. "Perhaps you're right."

Chapter Thirty-Four

Mara slept. She slept on the ship that took them back to Colendos. She slept in the soft bed of her palace room, Boden's body wrapped protectively around her like a cocoon. Rain came and went. Sunshine dried it up. Flowers bloomed and wilted and died, only to be replaced by a never-ending cycle of life.

She awoke one day on her own private veranda, head sagged to one side, warming herself in a chair. A shadow cast itself across her lap. Shielding her eyes, she looked up to find Boden smiling down on her.

"What is it?" she asked.

"Come, the island queen calls you. It's time."

Mara couldn't help but return his smile.

It had been weeks of waiting. While Hali had agreed to assist in the retrieval of Mara's throne from Iris, she said it would take time to call her fleet home. Her massive navy was flung across the archipelago, doing the bidding of Natan and herself. And while Hali retained sole dominion over Bastia, Natan would have to be *spoken with*. Hali had said these last words a bit tentatively.

But Boden and Mara had made the best of their time. Boden continued working to rebuild the strength he'd lost from his illness. Mara continued her training with the help of Hali's master at arms. He taught her to use the

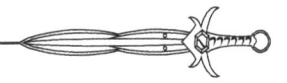

Bastians' thin sword, known colloquially as a Panther's Claw. Hali had even gifted Mara her own. It was silver-handled and perfectly balanced, shaped specifically for a left-handed fighter.

It hung snugly at her side as she walked next to Boden toward the throne room. Guards whispered down the hall but ceased when they drew near. Mara thought she heard Natan's name after they passed and took a corner.

"Do you think the crown prince has returned?" Mara asked.

"Possibly, if Hali is finally ready to return you to the Jeweled Realm."

Hali had not left Colendos since Natan's birth. She had remained the figurehead of the Bastian people while Natan traveled for her. But she'd insisted she would go with Mara. After Mara's defeat of Tachti's warrior, Hali looked at Mara differently. There was less pity. More reverence.

They found Hali in the throne room. A man sat on the second throne, previously always left empty. He stood when they entered. He was tall, much taller than Hali, with an angular, smooth face. But if Mara looked hard enough, she could see Hali in his features. The same oval eyes. The same nose. The way his hair met at a point on his forehead. It was obvious.

This was Natan.

Mara and Boden stopped simultaneously and bowed their heads.

"Greetings, Your Grace," Mara said in what little Bastian she knew.

"Likewise," Natan said in her own tongue. "Though, being dragged home only to be told my mother will be leaving the archipelago does not sit well with me."

"Natan," Hali growled, "we have already discussed this."

"No, Mother, *you* have discussed this with this so-called queen of the Jeweled Realm."

Natan descended the steps and stood in front of Mara. He peered at her, looking her up and down. She knew he was weighing her, measuring her worth. Boden moved to wedge himself between the pair, but Mara stopped him with her arm.

The man smelled of citrus. A freshly shaved face—an oddity among Bastian men—left Mara the ability to make out the freckles that speckled his cheeks. Eyes the color of sand glared at her.

Those were not his mother's.

"I apologize," Mara said to Natan. "I seem to have offended you in some unknown way. I'd be happy to make amends should you educate me on my indiscretion."

Natan frowned. "Hmmf," he said. "Tell me true: did you really beat Tachti's warrior?"

"Yes."

"I don't believe it." Natan turned on his heel and returned to his throne. "My army has spent many moons fighting Tachti's warriors back. He breeds them intentionally large. Intentionally fierce. I've hesitated to ask for a Champion's Fight because I feared losing the ground I've taken." He stared down at Mara, still looking her over, still uncertain.

Mara rolled her eyes. She was not there to argue with the crown prince. There had been plenty of witnesses. They'd all seen her defeat the warrior. "Well, now you need not worry." Mara shrugged. "You're welcome."

Natan's hands wound themselves into fists, but Hali spoke before he could erupt again.

"My son waged a tremendous campaign. I suspect he is sour because he was not the one to resolve it. But the Shipwright curates the events of our lives, correct, Natan?"

Natan nodded slowly, knuckles turning white.

"Good." Hali smiled. "Now, with Natan returned, the last of my navy has returned as well. In three day's time, we will strike out."

Mara glanced at Boden, who winked at her. "Thank you, Your Grace." Mara bowed her head to Hali.

She didn't know why, but the sanctuary called to her. It dragged her toward itself like Osanna had described young Bastians and the sea. Upon her first return to it, after defeating Tachti's champion, she had discovered there were indeed chairs to sit in. They formed a circle surrounding the center. It was Hali who asked to have them removed when she worshiped alone, or so a guard had informed Mara. It kept others away.

Visiting once again, Mara sat by herself in one of the many chairs, staring up at the chandelier as she had done every time she entered the sanctuary. It confused her, the size. She wondered how it was held up and why it didn't come crashing downward. It must have been a tremendous weight. And yet it was so fragile, so delicate. The white fingers of coral protruded in various directions, all reaching for something outside the circle.

It was eerie, the way it reminded Mara of fingers grasping.

A noise startled her. A gentleman's cough alerted her of his presence. She turned to find Natan standing idle in the doorway.

"I beg forgiveness, Your Grace," he muttered, not looking at her but around her. "I was told I'd find you here. I assumed you wouldn't be praying."

Mara smiled. "No . . . no, I'm not. Join me?"

Natan entered. He stopped short of the circle of chairs and bowed his head. Unknown words were uttered while he rubbed the top of each hand with the opposite palm, then held his hands together to finish. When he looked up, Mara observed him with twisted eyebrows.

"I understand that in the Jeweled Realm, you do not favor any gods," Natan said, climbing over a chair to join Mara.

"It's not that we don't favor them, we don't believe in them at all," Mara returned.

"But I wonder," Natan said, "if actively ignoring a god is just another form of believing in them?"

Mara sighed.

"Do amazing things not happen in the Jeweled Realm? Unexplainable things?" he asked.

"Certainly," Mara said.

"And you're willing to just let them be . . . mysterious?"

"Yes, I am."

Natan rubbed his chin. "Like your sword? The Sacred Sword. Supposedly magic, but you don't believe in magic. And since you trust in no god, well, then certainly it is not blessed."

Mara thought back to Boden's words on the beach, Tachti's warrior lying in the sand behind her. "The Sacred Sword is but a sword, island prince."

Natan gazed at her thoughtfully. "The First Queen would say otherwise. Certainly the Red Queen."

"They are dead." Mara's eyes bore into Natan's. "Let their silly beliefs die with them."

They sat in silence for several moments. Mara counted Natan's breaths. She didn't know why counting another's breaths made her feel better. It distracted her, she supposed. It made her be present.

"I must apologize for my behavior in the throne room." Natan stared down at his feet, his toes shifting in his sandals.

"That isn't necessary," Mara said, batting his words away.

"Please." He turned to Mara, grabbing her hand gently. "I am but a man. I had wanted the victory for myself. When I learned Tachti had accepted defeat . . . I was jealous."

"Really, this isn't necessary." She pulled her hand from Natan's. "I understand the need for victory." Mara looked up at the coral again. It suddenly reminded her of Iris's hands. The way she'd appeared skeletal and pale on the dam that day. "It makes you do . . . strange things."

Natan nodded, his gaze traveling upwards as well. They sat silently again, staring at the chandelier.

"My father had it made," Natan finally said. "A gift for my mother."

"Oh?" Mara asked. "Hali has never spoken of him. As a matter of fact, I've heard little about the king."

Natan smiled sadly. "Oh, he was never king. He married my mother shortly before she ascended to the throne. A marriage of convenience. Of duty. Nothing more."

"I see," Mara said. She studied Natan's face, seeing the smooth planes of his cheeks and sharp chin. A face unlike Hali's. Which meant he looked like his father. A handsome man, Mara thought, for Natan was handsome.

"He wanted her to love him," Natan carried on, ignoring Mara's stares, "so he commissioned this chandelier. A beautiful thing for a beautiful woman."

"And . . . did it work?"

Natan finally looked at Mara, meeting her eyes. It amazed her how much they'd change since she last saw them in the throne room. There, they had been sand, but now they were wheat in the field. Golden and life-bringing.

"My mother has loved one man. A man she knew when she was but a girl and he a boy."

"What happened to him?" Mara asked.

Love was a topic of little care in the palace of the Jeweled Realm. Her mother and father were matched as children. Her grandmother had insisted. Even her grandfather had been chosen, in a way. He was a warrior who'd helped her grandmother hold the line the day she won her first victory. She had felt the need to reward his loyalty.

And while Boden was right—Mara had fallen in love with him—she didn't know what that was meant to look like. She was raised in a realm focused on strength and power. That left little room for love and its presentations.

Natan shrugged. "He did not wish to be king. He refused to follow her to the palace when she was crowned."

"He refused?" What man refused power? This was not the way of the Jeweled Realm, where all those with ambition aimed to rule in some way. To possess power in their lives, whether merchant, miner, or magistrate. No one wanted to remain where they were. Upward mobility was something Mara's grandmother had insisted be open to everyone.

"My mother will rattle off something about the sacrifice of power. To rule is to pay a price."

Mara nodded. That sounded like Hali alright. But she wasn't wrong. "I am very grateful for your mother's friendship," Mara said. "I want you to know that."

Natan smiled. "My mother is kind when others are not. She is calm when others are uncertain."

"Must've been nice growing up with that kind of mother," Mara murmured.

Natan nudged Mara with his shoulder, bringing her eyes from her lap to meet his. "I learned. I learned when she was and was not in a pleasant mood. She has a tell, you know."

"A tell?"

"Yes," Natan nodded. "When she's upset, when she's lying. She'll mask herself with a face of serenity, as if she isn't upset, but she'll place her hand on her throat. She'll usually make it look like she's grabbing a necklace, but in truth, she's upset."

"So you knew you were in trouble when she did that?"

Natan smiled. "Oh yes. Many times."

Mara drifted backward in her mind, thinking of her own mother. Her mother had never shied away from demonstrating her anger. She'd been known for it. A day did not pass in Mara's childhood in which the Red Queen did not lose her temper.

Sometimes it was large things. Things that were so shattering that anyone would be upset. A handler's mistake caused the lameness of her favorite horse, resulting in having to put it out of its misery. Or the day her mother let Mara wear her grandmother's pearl earrings. They were the largest pearls Mara had ever seen and hung from a stud encrusted in diamonds, but Mara lost one when she—characteristically—jumped into the pond to have a swim in her clothes after Iris dared her to.

But small things could also set her off. The way Mara parted her hair on any given day. The way her father always cleared his throat while reading. Iris ... just her sister's presence would cause their mother to erupt with venomous words of distaste.

Mara inhaled sharply, realizing Iris suffered just as much as she had as a child. While Mara was never safe from their mother's tirades, she certainly did not receive the brunt of it like Iris. And their father's anger was leveled, easily concealed, malicious. It had stung, while their mother's anger had been a blunt force.

"What's wrong?" Natan asked.

He seemed genuinely worried. Mara wondered if he'd understand. The Jeweled Realm was a world apart from Bastia, where families were happy and loved one another. Mara swallowed hard, suddenly feeling sick again. It came in waves sometimes, and she'd feel adrift in the ocean, or lost in the river off Roully Dam.

The only thing that made it stop was Boden. He was her anchor. He was the foundation in which she'd build her future.

Mara stood. "I must go. Thank you, Natan, for your words."

She excused herself and left, feeling the pull of Boden even from the depths of the sanctuary. It was almost like going home.

Chapter Thirty-Five

Mara rose with the sun to dress and prepare herself for the procession to the harbor, but Boden dragged her back to bed, teasing her with kisses.

"It is as I feared," she said, stroking his hair while he rested his head on her chest. "You are a distraction."

"It is a heavy burden," Boden sighed, "but someone must do it." He kissed her, running a hand into her hair and grasping it tightly. He pulled her head away and stared at her. "It *is* a difficult duty. You and your people make things so complicated at times."

"So what do I owe you, Prince Boden, for your services?" She kissed him once. "My bed?" She kissed him again. "My crown?"

Boden twisted his lips as if in thought before offering her a sideways smile. She could see his dimple now, hidden amongst his regrown beard. Mara was glad to know it was there, like a mysterious, intimate detail only she knew. Though, no doubt Boden's mother had spent years lamenting the adorable, dimpled face of her youngest son.

"Six," he said.

"Six? Six what?"

"Children, of course."

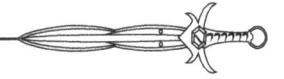

She stared at him, surprised, searching his face for a hint of the joke he played on her. His mouth twitched, and she broke. The laugh erupted from her belly, and for a brief moment, she couldn't remember ever feeling so happy.

Hali walked ahead of them, waving dramatically at her people as she sauntered past. Natan was at her side, waving along with her. Guards surrounded both of them.

The entire capital seemed to have come out for the departure. People stood, crowded together, filling every available space as their group descended the hillside toward the water. Bastians crowded the pier, their large cats skulking around their legs. Solara slunk next to Hali, but looked back at Mara every so often.

When they reached the docks, the captain of Hali's flagship—a short young man named Heron—met them. He bowed his head to Hali and Natan, then did the same for Boden and Mara.

So many faces were turned toward them. Mara's skin prickled along the back of her arms and neck at the attention. She suddenly felt sick with the thought and grasped the nearby banister.

"Your Majesty," Captain Heron said to Hali, "the sea does not seem to agree with the Jeweled One."

Hali turned her gaze toward Mara. She offered a sympathetic look and wrapped her bangled arm around Mara's shoulders. "She will stay with me, Captain Heron, in the captain's quarters. Surely, she'll find it more comfortable there." Hali smiled, assuring Mara that her words were final.

"As you say," Mara moaned. She didn't dare tell Hali that her sudden sense of sickness stemmed from the hundreds upon hundreds of Bastians looking upon them. Their eyes, along with their cats', multiplied tenfold in her mind, making the sea of people too many. Impossible. Impossible to count. Impossible to know.

"Would she not do better below deck, with me, as before when we were aboard the *Queen's Eye?*" Boden asked.

Mara smirked at him. They had spent the morning wrapped in silk sheets, building an imaginary future together with their words. Mara wanted it to be real more than anything, but it was not yet time.

She glanced from Boden to Heron. "I appreciate the use of your cabin, sir. I'm sure Queen Hali and I will be very comfortable."

Heron returned her smile and then turned his attention toward Natan.

Boden pulled Mara back by her shoulder and whispered in her ear. "How can I protect you if you're out of my sight?"

Mara shrugged his hand off her shoulder. "I will be fine, my dear distraction." She patted Boden's cheek. "Don't worry."

He fought a frown but said nothing more. He turned and marched across the deck, as if he wanted to catch a view of the harbor from the port side. Mara knew better.

She allowed herself to be swept away in Captain Heron's arm as he guided her toward his quarters, Hali and Natan ahead of them.

"I must admit, I find you quite beautiful, Jeweled One," Captain Heron purred in her ear.

Mara faked a smile and pulled away from the small man as much as she could on the crowded deck. Hali and Natan had made significant headway toward the cabin, but Mara and Captain Heron were stuck among the crew and the many soldiers joining them.

"Thank you, captain," she said. "Most people in my realm find my crown far more beautiful than I."

Captain Heron offered her a frown, one perfected by a fine actor. "Oh come now. I don't believe that. Such beautiful skin, like coffee with milk. And eyes like gold!"

She tried to laugh, to seem amused, but she wanted nothing more than to leave the man. Thankfully, Hali turned and saw her pinned to the captain's side.

"Captain!" Hali called over the noise of the deck.

Captain Heron's shoulders drooped at the sound. He dragged Mara through the mass of people to meet up with Hali and Natan at the cabin doors.

"The deck is crowded," Captain Heron joked. "We lost our way, I'm afraid."

Hali stared down her nose at Captain Heron. "Ah, yes. So many extra hands on deck. Speaking of hands"—she let go of Natan's arm and leaned in low to Captain Heron's face—"though you may find my jewel precious, I'll remind you only once she is not yours. If I see your hands upon her again, I will let the Ursan do with you as he will. Are we clear?"

Captain Heron nodded slowly, his eyes expanded with fear. He bowed curtly to Mara before scuttling away, crowing orders to his crew.

Hali watched him go, her eyes much like Solara's when the large cat stalked birds inside the palace grounds. "He's a good captain," she said to Mara. "He understands the sea well. But we all have flaws."

"And Heron's is?"

Hali lifted her hand in demonstration. "He can't seem to figure out where to keep his hands."

Mara nodded. "Noted."

Boden appeared from the crowd. "Everything alright?"

"Yes," Hali assured him. "Captain Heron was just making himself acquainted with the Jeweled One. He'll be of no trouble again. This I promise."

Boden looked from Hali to Mara. It was then, in the way he looked at her, that made Mara catch her breath momentarily. It was imperceptible to others, but she felt the hitch in her usual rhythmic inhale and exhale. The way he cared. The way he waited on her.

And no one else.

"I'm . . . fine," she said.

He dipped his head to her and returned to the mess of the deck. Mara watched him go and briefly wished to be back in the palace bed with him, the morning light spilling through breaks in the curtains, whispering dreams in the growing light of dawn.

"This way," Hali took Mara's arm gently and led her into Heron's cabin.

With the doors shut behind her, the commotion of the deck seemed less momentous. She found she could think better. With her mind actually working, she wondered about the captain's audacity.

"Would you really let Boden hurt him?" Mara asked.

Hali lounged in a velvet chair the color of a dusty rose. She languished in it, her limbs sprawled out. She seemed surprised at Mara's question.

"She's done worse herself," Natan mused as he leaned against Heron's large desk.

"Surely not," Mara said with a smile, but it quickly faded when she saw the pair were serious.

Hali sighed. She sat up and leaned toward Mara. "Just because Bastians do not wear our brutality on our sleeve like you, jewel, does not mean we cannot be ruthless."

"You speak as if you know much about my people," Mara said. "I apologize for knowing little about yours. Even after spending so much time in your kingdom."

Hali shrugged. "It is the nature of the Jeweled Realm's people. The First Queen sought stability. She raised up the people of the gutters, deposed and abandoned, and created the foundation for an entire country. Your kingdom is still so young. It is only natural to be so self-centered. Your time will come."

It jilted Mara to hear someone, a stranger, speak of her grandmother in such a way. But it was obvious Hali knew about much of the world, despite the size and position of her own country. The Isles might have been islands, but Queen Hali was not.

"Do you know of the nomads?" Mara asked.

Hali nodded slowly.

"Tell me about them?"

Hali accepted a glass from Natan. He had helped himself to Captain Heron's private cupboard. He offered Mara one, but she refused. She needed to remain lucid, of solid mind, from here on out. If she were to defeat Iris, she'd need to be at her best.

Whatever that meant anymore.

"There is little to tell," Hali said after gulping some ruby drink. "They keep to themselves and like it that way."

"As do I and my people," Mara said, "and yet you know of us. Our customs. Our language."

Hali stared at Mara over her glass, her eyes stone. Finally, she relented. Her shoulders relaxed, and she spoke. "They are nomadic in the sense that they travel up and down the Waste, following a path laid down for them long, long ago."

"To follow food," Mara said.

"No," Natan corrected. "The moon."

Her confusion must have appeared vividly on her face, for Hali stood and walked to a map pinned to Captain Heron's wall. It displayed all of what Mara knew of the world. She saw the Jeweled Realm, separated from Ursa by the swath of the Waste. The smaller countries were north, ones barely worth her time. And south was the Lion, leaping across the ocean, east to west.

Hali placed her hand on the Waste, dark and empty, save for a few landmarks.

"The nomads worship the moon. They see it as their celestial mother, for only a loving force would offer light amidst the darkness." Hali traced her fingers from the rocky beaches of the south along the desert toward the north. There, she let her finger linger over a black dot. "In the north is their nest, as they call it. They all return there, once yearly, to celebrate. A moon of red emerges, demonstrating their mother's love, that she is willing to spill blood for them. And in turn . . . " Hali trailed off, her hand dropping to her side.

"And in turn, what?" Mara asked.

Hali stared at the dot. "They spill blood for her. There is a legend amongst them, that one day the moon will descend upon them, personified, and lead them to freedom from the Waste, spilling blood for them as she goes."

Slowly, Hali turned to face Mara. She stared at her, clearly uncomfortable with the truth. But despite already knowing what Hali was going to say, Mara needed her to say it.

Hali sighed. "If Iris has convinced them she is this version of their mother, then they will do anything she says. Anything."

Mara swallowed, considering Hali's words. She had long wondered what Iris held over the nomads. Now she knew. Iris had always been good at lying. Mara just didn't know she could convince an entire nation of people.

But was that not what she had done herself?

"If I kill her, will they return to the Waste?"

Hali shook her head. "I don't know," she whispered.

Killing Iris might not be enough, Mara realized. If the nomads were unwilling to honor the Jeweled Realm way of sister fighting sister, if they were unwilling to standby while their honored mother fought Mara for the

Jeweled Realm's throne, then Mara's work would not be finished when she killed Iris. Mara would have to defeat a nation, too.

She'd have to wage an entire war.

Her heart thudded inside her chest, and she suddenly felt out of breath. Not wanting to appear weak in front of Natan and Hali, Mara excused herself.

She emerged onto the deck, where only a few crewmembers remained ambling about, and sat on the nearby steps. The salty wind whipped at her hair and stung her eyes, but it was easier to hide the tears that sat on the corners of her lashes that way.

"Are you alright?" Boden's voice drifted in on the wind.

Mara turned, not knowing from which direction his voice had come, and found him standing above her on the steps. He descended and thumped down next to her, agitated. He didn't like the ships. He didn't like the ocean.

At least they had that in common.

"I . . . I was talking to Hali about the Waste." She attempted to discreetly wipe the tears from her eyes before they fell and gave her away. Boden watched her before reaching out and wiping the tears away for her with the rough edge of his hand.

"And?" he asked, drying his hand on his pants.

Mara watched his face shift beneath his beard. He had cleaned it up since their arrival in Bastia. Bastian men, those that wore facial hair, kept it neatly lined and combed. Boden appeared to be trying out the trend. Mara admired the straight lines along his jaw and cheeks, making it easier for her to see the freckles hidden beneath.

"I now know why the nomads follow Iris."

"Oh? Has she bewitched them with her powers?" Boden mused.

"No." She felt the fear rise again. "She's convinced them she is a god. The moon, no less, here to save them and deliver them from their desert prison."

He wiped the start of another tear from one of Mara's eyes. "I've heard it said in Ursa that the nomads worship the moon."

He seemed amused by the prospect, which only made Mara angry on top of her fear. An entire nation was willing to die for Iris, and Boden found it funny.

"I don't see why you need to smile about it," Mara said.

Boden cleared his throat, attempting to hide his smile. "Forgiveness, Your Grace."

"What's so funny?" She couldn't decide if she wanted to slap him for his aloofness or kiss him for his gentleness. Her sense of frustration mixed with her feelings for him, and she felt tossed about like flotsam on the waves.

"Well, one sister despises gods, and the other thinks she is one." Boden choked on his own laughter then, leaning against the banister.

Mara glared at him, but slowly, a smile formed. She laughed, too, feeling her fear drain away. "She's crazy," Mara admitted. "Absolutely insane."

"Yes," Boden agreed, "we've established that."

She looked out at the deck, mostly cleared of soldiers now. All crewmembers were in their assigned stations, preparing to push the ship from the dock. Natan stood stoic on the dock, having finally left his mother's side and disembarked.

Mara's eyes grazed across the island that surrounded them. The green was so vibrant. The buildings looked like precious gemstones along the mountainside. Large cats strode through the streets, unhindered and unbothered. She made a vow to return. She'd come back and broker a trade with the Bastians. If only for the chance to see Hali again.

"What does Kalda say?" Mara asked.

"What?"

"Kalda. What does he say of the nomads and their moon worship?"

Boden sighed and rubbed his head, attempting to remember. "He said while the moon may be lovely, a woman it is not."

Mara laughed.

"And while a woman is also lovely," Boden's tone changed and his voice lowered to a whisper, "a celestial being, she is not. For while the moon may rise and fall, and a woman may live and die, these things matter not in time. As do all things."

Mara frowned. "Bleak."

Boden nodded. "At the end of his life, Kalda was very focused on the continuation of time and his place within it."

"And what of your place, Prince Boden?" Mara leaned back on her hands, studying Boden's jaw, admiring the way it moved from frown to smile and back again seamlessly, revealing she could still find his sensitive places. She could still ask the questions he didn't enjoy answering.

"I don't follow," he said, eyeing her between slotted lids.

The ship had shoved away from the dock, and the sun was in full force, pressing down on them, bathing everything in warm, bright sunlight. Mara held her hands to her brows, shielding her eyes. She could feel sweat bead upon her neck, sliding its way down her shoulder. Boden's forehead glistened with salty sweat. They'd need to find shade soon. The Bastian sun of midday did not entirely suit their mainland complexions.

"You needn't follow me to war," Mara said. "I have the Bastian military at my disposal now. You already nearly died for me. I don't need you to do it for me again."

Boden gazed at her. He smiled, then lost it, then chuckled to himself. He shook his head and stood. "You've no idea, do you?" he asked.

"What?" Mara hated when he belittled her like that, making her sound like a child.

He just stared down at her, a look so reminiscent of Iris that Mara suddenly felt sick. Boden looked away for a moment, watching the Bastians work. They performed their duties in constant song, throwing their voices into the mix of wind and gulls crying. It was beautiful, in a way. Strange, but beautiful.

Boden turned back to Mara, the corner of his mouth slightly upturned, and said, "I would die for you, over and over again, if that is what it took."

Mara's breath caught. "You don't have to, Boden. I prefer you alive."

"But that's what love is, Sword Queen." His half-smile was back, and Mara felt her heart pounding in her chest.

"Boden, I'm afraid I don't know how to love in the way you deserve to be loved."

"Don't worry. I'll teach you."

Chapter Thirty-Six

Mara had not seen land for many days. Only the constant color blue, in its various shades and hues, filled her vision. In the mornings, the water remained the beautiful, saturated azure that surrounded the islands. The sky was a friendlier shade of her sister's eyes, the color they'd been when they were young and still friends. In the evenings, the sea bled dark like ink, and the sky caught fire before weeping into a blue-black so clear she could see more stars than she'd ever known existed.

She took her meals with Hali. Heron joined them, usually. Boden less so. He claimed to like the crew and the stories they told. Mara assumed that was less true than the fact that Boden despised Captain Heron, but she appreciated that he did not smother her.

She'd find him, when she needed to, in the dark of night below deck. They'd lay smooshed in his hammock while Boden whispered stories of Kalda or his childhood in her ears until she fell asleep. Sleep was no longer a stranger to Mara. She fell easily into dreams now, wrapped safely in Boden's arms. But during the day, she needed air. She needed the space between them to breathe and think.

During dinner one night, talk arose of where to land the fleet.

"Should we not land in the Jeweled Realm?" Mara asked, sipping the fizzy drink the Bastian sailors favored on long voyages. The bubbles tickled her nose.

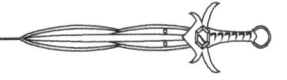

It was malt-like and stunk, but with fresh-water reserves limited, she drank it anyway.

Heron shared a look with Hali. "What would be the logic in that?" he asked.

Mara scowled and set her glass down a little too hard. "It is *my* kingdom. A triumphant return seems it would be most welcoming after being under the rule of a woman claiming to be a moon."

Heron laughed and sipped his drink. "She has a point," he said to Hali.

Hali smiled but shook her head. "It will not do, my jewel. While my navy is great, it will do little good if we cannot make landfall. Your sister will have the southern borders closely guarded."

"So, what do you suggest? Ursa?" She knew as soon as she said it that it wouldn't work. Boden's father and brother had chosen their side. They'd bet on Iris and used their kingdom as collateral. Landing there would be possible, perhaps, but they'd never make it out of Ursa alive.

"The Waste is our only choice, my jewel," Hali said, her eyes reading Mara's realization on her face.

Mara shook her head. "No." She sounded like a child, and heat filled her chest with frustration from it, but she set her fork down and attempted to even her temper. "We cannot land in the Waste. You said yourself that my sister controls too much there. It's too dangerous."

Hali leaned back in her chair. They locked eyes, neither wishing to look away first. To look away was to admit a weaker will. But Hali did not play games. She reached for her glass and sipped it, keeping her eyes ever on Mara. When she was through, she set her glass down neatly and smiled. "You fear the Waste."

Mara choked on a laugh. "And you don't?"

"I fear many things. But the Waste and its people are not among them."

"But y-you said . . ." Mara stuttered and looked away, the heat of Hali's eyes too much. She settled on the map, the Waste a dark scar across the mainland. "You said they'll do whatever she asks. That they think she's a god. Would it not aid them to fight on land they know well?"

"Ursa despises you," Heron interrupted, "and the Jeweled Realm only follows she who wears the Sacred Sword. This limits our choices, Jeweled One."

"Exactly." Mara felt vigor in her voice for the first time in a long time. She would not lose this argument. If they were to land and fight, they'd land in the Jeweled Realm.

They'd land in her home.

"The Sword is lost. Neither of us carries it, so loyalty lies with no one."

Heron stared at her. Hali slowly shook her head at him, clearing her throat. Heron pursed his lips, attempting to keep his mouth shut.

"What?" Mara asked.

"My jewel... she bears the Sword." Hali's voice was low, grave, more serious than Mara had ever heard it before.

"You're lying."

Hali shook her head again. "We received word shortly after you arrived. Your sister retrieved the Sword somehow and walked into your palace wearing it. The Jeweled Realm bends its knee to her fully."

A rope cinched itself across her chest. She couldn't breathe, though, her chest heaved as she tried desperately to catch her breath. Heron stood at the sight of her so upset. Her vision darkened around the edges. All she could see was Hali, sitting tall, beautiful, and serene, as if she had not just spoken words that condemned Mara to ruin.

"And you didn't tell me? Why?" Mara stood, her chair daring to tip and tumble behind her.

Hali held her head high. "Because it doesn't matter."

"Doesn't matter?" Mara laughed out of anger. "My kingdom bends its knee to someone else, and you say it doesn't matter? I'm sure that's easy to say with your throne intact."

Hali sighed as if she was tired of dealing with an insolent child. She stood slowly, ensuring her own chair would not fall behind her. Then she walked, in her graceful manner, to the map.

"Your sister's power is not real." Hali focused on the black slash of land denoting the Waste. "Whether or not you believe that. The people of the Waste use their knowledge of minerals and nature to perform parlor tricks and glamours. She's learned these ways and uses it to create her own illusions."

Hali peered at Mara over her shoulder. "Much like your Sacred Sword, it means nothing. Its value comes from those beholden to it. Your grandmother created a grand shroud of mystery surrounding the Sword, ensuring it would always remain as a symbol for the Jeweled Realm. But it means nothing, Jeweled One. You are power. Not the Sword."

"I know that now," Mara argued. She presented her left hand to Hali, so empty without the hilt of the Sacred Sword. "But my people don't. They will still see the Sword in Iris's hand and in turn, see their queen."

Hali slowly made her way toward Mara, her hand trailing down the edge of the wooden table. "You are an amazing warrior, as we've seen. When you defeat your sister, what then?" Hali smirked. "You think they'll still bend their knee to a piece of metal and a giant gem? Come now, Jeweled One, you are too smart for that."

Mara fell silent, a thousand images appearing in her mind at once. Memories of long ago, of watching the giant emerald glimmer at her grandmother's side. Of the Sword being bestowed upon her mother following the death of the First Queen. The nightly ritual of sitting at her mother's feet, watching and learning the perfect way to sharpen the Sword. The smells of the whetstone, of metal, of her mother's perfume.

Her head felt dizzy, and Mara rocked on her feet. Despite knowing the Sword no longer meant something to her, deep down, Mara knew it wasn't simply a sword, it was a symbol. And her people still bowed to that symbol. If Iris possessed it, Mara wondered if the Bastian army would be enough to take back her throne.

A hand rested on her shoulder. It was cool to the touch on her hot skin. She turned to see Hali's bejeweled hand resting there.

Hali reached and delicately petted Mara's sharp cheekbones. "It is not all loss, my jewel," Hali cooed. "For this lie of your grandmother's was like a womb, wrapping you within, growing you into the warrior queen you are. The Sword might not be real, but your skill certainly is. Your people will see that. It is time you dismantle this lie."

Mara nodded in agreement, choking down a sob. She wanted to cry. She wanted to scream out. But that was not her way. She straightened and turned toward the door. "I need air," she muttered.

Neither Heron nor Hali followed. Neither dared to. Mara felt their eyes on her back as she retreated into the sunshine and spit of sea swells. Outside, the rope around her chest loosened. The salty air seemed to ease her breathing, if for a moment. She inhaled deeply several times and found her way to a railing.

She stood staring out at the waves for a long time. The sun roamed over her head and found its descent in the west. The sailors worked around her, none daring to address the Jeweled One. They whistled and hummed foreign songs, occupying their mouths so they wouldn't slip up and bark something at her.

With the sunset, she found the horizon. It revealed itself, delineating the water from the sky for the first time since sunrise. It puzzled Mara how easily the sailors found navigating in the ocean. The surrounding blues blurred so seamlessly sometimes she wondered why they didn't drift off into the sky, a ship in never-ending blue.

Boden appeared just as the stars did. They peaked out from behind their dark curtain, one by one, some brilliant and some dull, but all beautiful. She enjoyed counting them, and did so now, though, she always ended the evening by giving up. There were simply too many.

"Have you supped?" His voice broke her thoughts, interrupting her counting.

She sighed, knowing she'd never count them all. "Yes," she replied, still staring at one particularly bright star.

It glimmered red at times, other times white. Not amongst the first stars to appear, Mara waited diligently for it every night. She didn't know why, but it was like waiting for a friend.

Boden followed her gaze and settled on the star as well. Mara waited for him to speak. He always offered some musing from his day, some heard story or learned fact from his time spent on the ship. It was their nightly ritual.

She found it strange how temporary their time on the ship would be, and yet still they yearned for routine. They drifted daily in and out of tasks meant to occupy them, but always seemed to meet in the evening, in the same spot, to end the day.

Together.

"Word is we're aiming toward the Waste," Boden said, still staring at the star. His breath was barely visible in small gusts of moisture. The farther north they traveled, the colder the evenings grew. The skin along her arms prickled at the cool breeze. Boden glanced at her pin-pricked arm and immediately removed his cloak. He draped it over her shoulders but said nothing more.

Mara couldn't pull her gaze from the star. It seemed the only thing rooting her feet to the ship's deck, anchoring her. Without it, she might drift away, unsure, uncertain, and afraid.

"She has the Sword," she finally said. She hadn't meant to whisper it, but didn't try to repeat it louder.

Boden must have caught it, because she heard the hitch in his breath as he inhaled. He looked at her, but quickly looked away.

"So?" he said. "It's just a sword."

Mara let out a small laugh. "You sound like Hali."

"Well"—Boden leaned on the railing—"is she wrong?"

Clouds rolled in, nearly invisible in the darkening sky, and slowly enveloped the night. Her brilliant star disappeared, breaking the spell it held on her. She looked at Boden. He stared at her so intently, as if he could read her without the need for her to speak. But what fascinated her most was that it didn't seem to matter. He waited for her to speak. He *wanted* to listen.

"My people still believe in the Sword, Boden, even if I've learned the truth."

His arm was around her, pulling her close. She inhaled the warmth he offered, letting it settle over her, soothing her for the evening.

"Show them the truth," he said. "Show them it isn't the Sword, but the woman that rules the realm."

Chapter Thirty-Seven

The Waste stared at her from a distance, dark and empty. Sharp spires of rocks erupted from the bay, but Captain Heron expertly led the armada through the rocky waters. A long sandbar melded the water to the rocky shore, and it was there that Heron made their headway.

"I've sailed these waters several times before," he assured Mara. "There is no proper port in the Waste for the nomads to trade their goods, but you can occasionally find them camped out waiting for a ship to pass."

"What sort of things do they trade?" Mara asked, hanging tightly to the nearby railing. Boden stood behind her, his hand quick to steady her around the waist whenever a strong wave rocked the ship.

"Precious metals mostly," he said, spinning the large wheel of the ship frantically to correct its path. "Medicinal plants. Some small animals. Lizards and things."

"Smoke," Hali added, clinging to the railing opposite Mara. "A drug. They use it in their rituals. Black as night, it blinds the user temporarily."

Mara turned toward Boden. "Perhaps that was what Iris used on me on the dam?"

Boden nodded in agreement. "Aye, it made me nauseous as I jumped to grab you," he said. "I was disoriented. Probably why I lost you in the fall."

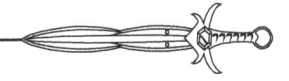

"Or that was the fall itself," Mara smiled.

An hour passed, and still they struggled through the waves. The spires grew thicker the closer they came to the sandbar, erupting from the water like skeletal hands reaching for the sun. Made of a rough red stone, Mara felt she could reach out and touch a few as they passed so close by.

"The rock is plentiful here," Heron said, "but the water is deep. We'll anchor ahead and use the rafts to make landfall."

"As you say," Hali said. "The sooner the better." It was the first time she looked uncomfortable on the water. Her skin was no longer clear and vibrant, but dull. She held her stomach and took a deep breath. Mara remembered Osanna's words, and how some Bastians never made it on the sea.

A useful life, but not dangerously so.

Mara watched Hali squeeze tightly to the railing, her knuckles turning white. Her chest would still while she held her breath amidst the incoming sweep of a wave, and then she'd slowly release it with the water. Hali was not dangerous looking, but beneath the surface lay something so much more threatening. She was smart. Cunning. She knew when to withhold and when to give.

A true queen.

Hali turned a nauseous face toward Mara. "I bet I look a wreck," she said. "Osanna would be ashamed."

Hali's voice caught on her sister's name, the first time Mara had ever heard her speak it. She offered Hali an encouraging smile. "No, she wouldn't," Mara said. "Not of you. Never."

Hali bowed her head to Mara in time with the next swell. She slipped on her feet, but Boden reached across and caught the island queen in his other arm. He pulled her to Mara, and the three huddled together as Captain Heron laughed in the face of the next swell.

"Yes!" he screamed into the wave, water dripping off his forehead and down his face. Water soaked him through and hung his clothes to his miniature frame, but fear was nowhere upon him. "This is the ocean!" he yelled back at them. "Feel her power!"

The closer they came to the sandbar, the smaller the waves became. Finally, they found relief from the surf within an inner circle of spires near the beach. Mara retched once while Hali threatened to follow her should she not retire herself to the cabin to rest. Boden remained with Mara, assisting her in cleaning her face.

"I would make a pathetic Bastian," Mara joked as Boden offered her his cloak to wipe her face on.

Boden laughed. "No, the sea doesn't suit you. It doesn't seem to suit many. You're better suited for comfortable thrones, delicate vins, and diplomacy."

Mara punched him in the arm before kissing him quickly. "I'd like to think I'm suited for more than that."

She left him there and descended the steps to the main deck. Sailors ran in a chaotic rhythm, loading rafts with sailors and soldiers of equal measure and supplies before lowering the small crafts down to the water.

Mara watched as they lowered a raft. The sailors on it struck out immediately toward the beach, rowing in a rhythm sung by the soldiers. It did not take long before several small rafts occupied the beach, their occupants spilling out across the sand.

"Ready, Jeweled One?" Heron called to Mara. He stood next to the railing, a raft hoisted onto the pulleys that would drop it down into the water. He helped Hali into the raft and waited for Mara. She accepted his hand and gingerly stepped into the swaying craft next to Hali. Boden followed. Three of Hali's guards joined them, followed by two sailors. Captain Heron stood on the deck, his hand on the rope that would drop the craft.

"I await your return, Your Majesty," he said to Hali.

Hali dipped her head toward the man with a smile. "A pleasure, as always, Captain Heron."

"The pleasure is always mine, Your Majesty." He yanked the rope, and the pulleys whizzed to life, dropping the craft much faster than Mara expected.

Boden's hand found hers when they hit the water, and he squeezed it twice. "It's okay," he whispered to her.

Mara squeezed back.

The sailors began rowing. It amazed Mara at how smoothly they accomplished their task. Their raft glided across the bay like skaters on the Mousseaux when it froze over during mid-winter. They made such quick work, they were lurching upon the beach before Mara had time to feel the salty breeze on her face.

The sailors jumped out first and hauled the small boat as far onto the beach as they could. The soldiers then jumped out and assisted them in pulling the craft farther out of the water so their queen would not wet her feet unnecessarily. A soldier assisted Hali in stepping out onto the sand.

Boden jumped out and reached back for Mara. "Are you ready?"

Mara took his hand and jumped onto the sand. It differed from the beach of Bastia. There, where Warlord Tachti's champion had died, the sand was soft, luxurious in a way. The sand of the Waste was hard-packed and dry. The breeze cut across the sandbar like a whip, bringing with it a cold smell of salt and fish. It was, much like Mara imagined the Waste to be, unwelcoming and barren. Even its color was an unwelcoming shade of red.

"Well," she sighed, "we made it."

Hali reached to her and squeezed her shoulder. "Now the actual work begins."

The soldiers made their way across the dunes then cleared a path among the rocks to reach the cliff top. It was a scramble to reach it, but by the start of sunset, they had climbed the highest point.

Before them, the Waste spilled out. Plains of sand rushed forth like a red sea interrupted only occasionally by scrub brush or a barren river wash. Nothing moved. Nothing even looked alive. A series of hills started their slow roll a short distance off. It offered the only possible protection in the area. Hali instructed the soldiers to set up camp there, amidst the hills.

"We'll set lookouts at the top," Hali assured Mara. "It's the best we can do."

A short and square woman wearing a beaded necklace that covered her chest approached. "I'll send scouts out to see what there is to see. The witch would be a fool to not have the entire coastline watched. I'm certain she knows we're here."

"Very good, general," Hali agreed.

"We know your sister is mad," Boden said to Mara. "Perhaps she's a fool, too?"

Mara sighed. "Doubtful. She learned warcraft from our father. While not the Red Queen, he was equally brutal."

Boden winced. "Well, we might want to reconsider the entire campaign. Return to bed?"

"Too late for that." Mara elbowed him. "Come on."

They fell into line with a platoon of soldiers, all hauling gear toward the hills. Later, the ships would offload pieces of wagons to be reassembled on the beach, but with the dying light, there was no time for that now. They'd have to bring what they could by hand.

Mara offered her help to a soldier struggling with several tent poles. The woman scoffed at Mara when she reached for the other end, but upon realizing who Mara was, she dipped her head low.

"Apologies, Jeweled One." The woman held tight to the poles. "I meant no insult. But I am certain I can carry these myself."

"As you say," Mara said, letting her go.

The woman lurched on, half carrying, half dragging the poles. She was tall, muscular, with black hair knotted above her head. In the dying sun, her skin blurred with the darkening sand, making her an illusion of the night. Mara blinked, and she was nearly gone, disappearing into the darkness ahead.

"Here," Boden's voice came from behind her.

She turned in time to receive a wallop of something in her arms. A burlap sack with a yeasty scent wafting out the top found its way into her arms. The smell of bread was welcome, and the sack wasn't particularly heavy. "What's this?" She slung the bag over her shoulder.

"The Bastians may have trouble treating you like a commoner, but they don't have a problem with me." Boden tipped his chin toward his own large sack over his shoulder.

It took a moment for her to realize what Boden had meant. She offered him her largest smile and turned to follow the soldiers farther into the desert.

They walked in silence, their footfalls softened by the sand. It was an eerie sound, one that Mara found more cage-like than freeing. She found she couldn't think beyond herself, beyond where her foot was going to fall next. A warmth spread across her cheeks and heat pressed into her neck where the sack rubbed against her skin.

Stars peered at them from above, but Mara didn't dare look for her star. To stop and look would mean staying still, and she feared that if she stayed still for too long, she'd never move again.

Finally, a gruff voice ahead called a stop. It was the small general, her voice gone hoarse from the effort of moving through the dry terrain.

"Set it up here," she barked. "The queen's tent first."

Mara threw down her sack and sank to the sand. The backs of her heels were rubbed raw where sand had worked its way into her boots. She had cinched them tight before they started, but it didn't matter. Sand always found a way to bite. To irritate and agonize. She rubbed her eyes to push the sleep away and instantly regretted it. There was sand there, too, blown in by the steady breeze.

Curses flooded beneath her breath. A soft laughter fell nearby.

"The desert is fickle," the voice said.

Mara looked up with bleary eyes to find the soldier from before. Her tent poles were gone, her hands instead filled with a waterskin. She drank heavily before passing it off to Mara.

"Thank you," Mara said, her voice scratchy.

The water was sweet upon her lips. She hadn't realized how thirsty she had become, but she remembered her mother's warnings. *The Waste is no place to venture,* she had always said. The land was deceptive. Quiet and somewhat serene, death lay just below the surface. One would find themselves dying long before they realized it.

"Keep it," the soldier said. "I have another." She headed toward the beginnings of Hali's tent. Mara watched her go as she vanished into the night. The Bastian warriors were tall and lithe. A different creature altogether from the soldiers of the Jeweled Realm, where they favored muscle and mass over leanness and speed. She wondered what the nomadic warriors of the Waste would be like.

Boden found her sitting there, considering this. She stared at the sand but wasn't really looking at it. He sank to the ground next to her and reached for the waterskin.

"Mind?" He didn't wait for an answer.

She broke the silence during his second swig. "What if the nomads are better?" she asked.

Startling him, water spilled down his chin and into his beard. He choked on his own laugh. "Better what? Fighters? Than the Bastians? Doubtful."

"You say that knowing nothing about them," Mara argued.

"I know a little about them." Boden pointed the waterskin at her authoritatively.

Mara raised her brows. "About their fighting? Their army?"

Boden frowned. "Well, no. But you don't know any more than I do. Your worry is pointless."

"Focusing on your enemy is always productive," Mara huffed.

"Are those your mother's words?"

"My grandmother's," she admitted.

"Look . . ." Boden leaned in close to Mara, their shoulders touching. She didn't pull away as she felt the sweat of his arm slick against her skin. His breath fell on her face, cool from the water. "We are here, in the Waste. It's a little late to worry. Surely your grandmother has some pearl of wisdom about worrying on the eve of battle being useless or something."

Mara's lips turned down in thought. "On the eve of battle," she said, "it is best to withhold oneself from drink and luxuries, lest they dull the mind in battle."

"Of course she said that," Boden muttered. "Okay, well, Kalda said something better. He said, 'The night before blood be spilled, one should do naught but sleep well, knowing all paths led to that night, and none shall lead away save for the morrow.'"

Mara wanted to laugh and poke fun at Boden and his belief in his ridiculous saint, but she found truth in Kalda's words. There was no other way. The only way out was what tomorrow brought. And the next day. Onward. Forward.

But never back, she thought.

"Jeweled One!" The general's voice broke through the glittering darkness of the sand. "Queen Hali's tent is raised. She requests your presence."

Mara cupped Boden's cheek before pushing herself from the ground. The sand stuck to her pants, and she wiped it away.

"Mara," Boden's voice caught her before she could take two steps. He didn't appear as if he were going to say more. He stared at her, a ghost of a smile on his lips.

"Yes?"

"Do not let her keep you long," he finally said. "I've thought of several other things you can do to repay me for my devotion." The clouds hid the moon, shrouding his face in darkness. Only a slight orange glint glimmered in his eyes, a reflection of the fire built for Hali's tent. It was strange, but Mara found she missed the blue that usually penetrated her shield.

"Oh?" She smiled. "You've piqued my interest, Prince Boden."

The light reflected in his eyes seemed to glow brighter. "I'll be waiting."

Chapter Thirty-Eight

Hali's tent was sparsely decorated. More amenities would come, Mara was sure, once the ships were fully offloaded. But until then, Hali would sleep on a pile of furs—some sourced from Ursa, no doubt by the look of them—and sup upon meals at a table with chairs formed from bent branches. They weaved in and out, intertwined to form legs, a seat, and a high back. The table was round with enough room for two to sit and share a meal. Hali, seated in one of the chairs, gestured for Mara to take the other.

"Sit, Jeweled One. Rest your feet."

Mara obeyed. Her feet were screaming at her to stop moving. She wanted nothing more than to remove them from her body. A steward entered, carrying a silver pitcher and two silver goblets. She placed them on the table and poured deep-red vin into both cups.

"A nomadic wine," Hali said, lifting her own cup to her nose. She sniffed it before sipping.

"Nomadic?" Mara hesitated.

"Be at ease, my jewel. This wine was purchased many moons ago. Captain Heron procured it himself and kept it for some special occasion. He told me today he saw no other occasion better suited than the campaign of the Jeweled Queen across the Waste."

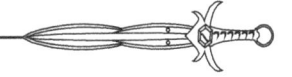

Mara swirled the vin in the goblet, staring down into its depth. She had wanted to remain vigilant. Death by poison would make a sorry end to her story. She smelled the vin herself. It was bold and strong. Even the color reminded her of blood. Reluctantly, she sipped at it, embracing the bite of it on her tongue.

"And where do the nomads find acceptable land to grow for their vineyards?"

"To the north," Hali answered. "Everything they love is to the north."

"Near their nest?"

Hali drank deeply and poured herself another glass. "Yes. No one knows much of what lies past their fortressed city. Perhaps the desert retreats, allowing forests to prosper and water to flow."

"And vineyards to flourish." Mara held up her glass to study it in the light. A red drop sought its way down the silver, leaving behind a cloudy trail marking its way. She licked it, admiring the way the metallic taste blended with the vin's sour.

"Has the general heard from her scouts?" Mara asked. She leaned back in the chair, attempting to make herself comfortable. The twigs seemed to dig into her legs, and she couldn't help but adjust how she sat every few seconds.

Hali seemed perfectly content as she leaned back in her own chair with her legs crossed, exposing them through the high slit of her linen dress. Bangles stacked one atop the other on her ankle. Their brilliant colors contrasted with the darkness of the sand-filled tent floor and the umber of her skin.

"No, but soon, my jewel. When I know, you'll know."

They sat together in silence for some time, sipping their vin, thinking. Mara wondered if two queens ever shared a tent during her grandmother's time, or if war was the only answer the First Queen ever found.

Outside, the noise of the camp filled the still night. The constant rumble of voices bounced off the tent walls while the heat of the day, rising from the ground, filled the inside. A golden lantern hung above their heads was their sole source of light. The flame flickered in its cage, casting off brilliant flashes and dancing shadows.

Mara's skin was sticky from sweat. She yearned to take a bath. When she sighed, she gained Hali's attention, her dark eyes sidling toward Mara like a snake.

"Will you kill her this time?" Hali broke their silence. Her voice was low. Tired. But she leaned forward, eager to hear Mara's reply.

"I must," Mara said between sips of her vin. "I've come this far."

"But you don't want to. Still."

Mara twirled the stem of the goblet in her fingers. It was cold and smooth to the touch, a brilliant sensation for her stiff and dry skin. She looked at Hali over the edge and smiled. "You sound as if you don't want me to."

Hali slumped back in her chair, frowning. "I want my jewel to be who she is. Brilliant. Sharp. I hate to see your hand forced to do something you think is wrong."

"I forced Iris's hand when I chose not to kill her."

"You gave her a gift," Hali returned with a scowl.

"A gift she didn't want. I should have killed her. I know that now."

Hali watched Mara for a moment. Mara could see she was thinking, considering, attempting to choose her words carefully. "And you're ... certain this time?" Hali finally asked. "That you'll kill her?"

Mara bowed her head. "Yes, I'm sure."

Hali stood abruptly, the branches of her chair kicking up sand when she pushed away from the table. "Then there's nothing left to discuss," she said, her tone sharp-edged and dangerous. "You'll need your rest, my jewel, if you are to conquer your sister in battle. I suggest you sleep." Hali pointed to the pile of furs laid out neatly in the corner of the tent. "I must have a word with the general. If you'll excuse me."

Hali disappeared beyond the flap of the tent's door before Mara could stop her, before she could utter anything in reply. The island queen was angry with her. But why? She wanted Mara to remain true to herself. Isn't that what she had said?

Mara slouched in her chair, tapping her fingers to her forehead. Since leaving her palace, there was no alternative. Iris must die. If Mara were honest with herself, there had indeed been a time when she was willing to forgo the entire thing—to let Iris live, even let her have the throne. But that time had passed. The situation had changed.

Mara had changed.

Boden appeared at the flap, startling her. "Apologies," he muttered, taking up Hali's seat. "I saw Hali leave in a hurry. What were you talking about?"

"She asked me if I still planned on killing Iris," Mara said, staring down into her empty goblet. The dregs of wine left various shapes in the bottom. Some claimed to read them, in the alleys of the Jeweled Realm, like sorceresses. Most paid them no mind. Mara wondered what they'd see in the bottom of her glass. Victory? Defeat?

Betrayal?

"And what did you say?"

"I said of course." Mara set her goblet down a little too hard. The potent vin seemed to have had an extreme effect on Mara. She felt drowsy and her head ached behind her eyes.

"Really?"

Mara glared at Boden. He had watched her kill Henri and his cronies. At the beach in Bastia, he'd stood behind her, a captive audience as she slaughtered Tachti's warrior. Why did everyone suddenly think she wouldn't kill her sister?

"I am of a resolved mind," she said.

"I see that." Boden fiddled with Hali's goblet, distracting himself from looking directly at Mara.

She watched him for a few moments, waiting him out, trying to get him to look at her without making him. But he seemed to thoroughly enjoy twirling Hali's glass. The vin was hot in her blood, and she felt dizzy. She eyed the furs nearby and felt the tug of desire to lie down and sleep.

"Boden," she said, "what were you saying earlier, about payment for your devotion?" The smile that curled at her lips wasn't hers, not really. It was painted on with the heaviness of the vin. Boden knew it, too, by the look on his face.

"It can wait, Mara."

Mara bit her lip. She felt off-balanced. She glanced at the furs again. Sleep would be a sweet relief, but her stomach rolled, and she knew it'd be impossible to close her eyes. Not without Boden there, whispering his secrets in her ear, lulling her to sleep in the safety of his arms.

"Lie with me." She gestured toward the furs.

Boden scowled. "In Hali's bed? I think not. She could return at any moment."

Mara shook her head. "I only want—" She stood lazily. What did she want? Her mind trailed off from her thoughts, leaving her abandoned in the middle. "Boden," she murmured, "it's just so . . . I don't feel well. I can't think."

The tent slid in her vision, tilting severely to one side. By the time she saw black, it was too late.

Mara kicked off the heavy furs pressing down on her, the heat like a heavy blanket of its own over her. The night beyond the door was dark, but inside the tent less so. The golden lantern that had brightened her drink with Hali earlier barely glowed, its wick having run nearly to its death.

She groaned. The heat clutched at her and made her feel sluggish. Her cheeks burned, but she considered that might just be her shame. Boden had carried her to Hali's furs and tucked her in. His face had flashed before her fluttering eyes. She had barely been coherent. Nomadic vin was potent, it seemed.

Subtle movement nearby jerked her head. Hali sat at the table, drinking alone.

"Hali," Mara whispered, "what's wrong?"

"I couldn't sleep, my jewel. All is well. You rest."

Mara scrambled to her feet and felt her way to the table. She sat opposite Hali, relieved to feel the heat dissipating off the skin of her arms and legs. Her mother had taught her the desert was cold at night, but her body felt nothing but heat. It scorched her face and pricked at her limbs. Her hand gingerly touched her face, and she instantly recoiled at the feeling.

"You're hot," Hali said. "You've had too much sun."

A small glass jar skittered across the table. Hali had pulled it from a leather satchel slung over the back of her chair. Mara picked it up and stared at the cloudy goo inside.

"It's a healing ointment. Put it on your skin where you feel hot, and you should find relief." Hali instructed.

Even in the dark, Mara could see the tired lines of Hali's face. Bags beneath her eyes were visible. Hali's hair, usually done up in some elaborate form, spiraled out in all directions.

Mara, not wanting to disturb the serene quiet of the evening, continued to whisper. "Hali, is something wrong?"

Hali shook her head. "No, no, my jewel. Not now. Not yet."

"Not yet?" Her words sounded ominous in the dark.

"I just have a bad feeling." Hali finally looked up at Mara. "Bad dreams."

Mara knew what that felt like. She had known bad dreams since childhood. Ever since she first learned of her fate, of the enemy Iris was meant to be. Some nights, she'd wake up in a cold sweat, her skin hot to the touch, having dreamt of Iris holding a knife to her throat. She'd wake up choking, sputtering, lashing out at anything around her. Sometimes she'd be so loud, a guard would burst into her room, demanding to know what bothered their queen. She would tell them it was a night terror, but she never told them of what. The nightmares might have left Mara, but their imprints were still pressed deep into her mind.

Mara wondered what Hali dreamt of. She had told Mara she didn't fear the Waste, so what did the island queen fear so much that it terrorized her in her sleep?

Mara prepared to ask, but voices cried out outside the tent. Mara was unsure if it was with joy or dismay. The rumbling of talk grew close. Mara felt her heart pounding in her chest. She glanced at Hali, only to find the queen reclined in her chair, her face serene. At ease.

Mara turned just in time to see why. The general pushed past the tent flap, bringing with her the cool desert air.

"General," Hali cooed. She stood and embraced her. "I dreamt you had fallen and that you would not rise."

The general held Hali at arm's length, her eyebrows lopsided. "Me? General Kassia of Bastia? Second General of the Panther Army?"

Hali laughed, though, it appeared painful to do so. "I know." She reached out and stroked Kassia's cheek. "But you are an old friend. Dear to me. Forgive me for my worry."

Hali held her hand against Kassia's face. They bowed their foreheads together and stood in silence. Mara shifted on her feet, wondering what to do with herself.

Hali cleared her throat. "General, what did you find?"

Kassia turned to Mara, surprised to see her there. "Forgive me, Jeweled One," she said, pulling away from Hali. "It seems your sister has cobbled together a mighty army for herself. Half jeweled, half nomad."

"As we suspected," Hali said. "This isn't a surprise."

"No," Kassia agreed, but she frowned at Mara, "but there is a considerable Ursan presence as well. More, much more, than the small group that traversed the Waste with Prince Boden initially. They outnumber our warriors two to one."

"Not a damning match for Bastians," Hali said. She looked at Mara, quick to read her worried face. "She will not prevail, my jewel."

Mara nodded, though, she didn't know if she completely agreed with Hali. While her mother had taught her that most sieges were a numbers game, she had also taught Mara that numbers could be skewed to one's favor with proper training and some grit.

She wondered which would prevail this time.

CHAPTER THIRTY-NINE

She slept fitfully again. Hali slept close by, beneath the furs with her. She found the queen's presence comforting, but not her body heat. She would have preferred Boden's body pressed up against her but feared the distraction. She needed to remain focused.

By morning, Mara was shoving all the furs aside, instead choosing to let her skin feel the cool morning air of the desert.

It felt strange to wake up in the Waste. In the Jeweled Realm, mornings were often cool, cooler still, depending on the time of year. The seasons followed a neutral path. Trees denoted the passing of time, and the temperatures walked hand in hand with their cycle, rising and falling with the year. But there were no trees in the Waste. Nothing to speak to her of nature's temperament. Winter approached the Jeweled Realm, but she couldn't tell what was happening in the desert of the Waste.

Bastia had been warm—a wet warmth that permeated every space of every room. Flowers bloomed in a continuous loop year-round. It was their death and resurrection that denoted the passing of the seasons. And yet, there were no flowers in the Waste to tell Mara their secrets. The air was dry, gratingly so, and left her thirstier than she had ever felt before.

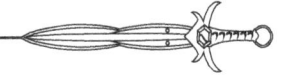

The sun peeked through a crack in the flap of their tent. Shadows danced back and forth from the guards standing watch out front. But their movements were not methodical, practiced. Instead, the guards moved about neurotically, their voices barking at others nearby.

Mara pushed herself into a seated position. "Hali." She nudged the island queen, who stirred beside her. "Hali, wake up."

"What?" Hali growled. "I've no interest in the sunrise, Jeweled One."

"No, Hali, something is happening outside." Mara crawled to the edge of the furs and peered out the door.

Both guards had their swords drawn, but past them, Mara could see some commotion. Bastian warriors ran, weapons drawn, while others moved past with empty buckets. She watched them run between the tents, farther and farther away. Their city of tents had grown overnight. With all soldiers offloaded from the ships, they were now spread out across the hillsides. The largest gathered army Mara had ever seen.

And then she saw it. In the distance, black smoke swirled upward, a deathly omen. The distant screams of people fighting fire reached her. She turned back to Hali, who was now seated upright, her face straining to hear what Mara heard.

"There's smoke," Mara said.

"Get up," Hali commanded. "Let us go."

Outside, the guards attempted to usher Hali and Mara back into the tent.

"It is not safe," one spoke in Bastian. The words were simple enough that Mara understood.

"What is it?" Mara replied in her best island speech, which fell limply off her ill-practiced tongue.

The guard raised his brows judgmentally but spoke nothing of her accent. "Nomads," he answered.

Hali pushed past the guards at the appearance of Kassia, who ordered the guards to leave them be.

"What happened?" Hali asked.

"We were attacked," Kassia said. "Early this morning, before the sun broke above the horizon."

Hali's eyes grew in fear. She turned to Mara. "Is it customary for the Jeweled Realm to infiltrate its enemy's camp at night? Was your grandmother not a follower of the Laws of War?"

"She was," Mara said. "I don't understand."

"Your sister sent Nomads to attack our army while they slept. Many were killed." Kassia. turned back to Hali. "We've lost a quarter of our warriors. If not from the blade of a creeping Nomad, then from fire, tent collapse, or crushed beneath the furor of madness created by it all."

Hali bowed her head, the weight of the moment already on her shoulders. "Call your lieutenants," she said. "We'll need to address this immediately." She disappeared back into the tent, her hand fiddling with her necklace.

Mara reached for Kassia, desperate. "Have you seen Boden?"

Kassia shook her head while she pulled away, her mind already someplace else, on the smoking remains of a part of her army. "No, not since last night, Jeweled One."

Mara needed to find him. This betrayal went too far. Iris knew better than to attack amid dreams. *Only beasts do that,* their grandmother would say. War was fought with death and destruction, but it need not drop to the level of savagery. There was an art to it, allowing it to be beautiful when done correctly.

Mara found her way through the tents, aiming for Boden's. Bastians still ran, shouting in their fluid language, dodging around her as they went. She wondered what they'd do with the empty buckets. With no water, the fire was sure to consume what it wanted, unhindered. It was too far to the beach to collect sea water.

Boden's tent was empty, as Mara had feared. She looked around frantically, hoping to catch sight of the tall, bearded man. Hoping his skin, like milk, would betray his presence amongst the red sand and dark-skinned Bastians.

Hoping to find the only man who had ever confessed to love her. The only man she believed.

Her eyes grew weak in the rising sun. A soft breeze brought her attention to her body, half naked from sleep, and she rushed back to Hali's tent. The Panther Queen paced, her hand constantly rubbing the large pearl of her necklace.

"Hali," Mara croaked. "Hali, I'm so sorry."

Hali batted her words away. "It is the cost of war, my jewel. Their lives for mine. Or in this case, yours."

Mara couldn't help but watch Hali. Her brown legs brought her across the small tent quickly, where she turned and strode the other way. Were the pearl upon her necklace not already smooth, Hali would have worn it away in little effort with the way she rubbed it.

Mara's stomach soured. She sank to her knees, tears coming unbidden to her eyes. "Do not be angry," she pleaded. "You are the last of whom I call friend. Boden is missing, and I cannot . . . I cannot live knowing you regret aiding me in my ludicrous return to the throne."

She clamped her eyes shut to keep the salty tears from stinging, but she heard Hali cease her walking. She felt Hali's body heat as she neared and felt the queen's small hands upon her shoulder as Hali, too, knelt in front of her.

"Regret? My jewel, have you learned nothing from your time in the Isles? The Bastians regret nothing. All is laid out as it should be."

"But Iris . . . she's a monster." Mara dared open her eyes, Hali's figure before her awash in her liquid vision like a painting. "I . . . don't know her anymore. I don't know how to defeat her."

Hali smoothed Mara's hair, considering her words. Finally, she stopped and brought her hand to Mara's chin, lifting her face to her own. She grabbed Mara's hand and wrapped it tightly in hers.

"Like this," she said, squeezing Mara's hand, forcing her to meet her gaze. "Eye to eye."

Mara wanted to speak, to ask Hali to tell her more, but Kassia rushed in, out of breath and smelling of smoke.

"The lieutenants come. Dress yourself, my queen."

Hali stood and helped Mara to her feet. "Send someone to search for the Ursan. My jewel seems to have misplaced him and requires his presence immediately. I want him found."

"As you say, my queen." Kassia bowed her head. She disappeared, only to return a moment later. "The order has been given. If he is to be found, my men will find him."

Hali's stewards arrived, carrying trunks of the queen's clothes. She ordered them to dress her and Mara. Mara stood motionless as the women tutted, whispering in Bastian while they dressed her. When they finished, she wore a dress of green linen. A sash of rust-colored silk draped across her neck. They instructed her to pull it over her head should she wish to protect herself from the sun. She bowed her head to thank them.

All was done mechanically. Mara did not feel herself in true control of her body. Something else had taken over. Something baser. Her grandmother might have called it the survival instinct. The one that takes over when one's will disappears.

Once dressed, the women departed from the tent. Outside, Hali was greeted by her guards and Kassia.

"This way." Kassia took Hali's arm.

Mara did not follow. She couldn't bring herself to do so. Instead, she fell back into her steps from that morning. One after the other, her feet took her to Boden's tent. She entered without hesitation and stood in the darkness that once held him.

His own bed of furs lay disheveled in the corner. A small book, laid flat to save Boden's page, was laid on top. A glance revealed it to be a study of Kalda. Of course it was. She picked it up and looked at the page, wondering what thought had struck him so hard that he'd left in the middle of reading.

The page described a story of Kalda on a day he happened upon a crying man. The man begged Kalda to kill him, for he had killed his own brother. When Kalda asked why he would do such a thing, the man said he had thought their inheritance split unfairly. A discussion between the brothers had turned into an argument, and the argument ended with the death of one.

Kalda told the man there would be no relief in death. What was once half his was now fully his. The best thing for him to do was to live out his days as generously as he could, lest he shame his brother's memory.

Mara set the book down. She straightened out the furs and laid herself upon them, inhaling deeply to get a scent of Boden, but everything smelled of sand. She rolled over onto her stomach and picked at the fur, wondering where he was, hoping he was alright.

The length of the night and her fitful sleep weighed on her, and soon her eyelids grew heavy. As the ruckus of the camp outside died down, she fell asleep with her face pressed into the furs where Boden's would have been. She dreamt of his face. His smile. His eyes.

Someone shook Mara's shoulder violently. She pushed herself upward, attempting to fight, only to be wrapped tightly in arms.

"At ease, Jeweled One," Kassia's words came out through gritted teeth as she attempted to stop Mara from swinging at her face.

Mara sagged in Kassia's arms, blinking, trying to force herself awake. "Kassia?"

"Yes," she whispered, "I've been looking for you. We have found your Ursan prince."

"Boden!" Mara stood up too quickly, her body still sleepy, and she fell back into Kassia's arms.

Kassia steadied her on her feet and grasped her shoulders. "Let us rouse that mind of yours, Jeweled One, before you injure yourself."

"Where is he?" She struggled to get away from Kassia, out of her arms and to the door.

Kassia held tightly to Mara, not letting her leave. "He is with my queen, in a physician's tent. Jeweled One . . . he is terribly wounded."

Mara's throat cinched shut, stopping her many questions. Kassia's mouth continued to move, but Mara couldn't hear her words. She heard nothing but her heart beating in her ears. Kassia's arm encircled Mara, and she escorted her out of the tent. They walked for what seemed like hours, time slowing to increase Mara's agony. The sun was high overhead, bearing down on them, but she did not move to cover her head. She wanted to feel the sting, the pain.

Above all else, she wanted to feel present.

The tent city flowed over the hillside, even with its massive black wound where the fire had broken out the night before. Kassia wound them through and around makeshift armories, kitchens, and latrines. Finally, they arrived at the blue-dyed tent, marking it as a tent of medicine.

Mara ran to the door and flung the flap open. The sun fell brightly on Hali as she leaned over Boden's body, singing softly to him, mopping his forehead with a wet sponge.

When she turned to see Mara, her face drew tight, and her singing ceased. "I tried to comfort him as best I could," she cried, tears filling the corner of her eyes but not falling. "Knowing it is what my jewel would have done."

Mara walked slowly to Hali, delaying the moment Boden's body would come into view. She edged around Hali, who kept her head down, until she saw him.

His body lay splayed out on a gurney. A deep red, almost black, soaked through his side, dyeing his linen shirt. His chest moved with shallow breaths and his eyes flickered beneath his eyelids, like one does when dreaming.

"He's not dead," she whispered.

Hali shook her head. "No, not . . . yet."

Hali petted Boden's hand, the contrast so stark Mara realized Boden was far paler than usual. Her eyes trailed back up to the bloodstain as she tried to calculate how much he had lost.

"My physicians have done what they can. If he lives, it will be a miracle."

Mara sank to her knees beside Boden, surprised to feel completely in control of her emotions for once. Tears did not find her eyes. Her heart had learned to tame itself. She held his hand in her own and stared down at his resting face.

"I don't believe in miracles, Your Grace," Mara whispered. "What has been laid out will be."

Chapter Forty

His chest continued to rise and fall. Mara found herself counting his breaths again, like she'd done before in Bastia. She'd stop at one hundred before starting over again—always back to one.

The noise outside the tent had disappeared. She no longer strained to hear what was going on, no longer wondered what existed outside the tent. Hali's physicians would come and go, administering medicine, checking his wound, but never spoke. Never stayed.

A long line of sun snuck in through the tent flaps. Mara gauged the passing time by watching the line crawl across the floor. She spent the rest of the day and night knelt by Boden's side. At one point she woke, having dozed. She leaned heavily on her knees onto Boden's gurney with her face snuggled into his forearm.

She froze when she saw the moonlight fall on open eyes. They glittered with the soft glow, staring directly at her.

"You're awake." Mara looked around for a physician, but they were alone.

"Please," Boden's voice was hoarse and weak, "don't call them. I just want to look at you a little longer."

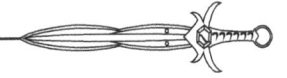

Mara fought the urge to disobey. If he was awake, then perhaps he would recover. If the physicians knew, they could administer some other medicine. But he looked at her as if far away, like someone searching for something they knew was there but couldn't quite find.

She held his hand to her face to help him see her. "Where did you go?" she asked him after watching his eyes read her face.

He struggled to swallow. He adjusted himself on the gurney, wincing as he did so. Mara did her best to aid him. When he finally settled, he answered, "I went to find your sister."

Mara was surprised. "For what purpose?"

Boden gave the slightest shake of his head. Useless, Mara knew. The purpose had been useless.

"You were reading Kalda," she said.

Boden stared evenly at her.

"I saw it—your book—on your bed."

"You were in my tent?" He seemed amused, or at least, he was attempting to be. His breathing was still labored. Mara could tell every movement for him was painful. She squeezed his hand tighter.

"When I couldn't find you after the attack, I sought you in your tent. I saw the book there."

Boden swallowed again. "Kalda always inspired me. Had you stayed with me, perhaps you could have convinced me of my foolishness." He squeezed her hand in his.

Mara smiled. "You're right, I would have stopped you, because you read it wrong, Boden."

"What?"

"The text. You read Kalda's story of the brothers and thought you could help me. You thought you could make what was partially mine . . . completely mine."

"A lot of good it did," Boden grumbled, grimacing once again. The linens that covered his wound glistened with wetness. The wound still oozed blood. Mara wondered how much time she had left.

"I don't believe in your Kalda, Boden, but I believe in you. I don't deserve such loyalty and devotion."

Boden attempted a smile but winced in pain. "I love you, too."

He knew she couldn't say the words, not right now. His eyes displayed his understanding. Boden knew her better than she knew herself, it seemed.

"Mara, there's something you should know," he said, his eyes turning hard. "Something I saw when I sought your sister."

When she finally emerged from the tent, the moon was full and high. She left Boden snoring quietly. Once he had explained to Mara what he had seen, he allowed the physicians to enter and administer their aid. They warned her he may not live to see the sunrise.

Her belief in him would have to be enough.

At once, she went to Hali's tent. The queen sat awake at her table, staring down into her glass of vin. She stood abruptly upon seeing Mara, her face at once full of relief and fear. "How fares the Ursan?"

"He lives," Mara said, rummaging through her bags. Someone had brought them earlier when the stewards dressed the women for the day. "For now."

She had tucked Edda and Liv away while they traversed from ship to shore. Her fatigue had taken over, and she had yet to retrieve them and bear them on her hips. She found them wrapped in her leather pants, safe from the terror of water and sand.

"What are you doing?" Hali asked. She watched Mara undress and dress again, this time donning her clothes favored for fighting. When Mara struggled with her belt, Hali came to her aid and helped cinch it down. "So it has come to this?"

"It's always been this," Mara answered. "It was laid out this way."

Hali stared at Mara, but finally bowed her head. "As you say, my jewel," she whispered.

Mara blew through the tent door and marched toward the edge of the camp. She'd have to walk through the burned debris to reach her destination. Her eyes traced the moon and her path in the sky, where she had been and where she would go. There was still time.

At the edge of the damaged tents, soldiers stopped her.

"We can't have you getting injured, Your Majesty." The soldier barred her way with his sword.

She stepped close to the man, so that her face was only a breath away. He smelled like an herb Mara knew but couldn't remember. She smiled at him. "Unfortunately, that is not for you to decide. Let me pass so that I may seek my path."

The soldier looked at his companion. The woman chewed on a sweet stick—a Bastian habit Mara never understood. The woman pulled it from her mouth and spat on the ground.

"Where are you off to, Jeweled Queen?" she asked.

"That is not your concern."

The woman nodded. "As you say, Your Majesty."

The woman stepped aside, suggesting to her companion he do the same. He seemed reluctant, but ultimately stepped aside as well. Mara's first step into the ash sent it flying high into the breeze.

It was quiet in that part of the camp. If Mara listened closely enough, she could still hear it smoldering in places. Hot spots would last for days. If the wind shifted, they risked an ember drifting and catching more tents on fire.

She left the burned remains of tents behind her, emerging onto smooth sand. Above her, the moon drifted toward a large dune. A shadow peered down at her from its peak. Mara hardened her heart and pushed herself onward.

When she was a few steps from the crest of the hill, the figure called out to her. "You came."

Iris sounded as tired as Mara felt. Her head was bare, and the brilliant moon illuminated her face. Iris had put on weight since the last time Mara saw her, but not enough to hide the sharp chin of their father. Not enough to fill the void in her eyes.

"Your Ursan dog *can* follow directions." Iris flung her cloak aside, allowing the light to strike the emerald of the Sacred Sword. She watched Mara's reaction, pleased to see Mara's feet stick where they were. "How is he, by the way?" She kept one hand on the Sword. "I'd hoped he'd make it back to camp before the poison set in so he could pass along my message."

"He'll live." Mara sidestepped around slowly, bringing Iris around so that her back was to the Bastian camp. "The physicians of the Isles have been practicing medicine since before the Black Rains ruined the Waste."

Iris rolled her eyes. "You always were such a poor liar."

"As were you, sister. A deity? The moon itself?"

Iris snarled at Mara. "Careful sister, you know not of what you speak."

"I know this"—Mara stood tall, using every inch she held over Iris—"there is only one way to end this. *My way.* So withdraw your weapon and let us begin."

Iris smiled as the Sacred Sword slid smoothly from its scabbard on her hip. "Gladly."

Mara withdrew Edda and Liv and prepared her stance. The pair circled each other, their faces moving in and out of the shadows. As they turned, Mara's eyes adjusted to the darkness. She could see the many masses crouched in the darkness on the opposite side of the hill. Iris had not come alone.

The nomads stood one by one and encircled them. Mara tried not to let the fear show in her eyes, though, the hair on the back of her neck stood up and her stomach would not settle.

But this was the only way.

Encased within a wall of nomads, Mara focused on Iris. The Sacred Sword, once worn at her side, seemed to sit comfortably in Iris's hand. Her mother's voice was in her mind, telling her she could not win, telling her the Sword was unstoppable.

But then she heard Hali's voice. And Boden's. She looked down at her own hands, wrapped tightly around the handles of Edda and Liv.

The power was there. The power had always been there.

Iris attacked first. She swung the Sword around her head and thrust. Mara twirled out of the blade's reach. Iris attacked again and again, and Mara continued to dance away. It was a farce, Mara knew—a play. Iris was trying to disorient her. Tire her out.

"Are you quite finished?" she called to Iris.

Iris wasn't even panting. She chuckled and smiled, bowing her head to Mara. "As you wish, dear sister."

With a wide stance, Iris prepared her own defense. Now she was ready to really fight.

"You're a fraud," Mara said to her. "A liar."

"*I'm* the fraud? Your entire legacy is a lie! You weren't suited for the throne because you never won the throne." Iris relaxed her stance as she argued with Mara. "You cheated. And were caught. And now you're angry."

She pointed the Sword at Mara, and Mara seized the opportunity. She sprung her attack, swinging Edda and then Liv, over and over again. Strike after strike, she swung at Iris as hard as she could, pushing Iris backward, sending her toward the circle of nomads.

Her victory was short-lived. Mara lost her footing in the sand, stopping her onslaught. Iris screamed in Mara's face and shoved her backward. Mara tripped but managed to roll onto her shoulders and then to her feet.

Iris breathed heavily. Mara, too. She laughed to herself. It reminded her of training in the gardens, of fighting until they were too tired to lift their weapons. Of their mother's never-ending displeasure with their performances. Of their father's constant scowl.

Bastians were leaving the camp now, slowly trekking up the dune toward the gathering of nomads. No one raised a weapon at each other. Instead, the silent people of the desert moved aside, allowing room for the Bastians one by one. Mara watched as the soldier with the tent poles appeared. A physician from Boden's tent. Kassia. They each arrived, expecting to begin the battle, only to find there would be no need for one.

"You are a stain to our family's name," Iris hissed. She lunged at Mara, but Mara used Liv to strike the Sword away. The metal of each blade echoed sharply in the cool night air. "You are an embarrassment to the Jeweled Realm." Iris struck again, and Mara used Edda to knock the blow aside. "But worst of all, you are dead to me," Iris snarled. She kicked sand in Mara's face, blinding her, and spun with the Sword.

The blow landed on Mara, but not where Iris intended. She had aimed for Mara's neck, but with sand in her eyes, Mara had stumbled, turning her side to Iris. The sword landed on Mara's left arm, slashing it open like paper. Blood poured forth, and she dropped Edda.

Searing pain cut through her arm. It shot up her neck and she involuntarily ground her teeth against the pain. Iris seemed surprised but smiled.

"I had meant to offer you a swift death," Iris laughed. "But a drawn out, painful one will do just as well."

The Sacred Sword dripped a trail of blood as she walked toward Mara. Mara gripped Liv tightly with her right hand. Her arm burned red-hot, but she forced the pain to be silent.

She needed only a few more moments. Iris was strong. Iris was a good fighter, but she rarely saw the complete picture.

Mara backed away from Edda, leaving her in the sand, feeling only slightly bad about abandoning her. Iris kicked the axe when she reached it, sending it flying toward the circle of witnesses surrounding them. It landed near Kassia, who reached down slowly and collected it.

"I will burn your body." Iris watched as Kassia retrieved the axe. "It is the only honorable thing I will do."

Mara bit her lip, attempting to still her racing heart. With every step that Iris drew near, Mara's stomach lurched. Dressed from head to toe in black, her sister was a phantom, a specter of herself. The hint of fuzz from her shaved head was lit up by the moon. The black paint around her eyes was so saturated, so flat, it absorbed any light that fell across her face. *She's the moon,* Mara thought, *so ethereal and yet so dark.*

"It needn't be this way," Mara panted.

Iris laughed. She charged quickly toward Mara, attempting to land her final blow, but Mara saw the move coming. Like they were playing Cavaliers again. She rolled to her left, ignoring the singing of pain, allowing her momentum to carry her. Pushing up from a crouched position, she vaulted to her feet. Before Iris could react, Mara circled and whacked her with a fist across the side of the face before kicking her.

Iris fell to her knees.

"We can rebuild the Jeweled Realm," Mara said between breaths, Iris's back to her, "in a better way. Together."

Iris stood and turned slowly. It was hard to read her face. Her hand reached for her cheek, only to be brought back down coated in blood.

"Never!" Iris snarled. "There can only be one."

Mara shook her head. "I thought so, too, once." She looked down at her hand, clinging to Liv. She frowned before tossing Liv to the ground. "I won't fight you anymore, Iris. I won't be a part of this . . . tradition." She held her chin high, staring at the black depths of Iris's shadowed eyes. "The throne is yours, Iris. I don't want it."

She turned to leave, to walk to the edge of the circle, and hoped they'd let her through. There was no need for more bloodshed. Not for her. Not for a throne that cared little who sat upon it. For a kingdom that cared little.

Iris screamed behind her. It was bloodcurdling, and Mara instantly tensed her shoulders. "You left me with no choice!" Iris yelled. "No choice! I couldn't go home!"

Mara turned to face her sister. Iris's neck bulged with the tension she carried. She screamed again. Her chest heaved, and spit flew from her mouth.

"You dishonored me!" she screamed.

Clouds drifted away from the moon and finally, for the briefest of moments, light fell across Iris's eyes. Mara could see them then, the icy blue. The sadness. The anger. But mostly, she saw the hurt she had caused.

"Iris," Mara whispered, "I never meant to."

"Liar!" her sister cried before rushing at her.

The moon's light glowed white in the blade's mirrored edge. Mara took a deep breath, and for just a flicker of a moment, nothing else existed. It was as if all paths had led Mara to that spot in the sand.

Mara's body took control in a moment of self-preservation, and she withdrew the Panther's Claw hidden at the small of her back. Her arm instinctively swung the thin blade upward.

Iris's charge faltered. She fell forward, leaning her body against Mara's.

Mara's blade had caught Iris along her inner thigh. She'd thrown a killing blow.

"Iris," Mara gasped. The pain in her left arm erupted with the weight of her sister's body. "Iris, no. I didn't mean to."

There was blood. Already so much blood.

At such proximity, Mara could see Iris's eyes easily. They weren't angry. They were afraid.

Their weapons fell to the sand in a deafening silence. The pair sank together. Mara clung tightly to Iris as her body grew limp. A rush of heat coated Mara's leg from the blood that flowed freely from her sister.

Mara laid Iris down gently, cradling her head, apologizing continuously. She watched the movement behind Iris's closed eyes slow, and then her breathing ceased entirely.

A shadow overcame them, blocking out the moon. Mara looked up to see one of the nomads. Tendrils of hair outlined the moonlight. A beard of salt and pepper covered his face, though, Mara spied youthful eyes beneath.

The nomadic warlord. Boden had described him to Mara inside the medical tent.

She turned back to Iris. "I didn't . . . " she murmured, "I didn't want to."

Iris tried to form words with her mouth, but nothing would come. Mara bent her head over her sister's and cried, the tears leaving streaks amidst the paint of Iris's eyes.

"I love you," Mara whispered to Iris. "I always have."

"We honor your victory," the warlord said through his thick nomadic accent, "and will fight no more."

Mara turned to him, hot tears still streaming down her face. "You will not fight? Not anymore? Not for her?"

The warlord stared at Mara. His eyes were the strangest shade of green. Like the oak lichen that grew between bricks. Nearly green, but not quite. He glanced past Mara at Iris.

"I loved her, too," he said with a nod. "And we will fight no more."

Mara looked at Iris one final time. She wiped a tear away and gently kissed her sister on the forehead. When she stood, she reached her right hand toward the warlord. They embraced forearms and stared at one another once again.

"What will you do with her body?" Mara asked him.

"We will entomb her in the temple of the Mother, as is her right."

Mara nodded.

"What will you do with the Sword?" the warlord asked.

"It's not mine," she said. "Bury it with her." Mara smiled broadly at this man, a man she felt somehow connected to. In a normal life, he would be like a brother to her. Family.

The other words Boden had spoken to her, the secret he'd whispered so intently as he lay struggling to breathe, surfaced in Mara's mind. She gripped the warlord's forearm harder, yanking him closer. She took a step toward him so that she only needed to whisper to be heard. The warlord froze, surprised by Mara's words.

"Bring me the baby," she said. "Bring me my sister's child."

Acknowledgements

I'd like to thank Rebecca Alexandru. Without your writing parties, Mara would never have been born. Your continued friendship as we both traverse our own writing paths has been a comfort and your encouragement and enthusiasm for my work is a balm for my soul. Your early reading of Liar Queen helped me realize that Mara's story needed to be shared. And to Nova McBee, who made me truly believe I could follow this path, whose own writing career is a shining example for me of sharing stories that honor our values.

To Joseph I give my undying love. We've grown up and now we're growing old together and I wouldn't have it any other way. With every adventure we've had, you've fueled my imagination and filled my days with wonder. I couldn't do any of this without you. Thank you for understanding my obsessive need to put words to paper and for being my first reader, every time.

To the Badger Boys—Matt, Tenn, and Sol—you are my everything. Being your mother has been the greatest gift and it was you three that finally pushed me to follow my own dreams and to be the best example I could for you. Thank you for all the love and reminders to take a break and play. Thank you for the adventures and the laughter. You've taught me so much more than I've ever taught you about life and love and the pursuit of happiness.

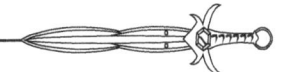

To my parents, thank you. Thank you for a childhood that was safe. A childhood that provided me with room to play and imagine. A childhood spent in the forests and mountains. Thank you for loving me for the dreamer that I am.

I must give thanks to God, who has been my constant guide and strength through this journey. I am grateful for the faith that has shaped me, and for the blessing of being a storyteller.

I have heaps of thanks for Morgan Macedo, my editor. You took the rough version of Mara's story and made it beautiful. You saw the story I wanted to tell and helped me get it right.

To Nicole and Kyera of Golden Scales Publishing, thank you. Thank you for believing in Mara's story as much as I do. Thank you for your trust in my storytelling and your patience with my incessant need to get the cover and map just right.

I must mention my history professor, Doctor Pearce, who merely uttered the words "I'd like to read your work someday," and instantly solidified my confidence in my writing and Professor Reese, who taught course after course on women authors at Portland State, filling my desire to learn and understand every which way a woman can use her words. And to Professor Ceppi, who was a hard grader but made me think: you introduced me to Coetzee and Woolf, and my thoughts on storytelling have never been the same.

And lastly, to the greats that inspired my words from the beginning: to Margaret Atwood for showing a fifth-grade girl what words could do. To Lois Lowry for showing me why words mattered. And to Alice Hoffman for demonstrating what magic really meant.

About the Author

Born in the American South and raised in the remote wilderness of Alaska, M.T. Solomon has been writing books since she was six years old. She graduated from Portland State University in 2012, where her studies focused primarily on women writers throughout the world. Solomon's writing takes cues from her childhood, where the vast setting of Alaska seemed just as much a character in her life story as she did. She resides in Alaska with her husband and three sons, where she coaches high school volleyball and is an avid advocate for female athletics.

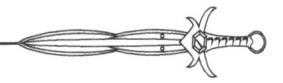

Photo by Joseph Keith